The Skifter

Martin Turner

First Edition 2010
Second Edition 2015

ISBN-13: 978-1517132712
ISBN-10: 1517132711

CONTENTS

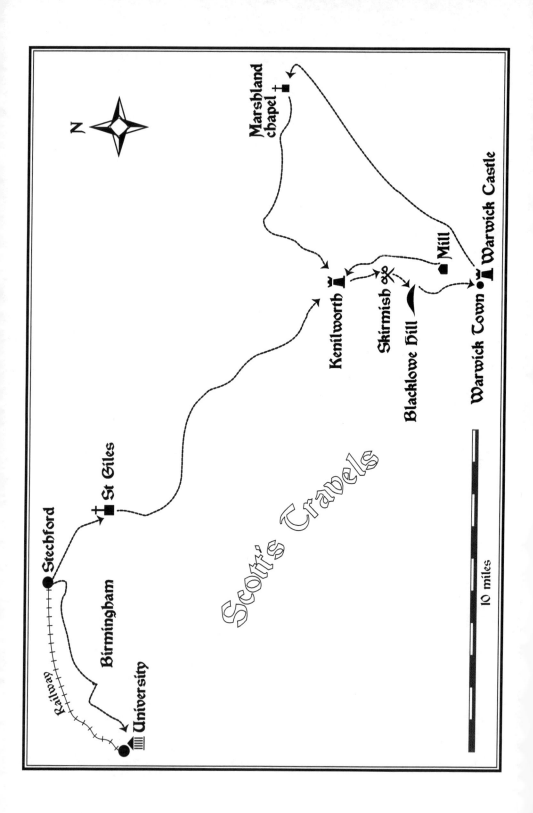

N

Railway

Stechford

Birmingham

University

St Giles

Scott's Travels

Kenilworth

Skirmish

Blacklowe Hill

Mill

Marshland chapel

Warwick Town

Warwick Castle

10 miles

Fitt 1

Skifting

1 Snow

For sno is slepe ond slepe is sno
Ond old things lang forgot whan sno is depe
Wandel on Godes erthe that elsewise
Onder erthe must slepe

Whan safe and sound thou thinkst to walk
Then quite thy steps and stil thy talk
For dark things lurk benethe the night
That hide ther faces from the light

he sixth of December began like any other December day. Dull, dark and damp.

At first break there was a gnawing wind across the playground. Scott groaned: there was a whole afternoon of cross-country running to come later. It was what the school did when someone decided it was too cold to play rugby. The only thing that could stop cross-country was really, really thick snow.

"I wish it would snow," said Scott to himself. "I wish it would snow for a week."

Perhaps he was unwise to wish such a thing, even to himself. Wishes have a way... but we are getting ahead of ourselves.

After break Scott dozed through geography. It was not that he disliked the subject. But the long trip to school—it was almost an hour with the autumn traffic—and the cold break, and a late night the night before, sent him into a daze, like human hibernation.

After geography was French, which was not a good subject to sleep in. Scott tried to pay attention, but his mind wandered, and his eyes slid slowly towards the window.

So he saw flakes of snow before anybody else did.

Snow is strange to watch. First a few splodges of white, and then a whirl in the dull sky. The whirl goes on but the ground does not at first change. And then—if you watch carefully—you see a speck of white somewhere. Perhaps it's just a plastic bag that someone has left lying around... but just when you're afraid that it probably is, you see another speck here, and a dusting of white there. Then suddenly—but it's not sudden at all, because you are watching it happen—there is white every-where, and the dashes of green and brown and grey are shrinking, and, if the falling continues, and the snow whirls thicker, you see the last islands of colour disappear, and the whole world is lapped in thick, creamy, crisp whiteness.

By the end of French it was three inches deep.

By the end of double Chemistry it was a foot.

The chemistry teacher held them back for a moment after the bell.

"Right, everybody. The Chief Master has been looking at the weather forecast. School is closing at lunch-time today. Everyone is to have their lunch and make their way calmly home.

"It's possible—although I'm sure you would all hate this to happen—that there will be no school tomorrow. You can look at the school website tonight, if you still remember how to find it."

And that was the end of that.

They piled out of Chemistry, and there was a scuffling struggle to get into the locker room because everybody in the entire school was af-ter their bag at the exact same moment.

Ten minutes later Scott was waiting at the railway station. To get to the station you had to go through the university. It was strange in the new world. The wind whipped round huge flakes which made it hard to see. Buildings loomed without warning, as if they had silently shuffled into new locations while your eyes were elsewhere.

The train was late, and full: other schools further down the line had sent their own hordes slipping and shuffling early away. Scott squeezed himself into the last carriage just as the doors closed. He was crammed up against an old woman's knees on the one side and two tall men on the other. The carriage was hot, the windows covered in condensation. He almost fell over as the train lurched forwards.

"You should watch yourself, young man," said the old woman. She had thick russet hair, that seemed to merge with her coat.

"You should watch yourself," she went on. "All nice in your school uniform. They obviously don't teach manners at your school. If I'd done such a thing in my time it would have been the cane…"

Scott looked the other way—which meant looking straight into someone's back. This did not stop the old woman.

"You should watch yourself," she said, and much more followed to the same effect. But, just as they were reaching New Street station, her voice changed, as if she began to sing a song with no tune. "The snow might seem mighty fine to you, but there's things about the darkest winters that few remember and none tell. Snow things will be out in the moonlight, and devil take the last to reach his door. Old Peter, now, he was the last to reach his door. Old Peter, in the winter's roar. Old Peter that was last to reach his door told no man his tale nor no man asked."

It was most peculiar. But, thankfully, the train stopped, and Scott managed to get his schoolbag from the ruck of feet and knees, and so he got off the train first.

He caught one more snatch of the old woman—and now he was sure that she was singing:

"For snow is sleep and sleep is snow
And old things long forgot when snow is deep
Wander on God's earth that else-wise
Under earth must sleep."

He scuttled off, ducking between the baggage cages that are known as 'brutes', and reached the escalator before the press of the crowd. Standing on the rising steps he saw the old woman waving. She seemed still to be shouting. The hubbub and the rush of bodies was too much for her voice to carry, except for one last shout that perhaps caught a gust of air.

"So watch yourself young man."

Now that he had escaped the crowd, there was more of a holiday feel in the air. No school today—perhaps none tomorrow. He thought for a moment about wandering through the centre of Birmingham and catching the bus home, but then he noticed that his train would be gone in less than a minute, and somehow, the urgency persuaded him to go with the train and get home soonest.

The train was not ready. It stood with its doors open. There were just a few passengers, so Scott found a seat in the corner and huddled up against the heating. He must have fallen into a kind of doze, because the next thing he knew one of the guards was shaking his shoulders.

"You'll have to change trains, mate," he said. "Platform ten. Get a move on, or you'll miss it. And watch yourself."

Platform ten was almost the other end of the station. Scott had to dodge to and fro among clumps of people who seemed to have nothing better to do than stand in his way. He rattled down the escalator, made a big jump at the end to avoid falling over, and bustled himself into the train.

"Aren't you going to close the door?" said someone. Scott turned to see who had made the joke, and then realised that it was an older train—a very old train—with doors that didn't close themselves. He pulled it shut.

He turned round again to see who had spoken.

It was a tall man—neither young nor old. He wore a long coat, and very dark, fine hair fell half-way to his shoulders. Scott would have guessed he was a biker, except that he was cleanly shaven. His finger nails were precise, and he wore a heavy ring on his left hand.

His voice had a hint—just a hint, mind you—of Irish or Welsh or Scottish. The man had a big bag with him. It was five foot long with wheels at one end. Scott might have taken it for a golf bag, except that he knew what it was—or thought he knew. Scott had joined the school fencing club that term, and the coach had a bag just like it.

He sat down opposite the man, and said:

"Excuse me, but is that a fencing bag?"

The man raised his eyebrows, and smiled.

"Ah, but indeed it is. Is that something which interests you?"

"I do fencing at school—but only since this term. Are you a fencing coach?"

"Sometimes, a little, when I turn my hand to it."

That seemed to finish the conversation, so Scott looked out of the window. The guard's whistle blew, there was a soft lurch, and the station slid slowly out of sight. Then there was the grey of sidings, with clumps of snow here and there, and then the railway world disappeared and they were in the utterly, utterly white world of snow. You could see a lot of Birmingham from this particular place, and Scott raced from one side of the carriage to the other. He had never seen it like this before—blanketed, muffled, cleaned as if with a fresh coat of ice-cream.

The train rolled on. It was a clicketty, clacketty rattling train, and it rocked from side to side.

A ticket inspector came bumbling along from the guard's van. He checked the fencing man's ticket carefully, as if he hadn't seen one like it for a long time. He smiled when he saw Scott's travel pass.

"Ah. You'll be out of school early because of the snow. I'll hope to see my son early today too. But you're lucky—the snow's still falling and this is the only line they've got open. It's the main line to London, see. There's snow ploughs out on the other lines, but I think some of your school friends will have a worse journey. Going far?"

"Just Stechford," said Scott.

"Ah, my granddad was signal man at Stechford, back in the day. I was just old enough to see the steam trains when they were running. Just the thing for this weather. The smoke and the steam was just the thing."

Then he bumbled on down the empty carriage.

"Ah, the smoke and the steam," murmured the fencing man. "And all the common folk on the wooden seats in third class, and the noble in first."

Scott looked away, unsure what to make of the man's strange remark, and noticed an old newspaper which had got caught in the gap between the seat and the side of the carriage. He fished it out, and pretended to read it, while he cast surreptitious glances at him. The man, for his part, settled back and closed his eyes.

The newspaper was almost two years old. The news did not seem to have changed very much. A mugging in Bordesley Green, a car driven into the canal in Aston. Then a story caught his imagination for a moment: "Baffling loss ends film hope." It was just a short article. "Insurers have refused to pay out for a missing multi-million pound film set, putting paid to hopes for another all-British historical blockbuster. Filmmakers claimed the set mysteriously vanished on its journey from Basingstoke. But insurers are not satisfied that the set, due to be assembled in West Yorkshire, was ever despatched. The decision effectively ends the chances that the Lottery-funded drama, based on a Walter Scott novel, will be completed."

The train drifted into Adderley Park, the platform crusted with creamy snow. A couple of people got off and nobody got on. Then the motors whirred with a warm whine and they slid out between steep embankments. A tree had fallen close to the track at one point. The driver pulled back to dead slow as they went past it, but the way was just clear.

They clanked up to speed again, and suddenly the country opened out, which meant it was almost time to get off. Scott got a good look at the whitened rooftops, and wished that he owned a camera and that he had brought it with him.

This was one of the trains where they had taken off the door handles on the inside for some railway reason that made no sense when explained to ordinary people. Scott pushed the window down and was met with a blast of cold as the train reached the platform. It was such an old train that he was able to open the door before it had really stopped, and he jumped onto the platform with his school bag waving behind him for an exciting four yards slide in the snow. Of course, he fell over at the end, but it was worth it.

He was going to go back and close the door behind him, but he saw that the fencing-bag man was also getting out at Stechford. He wondered for a moment about giving him a hand, but the man was already out of the carriage and closing the door himself.

Scott pelted up the stairs, over the bridge and down the other side. Stechford Station had been designed by a man who clearly felt that stairs were without a doubt the very best thing about a station, and had put in as many stairways as could be fitted onto the site. So, having gone up one flight and down another, Scott set off up the final flight to the road. He always felt that you should be able to run up and down all three, but by the middle of the last it was always trudge, trudge, trudge. Perhaps the man who had designed the station disapproved of running, and had done his best to stamp it out.

Running in snow was—in any case—never as much fun as it looked because you had to put in twice the effort for half the distance.

The ticket collector waved Scott past.

Stechford was not quite as crisply white as the rest of Birmingham. Old, smoky, leaky cars had already made deep ruts on Victoria Road, and it was grey and ground down. They were gritting on the Outer Circle, so Station Road was already back to its usual asphalt black, with a grey ribbon of slush running either side and down the middle.

Scott had read somewhere that Station Road was the oldest thing in Stechford. It had only been 'Station' Road since the railways, but the old name, Stoney Lane, went back to the Saxons, and maybe the Romans had had their own name for it before then. Stechford had been a prosperous village in its heyday, but that was a century ago, and now the shops were slowly dying, squeezed between the big trading estate at the bottom of the hill and the Yew Tree a mile in the other direction.

Birmingham was not an especially posh place to live, and Stechford was one of the most especially unposh parts of it. Nobody else from Scott's school lived in Stechford, and sometimes he felt going from one to the other was like crossing continents.

Scott slithered through the slush by the pedestrian lights. His shoes were beginning to leak and his hands were getting cold. But a free afternoon was a free afternoon, so he stuck his best foot forward.

To get home you had to go up Manor Road, past the old people's home that had once been a bakery, and across the huge patch of grass that ran up to the blocks of flats. The grass was a good place to toboggan when the snow was really deep, but it always took longer for it to settle there. He had heard that there were hot water pipes running from the swimming baths at the bottom of the hill up to the flats at the top, but he wasn't sure that he believed it.

Before Manor Road, you could take a short cut down Lyndon Road. Scott didn't like going that way because it was rumoured to be where a family of criminals lived. It was so cold, though, that he decided to risk it. There was a maze of garages and workshops on one side as you went down. Somebody was working on a car in the front. It was dark inside except for the flash of a welding torch on bare metal. Someone had once told Scott that this was the kind of place where they bring stolen cars and wrecks, to chop them up and weld them back together and sell them as 'bargains' to the unwary.

The best thing to do was to walk past with your hands in your pockets not looking, but Scott could not resist a look. His eyes wandered down the alleyway where the most secret workshops were. Apart from a brazier at the far end, most of the lights were out and the doors were barred. The snow was piled thick.

He looked away and plodded on, but just as he passed the point where you could see the furthest into that nameless place, he turned his head for a final glance.

He distinctly saw a huge pair of green eyes, larger than a man's, glowing. As soon as they saw him they blinked out. Scott stood stock still for a moment. He was sure that he heard something like a low growl.

"Just a guard dog," he said. But he hurried on as quickly as he could without actually running—Scott knew that the worst thing to do was to run away from a guard dog.

Lyndon Road turns a corner before it joins Manor Road. As he passed out of sight, Scott risked one final look. The blow torch was still flashing at the front, but all else was still. The fencing man was just coming into view, dragging his bag behind him on its wheels, making a deep rut in the snow, following the path that Scott had already taken. He also seemed to be interested in the workshops and garages, and stopped to peer at the man with the blowtorch.

That was when it happened.

There was a rush and a flurry of snow. The fencing man jumped back as a huge animal came bounding out of the alleyway. He threw up his arms to protect his face but the animal swerved and set off down Lyndon Road, straight for Scott.

And now Scott did run. The thing was after him and he knew it. But he could not run fast: his worn soles found little to grip in the snow, and he slithered and slid and struggled to keep his balance. All the while the beast gained on him, bounding lightly on padded, clawed feet. Scott looked desperately around for somewhere to run to. All the gardens had low fences that even an ordinary dog would be over in a flash. There were no walls to climb onto and no trees with low branches.

All Scott could think of was the red pillar box on the corner—if he could get there he could perhaps scramble on top.

"Help, help" he called out, but there was nobody to hear him.

Now he could hear the flapping, padding, bounding sound of the animal just a few paces behind.

He turned round at bay, holding his school bag in his hands to fend it off.

He saw three things at once. Very close, a huge beast, like a German Shepherd dog, leaping towards him. In the distance, the man with the fencing bag running towards him. Between the two, a flashing blur of something in the air.

Scott screamed.

Then the flying, flashing, blurring thing struck the animal.

The beast came crunching down in the snow, writhing as it skidded. It stopped two feet short of where he stood waving his bag. The huge teeth were fixed in a snarl.

But it was the snarl of death. A long knife, the size of a meat clea, trailed from its neck.

If he had been a little younger, Scott would have wanted to cry. Instead, gingerly, he waved his bag at the animal as it lay in the cold snow.

"No, it's dead," said the fencing man, who had come up. He turned it over with his foot. Even in death the beast was fearsome. It was the length of a motor bike, and the huge, green eyes might have belonged to a young horse.

"Come on," he said. "It's time we got you home. Which way is your house?"

Scott's house was number seventeen, Giles Close. Giles Close was an intricate road that branched left and right and back in on itself, and nobody but the postman and the people who delivered political leaflets knew where all the houses were. The council had already closed some of the houses off, but there were still a few like Scott's. The council didn't usually keep people in them for long, but for some reason Scott and his mother had been in number seventeen almost since the day he was born. A woman had come a few times to talk to Scott's mother about where they should live, but Scott had the idea they didn't get on with each other very well, and after a few meetings she stopped coming.

Scott's mother worked at the museum some days, at the university other days, and some days she stayed at home. On Mondays and Thursdays she often came home late. However, the light was on, so it meant that today was a home day. This was good because it meant the house would be warm, but it was bad because there would be some explaining to do, and probably an embarrassing phone call to the school. Scott's mother was unnaturally sceptical when it came to unscheduled holidays, and, more embarrassingly, occasionally explained to the luckless person on the other end of the telephone her views on education, which were somehow connected with Alfred the Great, and a fellow called Waferth, who had once received a letter.

One of Scott's teachers had once indicated that his mother was believed to be ever so slightly batty. What he had not mentioned was that she was also considered (although Scott would not have noticed) to be startlingly beautiful, and more than one of the unattached male teachers had tried (thoroughly unsuccessfully) to lure her out for a cup of coffee. The school being so close to the university ought to have made it easier, but nobody had ever made much progress.

Snow was piled in drifts around the house, but somebody had cleared a path. Almost as soon as Scott rang the bell, the door whisked open. His mother was standing there in her best dress. Before she had a chance to say anything, the fencing man said:

"Lady, I have brought your son."

"Indeed," she said, rather coldly. "I wasn't expecting him for some hours. What happened?"

"School closed early," butted in Scott. "This man rescued me from a huge dog."

"Indeed?" she said again, with even less warmth. "Well, you had better both come in."

Scott's house was what used to be called 'two up two down'. Its previous occupant had made alterations so that the ground floor was now what is known as 'open plan', which is to say that, aside from a small hall which led to the stairs, there were no door or walls separating the kitchen from the living room. Most families in Giles Close had done something of the kind, as it made the ideal space for home cinema.

Scott's mother had never bought a home cinema, or a television at all. Instead the living room was lined with shelf upon shelf of books. The dining table was at the far end, next to the kitchen, and there was a settee and two (non-matching) easy chairs at the end nearest the door. Normally if Scott's mother was working at home, the dining table would be covered in papers with books piled around. But this time there was just one book out, and it was on the settee, not the dining table. Scott noticed it had a green back, and its tattered cover had been well used.

"Why don't you go upstairs and change out of your school uniform, Scott?" she said. "I will make a cup of tea for your rescuer."

Scott raced upstairs—not because he particularly wanted to change his clothes, as he had already kicked off his wet shoes at the door—but because he had a strange sense that his mother already knew this man, and that she had even been expecting him. There was a particular place in Scott's bedroom where you could pull back a plank and hear everything that was being said downstairs.

His mother was talking. Scott wished he could see her face, but the tone of her voice told him that she had a severe expression, and was giving this man an interrogation.

"So, my son was scared by a dog."

"Your son was attacked, and by a wolf."

"It was a big dog, then. There are no wolves."

"It was a wolf. A great grey wolf—as large as any I have seen."

"Very well, then. Why have you come? I thought that perhaps you wanted to see me. But now it seems you have followed trouble here, or brought it with you."

"I am here on another matter. If I may beg your patience, I will sleep on your floor tonight, and then I will be on my way. But I did come to see you, because I need your advice."

"My advice. Well, really. That is how we first met, though you seldom took it after that."

"Lady, you will recall that you offered your advice in trade, and you demanded what seemed a heavy price."

"And yet later the price seemed less heavy to you."

His mother's tone seemed to have softened a little, but, as Scott strained to hear better, the voices became indistinct, as if they were speaking some language that Scott didn't know.

This reminded him that he had been sent upstairs to get changed. So he quickly put on some other clothes and rattled downstairs. He felt that if he crept down they might guess he had been listening.

The man and his mother were both sitting on the settee, but as far apart as was physically possible.

"Well, Scott," she said. "You seem to have met Mr Gavin Knight. He is going to stay with us for a couple of days, perhaps. At least until the snow has cleared, and he can be on his way."

The snow did not clear that night. The flakes ceased to fall a little after dusk, but the wind continued to whip the ground snow into eddies and currents, swirling upwards and blowing cross-wise over the roof-tops.

Gavin Knight did not seem a talkative man. He sat opposite Scott's mother for most of the evening at the dining table. He was writing—quite slowly—in a big book, like a ledger. From time to time he would steal a glance at her, but she didn't look back. Except once, late in the evening, when he had somehow dozed over his writing. She looked at him then, for a long time.

Scott went up to get ready for bed early. He did not feel particularly welcome in the living room. And he also thought that he might hear something from upstairs if he left them to talk.

This time it didn't seem to work. There was no sound at all from the living room. So he climbed into bed and lay thinking about the day's adventure. The snow, and then the wolf—was it really a wolf?—and then this man, Gavin Knight.

He had known from when he was quite young that there was something in the family that people didn't talk about.

He had once found a cutting from the Oxford Mail. It was in a pile of papers which his mother usually kept locked in an old tin box in her bedroom. It was a story about a young woman who had gone missing for five years, and had suddenly arrived back without any explanation of where she had been or what had happened to her. The woman, said the article, could not be named for legal reasons.

Whenever he asked his uncles or aunts what his mother had done before he was born, they always became suddenly vague. It was all such a puzzle… all such a puzzle… all such a…

Scott woke with a start. Moonlight was streaming in through his window. He looked out across a world of whiteness. The clouds were gone, and the stars sparkled fiercely on the gleaming landscape.

There was a rush of cold air, and a click from below. Somebody had gone out through the front door.

Very quietly, so as not to wake his mother, Scott pulled on his trousers and a thick sweater and crept downstairs. His shoes were still drying, but his Wellington boots were standing ready in the hall. Making sure he had his house key, he lifted his coat from the peg, eased open the door, and slipped out into the night.

The world was silent. Scott zipped his coat and pulled the hood over his head. Fortunately he had left his gloves in his coat pocket, along with a tube of mints. He breathed out and watched the little cloud of condensation in the chilly air.

There had been a slight thaw and the surface of the snow had re-frozen. It made it brittle, like walking on a thin sheet of glass. The path to his house was covered in tracks, which surprised him, because they had had no other visitors that evening. One set only, though, led away from the front door. He set off to follow them.

Outside the gate the tracks got muddled, and Scott was on the point of giving up, when he caught a glimpse of a man's head in the distance. Guessing that it was Mr Knight, he set off, half-walking, half running to catch him. He wasn't yet sure whether he would ask him what he was doing, or just track him from a distance, like a hunter.

In the event, he almost ran into him. Gavin Knight—it seemed—was also looking for tracks. He was casting around on what was usually the grass between the blocks of flats and the swimming baths. He didn't see Scott, and Scott had the presence of mind to get behind a low wall which ran at the back of the Pennycroft flats.

Between the moonlight and the snow, and the extra-strength orange street lights the council had put in to deter criminals, it was almost as bright as day. But the shadows were all mixed up, and it was hard to make things out. He saw Gavin Knight casting about, looking forwards and back, going a little in one direction, then in another direction and … without warning … he was suddenly not there any more. Gone.

Scott rubbed his eyes. Still gone. He watched a little longer, and then curiosity got the better of him. He climbed over the wall and made his way across the crunching snow to where Gavin Knight had been.

He was planning to follow the man's tracks, but something else demanded his attention. Fully five feet long: a footprint—almost as long as he was tall. It had sunk through a foot of snow, tearing up grass and earth where the toes pressed down.

Scott found himself doing exactly what Gavin Knight had done. Going a little forward, a little backward, he tried to sight where the next footprint would be. It should be just… yes, that was it. It was funny light. If you looked in just the right way, you could see the footprints headed off, left, right, left, right, left, right, into the distance. But if you moved a little to the right or to the left, they disappeared.

It was like one of those puzzle pictures that just look like a pattern until you defocus your eyes and look through the picture, which suddenly becomes a butterfly, or a bird, or a blade of grass.

There was just a faint shimmer or shadow that somehow marked the place where you could just-to-say see the footprints and then just-to-say couldn't. Going quite slowly, so as not to lose sight of them, Scott set off to follow. And that was when he caught sight of Gavin Knight, a long way ahead of him, making heavy weather of going up the hill on the other side.

There was a slight tingling in Scott's shoulders as he crossed what was not a line, but was definitely a something. He stopped, and took a step backwards. The tingling again. The light seemed a little different on this side. He looked around. How strange. If you stepped a pace forwards, the moon seemed to have switched places and be glaring down from a different part of the sky.

He moved back and forth a few times. There was just one place where you could actually see two moons. One in the North-West, the other in the North-East.

And there was something else odd as well. The snow was thicker after that line. The huge feet had made craters three foot deep. In the distance, Gavin Knight was floundering through a drift, buried almost to his waist, half pushing himself along, half swimming.

There was another thing. On the far side of the line, you couldn't see the blocks of flats. In fact, you couldn't see the houses either. If you turned round and faced exactly the direction you had come from, you could see the street lights on Station Road, and a solitary car creeping its way along. But, to the left, right, or ahead, nothing.

Scott turned right around. There was nothing but hill. Hill surrounded by trees. Lots and lots of trees, far more than Scott remembered.

And it was truly silent.

He now realised that the quiet of the night world he had heard before was really something else. As long as he could remember, there was a distant hum and rumble, the sound of the city which, even in deep winter, never really slept.

But here there was nothing. Only the distant crunch of Gavin Knight in a snow drift—and—

CRASH.

In the utter quiet, the noise was deafening. Far in the distance, far ahead, the sound of something—trees falling, rocks splitting, avalanche, even a bomb.

A huge head on massive, enormous shoulders, appeared over the brow of the hill. Scott thought it was coming back down its own tracks, then the silhouette bobbed and loped into the distance.

There was no time to be terrified. It was like the thrill at the top of a roller-coaster—a moment of pure terror followed by utter relief.

Just as he was getting over the fright, a long, ululating howl filled the night. Instantly it was joined by another, and another, and another. Scott spun round. His only thought was to go back the way he came, back to the world of the swimming baths, the blocks of flats and the house at number seventeen.

But he could not see the way. The shimmering line had faded. He moved a little to the left, a little to the right.

He was not panicking. Not yet.

He forced himself to turn around, to sight himself along the line of the giant's tracks, and then to turn back to look exactly where the giant had come from.

But still nothing. He tried the trick of defocusing his eyes and refocusing them, but that didn't help.

And then the howls began again. Wolves under the moonlight, just like in books, just exactly like in books, but infinitely more frightening.

Scott was on the verge of terror, when he suddenly felt himself lifted off his feet. He thrashed about until he saw that it was Gavin Knight who had caught him, and was running, carrying him straight towards where the shimmering line should have been.

In instant it was all over.

Scott could tell by the light, the shadows, the shape of the houses at the top of the hill. He was back in his own world, where he belonged.

He felt himself sliding to the ground, landing in a crunching heap of icy snow and Wellington boots.

Slowly, he pulled himself to his feet. Gavin Knight stood, facing away, as if he still gazed across the border between the two worlds. In his hand was a drawn sword. Not a foil, or an epee, or a sabre as they used at the fencing club, but a long, double edged, huge handled sword. And the moon glistened along edges that seemed to cut the wind with their sharpness.

He stood there a long time. A very long time, as if waiting for something to happen, or as if something was happening that Scott could not see.

At last he raised his sword, in the manner of a fencer's salute, and made a long, sweeping motion to the ground.

Then he turned to Scott.

"Friend Scott," he said, and the Scottish or Irish in his voice was now quite clear—"Friend Scott, this is a dangerous night to go skifting. I'm guessing I'll be getting the razor side of your mother's tongue for taking you down this road. Do you often go hunting in the snow?"

Scott shook his head and looked up, wondering.

"Please, sir," he said. "I don't understand what you are saying. I followed you through the snow and then I saw you vanish. When I came to the place where you were, I found I could see you if I went a particular way. So I followed you. But that's all."

Gavin Knight frowned.

"That is a little unusual," he said. "Have you never done this before?"

Scott shook his head.

"And has your mother taught you nothing about skifting?"

"Skifting?" said Scott. "I don't know that word."

"Well—" said Gavin Knight, and stopped. "This is not a good place for talking. We must return to your house, and accept whatever adventure befall us."

"Adventure?"

"I mean, we must put up with whatever it is your mother will have to say to us when we arrive back in the middle of the night with no explanation that she wants to hear."

"I see," said Scott.

They climbed the hill without speaking. There was nobody about, and the only sound was the comforting throb of the city that never slept.

As quietly as they could, they crept along the path. Scott thought they had got away with it as he turned the key in the latch. There were no lights on in the house, no sign that anyone was awake.

He pushed the door open and was on the point of slipping inside and up the stairs, when—

"That's far enough young man." It was his mother's voice. Low, stern, and almost hissing with fury. There was a click as she flicked the light switch. She stood in her white linen nightdress, almost trembling with anger, eyes glaring.

"And you—YOU!" Scott thought she was going to shriek as she turned her attention to Mr Knight.

She seemed to calm herself. Scott knew by experience that the worst was by no means over. The calm was a prelude to whatever punishment she thought would fit the crime.

"Right. Both of you. In the living room. NOW."

Scott found himself more or less slinking as he obeyed her instruction, but he saw that Gavin Knight walked very upright, with only his head bowed.

Scott's mother turned only for a moment to close the door behind her, but in that moment Gavin Knight gave Scott a look which was not quite a wink, but which said, as clearly as if he had said it, 'don't worry—we'll get out of this together'. Scott wanted to wink back, but his mother had turned again and was bearing down on them.

She gestured them into the settee, and sat down in the seat opposite.

"Well," she said. And she turned first to Scott. "Scott, I am astonished and disappointed that you have stolen out into the middle of the night with this man about whom you know almost nothing. We shall talk about this later."

"And you, Gwalchmai," she said, using a name that Scott had not heard before. "I should say 'how dare you come here to rob me of my son', except I should have known that this was just the sort of thing your foolish, idiotic, dull-witted and dishonourable mind would conceive. What I was thinking of when I allowed you into this house, under my roof I do not know. But know this, once the sun is up, be gone! I do not care where, as long as it is not here."

"My lady—" began Gavin.

"Do not 'My lady' me!" she said. "If you have anything, anything that you can possibly say in justification of tonight's debacle, say it without ornament or flattery."

"It was my fault," said Scott. He knew he was making things far worse for himself saying it, but, in some peculiar way, he felt he owed it to Gavin to rescue him from his mother in the same way that Gavin had rescued him from the wolf in Lyndon Road.

"Scott—stay out of this," she said.

"No, mum, it was my fault. I noticed that Mr Knight had gone out for a walk in the snow, and I realised that he didn't have a key. So I set off after him. But then I fell over in the snow and he brought me back."

"Is this true, Gwalchmai?" she said, turning back to Gavin.

He bowed his head.

"I am at my lady's mercy. No words that I can say will convince her, so I will remain silent."

"And what then should I believe?"

"My lady, all I can say—as to what you should believe—is 'you choose'."

This provoked an absolutely startling reaction from Scott's mother. Her eyes narrowed, she raised her finger, and for a moment she seemed lost for words.

"You—you—" And then she seemed to compose herself. "Right. Both of you. To bed. If you are going to behave like young children, I shall treat you both like them. Go. GO!"

"But, my lady, I was sleeping here."

"I shall stay here," she said. You may go and lie down on the bed in my room. I shall stay here by the door to make sure that neither of you get it into your heads to have any more night time adventures."

"And you—" she said to Scott "—fortunately for you, your school has decided not to open tomorrow. But I am going into the University, and you can just come along with me and work in the library, rather than hang around with this good-for-nothing layabout who hasn't done a proper day's work since before you were born."

Scott and Gavin exchanged looks on the landing, but neither of them spoke.

2 TIME LIKE SILK

Breakfast was surprising. Scott had expected the nutritional equivalent of a stern talking to. Perhaps dry toast and a cup of cold tea. Instead he woke to the smell of sausages and kippers and tomatoes frying, and the sound of coffee dripping through a percolator.

His mother and Gavin Knight were already sitting at the table when he arrived. Gavin insisted on saying 'grace', which seemed to consist of everyone bowing their heads while Gavin mumbled something in what sounded like Latin. It was odd and uncomfortable, but it only lasted a moment.

His mother, it seemed, was in the middle of a story about himself. Both she and Gavin seemed to think it was very funny, but Scott couldn't see what was especially interesting about some comment he had made to his teacher when he was six years old. He looked resolutely at his plate and ate his way through the sausages.

His mother seemed to get more and more frolicsome—almost giddy —as breakfast went on. By the time they had finished she was almost giggling, which was something he had never, ever seen her do. If he had been a bit older, he might have imagined that she had been at the brandy, except that she didn't hold with drink and there was no alcohol in the house.

All talk of putting Gavin Knight onto the street seemed to have evaporated. Instead, she presented him with a list of chores and errands to do around the house, as well as a long list of things to buy at the nearest supermarket. The nearest supermarket was a good two miles away, and Scott wondered, what with the snow, if there wasn't the slightest element of malice in that seemingly innocent instruction.

Then it was time to set off, and she was bundling him into their ageing Fiat Punto, and suddenly they were waving Gavin Knight good bye.

Usually Scott's mother went by train to the university, although she generally took a later train to save him from the embarrassment of being taken most of the way to school by his mother. But this morning she muttered something about the trains probably not running, and they set off down the hill straight into an enormous traffic jam.

The journey by car might normally have taken three quarters of an hour. This morning it was more like two, and it gave them plenty of time to talk.

Scott had a number of questions. He had shrewdly guessed that the chances of getting them answered depended on the order in which they were asked. After careful consideration, he decided to go for the softly-softly approach.

"Mum," he said. "Who is Gavin Knight, really?"

"Well, he's an old friend of mine."

"From university?"

"Well, not from the university as such. But I knew him while I was studying the dark ages."

Strange as it may seem, the words 'the dark ages', which Scott had heard countless times before, had a strange effect on him. He thought of silent, frozen hills, and wolf howls, and the huge footprints. He shuddered.

"Were the dark ages very dark, and cold, and … silent?"

"Well, I suppose they were some of the time. But they weren't anything like as bleak as people sometimes make out."

"Oh. I see. So who is Gavin Knight?"

"Well, he's someone I used to see a lot."

"When you were away?"

"Away? Away where?"

"Mum, you vanished for five years. It was in the Oxford Mail, but everyone in the family tries to pretend it never happened and they always avoid talking about it."

"Well, yes, I suppose I did know him then. But I knew a lot of people then, and I haven't seen any of them for twelve years, until Gavin arrived yesterday."

"So why do you call him Gwalchmai, if his name is Gavin?"

"Well, where he comes from most people have more than one name."

At this point Scott thought he had gathered as much information as he was likely to, and so he changed the subject to Latin verbs. He had only done a term of Latin—his school was one of the last schools that still taught it—but it was something he knew his mother strongly approved of, and so it was a safe subject to keep them going until they reached the university.

A thaw had begun to set in, and all the roads were grey and slushy. But the university was still bright with clean snow. The car-barriers at the East Gate were up, and the man there was waving cars in and out by hand. He saluted Scott's mother as she drove up.

"Doctor Raynall. Glad to see you made it safely through the snow. Are you teaching today?"

"Just a seminar on Old English poetry, Michael. It isn't until eleven o'clock, which just gives my students a chance of waking up in time."

"Very good Doctor Raynall. I'll keep an eye on your car if you park it in the usual space."

Scott considered asking to join his mother's poetry group, but he decided there were more exciting things to do in the library. So he agreed what time they would meet for lunch, and then set off on his own.

A university library is not like any kind of library you might normally walk into. For a start, there are few books on the shelves. If you want anything you have to look it up in the catalogue and fill in a form to give to the librarian. Sometimes you can order the books by computer, but this doesn't always work, although you can find most of what you want more quickly this way.

Scott was often in the library in the school holidays, and the librarians knew him well enough. Otherwise the presence of a young teenager might have prompted some difficult questions.

He sat down at the first available computer. The first place to look was the internet, although he was fairly sure he wouldn't find what he wanted. So he typed in 'Skifting' into Google. The result was a bit of a surprise. There were more than 8,000 websites that referred to 'Skifting'. But when he looked at them, they were all in Swedish or Danish or Norwegian. He tried 'Skift', but it produced more or less the same result.

So then he went to the library's database and tried 'Skift'. There were some Swedish references, but nothing in English. Helpfully, the computer said 'Do you mean 'Skiften'?' Scott searched for 'Skiften'. Another pile of Swedish books. But, right at the bottom of the third page there was a link to 'Department of English: restricted manuscripts in Middle English. Skiften.'

He clicked the link.

There was a pause, as if the computer was not quite sure whether was going to go there. And then a new window appeared. It said:

"Restricted Manuscripts. Please enter your name and password to continue."

Scott thought for a moment. He pressed 'Enter' to see if it let him in anyway, but it didn't. Then he tried putting in his name and his library password, but the message came back: "You do not have sufficient privileges to access this information. Contact a librarian for help."

Then he thought again. This time he put his mother's name in— 'Anne Raynall'. What about a password? He tried 'Scott', but the computer wouldn't accept it. Then he tried 'Perceval' which was his secret middle name that he never told to anyone. But it wasn't that either. Then he thought long and hard. A lot of computers would lock you out if you got the password wrong three times.

At last he typed in 'G W A L C H M A I'.

"Password accepted," said the computer screen. And it displayed a window of miniature manuscripts. Scott clicked on one, and it expanded into a facsimile of a faded, browned piece of vellum, written over in a precise script. It was not Latin, but it was not English either—at least, not any English that he could read.

He closed the window and tried three or four of the manuscripts. All were different, but each seemed to be written in the same way.

While he was looking, a message appeared on the screen.

"Doctor Raynall. I noticed you were accessing the manuscripts. Does this mean that you are joining us again? I do hope so. I look forward to seeing you at the next meeting. Or perhaps you would like to drop round and see me now? Yours, MLF."

Scott bit his lip. He hadn't reckoned on someone knowing what he was doing. If MLF—whoever that was—only looked at the timetable then they would see that Anne Raynall was actually teaching a seminar, and so could not be looking at files in the library.

There was a soft tinkle from the main desk. Someone was phoning the librarian. It rang for a few moments and then before it was picked up.

What if they were ringing to check who was using the computer?

Scott tried to log out, but the machine decided at that moment to go slow. Now the librarian was putting the phone down, and peering along the aisles of desks to see who was on the computers. He could hear the footsteps. A quick look round—it wasn't any of the librarians he knew.

His mind raced. Then, leaning forward, he casually pushed the 'Reset' button. The screen stayed steady with its incriminating information for a moment, and then flickered before telling him that he had not shut the computer down properly and it would now check for damage to the hard disk.

But Scott felt he wasn't in the clear yet. A machine that has just been reset is almost as incriminating as being caught red handed.

So he stood up suddenly, walked around the back of the next row of desks, and straight up to the advancing librarian.

"Excuse me mister," he said, in a voice that wasn't at all like his usual one. "'Ave you got any of the Judge Dredd comics?"

The librarian looked at him with infinite distaste.

"I'm sorry, I can't help you now. Try again later. Or try the university bookshop. I'm sure we don't have anything of that kind."

Scott hung around the university shops until lunchtime. He didn't have any money, but that didn't bother the shop-keepers, as most of the students didn't have any money either.

At twelve-thirty he went to find his mother in their favourite café. She was late. Very late. By quarter-to-one he wondered if he had the wrong place. So he scuttled off to the other café they sometimes went to. It was empty. Perhaps in that time his mother had arrived at the first. So he hurried back to that, but she wasn't there either.

At one o'clock two students wandered in who he had seen once or twice before. They both studied with his mother, and might have been in the seminar.

"Excuse me," he said. "Do you know Anne Raynall?" he said.

The student looked down at him, as if from a great height.

"That would be Doctor Raynall to you," said the student. "Yes, I know her."

"Well, have you seen her, because I was going to have lunch with her."

"Is that a fact?" said the student, and he exchanged a knowing look with his colleague. "Would this be academic or romantic?"

"She's my mother," said Scott.

"Ah, yes," said the student. "That would make you Scott Perceval, who loves sword fighting. She was teaching a seminar until an hour ago. But when it finished, two of the faculty seniors came to talk to her. She probably just got held up."

"Oh, right," said Scott. It wasn't like his mother to turn up late.

"Tell you what, why don't you give her a ring on her mobile?" said the student.

"I don't have one," said Scott.

"You can use mine. Just key in the number"—he winked at his colleague.

Scott dialled his mother's number. It rang for a few moments. Then a man's voice answered.

"Doctor Raynall's phone."

Scott put on what he thought was a deep voice, to try to disguise who he was.

"Hello. Could I speak to Anne please?"

"Oh. I'm sorry. Doctor Raynall is in conference. She has given strict instructions that she mustn't be disturbed."

"Oh. I see," said Scott, still trying to keep his voice as low as possible. "When will she become available?"

"Not until this evening," said the man. "Do you want me to give her a message?"

"No," said Scott. "I'll talk to her next week."

He rang off.

"Any luck?" said the student.

"It's very strange," said Scott. "But she didn't answer herself, and the man who did answer said she was at a conference."

"That is very strange," said the student. "Did you leave a message?"

"No," said Scott. "I didn't really like the man who answered."

"Mm. Well. That is funny. Perhaps he had the wrong end of the stick. Tell you what, why don't you have lunch with us while you wait for her to come."

Scott—who was by this time hungry—accepted the offer gratefully. The two students bought them each a mug of tea and ham in a baguette.

"Do you study Middle English or Anglo-Saxon?" said Scott.

"Well, 'study' is overstating what we do," said the other student. "But we're on the course. You'll find there's lots of dashing young men like us on the courses your mother teaches."

Scott didn't quite understood what he meant by this, but he thought they might know the answer to his other question.

"Do you know what 'skiften' means?"

One frowned, and the other looked away.

"We aren't in that group," said the first. "We don't really talk about that."

"Does my mother know about 'skiften'?" said Scott.

"No, she's not one of those either," said the other student. "Look, if it's all the same with you, we've got to be getting off now. Nice to meet you. Say 'hi' to your mother when you do find her."

They tidied up their plates as rapidly as they could without seeming to hurry, and made their way out of the cafeteria. But once away, Scott saw them dawdling as if they had suddenly discovered that they didn't have to be somewhere else after all.

He thought for a moment, and then he went up to the woman who was running the cafeteria. She was behind a long counter, polishing a rail, as there were by now few customers left.

"Excuse me," said Scott. "I was supposed to meet my mother for lunch and she hasn't arrived. Would you mind if I made a phone call to see where she is?"

"Phone booth round the corner," said the woman without looking up.

"Sorry, but I don't have any money. Please—it's really important."

The woman looked up. She was about to say something sharp when she saw that Scott was not a student.

"Oh, it's you. I've seen you here before. Make a call then, as long as it's quick. And no international, mind you."

Scott thanked her, and went behind the counter. You had to dial 9 to get outside the university phone system. So he dialled 9 and then his home number. If only Gavin Knight was at home—and if only, and Scott wasn't sure about this—he knew how to use a telephone.

The phone rang, once, twice, thrice... nine, ten, eleven.

'Click'.

"Hello," said Scott. "Is Gavin there?"

"Hello Scott," came the lilting, Irish-Scottish voice from the receiver.

"Gavin. Something has happened to my mother. She's more than an hour late for lunch. When I rang her phone a man answered and lied about her. I think it's something to do with skifting."

There was a pause from the other end.

"Scott, I don't like the sound of this. Are you able to come home?"

"I've got my travel pass."

"Right, well, come to Stechford Station, but don't come here. Do you know the old abandoned pub at the bottom of the Station Road hill?"

"I think so."

"Well, go there—but don't tell anyone. I will meet you there in one hour's time."

There was another click, and the phone went dead.

"Are you all right dear?" said the woman. She was now wiping down the hot trays behind the main counter.

"Yeah, thanks," said Scott. "If my mum comes in, can you tell her that I'm meeting my uncle?"

"Of course dear," said the woman, without looking up.

Scott left the cafeteria and took a long detour round by the Sports Centre on his way to the station. The train would be another ten minutes, and he felt that he shouldn't arrive earlier than he had to.

All the university roads had been cleared of snow, which made it a fairly easy walk out to the West gate and then back in towards the station. With half a minute to go he waved his pass at the ticket office and wandered nonchalantly down the steps. The train pulled in as he reached it, and he slipped into the nearest carriage.

There were two men in black coats and black bowler hats—the kind you rarely see these days—at either end of the platform. If they were looking for Scott they must have missed him in the crowd, but they seemed to be looking for someone, as they passed down the train looking into each carriage window.

They seemed to have some understanding with the driver. Normally the train would only wait just long enough for everybody to get on and off, but this time it waited patiently, doors open, until the bowler-hatted men were satisfied. Watching at the edge of the window, Scott distinctly saw them wave to the driver, and, a moment later, the doors closed and the train pulled away.

At New Street, Scott thought he saw more men of the same type. Long, black coats, and hats. This time they wore trilbies, rather than bowlers, but since they were the only men wearing hats in the whole station, it was hard not to believe they were somehow connected to the bowler men.

Rather than risk another train journey, Scott slipped out past the Stevenson Street exit, through the pre-Christmas shopping crowds which already filled Corporation Street, and along to the Number Fourteen Bus stop. The Fourteen took much longer than the train, but it dropped you almost right outside the derelict pub that Gavin mentioned.

He lurked in the shadows of a doorway until the bus appeared, and made a furtive dash. It was probably not a wise choice—the bus driver was suspicious and he made Scott show him his pass three times before he let him on. Scott settled himself on the side-facing seats between the front door and the middle-door. He reckoned that if someone he didn't like the look of got on at one door, he could quickly leave through the other.

The journey—down through Saltley and Alum Rock—took even longer than usual. Many of the side roads had not been properly cleared, and there were traffic jams everywhere. By the time they reached Stechford, it was almost four o'clock, and the sun was low in the sky.

He slipped quietly out at the stop nearest the pub. The Stechford snow was now completely scuffed and sludged, a blend of diesel grey and mud-brown.

The Manor House was a big old pub that had been abandoned for at least five years, after, so it was said, a young man was shot there one evening. There had been talk of new owners, or of replacing it with a medical centre, but in truth it was lost on an island between the river and the traffic. In the olden days working men had stopped off there on the way home to their wives. But most of the work round there had closed down years before, and what with busses and motor cars, few people walked that way now, whether on the way home from work or for any other reason.

Many of the windows were broken on the second floor, and all of the windows lower down were boarded up with thick, ugly boards. It had been a grand place once—not just a pub with a bar and a saloon, but an inn with rooms to let and a flat for the landlord.

"Scott, Scott," called a voice from among the bushes. It was Gavin. Scott walked across to him, nonchalantly, not looking where he was going, hoping to throw off any watchers.

"Scott. This is important. You're my younger brother, and we're both looking for work in the coal trade."

"But there is no coal trade in Stechford," said Scott.

"Not now, but once there was. Be careful what you say. You don't know anything about television, or any modern music—in fact, pretend you don't know anything at all. I will do the talking."

"But what are we doing?"

"We're going to hide for a little while in this pub. We can get a good meal here, and maybe a bed for the night."

"But Mr Knight, it's been closed for years."

"Never mind that. Just stay with me. Do you know the story of Good King Wenceslas?"

"The one who liked his pizza 'deep pan, crisp and even'?"

"Something like that. Wherever you see me put my feet, put your feet in the same place. Now."

Gavin set off slowly across the snow, making—for him—ordinary strides. Scott had almost to jump to match them. Walking in Gavin's footsteps, he could again see the slight shimmer in the air that he had seen the night before. On the far side the snow was much less—just a smattering, a sprinkling here and there. There were museum-piece motor cars in a car park, and the din of voices.

He crossed the line.

Now there was no doubt about it. It was another world, or another time. The pub which they had just left ruined and desolate stood in all its glory, lights streaming from the windows and doors, a good natured hubbub coming from the public rooms, and small crowds of men in caps standing around outside, drinking and smoking pipes or thin cigarettes.

Gavin pushed a path for them through the doorway. Scott noticed that he had a bag like an army kit back over his shoulder.

Inside it was warm and steamy. The saloon was closely packed with men like those outside. It was filled with the sickly-sweet smell of tobacco and stale beer. Scott stood half stupefied by the dull air and the din of voices, until a woman came and ushered him and Gavin into a side parlour where she laid out a meal of bread and corned beef.

Mercifully, the air was clearer. Once the parlour door was shut, the din fell to a rising and falling murmur, like distant water.

"Now," said Gavin. "Tell me everything that happened from the moment you set off this morning until you arrived here."

He munched bread and corned beef while Scott told him all about the library, and the computer, and the librarian, and waiting for his mother, and the students, and the strange man on his mother's phone. Gavin asked him some sharp questions about what he was looking for in the library, and then he let Scott finish his story about the men in bowler hats and trilbies, right down to getting off the bus in Stechford. Scott put in a lot of questions of his own, but Gavin said he would answer them when Scott had finished.

Then Scott ate while Gavin answered his questions.

"I can't tell you much about skifting," he said. "There's a great deal to tell and I am not the right person to tell it."

"But skifting means travelling through time, doesn't it?" said Scott. He had been thinking about it all day, and putting all the things together that he had seen since last night.

"In a certain sense, yes. You can only skift at certain times and in certain places. You can't skift in your own lifetime, and when you skift and you arrive back in your own time—if you ever do—you arrive back later than when you set off. If you spend a week skifting, you arrive back a week after you set off, if a year, a year, if ten years, ten years."

"How does it work?"

"I don't know the answer to that. I don't know if anybody does. A skift door opens in one time, and it lets you walk through into the same time, the same day, the same month, but a different year. You can't set off in Summer and arrive at Christmas, though, sometimes, things seem to happen out of sequence when you skift, and there may be a day of summer in the middle of Christmas.. Most often, the weather where you arrive is like the weather where you set off. And, the worse the weather, the more chances there are to skift. Bitter winds and deep snow—they are the ones that bring out the skifters.

"It's as if time were a roll of silk. Fine silk rolled tight. We creep in the space between the layers all the long days of our lives. But sometimes we find a tear, and we can go through a layer, or maybe ten, and we creep along again. And when we find another tear, we can go back to the layer where we began, but not the same place, because we have crawled on that much further.

"The skift door stays open for a while. Sometimes for a few minutes, sometimes even for days. But if you miss the door back to your own time, you may have to go through many, many doors to reach it again. If you ever do. There are tales of skifting-wanderers who have visited every time and yet never found again their own."

Scott thought about that for a moment, and missed the next part of what Gavin was saying.

"...when you are going. You don't know. You can feel if you are foreskifting or backskifting, and sometimes you can sense whether you are moving a long time or a short time. But you always know one thing—skifting always takes you to where the trouble is. You can sometimes find someone else's skiftdoor and go back to where they came from, but a new door means trouble ahead."

"What sort of trouble?"

"Oh, the usual kind. War, famine, plague. Murder, pillage, kidnapping and hostage taking. Massacres and burnings. The greater the trouble, the longer the door stays open, and the further in the future or the past it can be."

"So are we in trouble now?"

He was answered by a screaming, crunching, scraping sound from the road outside.

"Scott, I have to help," said Gavin. "This isn't something for you to look at. There's a room for us upstairs. Get what sleep you can." And with that, he was gone, struggling through the parlour door and out onto into the dark.

3 THE GATEHOUSE

Scott woke to see Gavin Knight crouched over a single, flickering electric light bulb. The fire had died in the grate, and the air was icy. He pulled the blankets around him.

Gavin was studying a book—what looked like an old notebook, leather bound, repaired many times, written in crabbed script.

"What are we going to do?" said Scott.

"We must set off to rescue her," said Gavin. "But we are not in a good place to do that. This place has only been here a handful of years. We might walk along Station Road and hope to catch a highwayman or so, but these were peaceful parts and poor, with little to catch a robber's eye. To the north is Sutton Park, which has seen many adventures, but I would rather strike out east towards Kenilworth. There were many dark days at that castle, and it will take us a good stretch backwards."

"How far do we have to go?"

"Well, their side was strong at particular times in history. They were strong in the Civil War, and they were strong in the time of Mary, and Richard the third. They were bad times all of them, easy to reach by skifting. Then we go back through bad king John, as we called him, and then the days of Stephen and Matilda, while, as they said, 'Christ slept, and his saints'. They were strong in William's time as well, but they didn't like what you call the Dark Ages. But they began in Arthur's time, and that is where they will always be strongest."

"Which side is their side?" said Scott, and, without waiting for an answer, he added: "Will we go to Arthur's time?"

"I would think not. If they just want to question your mother, then they will take her somewhere quite near, not so long ago, where they feel secure. In any case, they will not have had time to go far back. If we go swiftly we will catch them yet."

Scott wanted to ask, but didn't quite say the words: "What if we don't catch them?"

He climbed out of bed and pulled on his coat and boots. There were strange patterns of ice inside the window, which was something he had never seen before.

A few minutes later he was standing in the courtyard.

Scott was just wondering how they were going to get to Kenilworth in the middle of the night ninety years ago in the snow, when he heard a jingle and a neigh. Gavin Knight came round the corner with two horses, or, rather, a horse and a pony.

"Can you ride, Scott?" he said.

"Well, I suppose so, I've never really tried."

"Humph," said Gavin. "Did your mother never teach you anything?"

Scott shook his head dismally. He had, in fact, often wanted to learn to ride, but she had always said they were too poor. She had not liked the idea of him fencing either, but he had already started by the time she found out.

"Well, you'll have to do the best you can," said Gavin. "I'll help you into the saddle, and you'll just have to let your pony follow my horse. It's not so hard. Look at what my horse is doing, grip with your knees, and use the stirrups to keep you upright if you have to."

He helped Scott put one foot into the stirrup, and then heaved him up, as if he were the lightest thing in the world. For a moment Scott wobbled, but then he managed to get his other foot into the stirrup, and, precariously, he was up. The pony's back was beautifully warm.

Then Gavin mounted his own horse. He did it so lightly and easily that Scott wondered how many years practice it would take for him to do the same.

"Where are these horses from?" said Scott.

"Never you mind about that. Keep your eyes on me, and try to stay up."

And they set off. The snow was thicker than it had been in Scott's time, and it seemed that there had been less traffic to churn it up. Very quickly they passed onto quiet lanes between open fields.

"Where are all the houses?" Scott called.

"They don't come for years yet," said Gavin. Now that they were out of earshot of the pub, the night was absolutely silent. The horses' hooves made almost no sound in the snow. The moon was bright, and the air crisp.

After a while, Gavin's horse began to trot. Scott's pony did the same. For a moment he felt he was going to fall, but somehow he managed to keep in the saddle. He wondered what would happen if Gavin decided to gallop.

After about half a mile they passed a solitary farm house—big and white, it was a house Scott recognised. Then hedged fields, and an old church with a tower.

"That's Saint Giles," said Gavin. They passed an inn, and Gavin drew them in a wide circle around the inn again, slowing the horses to a walk. Scott saw him shifting this way and that, just as he had done on the hill by the swimming baths. Then he saw the faint shimmer himself. It was a little like the shimmer of silk.

"Here's a piece of luck," said Gavin. "A skift door—and sooner than I had hoped. Come on." He spurred his horse on, and Scott followed a little distance behind through the shimmering.

On the other side was an ugly crowd of people with pitchforks and mattocks and scythes and axes. One or two had lanterns such as Scott had seen in films, and one had a musket. He could not make out the voices, but the crowd seemed to mumble and murmur as one man. Then a single voice raised itself above the others: "Never you mind about that," it said in a thick accent, like something you sometimes hear from the oldest of old Birmingham men, but slower, richer. "Never you mind, John Bartlett," the man went on. "We got her old ma and we'll get her next. We've no need for witches in these parts. You just push her out now and let us deal with her, and we'll make that an end to it."

"Not while she's a guest in my hostelry," shouted a voice from the inn. Scott looked up and saw a man leaning out of an upper window. He looked frightened, but something in the set of his jaw told Scott that he meant to stand his ground.

There was a thud from down below. Scott saw that four of the men had got a log and were starting to batter down the door. It was heavy, studded oak, and as yet showed no signs of cracking. All the windows were shuttered, "but it won't be long before they realise that those shutters will open easily enough," Scott thought.

"We've no quarrel with you John Bartlett," shouted the leader. "Push her out of the window and there's no hard feelings."

This was too much for Gavin Knight. From his bag he had drawn out a sword—not a big, cumbersome sword nor yet a finely tempered rapier, but something sharp and gently curved. He rode straight at the middle of the crowd.

They must have had good ears. With no more than a neigh and the crunching of hooves to warn them, they parted like water. Gavin rode into the middle of them, made the horse rear up and brandished his weapon.

"Who are you?" shouted someone. The crowd—which had given him a good couple of yards space—edged forward.

The horse reared again, and the crowd gave a little—but only a little.

"What manner of men are you, that threaten a lady with scythes and clubs?" he shouted. And then he wheeled the horse round until he had cut off the leader from the others.

"And you, sir? What have you to say to yourself. Speak man, or your life is forfeit!"

"There's a witch in that inn, your honour, sir. There's no call for giving hostelry to such as 'un. Her'll be the death of this village, and no mistake."

"A witch, man? Do you know what year this is?"

"Seventeen hundred and forty-six, your honour. I knows my letters."

"And you mean to come blathering about witches in these days of iron and steel and furnace and steam? Have you no knowledge of the advancement of science, man? And know you nothing of the laws of this land? Be off, at once, all of you. I've a mind to call out the militia and have you all thrown into jail."

"Who are you to tell us what's what?" shouted someone.

"A knight, sir. A knight and a soldier of the king. And a privy councillor to boot. And if you would not face my wrath, you had better be gone from here." He let the horse rear up again. This time it lashed out with its front feet at the nearest of the mob. Gavin raised his sword as if to strike.

And—suddenly—the crowd was gone. They slunk off to the left and to the right, avoiding his eyes, keeping their heads down, shuffling to be away from the hooves and the glinting blade.

When all was quiet, the innkeeper unbolted the door and let them inside. It was dark in the parlour after the moon-snow-brightness outside. A pair of tallow candles filled the room with choking smoke, in exchange for meagre light which did not quite reach the corners. The innkeeper made a great fuss of begging 'their honours' to stay for the night. But Scott could not help feeling that he really wanted rid of them.

In any case, Gavin wanted to push on. The innkeeper offered them a change of horses to speed their journey.

"You'd best take the witch with you then, my lord," he added.

"You believe she is a witch, then?" said Gavin. "Why did you not hand her over?"

"Witch or no witch, a paying guest is a paying guest. That lot'll be in here tomorrow night and the night after drinking their own health whatever I do or say. But if word got out that I abandoned my guests at the first sign of trouble, then that'd be an end to the gentry who stop here. But you mun best take her, since they'll be back the moment you're gone, any-road."

Scott did not much like the idea of continuing their journey with a witch.

Still, as Gavin did not ask him, he felt reluctant to complain.

And so it was that they set off again through the snow, three of them. Gavin had turned down the offer of a change of horses, though he took one for the witch-girl. But he did request thick winter cloaks, such as travellers wore.

"These will keep us warm, and keep prying eyes away from our clothes, which are not suited to these times," he said.

Scott had not yet seen the witch-girl's face. She had left the inn muffled in a cloak and hood, and she avoided Scott's eyes as she mounted her horse. He was surprised to see that she did not entirely mount it, but sat 'side-saddle' as he later learned to call it. He managed to mount this time on his own—not in the effortless, elegant way that Gavin had, but with enough independence not to embarrass himself.

As they rode, the snow began again to fall. It settled flake by flake on their cloaks, and filled the air with swirling.

They rode on. An hour through the dreamy landscape. Scott did not feel cold—the cloak, and the pony, kept him warm, and by drawing his hands deep within the sleeves, he was able to both hold the reins and keep them from freezing. He found himself the last in the line, with Gavin leading the way and the witch-girl keeping pace. His pony was content to trot along, making almost no sound. Nobody spoke.

He must have half fallen asleep.

Scott came to his senses with a start. They were in a wide space of white. Ahead was a large building. He had been to Kenilworth Castle before, and believed it to be the gatehouse. He strained his eyes through the snow to see the castle beyond. There was something …

"But it's still a ruin," he said out loud. He had expected to see the castle bustling with life now that they were in the past.

"Hush, my young friend," said Gavin. "Never let people know that you are not from their time. The castle was ruined more than a century before where we stand today. For now, it is enough that we are at the gatehouse. In the morning we will seek a way further back."

With that he rode up to the huge wooden gates and banged on them with the hilt of his sword. It was such a blow that would have knocked a hole through the front door of Scott's house, but it made little sound on the huge, hard grained oak. He banged again, and a third time.

Then they waited.

Scott felt as though he were going to fall again into sleep, when he saw a flicker of candlelight in a dark window. Then the light was gone, but not long afterwards a side door, called a postern, opened, and a man looked out.

He was grizzled, with grey hair, and he did not like the cold. Scott saw him hugging himself and cursing the snow. He moved erratically, this way and that.

"What d'you want?" he yelled, except that his 'want' sounded more like 'warned'.

"Guests seek lodging. A knight of the crown, and two young persons in my charge."

"W'll, this ain't no hostel," shouted the man. "Be off with you."

"This is no way to treat honoured guests," retorted Gavin. "Or do I have to break down the gate and leave the damage to your account?"

Scott thought he had as much chance of breaking down the gate as he had of jumping his horse over the walls, but the threat seemed—in a perverse way—to make an impression on the gatekeeper.

"You'd best be coming inside," he said. "The master'll no doubt be waiting for you, with all the other guests tonight."

Scott could not see the look on Gavin's face, but noticed that his shoulders twitched just a little when the old man mentioned other guests.

There was a rattling of bolts, and the gates swung open to reveal a tiny courtyard. The gatekeeper came out and took the heads of their horses and led them in. Now that he had decided to admit them, his surliness seemed to evaporate.

Five minutes later they were shaking off the snow in front of a roaring fire. Scott found that he had become stiff from the ride. Once they were dry and a little warm, the man led them across the courtyard to a spiral staircase. It was made of stone flags, tidily cut and newly cleaned. Scott had climbed such staircases in preserved monuments, but he had never been up one which was actually in use. It gave him a slightly funny feeling.

"The stairs turn this way to give the defenders an advantage in a siege," said Gavin. "The attacker finds himself constrained on his right, while the defender is free to attack. That is why it is wise to also learn to fight with your left hand."

This seemed such a strange thing to say that Scott asked:

"Please, Mr Knight. Have you ever been in a siege?"

"A siege, master Scott? Once or twice. But I have seen many fights on staircases, and I would always rather be the man at the top than the one below."

They soon found themselves in a hall or banqueting chamber. It was not as big as the school assembly hall, but it was much bigger than

Scott's house. It was set with a long table down the centre, and many guests were dining. But, alongside, somebody had marked out a piste for fencing, and a small crowd were gathered in ones and twos watching as two men fought a bout.

For a moment Gavin stood rigid.

"This is a strange gathering," he muttered. Indeed it was. Looking up and down the table Scott saw people dressed in many different ways, but surely they did not all belong to this time. One man wore a suit such as Scott's grandfather had worn, while another looked as though he had stepped out of a Robin Hood adventure.

But there was not much time to look, as people were now advancing on them. The first seemed to be the host.

"Greetings, friends," he said. "This is a sorry night to be lost in, but you see we have many guests and more cannot hurt. I do not imagine that you have travelled just to see me, and I long to hear your tale. But, first, here is food, and drink, to take away hunger and thirst, and to banish the memory of the winter cold."

"My lord is most gracious," said Gavin.

"By what name should we know you?" said the host. "Or do you prefer as many do to go incognito in these uncertain times?"

"My lord is most astute. Perhaps for this night alone he may call us Sir Gawain and Perceval, and let this young lady be our damsel rescued from distress."

"Indeed, my knights. Might I be so rude as to enquire if you are going forwards or backwards, since it is no secret to me that you are not of these times?"

"My lord is too kind," said Gavin. This reply seemed to catch the host off guard, and he stumbled on his next words.

"How rude of me to press. Sit, eat, drink. And when you wish to sleep, my steward will lead you to bedrooms presently."

Scott found himself seated next to the man from Robin Hood on his right, and the girl they had rescued on his left. He was about to tuck into the food that was spread across the table, when Gavin, who had not yet been seated, muttered in his ear: "Watch what you eat and on no account drink the wine. And don't say a word about why we are here or when we have come from."

After that Scott felt he could do no more than nibble at some bread rolls. This was a pity, because he had never in his life seen a table so amazingly covered in every possible kind of pie, cut of meat, and winter vegetable, with soup steaming in tureens, and potatoes piled high, while fat dripped invitingly off what seemed to be half a pig, roasted and glazed in the middle of the table, with an apple in its mouth.

But it did give him a chance to look more closely at his new companion.

She was a slight girl, a few years older than he was. She had mousey brown hair, and hazel eyes, and she wore a necklace of green and gold, with malachite and garnet swirled together between endless flowing snakes and dragons. It was beautiful, and Scott thought that she was beautiful as well.

But she did not speak. She looked straight ahead of her, neither to the right nor to the left, and ate slowly and daintily. Scott noticed that she only used her knife, and left the fork beside her plate.

Gavin was seated some distance from them, next to the host at the top of the table. There was so much noise in the hall from the general chatter, mixed with the snicker-snack of blades from the fencers that he could not catch anything of their conversation. But he did notice that other several heads were turning towards in that direction.

"And you are the young Sir Perceval," said the man on his right. Scott wasn't quite sure what to say, but felt he ought to say something. So he said:

"Just for tonight. May I ask your name?"

"Oh, I have no name of any real interest. I'm just a tourist. Are you from then, or from now?"

"Oh, that depends," said Scott. "When is now and when is then?"

"Ah, yes indeed. A fine response. Your guardian would be proud of you. And the young lady?"

"Oh, she doesn't say very much," said Scott.

Just at that moment he heard a voice behind him which made him spin round.

"Well, well, well. If it isn't young Master Raynall. Who would have thought of seeing you here?"

The man standing behind him was—no it couldn't be—yes it was, the fencing coach from his school. Professor Sutton was a kind man of no particular age with close cropped hair, a short black beard, and a slightly rounder stomach than you might expect from a sports coach. He had the trick of remembering everyone's name after the first time they met, except he spoilt it sometimes by forgetting the names of people he had known for years.

"Hello, Professor," said Scott.

"Have you come here for a fencing lesson?" said the Professor. "It's certainly a long way to come. Find yourself a mask and a jacket, and we'll see what we can do."

Scott looked up to see if Gavin had noticed what was going on. It seemed that he had, but as he made no effort to intervene, Scott—rather glad to be out of the conversation with the Robin Hood man—obediently excused himself from the table and made his way through the clumps of spectators to a pile of masks, jackets and fencing foils.

Scott had done barely a term of fencing, but he had worked hard and the Professor had told him he was a 'natural'. He had told his mother this, but this seemed to please here even less than when he started. This was a pity, as he was terrible at all other sports.

He hunted around the pile to find a jacket and a mask that fitted him. The materials were rather odd. Instead of Kevlar and cotton, which is what the jackets at school were made from, the jacket seemed to be thick canvass. There were no zips, but someone helped him with the buttons, which ran all the way up the side and across his left shoulder. The mask was made of the familiar wire mesh, but the sides and bib were padded with leather.

"Now, be careful with this equipment," said the coach. "It's not quite as safe as what you're used to, though it should look after you if you are circumspect. En Garde!"

The professor seemed intent on giving Scott a very full, very thorough lesson. He drilled him through his lunges, and his attacks, and his parries, and ripostes, and first counter ripostes, and second counter ripostes. Then he took him through attacks on the blade, including beats, and prises de fers of all kinds, with binds and froissements and coulés and glisses. Then he began to work on Scott's footwork—steps, and jumps, and appels, and balestras, and the fleche, which means diving through the air at your opponent. He paid special attention to the balestra, which was a move Scott struggled with. It was a cross between a jump and a step.

"The balestra is your greatest friend," he said. "It breaks the rhythm of your step, so you are not where your opponent thinks you will be, and it adds great penetration to your lunge."

As he taught, Professor Sutton mixed in other kinds of advice as well.

"I come here a lot," he said. "As there isn't always enough coaching work in our time. I have my ways of coming and going, and there's usually a welcome here."

A little later he said: "I've known young Gavin, as he calls himself, since he was your age. A fine fencer and the master of many weapons."

And later still: "It's no surprise that you would go skifting, having it from both your mother and your father."

"Do you know my father?" said Scott. It was almost a yelp.

"Don't you? Well, I shouldn't be the one to say. When you go skifting, there are many secrets you should keep and no one should be too quick to tell another's."

"Please, Professor Sutton, what is skifting?"

"Ah, that, young Scott, is something that I am not allowed to teach. It's one of the rules of the Academy. But if you've come this far, you must have a fair idea of your own."

"Why is that a rule?"

"Well, Scott, you couldn't have generations of fencers all skifting up and down time looking for fights. There would be no end to the trouble."

"Do many people you coach skift?"

"A lot of people start fencing after they start skifting. Guns and machines of all kinds do not travel well through time. And, as they're always skifting into trouble, they need a way to defend themselves. Then there are the people who think we should never have left the middle ages and start fencing because they think that somebody might tell them how to skift."

"Can anybody learn to skift?"

"Very few. Very few. But it runs in families, and if your mother and father were both skifters, there's a good chance that you are as well, whether or not they want you to be."

Scott was about to ask him more, but the lesson suddenly picked up pace, and they were at it, hammer and tongs, up and down the length of the hall. It seemed to Scott that he had learned more in that hour than in all the fencing he had done before. But as they came to the end, the coach said:

"Now, Scott, you've done well. But don't think about getting into any fights. There are people in the past who would chop you into mincemeat. And there's worse than people."

"Worse than people?"

"Giants, werewolves, dragons. Basilisks, serpents and worms. Trolls, wraiths, and witches."

"Do they exist?"

"Scott, I'm not sure I should tell you this. But whenever you skift, you make the holes in the cloth of time a little bit larger. The more people skift, the easier it is to skift. But other things come creeping back through those holes."

"But we'd be safe enough in our own time," said Scott. "We've got the army. And tanks. And missiles. And nuclear weapons."

"It would be nice to think so, Scott. But they are not merely flesh and blood. They cannot be destroyed with bombs and bullets."

"Then how do you fight them?"

"With a brave heart and strength of spirit. If you strike a monster with a sword, or with a lance, or even with a dagger, you strike with your heart. And if your heart is strong and your spirit pure, the wound will be bitter. But if you were to throw the same dagger, or shoot with a bow, or a bullet, or a missile, it would do nothing. And the same is true if you strike with fear in your heart, or with evil in your soul.

"Don't go picking fights with monsters, Scott. Not yet."

And with that he saluted, and the lesson was over.

Scott was now tired. Someone took his hand and led him down a long corridor with doors on the left and the right. At the far end was a door to a room with a fire in the hearth and a bed.

4 THE KNIGHT OF THE GREEN

Scott did not wake until the sunlight played across his face. He sat up in his bed, and remembered that this was not his bed after all. The blankets were heavy, but the mattress was soft, as if filled with feathers. A fire was burning in the hearth, and a large copper pot full of steaming water was standing beside a bath.

Of course, it was not the kind of bath that Scott was used to. There were no taps, and no plumbing, and it stood on its own.

It took him a few minutes with the copper pot and a jug of cold water to find the temperature he wanted, but when it was ready he sank himself to his neck.

A bath really was just what he wanted—all his muscles ached, partly from the horse riding, and partly from the fencing. His mother kept a bottle of something called Radox at home which was supposed to be good for muscles. Looking around he did not see (and did not expect to see) Radox, but there was a little bottle beside the copper pot, and he poured it into the water. It was a green vial, with a curious stopper.

Instantly a rich and rather heady smell filled the room, and his skin tingled. He felt his nostrils clearing. It made his eyes water a little, but, aside from that, it was quite simply the most delicious bath he had ever taken.

If there had been a hot tap, he would probably have stayed in there for hours. But the antique bath had one shortcoming—it did not hold the heat well. Even as the smell from the bottle began to fade, the water was lukewarm, and Scott could tell it was quickly on its way to cold.

He jumped out and dried himself.

His clothes, crumpled beside the bath where he had left them, looked decidedly the worse for wear. Mud spattered, salt crusted, and he saw now that one of his soles was peeling off.

He was just wondering what to do when an old man hobbled into the room.

"Everything right for you, my young master?" he said. He laid something on the bed and then busied himself with throwing away the water from Scott's bath. There was a rush of cold air as he opened the window, and he let out a strange, yodelling cry. It was followed by an enormous splash, as he tipped the whole contents of the bath out. Scott wondered what it would be like for anyone underneath, and guessed that that was the point of the cry.

But his attention returned to the bed. It took him a moment to work out what the old man had brought him. It was definitely clothes of some kind, but like nothing that Scott had ever seen.

"Here you am, young master," said the old man, and began to dress him. Nobody had ever dressed Scott before, except his mother, and that had been years ago when he was a small child. But the old man was so quick and deft with his fingers that it soon seemed the most natural thing in the world. Scott's new clothes, which would have been extremely old (in his own time), were nothing like his old clothes (that is to say, his modern clothes). For a start, there was no elastic. Instead they were fitted with an astonishing array of buttons, buckles, hasps and hooks. He felt that he would have been quite at a loss to put them on without help. The old man also helped him into a pair of soft leather boots that rolled down to just below the knees.

Scott caught a glimpse of himself in a mirror at the other end of the room. He did not look like himself at all. His narrow shoulders had been broadened out with layers of padded velvet and silk, while his waist was pinched tight. The colours were also colours he was not used to—deep reds, and greens, with hints of gold woven into the fabric.

"And there you am, young master. There'll be breakfast in the hall, and I've no doubt but you'll find many as wish to talk with you," said the old man, as he added the final touch—a richly jewelled belt, and hanging from it on the right hand side a dagger, and on the left hand side a sword.

A sword!

Scott brushed his hand against the pommel, just to get a feeling of its weight. It was surely far heavier than the fencing foils he had practised with.

"Her'll be nice and bright and sharp," said the old man, turning back as he hobbled his way out again. "I saw to her myself this morning."

Scott lifted the weapon a little, so that the blade slid out of the scabbard. It moved smoothly, and the sun glinted on a foot of polished steel. He let it fall back in, and made his way to breakfast.

There were just one or two people in the hall. He noticed straightaway that no one else was dressed as he was. Feeling a little self-conscious, he chose a place as far away from the others as he could, and sat down.

Almost as soon as he was seated a maid, with her hair tied back and wearing a stiff, white apron over a dark dress, set out a glass of milk and a bowl of porridge. Scott was hungry. Quite forgetting what he had been told the night before about watching what he ate, he made his way through the porridge, and then through a poached trout, and finally through liver and kidney.

When he finally looked up, a young woman had sat down beside him. She had long, slender fingers, and very white skin. Her lips were thin but quite red, and seemed hard, except when they opened into a smile. She could have been the older sister of the girl they had brought to the castle.

"So, young Sir Perceval. What is it like to travel with the famous Sir Gawain?"

Scott did not quite know what to say.

"You seem abashed," she continued, as if she had not quite expected him to reply. "We have many visitors in this place, skifting backwards and forwards on their way hither and thither. But seldom do we have two so famous as yourselves."

"I think you are making a mistake," said Scott. "You see, those aren't our real names. They are just names that my friend gave for politeness."

"Ah, but I see you are yourself a master of courtesy. Many travellers boast of deeds they have not done and sights they have not seen. But you hide your fame."

"No, it's not like that," said Scott. "They're just made-up names."

The woman smiled—a full lipped smile that softened her face. But Scott noticed that her eyes did not smile.

"I shall call you Perceval nonetheless, and you shall call me Viviane. But even if you are not Sir Perceval, your friend is surely Sir Gawain."

Scott shook his head.

"Young Sir Perceval, do not jest with me. Sir Gawain I have seen many times before, although always from a distance. At tournaments, and at occasions of state, and once, just once, at the court of Arthur the king, his uncle. Even if he had not given his name, I should have known him."

"How would you have known him, Viviane?" said Scott, caught up in the lady's enthusiasm.

"First, you should know that he has a small wound at the side of his neck. They say that a giant struck at him with an axe, but Sir Gawain survived. This I have seen on the neck of your companion."

Scott thought about this for a moment. He had noticed a mark, which could be like an old scar, on Gavin Knight's neck.

"Second, you will know that he always wears wrapped about his waist a green belt. A slight thing, barely more than twisted yarn, but a strange thing for a man to carry. This is Gawain's belt, that he had from the enchantress of Hautdessart. Surely you know this story?"

Scott did not say anything. He had not noticed Gavin wearing a green belt, but he could not convince himself that he had noticed him not wearing a green belt either.

"And, finally, everyone knows Sir Gawain by his courtesy, and especially by his courtesy to women. Come, look!"

She led Scott to a window that looked down on the courtyard. They were three storeys up, looking down on the heads of the people below. Scott saw four women crowded around one man, and the man looked up, and Scott saw that it was Gavin. He pushed open the window for a better look, and Gavin called up to him.

"Hey, lazybones! It's time we were on our way."

When Scott pulled himself away from the window, the lady was gone.

In the courtyard, Gavin—or was it Gawain?—was holding the heads of two horses. They were not quite like the horses of the night before. They were somehow heavier in the shoulder and in the calf. Scott's especially, seemed rather taller. There was no sign of the girl they had brought with them to the castle. Scott was glad of that.

Gavin was also dressed rather differently. He was wearing a long cloak, clasped about his throat with silver, and boots like the ones that Scott had been given.

"Good morrow, my friend," he said. Scott couldn't quite tell, but it seemed as though his accent, which was always on the verge of being Welsh, or Irish, or Scottish, had deepened and softened.

"Here, put this on," he said, and handed Scott a cloak like his own. "Your new clothes are just fine for the end of our journey, but they might attract a little too much attention this side of the middle ages."

"Do you know where we are going yet?" said Scott.

"Hush. Not until we are outside these walls. Not everyone here is a friend," he said, softly. And, then, much louder: "I think we will set off for Warwick next. The snow is still thick on the ground but the road is good and the day is ahead of us."

Gavin gave Scott his horse's reins, and together they led them out through the great gate. Scott eyed the stirrups suspiciously, but Gavin gave him a heave up, and they were on their way.

The road led out of the gatehouse and around the sides of the old castle ruin. It stood gaunt and sinister in the snow. Light poured over the red stone from the East. Somewhere, a raven cawed.

"What did happen to the castle?" said Scott.

"Oliver Cromwell happened to it," said Gavin.

"Wasn't he the one who had the king's head cut off?"

"Ah, he was. But you must listen carefully, as our road is likely to take us through Cromwell's time. Most of the roads do. It was a bad time, with trouble a plenty, and butchery and dark deeds on both sides.

"Charles the first was a foolish king. He thought that the monarch should be able to rule just as he wished. But times had changed and already parliament had become a voice to be reckoned with.

"They fought battles up and down the country. The Royalists had the best of it, but neither side was really winning."

"But what about Oliver Cromwell?"

"Oliver was a Parliamentarian general with a rare gift. Cromwell used to brood over his losses. He reformed his army and called it the New Model Army. He recruited only the best, most disciplined troops, and he demanded purity and good living from them."

"We did this in history at my old school. Were Cromwell's army the Roundheads?"

"They were, but you mustn't call them that if you come among them. 'Roundheads' is what Charles's Cavaliers called them, but Oliver punished his men if they used that word.

"The civil war lasted a long time, but Charles did not. He was captured by parliament, and Oliver himself signed his death warrant. They say Charles went bravely to his death, as a good man should."

"So what happened to the castle?"

"Many of the castles were in the hands of Charles's supporters. They were hard to capture, even with gunpowder, but they were not much use to Oliver in trying to defeat the royalist army. So, whenever he took a castle, he used gunpowder to destroy it. Most of the old castles in England were destroyed that way."

"Are there any that weren't?"

"Near here, just two. Tamworth castle is old—very old. But where we are going is Warwick. Have you ever seen it?"

"We went once with the school. Mum wasn't happy about me going, but she gave in, in the end."

Somehow the night's adventures, and riding through the snow in a forgotten corner of history with this man who might or might not turn out to be a Knight of King Arthur, had driven the real purpose of their journey out of his mind.

Now it came rushing back.

"We are—we are going to find her, aren't we?"

Gavin half turned in his saddle.

"Scott, I think I already have."

"How? Where?"

"Kenilworth gatehouse is a good place for giving away secrets, which is why I said we should be careful, and why I gave different names. But it's also a good place for hearing news."

"But you gave your own real name, didn't you?"

"There was little point in hiding it. I'm easy enough to spot, even at a distance. How did you guess?"

"Oh, this and that. The green belt, the wound on your neck."

"That's very good. Did your mother tell you about them?"

"They're just things I picked up."

"Well, the important thing was not to give your name away. Raynall is not a common name, and word would have got back quickly that your mother's son was skifting after her."

"So what did you find out?"

"Riddles—mostly. Anybody who skifts learns to keep their secrets to themselves—but a flat lie can tell a careful listener as much as the plain truth. So skifters play a game where they hide one truth inside another, and keep the listener guessing. But if you talk to enough people you can catch them in each other's riddles.

"The date was easy enough to find. It's in the twelfth century—dark days, and further back than I would have guessed. Closer to Arthur's time than to yours.

"The place was more difficult. A huge castle of red stone, set about with towers and battlements, impregnable to every attack. And not twenty miles from where she was taken."

"Do you know where this castle is?"

"There is only one castle that would match that description in the midlands. We are far enough away from it now. Turn your horse and look with me."

They wheeled their horses, and looked back at the ruins of Kenilworth, now barely a speck on the horizon.

"There you have it."

"Then why are we riding away from it?"

"For two reasons. One is that we don't want to skift into trouble under the castle walls. We need to find our way back somewhere close, but not too close, so that we can spy out the land and see what we should do. The other—"

He paused.

"—the other reason is that the huge castle of red stone was not built until much later. It was King John who enlarged it. I know, because I rode past it while they were laying the stones. Back in Matilda's time, I remember it as just a hill fortress, the kind of thing that the Normans threw up quickly to subdue the local people. A shell keep on a mound of earth."

"So where is my mother?"

"In Kenilworth. I believe. But there is something else strange about the castle. The legends say that Kenilworth was a castle in Saxon times, and was fortified by King Arthur."

"And was it?"

"Not to my knowledge. But the history of Arthur is strange, and the stories change and change about.

"When we skift, our time moves on. If we skift for a week, we return a week after we set off. Everything that happened in that time is as dark to us as if we were born a thousand years later. We know nothing of things that happened in the world's time after the days which we have lived through. And I have not seen Arthur's time for many long years."

"Why is that?"

"Because we have lost Arthur. We fought a terrible battle at Mount Badon. Do not ask me where that hill is, because we were guided there through many mists and secret ways, and we were many days on the march, pursuing a Saxon army.

"At the end of the battle, the Saxons were defeated, but Arthur was wounded. We never found his body, it is said that he had been taken across the water to the magical isle of Avalon, to heal his wounds."

"And was he?"

"Who can say? Knowledge—even reading and writing—seemed to empty out of Britain not long after Arthur's kingdom ended. I had never skifted further than the middle-ages at that time, but I had picked up stories of Arthur and Avalon, and how the king sleeps under a hillside with knights and horses waiting for the day he should be called to lead Britain once again. With a few others, I set off to find what certain knowledge I could of where he was and when.

"This has been the quest of my life these ten years.

"The centuries after the end of Logres were bleak. We found cities deserted where once we greeted friends. Invaders covered the land with wooden villages, avoiding our cities, but stealing our stone, and our gold and silver. They were brutal days. Villages made war on villages, and drunken quarrels became battles that spread across the land to the ruin of all.

"So I searched onwards into history. By the time of Sir Thomas Evil Ear, Mal Oreille, as we called him, there were thousands of tales of Arthur. Some I recognised—a little—from my own journeyings. Others were new to me, and others I knew to be false. But there seemed no way to separate the good from the bad.

"Then I thought of your mother, and what she had told me of your time. She talked about universities, and archaeologists, and libraries, and computers. I imagined that using the skills of your modern scholars, I could find Arthur and return him to his proper time, to build up the realm of Logres, and perhaps to fight the final battle at Camlann, years after the time I left.

"But your mother's time is also Morgaine's time."

"Who is Morgaine?" said Scott.

"Morgaine? Morgan le Fay. My aunt, and Arthur's half-sister. An enchantress and our greatest enemy. It will be Morgaine's people who have your mother hostage."

"What will Morgaine do to my mother? She won't—she won't kill her, will she?"

"Arthur's folk do not kill their enemies, except in battle or at great need. Morgaine will try to win your mother back to her side."

"Back?"

Gawain looked back, and wheeled his horse back onto the road.

"I've said too much. Come. We must to Warwick to find a skift-way back to Matilda's time."

And he set off at a canter, which Scott was hard pressed to follow.

The snow was thinning now—not into Birmingham slush, but into a fine covering as if it had fallen lightly here. The galloping hooves kicked it into a low mist. Scott was afterwards very proud that he stayed in the saddle for that ride.

In the distance he saw the highest turret of Warwick Castle. In the sun and the snow the road shimmered and shook ahead of him. He had seen mirages of this kind on long car journeys... except... except...

"Stop—Stop!" he yelled. It was not the shimmering of a mirage.

"Gawain! Stop," he yelled again, reining in his own horse. He could see the shimmering door quite clearly now. To the left and to the right the feathery snow of this time. In the centre a path cut through deeper snow, muddied and turned as by the wheels of heavy wagons.

"Gawain! A door! There's a door here!" he shouted.

His companion was some way ahead of him. Scott saw two things almost at once. Gawain turning his horse and looking back at him, and the skift door beginning to fade. Without thinking about the consequences, Scott spurred his horse on and rode straight onwards, into the other-time, into the deep snow.

The last thing that he heard as he crossed the line was Gawain's voice:

"Scott! No! I can't follow you. I can't see the door!"

The voice stopped, like a door closing. Scott looked back, and saw for a moment the eighteenth century world. And then that world faded, and the door folded in on itself, and shrank, and ended like the dot that is left for a moment when you switch off an old television.

He was alone. But when?

5 IN OLIVER'S TIME ALONE

There was an odd, acrid smell in the air. Like a mixture of fireworks and factory chimneys. And a sound. Intermittent, something between a crack and a bang. A few together, and then silence, and then a few more.

No—not silence. The shouts of men. Then a single, crashing, boom.

All of a sudden it came to Scott what these sounds were. Guns, and fighting men, and a cannon being fired. He had ridden straight into a battle.

But who was fighting whom?

He dismounted—wondering for a moment if he would be able to get back up again—and led the horse quietly up the hill to the ridge where he had last seen Gawain.

It was quite a scene that met his eyes. The country fell away sharply, so that the road had to wind down the hill. To the left there was a farmhouse, thatched with sooty straw and surrounded by scattered outbuildings. It was black beamed and white plastered, but battle-scarred, with smoke pouring out of one window, and the thick glass in many of the others smashed. Musket-barrels poked out through the windows and the door, and every so often there was a flash as one of them fired. There seemed to be men in the outbuildings as well, although Scott could only see what looked like the tops of hats.

On the right, and partly protected by a fold in the landscape, was a detachment of soldiers. They wore rounded, iron caps, and some of them had light armour, while others wore leather coats. There were a couple of tents—big tents, like the sort of thing boy scouts use—and, behind one of them, just visible, the spiteful mouth of a small cannon.

"Roundheads," thought Scott to himself, and then he remembered that Gawain had told him not to call them that. His next thought was: "So this is Oliver's time. I wonder if I will meet Oliver." It was followed by: "I wish I'd asked more questions about it."

He noticed that some of the soldiers were gesturing and shouting at him.

"Hey—you boy—get down here. It's murder to stay on that ridge."

He looked down again. There didn't very well seem to be a way of going further along the road without passing between the muskets of the two sides. Not that they seemed to be doing much damage to each other, but he felt that he would certainly have the worst of it if he rode between them.

"Hold on!" shouted the man again. "I'm coming up."

A minute later, hot and bothered, and both wet and mucky from the mud and the snow, a man in a thick leather coat came toiling up the hill.

"Now, young gentleman," he said, as he reached Scott, "You'll please be coming down by the side path, if you don't fancy bein' chopped into tiny pieces by Old Tom there."

He gestured at the little camp, and Scott guessed that Old Tom was the cannon.

"Are you Oliver's men?" said Scott.

The man gave him a sharp look.

"I don't know about Oliver's men. We are fighting for the people, and we serve Parliament against the rebels. Sir Thomas Fairfax leads this army, though the word is that Oliver will be soon back to join him."

He took the horse's reins, and led him down the hill and into the camp as sure-footedly as if there had been a new made road, though all Scott saw was mud and rocks and puddles between the drifts.

"Now what is this?" said a man in armour, who seemed to be the commander.

"This young fellow was out for a winter ride, if you ask me," said the man who had run up the hill. "And if old Toby here hadn'an been keeping a sharp eye out, he would have ridden straight between our muzzles, and been blasted to kingdom come. Friend of Oliver's, he said he is."

"Is this true, young master?" said the man in armour. "Do you come from Oliver's men?"

"I'm just riding my horse, sir," said Scott.

"Just riding? You didn't decide to feast your eyes on a battle, like a young David?"

Scott didn't know how to answer this, so he said nothing. Nothing, it seemed, was the kind of answer that the commander liked to hear.

"Well, you can't carry on riding on this road, at least not for some time. We're smoking out a crowd of bandits here, and as likely as not they'll make a break for it soon enough. If they try to cross open country the blizzard will have them—it's set to get pretty thick after noon. But my guess is they will take what horses they can and go north or south along the road. Either way, you'll not be wanting to be in their way."

Scott looked up at the man. His armour was polished and bolted on tightly, and the nose-guard of his steel helmet gave him a strong, military look. But under the helmet there was a hint of chubbiness in his cheeks, and his eyes looked like he was more used to smiling than shouting.

"Are they Cavaliers?" he said.

"Yes, if bandits are gentlemen. But these fellows are highwaymen and small thieves who expect reprieve by putting feathers in their hats."

Scott wasn't sure what this was exactly supposed to mean, but he thought it best to move the conversation along.

"Can't you blow them to pieces with your cannon?" he said.

"What, Old Tom, there? That's a demi-cannon, not a cannon proper, young master, but she was miscast and it's hard enough to aim her straight. You'll see we haven't had much success on the farmhouse yet. If you ask me cannon have seen their better days. They're fine for knocking holes in the sides of castle walls, but give me cold steel any day if it's man to man. And don't give me no pistol neither. By the time a man's cleaned it and loaded it and primed it, t'other fellow has run him through."

And he lifted his own sword in its sheath and rattled it back in to underline his point.

"Are you a master swordsman?" said Scott.

He noticed some of the men looking up and smiling as he said it. The commander went a little red in the face.

"Well, I don't know about being a master, but I hold my own."

"I've got a sword," said Scott. "But I haven't had it very long, and I haven't got used to the weight of it. Perhaps you could teach me some things." And he pulled out his own sword to show the man.

"Now, that's a mighty fine weapon," he said, taking it from Scott and letting it glint in the light of the low sun as he turned it. He swung it over his head, and then let his thumb run down the front edge, before handing it back to Scott.

Then he rocked back on his heels, as if he was about to deliver a lecture.

"Now, like all young men, you'll be proudest of the edge. And a sharp edge is the mark of a sharp soldier. Men fear a sharp edge. In a brawl, or on the battle field, or on a dark street late at night, that edge will see you safely home. But, if you are fighting for your life, and your enemy intends to kill you, then you must know that it is the point which is deadly."

The lecture might have continued for some time, but just at that moment something came whistling through the campsite, and everybody except Scott threw themselves flat on their faces. A hand reached up and pulled him down.

"Looks like they've got round the back," said someone.

"Two of you," hissed the commander, "muskets round to the southwest."

There were more bangs and whizzes overhead. There was a sound of groaning and creaking by the cannon, and then a huge boom shook the ground. Scott tried to lift his head to see what was going on, but he quickly felt a hand on his back pushing him down again.

More cries, and more shouts. Another boom, and a cheer from the roundheads. A moment later a shower of dirt and dust came flying through the air. The cheering was cut short by a sharp cry.

The firing went on for a few more minutes—not rat-a-tat firing, as Scott had heard on films, but once in a while a bang like a fire-cracker, and then hush.

And finally—silence.

Scott lifted his head, and saw that there was no one around him.

He pulled himself to his feet. One of the tents had partly collapsed, peppered with holes. There was crimson on the snow here and there. The fallen tent revealed the whole of the cannon. Just beyond it, the commander and four of the men were standing in a circle. Their heads were bowed and, although the commander's lips were moving, Scott could not make out his words.

Then the group broke up. Two of the men picked up shovels, and began to dig. Scott could make out something—something—a body.

Scott bit his lip. Somebody had died in the battle. They were burying him.

He looked away. The farmhouse seemed to have taken more than one direct hit. One end had completely collapsed, and the glass was now gone from all the windows. Smoke poured from one of the out-buildings, and he could see occasional flashes of fire. There seemed to be nobody left to put it out.

The commander came and stood beside him.

"They'll not be firing back, now," he said, and then, as if he was starting on a new subject: "He was never meant for a soldier, young Tobias. He believed in the cause. Believed in it with his heart. But he should'na been a soldier. Didn't have the knack for it."

And he handed Scott an apple.

Without saying anything, they munched together. Scott sensed the man's grief, but he could not share it.

Finally, when the apples were finished, the commander said to him: "You'll be wanting to be on your way again. If you're skifting, you might have some luck down by the castle."

Scott almost jumped.

"Do you know about skifting?"

"Never gone in for it me'self, but we get lots of skifters coming this way. Sometimes they fight with us, sometimes against us, sometimes they just pass through. I figured you for a skifter as soon as you opened your mouth. But you're just a lad. I never seen one so young. Are you skifting on your own?"

"I was with someone. But we got separated."

"That doesn't sound so good. Do you know where it is you're going?"

"I'm looking for my mother."

"Ah. I don't know as we can help you much with that. But we'll look out for you if you should come this way again. What name do you go by?"

"Perceval," said Scott.

"Ah. Well, young Perceval, my name is Smalbroke. We'll know each other if we meet again."

Then he turned away to supervise the men digging.

Scott went to look at his horse. It was stamping nervously, but otherwise seemed to have gone through the battle without hurt. A few minutes later he was back on the road towards Warwick. He stopped once, at the brow of the next hill, to wave to Smalbroke, and then on.

A strange calm had settled over the landscape. There was not a house, not a human in sight. Aside from the clippety-clop of horse on snow, there was no sound, not even the wind.

The day wore on. The low sun poured what heat and light it could through the still air, and a warmth slowly spread across Scott's face, into his eyes, down through his back.

Somehow he knew that the horse had ceased trotting, was barely walking, little more than dawdling. But the adventures of the night before were catching up with him. For a moment he knew that he was drowsing, that he was drooping over his horse's neck... that he was almost on the edge of sleep.

He awoke with a start. It was cold. The sunlight was completely gone. Snow was falling again. It had begun to pile on his cloak, on the saddle. The horse was flicking its head to keep the snow away.

He looked around. There was no sign of Warwick ahead, and no sign of anything behind. In fact, there was no real sign of the road—had he wandered off it, or was it completely covered?

He shook himself to dislodge the snow. The horse sensed something was happening and broke into a short trot. Scott spurred him on into something like a canter.

On the brow of the next hill he slowed and looked around. The falling snow made it hard to see much more than a few hundred yards. But from what he could see, there was nothing to see. Just more snow, and the brow of another low hill, and neither track nor road to tell him if he were riding towards Warwick, or back to Kenilworth, or across open country towards nowhere in particular.

No. There was one thing. A little flicker of light. Or smoke. Or smoke and light. Or nothing. No, there it was again. Definitely light.

Now certain, he spurred the horse on. The ground seemed to change, and he was sure that he was riding across field or broken country. They went more slowly. At times hollows opened up ahead of him, with flat bottoms covered thinly. He took them for frozen pools, and skirted them. After a while the pools became more frequent, and he decided to dismount and lead the horse by its head.

The flickering light became slowly clearer. It was a building of some kind. A single storey, one window, a wide door. Perhaps a barn or a granary.

They drew closer. Definitely a barn. There was no proper chimney: smoke was gusting out of the door, and through a crack in the window.

Scott wondered who might be inside. But he did not like the idea of spending the night in the snow.

He stood at the barn door for a moment, uncertain about what to do. He could not hear anyone inside, just the crackling of a fire, and...

His horse snorted.

"Who's there?" came a man's voice.

"A traveller," called Scott. "Lost in the snow. Can I come in?"

The door swung slowly open. A low fire was burning in a brazier. There was a tankard on a barrel, and a wooden plate with some bread and meat, and—

Whoomph.

Something soft and heavy came down over Scott's head. At first he thought he had been hit, then he thought he was being smothered. And then the bag was being pulled off his head.

"I'm sorry about that, young gentleman," said a rich, noble voice. "One can't be sure of one's visitors in these desperate times." The man slurred his words, and Scott—thinking of the tankard—wondered if he perhaps might be a little drunk.

Scott looked slowly round. The man was tall, with long, dark hair, falling in waves over his shoulders. Scott thought he had a rather long face, with sad eyes, and he had a short moustache that made his mouth look noble, but mournful.

"Who are you?" said Scott.

"I?" said the man. "A soldier of the king. A chevalier. A cavalier. They call us chevalier because of our long hair. It's French, y'see. Cheveux, Chevaux, Cheval. Hair and horses. Horses and hair. All the same. The same as each other. Tous les deux le même. Tous les dieux. All the gods. All the gods of the Greeks and the Romans."

"I see," said Scott. "But what's your name?"

"Sir Richard. Sir Richard Lovelace. Always have done. Born in the Low Countries. Best lace in the world. Bruges and Brussels, and Antwerp and mussels, and tulips that send the Dutch mad. Two lips so red that would send all the world mad.

"But you'll forgive me for my welcome." And he took Scott by the shoulder and propelled him towards the brazier.

"You'll forgive my welcome," he said again. "Here in this palace of my abode. Welcome welcome welcome welcome. Everything you could possibly want is here. Beer and meat and fire and heat, all out of the cold cold snow. The snold snold coe. The bold old show. In the wold's wild woe."

"My name's Scott," said Scott. He was pretty sure that this man would not be remembering his name the next morning.

"Scot, young man? Been there myself. Fought with them, fought for them, fought against them. All the Scots. All together. For the King. Against the King. On the left. On the right. In the middle. With cannon and horse and musket and pike."

Scott pulled himself out of Sir Richard's hands, and went back to the door to bring his horse in from the cold.

"Ah. A horseman. A chevalier like myself. But your hair is too short. Grow it out long like mine. Are you of the party of the cavaliers, or of the roundhead?"

"I've not really chosen a side. I'm still at school."

"Ah. A scholar. I was once a scholar. But now I am a Master. A master of all the arts, created so by the king. Have you met the king?"

"I'm afraid not."

"A pity. A gentleman of infinite wit, now gone the way of all flesh like a jester in a graveyard. Or was it the young king that you have not met?"

"I haven't met any kings."

"Ah. None at all. Nihil, as we say in the Roman tongue. A very round number. Invention of the Arabs, who discovered nothing in a sea of logic mathematical. But I have made a discovery more wonderful than the discovery of the Arabs. You wish to ask me what it was?"

"I suppose so."

"I found a gate into worlds past and worlds future. Worlds and time."

Until then Scott had been sure that nothing the man was going to say could make any sense.

"That's—very interesting. What kind of gate is this?" he said.

"Not a gate as you might find in a wall. Sometimes there, and sometimes not. The gates shift and slide, like yonder wicket gate, sometimes there, and sometimes not. I tell them I am going to Holland, and then I am free to roam this way and that. Even in a prison cell, for stone walls do not a prison make, nor iron bars a cage."

"Did you write that?" said Scott. "I think I read it somewhere."

"Write it? No, I never did, but I believe I shall."

"You believe you will?"

"All kinds of things will I write. But did I write them, or did another and I but borrowed? And were the words of other poets my words which they found in a book late in time and made their own? I know not."

He dipped the tankard into the barrel.

"But you, my young chevalier, my D'Artagnan, you are of the future, are you not? Even through this—this rather drinkable ale—I hear the modern tone of your voice. You are, perhaps, from the twentieth century?"

"The twenty-first," said Scott.

"The twenty-first? I never went so far. Do men sail from house to house in flying cars and take their holidays upon the moon?"

"I don't think so—at least, not in my part. It's the start of the twenty-first century. It might happen later."

"Then why are you travelling back here? Why are you not searching out the years and centuries beyond your own time? Why do you come to these dreary days, this civil war, this commonwealth of grocers and petty officers?"

"I'm on my way somewhere. I'm not expecting to stay."

"Whither are you going? That is, to where?"

"To Stephen and Matilda's time."

"Ah. When Christ slept, and his saints? A bad time, a very bad time. If you'll take my advice, my young traveller, you'll leave well alone. Most alone. A bad time indeed. Indeed.

"You go alone?"

"I was with someone, but we were separated."

"A bad business indeed." And then he got up suddenly and went to the window.

"But hush," he said. "What sound is this?"

Scott did not hear anything, but Lovelace evidently could.

"Quick young man. We must hide."

"What—why—where?" He looked around—there was nowhere to hide.

"Up here. Quickly." He gestured upwards. Scott looked and saw a sort of mezzanine where some other room had been built into the barn, with its ceiling making a platform two thirds of the way towards the roof. Barely visible in the darkness, a knotted rope hung down.

Scott stood a moment, doubting. He still could not hear anything outside. Even with the knots, he wondered if he could make it up the rope. He remembered the climbing ropes in the school gym—which he had never managed to climb.

"What are you waiting for, boy?" said Lovelace. His gentle, half-drunken tone had become an urgent whisper. "Here!"

Before Scott knew what he was doing Sir Richard had lifted him up over his shoulders, as if he were no heavier than a cushion, and pushed him halfway up the rope. Scott clutched at it, and managed to pull himself up on to the ledge. He lay there panting, and Lovelace's head appeared over the edge a few moments later. His body followed, and he drew the rope up behind him.

"Now, lie still," he whispered.

Nothing seemed to happen for a long time. Scott was about to ask what was going on, but then he heard it too: soft voices, outside the barn.

The door creaked open.

"Hello, my kind maisters," called a voice. It was a thicker, more 'country' voice than Lovelace's, but there was an edge to it that Scott did not like.

"Hello, my kind maisters," came the voice again. "We're lost in the blizzard, snowing as you would never believed how. We just want to share a bit of your warm fire. We've drink of our own, and victuals, and we're glad to share if you are."

Scott wondered if they should answer, but a sharp squeeze from Lovelace told him to stay silent.

"My maisters?" Now the voice was wheedling, ingratiating.

"Reckon they've skitted out," said a second voice. It was a lower, cracking voice, harsher than the other.

"Skitfers?" said the first. "You reckon that's what it is?"

"No doubt about it. They was here for definite. And now they ain't. Only one door, and we came through it, and they didn't. So they skifted."

"At least they left their drink," said the first. There was the sloshing sound of the tankard dipping into the barrel. "And the horses."

"Ah, that's all right," went on the first voice. "Good hospitality. A fine establishment. And we didn't n'even have to break no bones nor no heads."

There was another sloshing sound.

"No doubt about that," said the second voice. "There's a fine bit o' hops. Wait—what's that?"

Scott strained his ears to catch what had disturbed him. There was a faint rustling from one of the corners.

Suddenly—a bang, followed by a smell like fireworks.

"Was a rat," said the second voice. "You'd've been better not to fire that shot."

"There's no one to hear it," said the first. "What harm can it do?"

"Ah. That's what brings them."

"Who?"

"The skitfers. Who else? It's trouble as draws 'em out, and there ain't no trouble so good as the firing of good weapons."

"You seem to know a lot about them."

"Ah, that's what," continued the second, the low, cracking voice. "I know 'em 'cos I seen 'em."

"Everyone's seen 'em. They'se all over the place these days."

"Ah, but I'se seen one skitting. We was doin' a small hoperation with a lady and a genkleman as was making an unadvised journey. My mate Tiny—you remember 'im—was a little free with the shot. The genkleman was all right, but 'n 'orse wan't so lucky.

"We was just at the point of invitin' the gentry to dismount from their transport, when—clear as the day—a rider rides out o' nuffin straight at us. 'E lays about wi' a big sword as long as a pike staff. Me an' Tiny gets out the way o' the sword, and then we makes our way back through the forest. Tiny thought it was a ghost, and if you aks me, he weren't never quite the same after."

"Maybe it was a ghost."

"Bah. I never 'eard of no ghost as could charge you down."

"Maybe. And did you find out if you could shoot 'em?"

"Chance would've been a fine thing! Tiny 'ad already let off 'is shots, and I wasn't wasting mine wi'out some'at as stayed still long enough to shoot at. But I reckon as they'd fall same as any man if you got your shot in."

"So where do they come from, the skitfers, then?"

"That would be what they call—" Scott heard the man take a breath before spelling it out: "'A matter of Con-Jek-Sure.'"

There was a pause.

A rustling.

Then:

"We knows you'se up there. And we knows you'se listening." It was the second voice, the low, cracking voice.

"We can't climb up to you. But you can't come down here wi'out our pre-mission. And we've the drink. And victuals. And, most of all—we've the fire. We can stay here as long as we want, and then, when we 'as to go, an accident wi' the coals, and you'se all sparks an' ashes.

"So what do you say? Does you talk?"

Lovelace lifted his head.

"What do you want?" he said. Lying flat as he was, he still made his voice boom.

"Ah. That's better. Now we both knows what we both knows. How many of you is there?"

"Hundreds," bellowed Lovelace in return.

"Ah, you're a wit, sir. Show your face and we can talk."

Lovelace touched Scott's hand and pushed his head down. It was dark on the balcony, but Scott could see enough to make out that this was where Lovelace had been sleeping for quite a few days. There was a roll of blankets, and what looked like a pillow.

Now, stealthily, Lovelace pushed the pillow into a sort of roll shape, and stuffed it into his hat. Scott had seen something of the kind before in a film, so was not surprised when Lovelace pushed the hat up above the ledge.

Bang! Bang! Two flashes of light and more smell of fireworks. The hat went flying through the air. Lovelace muttered something. Then he leaned over the edge. Scott could not see much of what he was doing, but he seemed to taking aim.

A flash and another bang—this time from Lovelace. A grunt from below, and something that sounded like swearing. Lovelace pulled himself back, and set about reloading his pistol.

Scott wondered what he would do next—there were two men, and he could not see them falling for the hat trick a second time. But Lovelace had another idea. He gathered his blankets up into a ball, and then put his hat back on his head. Pulling himself up onto his haunches he peered over the edge once more. This time there were no shots.

With a huge roar, Lovelace stood up, sat down again, and pushed his blankets over the edge.

Scott couldn't help himself—he rolled to the edge to look.

He saw two men in the orange glow of the fire. One was on the floor, clutching his leg with one hand but holding a pistol in the other. The other one was crouching behind the brazier, also holding a pistol.

Then there were three shots, each like a firecracker going off.

Both of the men fired—but they weren't firing at Lovelace, and they weren't firing at Scott. Each hit the blanket in just the right place to

71

wound or kill a man. Scott saw their expressions change—first surprise, and then satisfaction, and finally alarm, fear, bewilderment, all in one. Then Lovelace stood up properly, took careful aim and shot the man behind the brazier. He fell.

It was at that moment that Lovelace did jump. With his cloak opening behind him, he looked like a man with the power of flight.

Sir Richard stumbled as he landed, but he fell on straw, and in a moment he was up again, drawing his sword. The firelight flickered down the blade.

There was no one to fight. One man behind the brazier, lay still, while the other man, with the wounded leg, whimpered.

"I think it's safe now," said Lovelace. "Perhaps you should come down."

It was a nasty business bandaging the leg-man's wound. He kicked and struggled whenever they came near, even after Lovelace tied his hands and feet. In some ways he had been lucky. The bullet had gone through his calf, causing doubtless intense pain but not hitting the bone. They found the bullet—or rather, a small lead ball, not at all like the bullets Scott had seen—in a pool of blood.

Bandaging did not seem to stop the bleeding, and in the end, to Scott's horror, Lovelace heated up the tip of the man's sword in the fire and closed the wound with it. The man moaned, then lay still.

"He will have a scar as long as he lives," said Lovelace. "But he will live."

The other man had not been so lucky. The bullet had gone straight into his forehead. Lovelace closed his eyes with his hand, and put two large coins over them.

"It's to pay the ferry man," he said. "For good or ill this man has a journey to make across the river, and the ferry man must be paid."

He picked up the tankard. There were dregs in the bottom, which he tipped out onto the floor.

"A libation to the gods," he said. "After battle, peace."

Then he filled the tankard again and sat down, looking into it. He did not speak for a long time.

Outside the wind had settled.

The flames in the brazier had died down, leaving only the embers to give heat, and a red light on tired faces.

"You are very young to be skifting," said Lovelace at length. "I was a little overcome by the goodness of this drink earlier on. But I think you said you were going to Stephen's time, the Anarchy, as we call it; is that not so?"

Scott nodded.

"You will forgive my asking, but what is your knowledge of languages?"

"We're learning Latin and French at school," said Scott.

"That would be, I think, what you would call 'Modern French'?

"Yes."

"Ah. And Latin. That would not, I suppose, be what one might term 'conversational Latin'."

"No."

"And would my guess be correct that this is your first journey?"

"Yes."

"I see." Lovelace sat looking at the fire for a long time, eventually poking it with a stick and making some marks in the dust of the floor.

"You will forgive me once again, but have you given any thought to how you will speak with the people of Stephen and Matilda's time?"

"Don't they speak English?" said Scott. But even as he said it he remembered books that his mother had shown him in what she had called 'Old' and 'Middle' English, neither of which he could read.

Lovelace watched his face fall.

"The peasants—that is to say, the Saxons and Danes conquered by the Normans—speak what scholars call Early Middle English. That is the scholars of your day. The scholars of my day were not as interested in giving such names. The priests and learned people will speak Latin, at least to each other—though you may find it very different from the Latin you have learned in school. And the nobility speak to each other in Anglo-Norman, which is a kind of French. But even if they spoke the pure French of their day, you would find it very distant from the French of yours."

"What should I do then?"

"I do not know. In my time—this time in which we now sit—all people of note learned Latin. We learned to converse in Latin. We wrote poems to each other in Latin. And of course many of us learned French and Low German.

"But I myself have never been back as far as the Anarchy. I have enough of war here in my own time. I do not need to go skifting to find bloodshed. But there was one war I did visit. A peculiarly bloody, nasty and useless conflict, even by the standards of such things. It was fought in France, and they called it the Hundred Years war. It is closer in time to today than is your time, but I myself struggled to speak plain English with the people, and I found my French to be of little use. Latin was my main means of discourse, though I found their accents barbarous and their vocabulary comic."

He sat and thought for a little longer.

"The only advice I can give you for now is to climb again that knotted rope, and give yourself over to a fine night's sleep. Mayhap the morrow will bring better counsel."

Once again, he helped Scott up, and then followed him. A few minutes later, curled up in a blanket, Scott fell asleep.

He awoke with a start. Something was wrong. Harsh winter air was rushing by gusts through the door, which stood open. The light from the brazier had died down, but some other, colder light filled the barn.

Peering over the ledge, Scott saw bull's horns, moving this way and that, set atop a head that was like a great bull's head. But the animal stood on its hind legs, and moved like a man. It was fully ten feet tall. The arms were the arms of a man, but the legs ended in cloven feet. And the beast was covered in fine, black hair, like the bulls bull-fighters fight in Spain. But it was the eyes that were the most wrong. They were great, slitted eyes, like a bull's. But they moved this way and that, searching the barn, like the eyes of a hunter, like the eyes of a man.

The bull-man filled Scott with strange dread, but also fascination. He watched the beast move to and fro, searching for something, hunting. Scott could not see the wounded man, and there was no sign of the dead man.

Suddenly, from his left, there was a flash and a bang, and another flash and another bang. Richard Lovelace had discharged both his pistols at the horned head. Scott watched for the creature to fall, or to bellow with rage, but it did neither. Instead it lifted its head and fixed them in the stare of a single, bull's eye. And then it pawed the earth, stalked out of the barn, and was gone.

"What was that?" said Scott, after a long time had passed.

"I know not," said Lovelace. "But I gave it both my pistols, and, as you see, it troubled him not. A spirit from another time or place, I fear. It had no thought for us. But I think we will not see our two friends again, in this life or after."

It was late morning when Scott awoke. The winter sun had climbed a little into a paper-white sky, strong enough to cast shadows through the window, but not to bring heat into the world.

He had wrapped his cloak around him for the night, and tried to snuggle into the straw. This was all very well as he drowsed, but he felt the cold as soon as he was properly awake. He was stiff and sore, and his head ached. Climbing back down the knotted rope seemed as much a chore as climbing up it had been.

There was a little charred wood left in the brazier, and some hunks of what looked like ham on a metal plate, set atop the cask from which Lovelace had been drinking.

There was no sign of Lovelace, nor of the dead man, nor of the wounded one, but Scott's horse was standing patiently in the corner, working its way through a bale of hay.

Scott poked at the brazier with a stick. There was a tiny glow of orange. Part of him wanted to put wood on it immediately, but he had read somewhere that the thing to do was to blow it. Scott had never been camping or lit bonfires or any of the other things that other boys of his age might have done, otherwise he would probably have had better luck. But, after ten minutes of frantic blowing, and several hand-fuls of straw (which frizzled up instantly and did nothing but smoke), he finally coaxed enough of a flame to set a couple of small sticks alight.

The work of getting the fire going probably did more to warm Scott up than the meagre flames. Certainly it gave him an appetite. He won-dered about trying to heat the ham in the fire, and thought fondly of microwave ovens. Eventually he settled for eating it cold.

It was not until he had finished with the ham that he noticed there was a piece of paper underneath the metal plate. It was creamy but un-evenly made, folded into three, and signed 'From RL'.

He opened it. It was a letter for him, written in beautiful copper plate handwriting which nobody seems to know how to do these days, but which you can sometimes see in old books. It took Scott a moment to decipher some of the letters. The 's' was like an 'f', and the capitals, although graceful and ornate, were unlike the ones he was familiar with. And then the 'u's, 'm's, 'n's, 'v's and 'w's, when they were next to each other, seemed to be a marching row of even up and down strokes joined by the slightest traces.

But this is what Sir Richard Lovelace had written.

"To my young friend.

"It was most agreeable to encounter you on our respective travels. I had thought to waken you from your slumbers, but you seemed resistant to the welcome of the early morning. Our guests, I fear, departed during the night. Whither, I know not, nor wish to.

"You will see I have left meat and some drink, and your horse is still with you. My own horse, alas, I lost in the blizzard, but our guests were well appointed with two serviceable animals, and I was able to acquit myself of a rustic transportation, namely a cart, by which means I will disguise myself as I ride. I shall make myself scarce, as these are not pleasant times for a man with a feather in his hat.

"In regard to your own journey, I give you what little advice I can. You will have to cross many thresholds if you are to find Matilda's time. I cannot think that I will dissuade you, but remember that skifting leads always to trouble, and you will have your fill of it by the time you find your journey's end, if find it you do. Spend as little time as you can in Elizabeth's time and Mary's. Skifters are unwelcome there.

"Be very careful in choosing your friends, and even more so in choosing your enemies. Better it is to walk by on the other side than to be drawn into another man's quarrel, and drawn in you shall be if you are too quick to bring help or harm.

"With the warmest regards;

Your friend, whether we meet again in the future or in the past,

Richard Lovelace (Knight of the King).

And it was signed with a huge, flourishing signature.

6 BLACKLOWE HILL

Scott led his horse back to the road. Though the air was cold, the snow was melting underfoot. He was glad of the thick boots—but he could already begin to feel the moisture leaking in around his feet.

The road—or what there was of it—was mostly clear of snow, and he could see now that it was partly old stone, partly mud, and partly grass. It was nothing like the road which had led out of the gates of Kenilworth just a day before.

He put his foot in the horse's stirrup and mounted. It was already much easier than two days ago. Once in the saddle, he set off at something between a walk and a plod.

"Of course," he said to himself, "the main thing is to find somewhere that will take me further back in time. But where do you find such a thing?"

He frowned, and pressed on.

By and by he came to a village. It was half a street of houses, small but in good order, with black timbers and white plaster, thickly thatched with grey straw. There was a church with a small, square tower. Even in Oliver's time it was old, and Scott wondered when it had first been built and by whom.

An old man was sweeping away snow from his doorstep with one of the brooms that look like witches' brooms and are known as besoms.

"I wonder if that girl really was a witch—perhaps witches have villages where they all live together," thought Scott, but the old man did not look like he had much to do with witches.

The man touched his head as Scott rode past, and he guessed it might be some kind of salute. There were children playing some-where—he could hear their voices, and thought of himself playing in Stechford more than three hundred years in the future.

Almost before he had reached the church, the village petered out. There was a stone wall around the church yard, and a covered gate. Beyond the wall were no more houses.

He rode on. The sun rose to its highest point as he reached the brow of a hill. It was a good place to reach, because for the first time he could see a little town in the distance, the glint of water, and, tiny, like a model, the turrets of Warwick Castle.

He slowed to a halt, and gazed for a few moments. The melting snow created eddies of air and tiny mirages, which made the landscape strange and enchanted, shifting and moving as he watched.

But it was not only mirages which were shifting and moving. He leaned backwards a little, and forwards, and began to make out the form of a door in the air, a skifter's door, ready for him to go through. It was just a little way down the hill. For a moment he wondered if it would take him back towards the future instead of into the past where he wanted to go. There seemed to be no real way of knowing, and yet it felt as if it were the right thing to do.

He set off down the hill. The light flickered a little as he crossed the threshold, and suddenly he found himself riding into a crowd of people. The gentle hubbub of their voices was a welcome change from the silent winter of Oliver's time.

They were dressed in many different ways. Most wore hats or caps, but no two were alike. A few wore dull, loose fitting gowns. Others had pleated jerkins that were pinched tight around the waist but billowing at the arms and shoulders. Scott glimpsed armour glinting in the winter light. Several of the men wore swords—big plain swords that looked cumbersome and heavy to hold.

Scott dismounted—nobody particularly seemed to have noticed that he had arrived. He had no idea what the year might be, but the look of the clothes and the people and the weapons made him think that this was the Middle Ages.

But when were the Middle Ages? After William the Conqueror, but before Henry the Eighth. He remembered that much from school. But what happened in the Middle Ages? He had a vague memory of Richard the Lion-heart and bad King John, and Robin Hood if Robin Hood really existed. People always talked about castles and cathedrals as 'medieval'.

The hubbub began to quiet. Something was evidently about to happen. Scott followed the eyes of the others to the hill-top. A company of men at arms stood to attention, and a huge man, wearing a heavy mail coat began to speak. He seemed oddly familiar, which of course he could not be.

Scott strained to hear the words, but he was some way away. With a little pushing he managed to make his way upwards, nearer the front.

He was close enough now to hear the man—his booming voice was as huge as he was, and the crowd had become whisper quiet. But, somehow Scott could not make out the words. Every now and then they seemed to be on the edge of a meaning, but never quite enough to follow.

Here is a little of what he heard:

"Sithen the Kynges fader, ure lauerd, yeferd is, ure lond onder yfils mony gefallen is thurh unwihtennessin ayin Godes wil. Fyl ond swaar be the dades of this dayes Kynges freonden, ond they leidde the yonge Kynge in the deop weies of helle. Ond of alle stench untholelich, that stench is meest thoster ond thik in tham lich af Gaveston Piers, Cornwals Erl…"

He rolled the sounds of the words around in his head, but he could do little with them.

The crowd seemed to like it though. Every so often they let out a cheer.

Then Scott noticed something behind the men-at-arms on the hill. It was man-sized, man-shaped, and occasionally it seemed to struggle. A prisoner, perhaps. Standing behind it or him was something else. A man in a mask, holding a huge axe.

"So," said Scott to himself. "That is an executioner, and the poor man is going to be executed."

79

He wondered what Gawain would do if he were here: would he ride in and rescue the man, or would he let justice take its course?

"You don't understand what they are saying, do you?" said a voice close by. A young voice, a woman's voice, with the slightest trace of an accent—French perhaps. Scott turned to look. It was the girl they had rescued on the road to Kenilworth.

Scott was not sure he trusted this girl. Had she followed him here, or had she bumbled down the same mess of skifts to this exact place at this exact time. Was this the kind of thing that happened? If only he had found out more when there was Gawain to ask.

"I will translate for you," she went on, "Or, at least, I will explain."

"Ok," said Scott, not knowing what else he could say.

"They are executing Piers Gaveston. The man with the giant's voice is Guy of Warwick. Piers is a close friend of the King, but all the nobles hate him. Guy takes a big risk. Who knows how it will turn out? They seized him in Deddington, which is two day's march from here. Gaveston should not be in England at all, because he was exiled by the King. Guy has just been reading out the order for his exile, which he says cannot be countermanded. The order is in French, which many of the people will not understand, so he has translated parts of it for them. He is being very careful to say nothing against the King, though every-body knows that the barons hate the King almost as much as they hate Gaveston. They remember the old King, whom they loved. But Guy is a shrewd man. He will say later that he was obeying the letter of the king's decree. Gaveston was a dead man as soon as he landed in England."

"Shouldn't we try to help him?"

"Help him? What business is it of ours whether he lives or dies? Are you going to fight all these people? He probably deserves it; most of them do."

"Oh."

"Listen, he calls on those assembled to stand with him. When he raises his fist you must be ready to shout 'Oyez', otherwise people will think we are with Gaveston, and it might be us next on the block... ready... OYEZ! OYEZ!"

Scott didn't shout. There was a sickening roar as the crowd belowed their cries. Everybody strained to get a closer look. Scott was tall for his age, but he could no longer see past the people in front. Somehow he was glad of that.

The roar rose to a deafening shriek, and people stamped their feet or rattled swords if they had them. Scott caught a glimpse of a head, held up in the air, for one moment. Then the chaotic shouting began to take on a rhythm of its own. "WARWICK! WARWICK! WARWICK!" they chanted.

Scott turned away, and began to lead his horse out of the crowd, down the hill, the way he had come.

This must have caught the girl off guard, because she had to run to catch up with him.

"You are leaving in a hurry," she said. "I'd almost think you were afraid. Where are you going?"

"Oh, down to Warwick," said Scott, airily. He trusted her even less now.

"I will come with you," she said. "I lost my horse, so I will ride yours. That is all right, as you can lead me."

Scott did not think much of the idea of leading his own horse while the girl rode, but he did not have a good answer for her. At any rate the snow had cleared up—if there had ever been snow in this time—so he would not be getting his boots wet.

She mounted effortlessly.

"Ah, that is better," she said from above. "I can be your lady and you can be my squire. Lead on, good squire!"

Rather than waiting for him to lead, she spurred the horse into a rather faster walk than Scott would have chosen. He wondered if she was planning to make off with the horse and leave him behind, and what he could do about it if she were.

Fortunately the ground broke beneath them. The horse was left confused for a moment, looking for a good footing. It gave him enough time to take the horse's head, and so lead the way down.

"You are very young to be skifting on your own," said the girl. "You were with that man. Did he get tired of you, or did you get lost?"

"I'm on a quest," said Scott, resolutely. He wasn't really sure what a quest was, but it seemed to fit what he was doing, and it sounded an awful lot better than saying 'I got lost'.

"A quest? My, my. A quest! Something in particular, or are you just questing around for anything that takes your fancy?"

"Something in particular."

"You must be a mighty hero, to be questing through time on your own. Have you killed many men with that sword?"

"No, not many," said Scott.

"A hero of few words. Have you a lady?"

Scott was caught between saying that he did not have a lady, and saying that his mother was his lady. But then he realised, quite suddenly, the danger he was in. This witch-girl, who was as likely to be a deadly enemy as a friend, had already got out of him far more information than he had meant to give her. She had a gentle, teasing, questioning voice, and every question left Scott feeling as if he had failed to live up to her expectations, and every answer he gave made him feel as if he wanted to please her more.

What would Gawain do? When they were at Kenilworth he had turned away sharp questions with his own gentle, jesting answers, tied together like riddles.

"You are silent, my young hero," said the girl. "Did my question about your lady offend you?" She had sounded quite English for the last few minutes, but now the hint of French came creeping back into her voice.

"No, my lady," said Scott, reaching for the words that sounded like Gawain's words. Then inspiration struck him. "No indeed, my lady," he went on, hesitantly. "For today, are you not yourself my lady, since our paths have chanced to meet?" He had learned some of this rolling language once for a part in a play he had wanted to get, and practised it with his mother. Somebody else had got the part, but the sound of the words, if not the lines themselves, were beginning to well up in Scott's memory.

"Ah, but you are suddenly full of courtesy," she replied, with something between a laugh and a smile.

"But how could I not be?" said Scott, "when there is such a model of beauty and favour before me."

What Scott did not know, and could not see, was that with the change in the way he talked, his whole body had changed. Before he had been plodding on ahead, leading the horse with such a slump in his shoulders that it was obvious that he thought he should be riding it. The girl had seen this, and was teasing him as she might tease a peasant. But now he was walking erect, head high, and with a hint of grace in his legs and strength in his shoulders.

"But my friend!" she said, clapping her hands together in delight. "Surely you hid your true self when first we met. But tell me, that man who was with you, surely that was Gawain, the knight of King Arthur."

"My lady" said Scott, wary again in case he gave too much away, "My companion's name and person are for himself to reveal, and not for me."

"Truly you are a paragon of discretion," she replied. "But if you will not say, then surely I must! It was Gawain, who is called Gwalchmai, and Walganus, son of Lot and Morgause. Hawk of May, King of Goddodin, the lightning sword, master of battle, whose strength is like the sun. Surely you know that it was he?"

"My lady, a man's ways are his own."

"But surely you know that this Gawain is the master of romance, king of chivalry, peerless knight of courtesy, beloved of all women?"

"As to this, my lady, I cannot say. But tell me of yourself: why should we talk of companions when beside me rides the sweetest of sweet ladies, whose beauty is like the moon. Except... except that I do not know her name?"

"Ah, my young hero, if you would know the lady's name, you must first prove your mettle. When you have won a battle for me, then perhaps you shall know my name."

On the whole, Scott thought he had got the better of the second half of their conversation. But he was still worried by how much she now knew or might have guessed.

By and by they reached the outskirts of Warwick. The sun was low in the sky, casting long, sharp shadows to the north east. The castle and a church stood proud over the landscape. Stones glowed golden in the failing light. Scott guessed that it was a substantial town for its day, but the whole of Warwick would have fitted neatly into the middle of his Stechford.

The Warwick of this age—he did quite know what this year was—was unlike any town he had seen before. The towns that Scott knew began gradually. The outskirts would be warehouses and petrol stations, with scattered houses clumped together as you went further to make broad roads and avenues, and then into new housing estates, and finally twisting, narrow streets of tiny shops and old houses, or perhaps hideous office blocks, flats and skyscrapers.

This Warwick was nothing—and then suddenly a wall with a gate — and then many houses thickly set together, higgledy-piggledy, some in stone, some in wood, and some in the dark beams and white walls which are called 'wattle and daub'. The gate was open, with men at arms standing sharply to attention. They carried pikes and wore thick leather tunics, their surcoats emblazoned with the Bear and Ragged Staff, the emblems of Warwick. They banged their pikes smartly on the paving stones and stood to attention as Scott led the horse and lady through.

Inside the gate, they followed the winding cobbles past street merchants and children playing. It would have made a picturesque postcard—but it was let down (in Scott's opinion) by the dreadful smell. There was raw sewage in the gutters, and every so often somebody would let out a yell and pour a pitcher of dirty water from an upper window, much as the servant in Kenilworth had done.

The girl knew of an inn that would welcome guests. Scott had been casting occasional glances at her. Sometimes he saw the witch-girl from their first meeting, and sometimes a noble lady, young, but stately and beautiful. And sometimes there was a hint of something else. It was hard to place her, not knowing her name, and Scott had already resolved to do some deed of valour or chivalry which would persuade her to reveal herself—if only he could think of one.

For all the trouble of the execution of Piers Gaveston, these seemed to be settled times. Lamps were being lit in the houses and shops, and the bustling streets had the cosy air of the last days before Christmas.

They made their way deeper into the town. The streets became crowded, with barrows set close together, traders yelling their wares, clumps of people huddling round this or that wonder from the East. It was market day, and many of the merchants and sellers were unwilling to leave despite the darkening weather until all their goods were gone. At one place the street was so narrow and the people so thickly packed that Scott had to squeeze himself between bodies to make any headway. He wondered how the horse would manage it, but the press parted, perhaps out of respect for a noble lady, or more likely because of a shrewd calculation about the damage the horse's hooves might do if it got restless. Packed this close, the air was full of perfumes—rich, thick scents that seemed more like something you would find in an oriental kitchen than you would want to wear yourself. It almost, but not quite, disguised the fouler smell from the gutters.

The streets opened out into a market square. It was bustling with more life than Scott could have imagined. Over here musicians were playing simple, rough made horns and pipes to the accompaniment of a loose drum. There a whole pig was being roasted over a great fire, while a small child turned the spit which kept it from burning. One stall sold huge furs, which looked as if they had been cut in one piece from some great animal. They were piled higher than a tall man.

There was a livestock auction in one corner. An enormous fellow bellowed out what Scott guessed were prices, as great horned bulls and short-legged, thickset cows were led out. Tempers seemed frayed, and Scott was sure that one of the auction crowd was having a fist fight with someone else, though nobody paid much attention. There were rolls of silk on another stall, blazoning rich reds and purples, with women standing marvelling at their colour and sheen. A man in a thick leather coat that did not look as if it had been tanned properly was selling hares. Some were in a basket at his feet, and others he kept inside the coat. An old man was sitting by himself at a table, slowly writing with a white-feather quill pen on parchment. There was no crowd of eager buyers around him, just one sour faced customer who kept looking over his shoulder. There were carpenters and blacksmiths and cheese-makers and lace-makers and leather tanners, all calling out their goods and services, though Scott could not understand a word of it.

There were butchers and bakers and—in all probability if Scott had looked hard enough—candlestick makers. In the furthest corner there was a huge, beautiful bear, standing upright chained to a stake. Some boys were throwing stones at it, but the bear only shuffled mournfully from side to side, staring at nothing in particular, perhaps dreaming of the forests and rivers where it was born.

Almost every stall had lamps lit. More lamps were hanging from the shops and houses that made up the square, but one building in partic-ular caught Scott's eye. It was at the corner of the market and another street, and a sign like a pub sign was swinging from its upper storey. The girl gestured to it, and he guessed it was the inn where they were headed.

Crossing the market was no mean feat, but they managed it in the end. The girl dismounted from the horse—his horse—and left it with a stable boy who leapt up from his game of tormenting the bear. Scott followed her inside. It was a wide, low room, with rough wooden pillars and many beams. Scott had expected the choking smell of stale tobacco smoke, but this time he was wrong. He smelt beer, bread and thick gravy, but the only smoke was wood smoke from the fire. He wondered if they would tell him he was too young to be there, until he noticed little children playing in one corner and boys of his own age nursing thick wooden mugs.

"You're not from this time," said a voice, and Scott found himself yanked down onto a bench by a balding man with a round back, and a rounder face. Scott was not sure what to say. They were the first intelligible words that anybody in Warwick had said to him, but he was not sure he wanted to tell his business to any stranger.

"Who are you?" he said.

"Me?" said the man. He had a croaky, chokey voice, and sounded like he might have come from London. "I'm Andrew Chapel I am. Antiquarian extraordinaire, counsellor to kings and princes."

"Oh," said Scott. "What do you counsel them about?"

"Love mostly. Romance. The affairs of the heart. I wrote the book on love, I did."

"Is that right?" said Scott, wondering if the man was mad or just drunk.

"Oh yes. Oh yes," he replied. And then added another "Oh yes" for good measure. When Scott didn't reply to this, the man started again.

"Oh yes. I wrote the book of love. Anything you want to know. The art of love, I call it. An art. An exquisite art-form that every man should know. Most of them don't. Even princes. Even kings. That's why they come to me. They send someone who knows how to find me. We agree our price. And then I travel to them. Oh yes. I write their letters to their ladies fair, to their lovers and their mistresses, to their betrotheds and wives to be. History wouldn't be what it is without Andrew Chapel. You've heard my name, of course?"

"I'm not sure," said Scott. Actually, he was quite sure, but it was easier not to say so.

"Ah, but of course, being a studied man, you'll know me as Andreas Capellanus. That's my Latin name you see. That's what you have to do, you know. Nobody ever got famous at this end of history writing anything but Latin. And if you write Latin, you have to have a Latin name. That's just common sense. I wrote my book for a boy called Walter. But in Latin that's Gualteri, d'you see? What's your name in Latin?"

"I don't know," said Scott.

"Well that's no good to man nor beast. What is it in English?"

"Scott," said Scott, and immediately wished he hadn't.

"Ah. That's tricky. You could try 'Caledonia', which was the old name for Scotland, or 'Ultima Thule', if you want to go a bit further north. But, of course, up to a point, all the Scots lived in Ireland, and the Irish lived in Scotland, which is well known. So you would call yourself 'Hibernia', except that it would sound like a woman's name. So perhaps 'Hibernius'. Of which century are you, Hibernius?"

"The twenty-first," said Scott.

"Ah. So far. We never believed that there would be a twenty-first. We were happy with our nineteenth. Some of us went looking in the twentieth, but it was a bad business—wars, and famines, and dreadful illnesses that wiped out half the world. We thought that the end had come, and if we went any further we would never come back. But that was long ago. That's when I busied myself with antiquity, and with love. I wrote a book on it, you know?"

"Yes," said Scott. "Someone was telling me about it, very recently."

"Were they now? That is nice. 'De Amore', I called it. Everything you need to know about love. Of course, it wasn't all mine. I borrowed from the classics. From Ovid, from Virgil, from the great writers. But even so, I surpassed them. The greatest book in history on love. Are you in love, young Hibernius?"

"I don't know. I don't think so."

"But you came in with a lady. A fair lady. Too young to be your mother, too unlike you to be your sister. A little older than yourself, but love makes light of these difficulties. You must woo her, and prove your love. What is her name, Hibernius?"

"I don't know."

"Ah. I see. But love desires to know its object's name. Why has she not told you?"

"She says I must perform some heroic deed if I want to learn her name."

"But of course, but of course. She already is smitten, for Cupid's arrows strike first one, or first the other, but seldom both at the self same time. Have you determined the deed that you will perform for her?"

"I was sort of waiting for something to turn up."

"There is wisdom in waiting, that is true. But love will not be held back. Have you an intermediary?"

"A what?"

"An intermediary. Someone who will go between you to smooth the path of love and to make all things ready. An internuntius. The lover must not leave things to chance, but seek the services of one he can trust—"

He was interrupted by the return of the girl.

"Andrew Chapel!" she said. Her voice was icy—quite different from the mocking, playful tone that she had taken with Scott. He noticed—though—that her accent was more obviously French.

"Marie-France," said the man. "How lovely to see you again. Are you still writing?"

"What are you doing here, Andrew Chapel?"

"I? I am fulfilling my life's destiny, instructing young Hibernius here in the ways of love."

"And what do you know of the ways of love, Andrew Chapel? Less than this young man, who knows discretion and courtesy as you will never know it."

"My dear, sweet thing. It is always a pleasure to discourse with you—". But Marie-France had already turned from him to Scott. She smiled, and tilted her head a little.

"My friend, it seems that you are expected at the castle. I may accompany you, unless you would prefer to have your new friend—?" She gestured to Andrew Chapel. "They will bring your horse, and for the rest there is nothing to be arranged. Do you wish that I accompany you?"

Scott got to his feet. He did not very well see how they could expect him at the castle, since he had arrived here by accident. He wondered if it was a trap, but, then, why would they want to trap him when they could send armed guards to arrest him? There was not much time to think. He offered Andrew Chapel his hand:

"It's been a pleasure meeting you, Mr Chapel," he said. "I will bear your advice in mind."

A company of guards had arrived at the inn door, ready to take them the short distance through the town to the castle walls. Scott was not sure if he was under arrest, or being escorted with honour. But Marie-France offered him her hand, which she raised to shoulder height between them, as Scott had seen in old country dances. He took this as a good sign. The guards seemed content to match his pace, which was also a good sign, and the crowd parted obediently before them.

The castle was surrounded by an outer wall, crenelated with battlements and pierced at several points with low turrets. In the gathering darkness the wall seemed to stretch endlessly in either direction, but the road took them to a gatehouse. Scott had been to the castle before, in his own time, and this gatehouse seemed somehow smaller than the one he remembered. But it was a very different thing to visit a castle as a tourist in the daytime of the twenty-first century than to arrive at night, perhaps as guest, perhaps as prisoner, when it was a fortress defended by many men.

The guards exchanged passwords with the gatekeeper, and they were allowed inside. Torches and braziers were set at intervals along a long passage. Looking up, Scott could make out the holes in the roof used for pouring boiling oil onto the heads of attackers. He wondered what boiling oil felt like, and how long it took to die from it.

He shuddered. To break his train of thought, he ventured a question to Marie-France.

"Did that man really write a book about love?" he said.

"Andrew Chapel? Yes, he wrote a tiresome treatise. He is the man who knows everything there is to know about love, except what it is like. He has a rule for every occasion, but he has taken all of them from books written by others."

"And is your name really Marie-France?" said Scott.

"He should have not told you my name, because you were to learn that when you had performed some deed of valour. Now our game of courtesy is broken, and you know me simply as Marie of France, or Marie de France, if you prefer."

"My name is Scott," said Scott.

"This I knew," she said. "You are Scott Perceval Raynall. Also, I knew your mother."

"You knew my mother? Where—when?"

"Many years ago, when I was a little girl, I spent one summer at King Arthur's court. I will never forget it."

"But how was my mother in King Arthur's time?"

"That I do not know. I was very small, and did not understand much of what I saw and heard. But I remember the colours, and the delights, and the sound of trumpets, and of many, many things. Arthur's knights had gone out into all of England, and into Brittany and beyond. Skifting from one adventure to the next, they visited many times, and brought back with them delights from every part of what you would call the Middle-Ages. So Arthur's halls were decked with banners and flags, and tapestries and embroideries, and in every courtyard was a statue or a fountain.

"Machines do not travel well through time, so they seldom brought back the later marvels, but they brought architects and musicians and poets and many others who desired to live a little in the realm of Logres. And so Arthur's castles in Carlisle, and Caerleon, and Camelot were wonders that will not be equalled by anything this land will see again.

"But hush, we are greeted."

The soldiers had brought them out into a courtyard inside the walls. There was one great tower, a keep, which soared upwards further than the eye could see in the darkness, for the sun had now set utterly, and they were left staring upwards at the stars that shone down so much more brightly in the clear air than ever they did in Scott's own time.

But there was little time to look at the stars.

"Well met, my young traveller," said a huge voice, and the man from Blacklowe Hill strode up to greet him. He bowed low, and Scott did his best to make the same gesture, though it made his sword drag along the flag-stones.

"You are a long way from home," he said. "Come, you must eat with us, and your lady. Tonight you will sleep safe in the strongest keep of Britain, though tomorrow you journey on into reckless danger."

Scott was not quite sure he liked the sound of the last part, but the idea of food and sleep was a welcome one.

"I thank you," he said in reply. He wondered if perhaps he should add something to it, but the man had already turned on his heel. Scott guessed that they should follow him.

"That is Guy de Beauchamp," said Marie-France. "He is a famous knight. He once skifted back to save England from the Danes, all for the love of a lady. He is a man who understands love—and valour."

"And did he save England—wouldn't that have changed history?"

"What do you mean, that it would change history?"

They were climbing up a broad but steep staircase now, towards a great hall. Scott thought for a moment: "Well," he said, "if you skift back, doesn't it change what would have happened—so that maybe things turn out differently later on, which could mean that you would be a different person, and wouldn't skift back to do it?"

"This is a problem for you? But surely if you are doing it, then that means you are not doing something that prevents you from doing it?"

"But it would change what actually happened."

"But we change what happens all the time. Listen, I write romances—histories and stories about the knights and heroes I have met. They are not known in your time, but in the time where we are now, they are reading them even in Iceland. Most often I try to stay with the true story, but sometimes there are parts I need to tell that I do not know. So I have to make up something that takes the story from one event to the next. Sometimes I find out later what really happened—most often it is not what I wrote, but it does not matter. At the end of the story, all the knots will be untied in the same way. But hush, we are here."

The hall where they were standing was many times larger than the hall in Kenilworth gatehouse. It was lit by lanterns and torches, though the light barely reached the high vaulted roof. Music was in the hall, tumbling down in a flurry of notes from players in a gallery above. At the far end of the hall was a long table on a raised platform or dais, and a servant guided them past many trestles where men at arms or knights and ladies sat, to a place near the middle of the high table.

"This is a great honour, Scott Perceval," said Marie-France quietly, "to be sat at Guy's high table, and so close."

Scott looked at the place set before him. There was a knife and a spoon, but no fork. And the knife was more like a dagger than an eating knife. Instead of a plate there was a shallow wooden bowl, close grained and dark. The cup was a goblet: brass, or bronze, or something more precious. He put his elbows on the table, but immediately felt the surface wobble and took them off. All the seats were on the same side, so that everyone on high table faced the assembled throng. There was barely light enough to see to the back of the hall, and the smoke from torches and lanterns thickened the darkness.

A herald stepped forward, and the hubbub of chatter died down. He began to declaim loudly. The sound of his voice and words stirred something in Scott, though once again he could not catch any meaning. He looked at Marie-France, but she was listening too intently to notice him. The herald moved the air around him with his hands, and torch-light caught on his golden buckles. Scott could feel the excitement in the hall, and he was not surprised when the knights and ladies and men at arms rose to their feet as one man. "Warwick," they shouted, and banged their cups or flagons or goblets on the table and stamped their feet upon the floor.

Then Guy of Warwick himself stood, and bade the feast begin. There was a sound of drums, and a procession of brightly clothed cooks and servants marched into the room with tureens and bowls and ladles as big as a man's head. They served the high table first. Scott wondered how long it would take them to serve everyone, until he noticed that other teams of cooks and servers were already at the other tables.

He had forgotten how hungry he was. The soup was hot and salty, but with a little of the bread—which was rather bland—it took the edge off his hunger. After the soup there was fish. Small fish, with the eyes still glinting at you while you ate. After the fish, something like a pancake, and after the pancake a little bird. After the bird there was music and more drums, and the cooks brought out a whole boar, roasted on a platter.

Scott had eaten more than he thought he possibly could long before the last course was served. He had also drunk several glasses of the vinegary wine in the goblet, and the effect of the food and drink was to make him very sleepy indeed. He may well have fallen asleep more than once: he found himself waking with a start as he nodded forward.

The herald was talking again. He seemed to speak several languages— one was like French, one was like Latin, and one which was like the one he had heard on Blacklowe Hill. He was about to ask Marie-France for translation, when the herald turned to face him, and spoke in clear English:

"And my lord bids welcome to a young knight sent to us by our illustrious cousin Gawain of Logres. His name may not be known, as befits such a one on his first quest, but our welcome is no less because of it, and for this reason we shall know him as the Chevalier Desconnu.

"And my lord bids welcome to our nation's greatest poetess and story-teller, Marie of France, Marie of Avalon. It is my small skill which would at this time be called upon to recount a tale fit for this day, but I gladly cede my place. Marie, my lord bids you, tell us a tale of Logres."

Marie-France rose to her feet. Slowly, and with great poise and dignity, she made her way to the space above the steps. She spoke briefly to the herald, and to Sir Guy, and then she too turned to Scott.

"My lord, Chevalier Desconnu, since you are here and know yet little of our ways and of the three tongues of Britain, the noble Sir Guy of Warwick, has bidden me tell a tale in your own tongue, which is called New English. Alas, I have not the skill to set my thoughts into such poetry as amuses us, so I beg the court's indulgence for my halting words. But perhaps, if I may have a harpist to assist, I will borrow from the sisters of Avalon, and even so weave a spell of thought to pass an hour. And my lord Guy's gracious herald shall retell my thought in today's tongue for our knights and ladies.

"Now watch."

Slowly, she spread her hands. There was a sound like slow chanting in the distance, and the strumming of a harp. But over the sound of music Scott began to hear the sound of birds singing, of wind in grass and in trees. Then the space between her hands began to glow. It was a ball of spinning fire in the darkness. The light grew, until it surrounded her, and filled the space around the dais, then the whole hall.

As the light grew, it dimmed, and became more solid, and shapes separated themselves into light and dark, and finally the whole became a living world of colour and form. It was like a picture, except that it moved. It was a little like a film, except that it was all around, perfectly sharp, perfectly solid.

They were standing in a clearing in the wide forest. Scott could not see beyond the trees, but he was aware of badgers digging, foxes snuffling, bears lumbering, deer running and hares listening.

Scott was marvelling at this when he became aware of scents. It was like starting to smell again after a long cold: crushed grass, pine needles, the mustiness of leaf mould.

The voice of Marie-France breathed into the open space. She seemed to speak quietly, very close, and yet her voice filled the hall. Scott was aware of the others sitting alongside him, and of the sounds and smells of the feast, but they were less real than this other world.

"Arthur was dwelling at Carlisle, and see, on a day he sets off into the forest with Gawain and Bors."

There was a jingling of harness and spurs from among the trees, and into the clearing rode three men. They rode on mares, not chargers, one white, one black, and one piebald. None wore armour, but each had a light sword slung by his side. The man on the white horse wore a circlet of gold about his forehead, and his beard was golden. The man on the black horse had the emblem of a boar's head on his surcoat, and he had a black beard. But the man on the piebald horse had no beard. Scott started forward, because it was his own friend Gawain.

They rode out of the clearing—Scott smelled the sweat of the horses and the new leather of their gear. Then the clearing itself softened and changed, and they were in front of a great castle.

"After many hours," said Marie-France's voice "they came to a castle with the drawbridge open. At the gate, a huge man stood, in black armour, carrying an axe."

Scott watched as the king and his knights rode to the drawbridge. The man was waiting for them. Twice their height, he was more a giant than a man. Behind him a gallows stood, and from it hung, upside down, three knights, dead, rotting in their armour.

"Ho, little men," he roared. "By the look of you, you would be knights, but you are children."

Arthur rose in his saddle, and wheeled his horse to face the man.

"A great fellow like you should give his name before he insults the guests at his gate," he roared in return. "What is your name, and what is your purpose?"

The giant laughed. A deep throated laugh that began in his belly and shook the ground they stood on.

"I am the Carl of Carlisle, and I am the strong man and the land man from these parts, and I capture all those who come to my gates and hang them up by the heels until they pay me ransom," he said.

"Then know that I am Arthur, King of Britain, and I tolerate no such wickedness in my realm. Prepare to defend yourself."

Instantly the Carl of Carlisle called a black horse to him. He drew a huge sword and whirled it over his head.

Scott winced as he looked at Arthur—without armour, on a light horse with no lance or helmet. But there was no fear in the eyes of the king. He spurred his horse on. The black knight did the same, but just as they reached each other he threw his sword to the ground so that it stood upright in the earth, quivering. Then he reached over and pulled Arthur bodily from the saddle. He reined his horse in, and, with a blur, tied Arthur's hands and feet and hung him upside down from the gallows.

Scott gasped. He saw that this was too much for Bors. Drawing his own sword he spurred his own horse straight at the giant. But the result was the same, and soon he too was hanging upside down from the gallows.

"Now my lords," breathed the voice of Marie-France again, "Gawain does not know what to do. He knows that he cannot defeat the giant knight. But if he goes for help the king may be dead by the time he returns. What must he do? What would you do my lords?"

Although the bright summer's day did not fade, Scott became aware of the knights sitting in Sir Guy's hall. He heard them murmuring. It seemed that some said "fight" and others said "seek help", but at length he heard the rumble of Sir Guy's own voice. "Parley," he said.

The hall faded. Gawain rode forward, but slowly.

"Good Sir knight. You hold my king captive, and my friend. I cannot fight with you, being not tall enough. Nor can I bring an army against you without abandoning my honour, for I would have to turn tail first and flee. So I do what all knights must do in such a state. Name your terms for my king's release."

The Black Knight roared, and for a moment Scott thought that he would strike him. But then he seemed to check himself.

"Some would call you coward, Sir Gawain, but I do not. If you would save your king, promise me one thing. Return with him a year and a day from now, and answer me then a single question. If you fail, then both your heads are forfeit. If you answer aright, you will be free to go, and Arthur will receive my fealty as my liege and king."

"I accept your terms," said Gawain. "Release my friends."

The Black Knight lifted Arthur in one hand and Bors in the other. With a tug he snapped the ropes that tied them to the gallows, and he set them backwards upon their own horses.

"Now fail me not Sir Gawain," said the Black Knight. "Return a year and a day hence with your king, and with the answer to my question."

"Name your question," said Gawain.

"Simply this: what do women desire above all things?"

The clearing in front of the castle faded into the blackness of the hall as Gawain, Bors and the king rode away.

"Now," said Marie-France's voice, "Arthur and Gawain have one year to find the answer. But surely in this place, in this court of Warwick, there is wisdom enough to answer them. My lords, my ladies, give us your thoughts—let the herald speak for all of you, and I, for a moment, will rest my voice."

For a moment everyone sat silent, and then there was a hubbub of noise across the hall. Sir Guy gestured to the herald, who took with him a scribe and set off among the trestle tables writing the many answers the knights and ladies offered.

Marie of France stood silent, pensive, her hands pressed together like the steeple of a church.

"What do women want above all things?" said Scott to himself. He wondered if Andrew Chapel had the answer, written in his book of love. He thought about the things his mother asked him—to tidy his room, to do his homework. These did not sound like the sort of thing that would answer the black knight's question. Then he thought about Marie-France. What did she want?

96

The herald returned to the high table. In just a few minutes he had made a list of many hundreds of ideas. With elaborate courtesy, he read his list, translating into New English for Scott as he went along.

"Money... jewels... a handsome lover... safety... freedom... a castle... a son... a daughter... the king's favour... the largest ruby in the world... beauty above the lot of mortals... eternal youth..." The list went on. Some of the items were more comical: "A different husband... a moment's peace... to be deaf for a day... clothes that washed themselves... a servant who did not lie... a husband who did not lie." Some were poignant: "To know her children were safe... to be sure her husband returned safe from battle... to die in her love's arms."

The herald bowed as the list was completed. Marie-France made a graceful curtsy.

"My friends," she said, "You are of a truth the wisest courtiers of any that I have known—excepting the court of Arthur the King, for where you have made a hundred answers and filled three parchments, his court made ten thousand and filled three books.

"But come with me now back to the road to Carlisle, a year on and one day, where Arthur and Gawain ride with mournful faces. For, though they have three books of answers, both know in their hearts that they have not found the one thing which women desire above all."

As she spoke the hall became filled with all sorts of noises—not the cheerful woodland sounds of the start of the story, but creakings and groanings, sly and furtive sounds, slinkings and whinings. Then the smells—the smell of burning thatch, the stench of death. In the deep distance Scott thought he could perceive robbers plotting, misers counting, ravagers pillaging, gluttons gorging. The colours came last of all. Sombre colours, dark, vaulting. They shaped themselves into lines, and Scott found that they were riding a narrow path through a thick forest. Huge trees thrust upwards into arches that held back the light. There were pits dug into the road with sharp spikes, and covered with leaves and netting so that they could not be seen. Each pit must be carefully avoided, because a horse that put a foot onto that false ground was lost. At times they came to deserted houses—a woodman's cottage burned and blackened, a hermit's cell empty and forlorn, a wayside smithy pulled to the ground, the charcoal scattered, tools rusting under the world's rain.

Gawain and Arthur—for it was Gawain and Arthur—rode on in silence. Strapped to Gawain's saddle were two huge books, and to Arthur's a third. The king looked older, much older, and Gawain was hunched over his saddle.

"Hold, fair sirs!" croaked a voice from in the shadows. Arthur reined his horse in sharply, and Gawain drew his sword.

"Hold, fair sirs!" creaked the voice again. It was neither a man's voice nor a woman's voice, neither young nor old. It was a cracking voice, a dry voice, a crow voice.

"We hold, good neighbour," called Arthur. His tone was kingly, but his voice trembled. "Show yourself to us, if you will that we stay to speak with you."

From out of the darkest patch of shadow between the trees, a hideous old woman hobbled out into the middle of the path. She was bent almost double, and pushed herself along with a heavy stick. Her face was gnarled like an old tree, and a breath of wind brought a terrible smell drifting into their nostrils.

"You are Arthur, king of Logres, and his nephew Gawain the lightning hand," she croaked.

"We have no need to hide our names, good lady," said Gawain. Scott marvelled at his kindly tone—he would rather have struck the old woman than speak with her.

"That is truth," she creaked. "For in the grave there is no concealment, and Arthur rides even now to his death, unless one can save him."

"What know you of this, good damsel?" said Gawain.

"What every one in this wide land knows. That Arthur seeks the answer to a riddle. But no answer can he find, and he must this day give his head to keep his word, or stand forever shamed."

"And what is this to you, good woman?" said Gawain.

"I, and only I can save him. But my price is high, and you will not want to pay it."

"My good maiden, if you can save the king then no price is too high, except a price which would be oath-breaking or shame or dishonour."

"My price is not for the king, but for you Sir Gawain. It is said that you are the most courteous knight in the world, and that you would give yourself to save a lady's honour."

"I count courtesy and a lady's honour to be among the first duties of a knight."

"Then make your promise, Gawain. If I can tell you the one answer which can save your King, then you must promise to wed me as your lawful wife, and to have me as your love and paramour alone, forsaking all others."

Marie-France's voice drifted once more across their minds.

"My lords and ladies, for certain Gawain is now in sore distress. He knows that the realm of Logres must fall to wrack and ruin without the king. And his duty as knight, and nephew, and subject, is to give his life for his sovereign. And give his life he would, without a moment's thought or regret. But what this woman asks goes beyond his life, because of all knights Gawain is the knight that loves women—the beautiful, and the comely, and the noble, and the delicate. And all know that Gawain is loved by women. For any knight to marry this crone would be a burden, but for Gawain it would end his world.

"But Gawain cannot think long, for noon approaches, and it is at noon that the King must appear before the Carl of Carlisle, or else forfeit either his head or his honour."

Scott wanted to shout out 'Gawain, don't believe her. It's a trap.' But the words would not leave his throat. He watched in anguish as his friend squared his shoulders and made himself upright in the saddle.

"My lady," he said. "These are strange ways to go about winning a husband. In my land it is the knight who must woo the damsel. But I will consent to your condition, except for one condition of my own."

"Name me your condition," snapped the crone.

"That you promise me faithfully and by all that is holy that the king's predicament is neither of your own doing nor your instigation nor of your planning."

"Pah!" she grunted, and spat at the ground. "An easy enough condition to meet. Your enemy is not me nor any friend of mine, but your own aunt, the King's sister, Morgan Le Fay, the enchantress who has long plotted his downfall."

"And how do you know of this, good lady?"

"That is simple enough. I was one of Morgan's maidens. But I would not share in this wickedness, and so she cursed me into this form, even as you see me, and thrust me out to die in the forest."

99

"My lady, you have my pity," said Gawain. "And if you truthfully and truly tell the king the answer that saves his life and honour, then you shall also have my hand."

"You swear it?"

"I swear it."

The woman scowled and chewed her tongue.

"But you're a crafty one. Swear by all that is holy that you will marry me in public before all the court, and that as long as I will have you then you will have no other loves, else may you become as hideous as I. Do you swear?"

"I swear it."

This seemed to satisfy her. She hobbled closer, so that she came between Arthur and Gawain, and Arthur had to hold his horse to stop it from shying at the horror of her.

"Bend down my king," she said. "And I will whisper the answer in your ear."

The scene faded into the blackness of the forest.

"Now Arthur and Gawain ride in haste," said Marie-France. The hall opened once again into living colour, but this time Arthur and Gawain were galloping between gorse bushes over the hills, as they raced to reach the Carl's castle by noon.

"And so they come to the gates of the castle one stroke before the noon bell, and Arthur beats upon the gong at the castle gate."

Once more they were in the clearing by the black knight's castle, but what a change had come over it. The stones were scoured and pointed as if they were new, and hideous war machines stood ready on battlements, and the steel helmets of many men at arms marched from tower to tower. And in the clearing, the black knight had built a gallows twenty feet tall, and from it hung an iron cage in the shape of a man.

The Carl of Carlisle came striding through the portcullis, over the wooden drawbridge, and in his right hand was no sword but a headsman's axe, and in his left the stump of a tree, five feet wide, which he set upon the ground as lightly as if it had been straw.

"So, you have returned little man. I had half expected that you would not. And you have returned almost alone. I fully expected that you would bring your army, and, as you can see, I am well prepared. But, see, I stand here ready with my axe and my chopping block. I will hang

100

your body from my gibbet, but your head I will place on a stake, and the stake I will place on a cart, and the cart I will have drawn throughout your realm of Logres, so that none will doubt your death."

"You speak as a man who has already won his game," said Arthur.

"And you speak as a man who has no hope but empty words. Or, if you know the answer to my riddle, give it to me."

"You did not say how many guesses I might make," said Arthur. "So I have assembled one or two, or three or four, or perhaps more, if you have the patience for them."

"Guess away," said the Carl. "I have all day, but you will not wear me out with your many guesses. Only the true answer will save you, and I know that none know that save my own lady, and those to whom she has confided it."

"So Arthur began to read from his books," said Marie-France. "Arthur turned page after page, reading many answers. The shadows lengthened into afternoon, and then into early evening as Arthur turned the final page in the final book and read the final answer."

The Carl of Carlisle let out a deep laugh. The ground shook with it.

"Ah, Arthur. You have entertained me greatly. Never did I imagine that you could have expended such effort and ingenuity. Nor did I believe that there could be so many wrong answers in the world."

"Then it is not rubies which women desire above all things?" said Arthur. "Nor youth nor beauty nor a handsome lover?"

"None of these things, Arthur," said the Carl. "Now, prepare yourself for the axe, as I have expended quite enough time on you, and I wish to go to claim your kingdom."

"It is as you say," said Arthur. His tone was mournful, but Scott caught a gleam in his eye.

"Indeed it is," said the Carl. "Make haste—I grow impatient."

"Then die I must," said Arthur.

"Die you must," said the Carl.

"Unless—but, no…" said Arthur.

"Unless what?" said the Carl.

"Oh, it is but a trifle, a final answer that I learned on the way. I would not be giving it, except that I promised a lady that I would, and I would not die with a broken promise on my lips."

"Hurry, then," said the Carl.

"I must whisper it in your ear," said Arthur. "It is such a simple thing, such a little thing, that I would not wish to be embarrassed before your men and my nephew."

"Very well, then," said the Carl. "But I warn you, I am wearing thick armour if it is your intention to knife me where I stand, and if you do, after I have killed you, I will eat your nephew who sits there quaking on his horse like a scarecrow."

Arthur rode up to the Carl. Even on his horse he came only as high as the Carl's ear. He leant across, and whispered something.

The expression on the Carl's face changed. First surprise. Then anger. Then rage.

And then his face relaxed, and he began to laugh. It was a huge laugh. The ground shook with it. The castle shook with it. The air shook with it. Shook and shattered into tiny pieces which fell to the floor of the hall. And there was only Marie-France, a finger to her lips, bathed in soft light.

"Friends, certain-sure Arthur had given the Carl of Carlisle the one answer in all the world that could save his life. And the Carl confessed that he was beaten, and swore allegiance to Arthur, and in years later came to serve him as the warden of his northern marches.

"Arthur rode southwards to Camelot with a glad heart, but Gawain rode behind him sickened and consumed.

"In Camelot, joy was great that Arthur had returned, but not so great as surprise when they learned that Gawain was to marry. Neither Gawain nor Arthur told any more of what had happened, and so the courtiers fervently believed that their own Prince of Romance had met some foreign maiden whose beauty was beyond any seen in Logres, and who doubtless was a royal princess of the highest birth.

"The preparations were made for a lavish ceremony, and on the appointed day the lady arrived at the castle. She rode on a mangy, hobbling horse that looked more a stray dog than a noble animal. And she wore a thick wedding dress, with a heavy veil. Some wondered if she was from some sunny clime, and had yet to learn to bear the British cold. Others argued she was ill, and said aloud that the wedding should be delayed.

"But on the appointed day, Gawain stood before the Archbishop, and Arthur there with Guinevere his queen, and with all the knights of the round table in attendance, and there before the assembled throng, Gawain gave a ring and received a ring, and the comeliest, most chivalrous and perfect knight of Logres and of the entire world was wed to the most hideous hag that ever thought conceived.

"But now our story takes us to that very night, as Gawain takes his lady to his bedchamber, and prepares to lift her veil. Sick he is in the stomach, but he has given his word, and he will keep it, or else end his life. He paces about the bedchamber, and looks at his sword, and wonders if it would not be better to fall on it. But he has given his word, and his honour is more important than life itself.

"But watch again, and see if there be hope for young Gawain."

Slowly the darkness of the hall faded, and they were in a marble room. Its pillars were twisted and fluted and carved as if they were the softest silk, yet with the strength to hold a roof of stone.

Scott felt a gasp from the knights and ladies. This was indeed a room more beautiful than any he had seen or dreamt.

A window stood open, and moonlight drifted in on a gentle breeze of roses and violets. Gawain sat in his shirt and breeches at a desk of polished mahogany, which seemed almost to glow in the moonlight.

"My love," called a voice from another room. "Come to bed, since it is our wedding night."

Gawain stood up. He was very stiff in his movements, abrupt as if he were wrestling with his thoughts. He turned, and it seemed that the whole room turned with him, so that they were facing a doorway.

In the doorway stood a young woman. Her hair was golden and it fell across her shoulders like foam from the sea or like the leaves of the forest. Her face was flushed, and yet perfectly coloured, and her eyes were azure.

"My love," she said, and her voice was like the sound of running water. "Come to bed, since it is our wedding night."

"Away from me, foul temptress!" cried Gawain, his face twisting in distress. "Restore to me my wife, for I have given her my word that I am hers alone and for always."

"But Gawain, my love, I am your wife. I am the lady Ragnall, whom Morgaine cursed, so that I would be the most hideous hag that ever mind conceived unless I should find the most pure and perfect knight, and persuade him of his own will to marry me. And you are that knight, my Gawain."

For a moment Gawain did nothing. And then he fell to his knees, sobbing, and saying over and again: "My lady, my lady."

She came to him, and laid her hands on his head, and then raised him to stand facing her, and they kissed as lovers do.

But then she turned away.

"My lady, what troubles you?" said Gawain.

"Gawain, my love," she said. "There is more to the curse than I have said. This night, this very night, you must make a choice which may leave you wretched for the rest of your days."

"Tell me of this choice," said Gawain.

"Now you see me as I truly am," she said. "But I cannot remain this way. For half of each day I must become again the toothless hag that I was when we first met. I must be one for the night time, the other for the day. And you must choose which it is to be."

"But my lady, how must I choose?"

"Wisely, Gawain. For, see, you may choose to have me beautiful at night, so that you may lie beside one as has not been seen since the love of Paris for Helen brought the walls of Troy tumbling to the harsh earth. But you will know, in your heart of hearts, that throughout the day you must endure the scorn, the pity, the derision of every courtier who sees the evil hag who is your wife. You will go about your business, you will do your deeds of valour, you will be perfect in chivalry, but all that people will ever say of you is that you are one with the foulest, most despicable, most wretched, most filthy crone that ever eye did see. Or you may choose that I be beautiful all day long. You will see the delight on every face as you lead me to dances and hunts and feasts and tournaments. Our love will be famous throughout time, and all men will long to be you, and all women to be me. But you will know in your heart that, at night, when lovers should share the most tender embrace, that you will come to bed with a drooling, retching, foul bag of bones and sickness. The stench of my body will drive you from your own bed, yet your promise to me before God will draw you back. Your nights will be misery, and the days will be darkened because of them."

"My lady, I cannot choose."

"But my lord, choose you must."

"But my lady, hard as it is for me, is it not ten times harder for you? If I choose for the day, then every night you will see the horror and loathing in my eyes. You will reach out to me, and before I can steel myself you will see me shrinking from your flesh, and where you desire love and companionship, you will find only bitterness and regret. Or if I choose for the night, to selfishly have you for myself throughout the long hours, then you must endure the horror in the eyes of all you meet. You will know that all speak ill of you behind your back. You will long for companions, yet when you approach a group idly talking, or weaving, or carding wool, or setting off to hunt, or choosing cloth, you will find them melt away.

"My lady—I cannot choose. You choose."

There was a flash of light, and a shriek, and a strange smell, and the marble bedchamber faded into the dark of the hall.

"The lady shrieked," said Marie-France. "And she fell to the floor sobbing. And when at length Gawain raised her to her feet, she told him that once and for all he had broken the curse, which could only be broken if he gave her the choice to choose her own destiny for herself.

"Gawain and the lady Ragnall lived years in bliss and joy together, and her beauty outshone even Guinevere.

"And this, my lords and ladies, draws the threads of my tale together, for now you may know the answer to the Carl's riddle, the answer which Ragnall told to Arthur, and which Arthur told to save his life.

"And the answer was that a woman desires to have mastery over a man, above all things in the world. And this was indeed the answer that Morgaine sought. For to her, in all the world, this was what she most sought—to have mastery over Arthur, her brother, and to rule Logres through him.

"But there is another answer, and it is the answer that Gawain gave to Ragnall—a woman desires herself to choose, not to be at the whim of man, but to make her own choices in her own world.

"And I, as a woman, speaking for all woman-kind, will give you a third answer, and then my tale is done. And it is this: a woman will have what she will—which is to say, that a woman desires what she desires."

Her tale ended, Marie-France stood for a moment, before making her way back to the high table. There were many shouts and calls from the hall, which Scott took to mean that they were pleased.

Pleased!

It had been the most marvellous thing that he had ever seen. But had everyone seen the tale in this way, had they all been part of the enchantment, or was this something specially for him?

"Is that really how Arthur looks?" he said to Marie-France as she sat down.

"I do not know how he seemed to you. If you have never seen him, then your imagination will have done the work. Was there anyone else you recognised?"

"Gawain."

"Ah, of course, Gawain. But nobody else?"

"I don't think so."

"I see."

Scott was now feeling extraordinarily sleepy. By and by a chamberlain came to lead him to his room. He followed obediently. They made their way through the castle to what must have been a luxurious apartment. To Scott, though, it seemed plain and cold. There was a brazier in the middle of the room, and a huge bed with its own curtains, of the kind that used to be called a 'four-poster' bed. There were hangings and tapestries on the walls, and there was a chair. But nothing else. The chamberlain helped him into a night gown.

There was no light to switch off, but the light from the brazier gave the room a warm, if not cheerful glow, though the air was icy. Scott buried himself under the bed-covers, which were also chilly.

He shivered for a few minutes until the sheets slowly began to warm, and wondered if everyone in the middle-ages was always cold. He could see a lantern on top of a tower through the window, and beyond that, somewhere deep in space, a single star burned down through the battlements. In the airy darkness, an owl hooted.

He slept.

7 WARWICK

Scott woke with a start. He had been dreaming of his mother. Somewhere, far away, she was calling to him. In the dream he was lost on a wide plain. It might have been a plain of grass, or a plain of gorse, but fire had swept over it, and there were now only twisted, grey stumps reaching out of bitter earth.

He heard her voice, but it seemed to come from under the ground.

And then the dream faded, and the light was floating across his face through the window. It took him a moment to work out where he was.

He put his foot out of the bed onto cold stone.

Clean clothes were lying ready for him on an ornate chest by the window. It was odd, but they were more like the clothes he was used to than the ones he was given in Kenilworth. And there was a note on top, written in what looked like biro on a scrap of ordinary paper.

It said: "Come and see me in the old chapel as soon as you are up. The servants will direct you. Do not tell Marie de France."

It was signed "G. Warwick."

It was most strange. Scott had a maths teacher for his first few weeks who was called Mr G. Warwick. He had only been there temporarily while the regular teacher was away. He was also a very large man—people said he had been a boxer, although Scott had not believed it.

He made his way down into the courtyard. In the daylight the castle was still enormous, but he saw that it was smaller than the castle of his own day. In fact, it seemed almost a different castle. The castle which he had visited in his day had slender, elegant towers at its corners. This castle had one, lumpish keep, huge, and haphazardly built.

A servant was waiting for him at the bottom of the steps. Without a word, he pointed Scott to a small door set into one of the walls.

Across the courtyard, he pushed open the door. A short flight of steps led down into a room that was set out as a study. Light was streaming through deep set windows. The huge man—Guy of Warwick—was sitting at the desk. In that posture he seemed more like a maths teacher than a medieval earl.

He turned to see Scott enter.

"Scott. Thank you for coming down," he said. He must have seen the look on Scott's face. "Yes, I wondered how long it would take for you to recognise me."

"Mr Warwick. That is, Sir Guy."

"Both. I imagine that you could do with some explanations, of various kinds, Scott."

"Yes, sir."

"Well, there's no need to call me sir, here. Even though I am, quite correctly, a Sir."

"No, sir."

Sir Guy gave him a reproving, patient look.

"I was to some extent expecting you. We have a system of passing messages. It's not very reliable and as often as not the message arrives after the person it was announcing. But a letter came to me yesterday afternoon that you were lost in time, and needed assistance. I thought I saw you on Blacklowe hill, but I had not yet received the message and had not imagined that you would be skifting—and skifting so far from home. It took some hours to get back to town, and you were ahead of me. But the gatekeepers told me immediately that strangers had entered."

"Did you really chop that man's head off?"

"Oh yes. Completely off."

"That's horrid, sir."

"Well, possibly. It's a matter of opinion, or, more precisely, it is not. And of time. In Birmingham, in your time I was a temporary maths teacher. You can't have temporary maths teachers going around chopping off heads. It would be entirely inappropriate, and questions would

108

be asked. There would be trouble with the law. But here and now, I am, in some respects and locally at least, the law."

"How long have you been here, in this time?"

"I was born here. Guy de Beauchamp. Formerly a loyal servant of King Edward, and a rather less loyal servant of his son Edward the second, who is by no means the man his father was."

"How did you come to be in my time then, sir?"

"Strictly speaking, I was looking for someone. I wanted to be close to the university, but for various reasons I could not be part of it. Your school has a long history with skifters. On our side, that is. You would be amazed at how many history teachers, sports teachers, French teachers and most especially Latin teachers have been skifters in need of a visible means of support."

"Are there any others there now?"

"I couldn't possibly tell you that, even if I knew."

"You said 'our side'. Which is 'our side', and what is 'their side'?"

"Our side, or, at least, my side and the side of your fellow-traveller Gawain of Orkney, is what we call Logres. King Arthur's side, although it was there before there was a King Arthur, and remains even if he is no longer there to be on it. The side of honour. The other side is what we call Avalon. Morgaine's side. The side of enchantment."

"Oh," said Scott, abruptly.

"Oh?"

"Last night, your herald introduced Marie-France as 'Marie of Avalon'. Is she on Morgaine's side?"

"Most certainly. Were you not enchanted by her tale? And not in the usual way in which we use the word?"

"But. I don't understand. She was kind to me, and you took her into your castle. Why, if she is an enemy?"

"I didn't say that Avalon was our enemy. These thing change and change about. You might better say the two sides are two factions, or two philosophies, or even two political parties. At times they work together, at times they work apart, and at times they are so opposed that death, murder and war break out between them. And then there are people who cross from one side to another, and there are people who never really declare themselves for one side or the other, and there are people who are caught between the two."

"So should I trust Marie-France?"

"Be very careful who you trust, Scott. Be careful of me, even be careful of your friend Gawain. Do not give your trust lightly. If someone earns your trust, then good. And you yourself should seek always to be trustworthy, so that you can earn the trust of others. But never trust someone because they seem to be on your side. There are games within games and wheels within wheels. Even in my little court here in Warwick there are people who are of Morgaine's party. I do not know who all of them are."

"Did you kill that man for being one of Morgaine's lot?"

"Piers Gaveston? Certainly not. That is purely today's politics. Edward the second is a bad king, and is ruining England. Gaveston was exiled by the barons because of the way he led Edward astray. But he returned to England believing the king would save him. He would have been better trusting the wind."

"Did he deserve to die?"

"Deserve? I've no idea, and it's none of my business. But the law said he had to die. We can let England sink again into lawlessness, as it did in Stephen's time, or we can uphold the law."

"Couldn't you have put him in prison, then?"

"We could, and the king would have let him out again as soon as he found out where he was."

"I'm not sure I see that," said Scott. "But there's a lot I still don't understand. What I want most explained is what skifting is, and how all these bits of history fit together."

"What has Gawain told you already?"

"He said he wasn't the one to explain it, but that time was like a roll of silk, and you could fall through the holes if it was torn, but you could only fall to exactly the same day of the year you had left, and you couldn't skift in your own lifetime."

"Well, I suppose it's a start. Nobody really understands skifting, which makes it hard to explain even what we do understand. But, as a mathematician, I suppose it's my job to try to make some sense of it. Forget the silk for a moment, and think of time like a chess board. The pieces can move from square to square, but they can only move onto whole squares. You can't have pieces between one square and another. But time isn't quite like a chessboard. Nobody really knows, but we think there are about ninety years of skift time. You and I, right now, are in about the fortieth year. You can't usually skift to earlier or later in those ninety years, so imagine that each square on the chess board is ninety years. I can go ninety, or I can go one hundred and eighty, or I can two hundred and seventy, and so on. But sometimes, just sometimes, it's possible to fall between the cracks, and that's when you really can meet yourself coming back."

"But doesn't it change the future, if you alter the past?"

"Most certainly it does. But the past is also the present. Think of it another way. Think of time as like the landscape of Britain. If you're on the beach, you can choose to make your sandcastle wherever you want—but the sea will come and knock it down in due time. If you want to build a proper house, then much more work is required, and you have to involve builders and architects, and surveyors, and, in your time, the local planning department. If you want to build a motorway, then thousands of people have to agree, and it will cost you hundreds of millions of pounds. But that in itself is a fairly small business compared to shifting the course of a river, or moving a mountain, or filling in an ocean. In time there are landmarks like rivers and hills which are almost impossible to change. Then there are things like towns and motorways, which you could change if only you were powerful enough. And then there are things which are quite trivial, such as what you have for breakfast. The little things don't add up to change the landmarks, any more than the sandcastles you make on the beach threaten to change the sea."

Scott thought he could see what Sir Guy meant. Any other time he would have wanted to ask more questions—he was one of those boys who like talking to grown-ups as long as they took him seriously, and liked working through a puzzle or a new idea. But, right now, he had something more pressing in his mind.

"Sir Guy, can you help me to rescue my mother?"

"Well, this is exactly what Gawain asked me to do. I can help you up to a point, which is to say, I can probably help you to find a place to travel back to Stephen and Matilda's time, which is where Gawain says you are going. Not skifting—the snow is gone, and skift doors will be hard to find, but by another means. But I cannot go with you—Piers

Gaveston's death could leave England in civil war unless it is carefully managed. I don't know if you know what civil war is like—"

"I've seen a little of it."

"Well, I'm afraid you are going to see more of it. Stephen and Matilda's time was the worst of all the civil wars that have tortured these islands."

"I don't understand. Were Stephen and Matilda married to each other? Did they quarrel?"

"I am not a historian, and cannot give you the rights and wrongs of it. But you need to know a little for your own safety when you are there. So here—with my own guesses—is what I know:

"It all began to go wrong when King Henry's son drowned in the wreck of the White Ship, leaving no male heir. Matilda was Henry's daughter, and he made the barons promise to make her queen after his death. But the barons didn't like the idea of a woman on the throne, and they particularly didn't like Matilda. So instead, they asked Henry's nephew, Stephen, to become king. It was a terrible mistake. Stephen was a weak, cruel, vain man. He could be charming enough, and he had a kind of recklessness that some mistake for courage, but he didn't have the qualities to be king."

"Couldn't somebody go back skifting and sort this out?" said Scott.

"Well, that's the funny thing. I think somebody tried to. Instead of helping, they made things a thousand times worse. There's all kinds of odd coincidences and backtracking that happens when you try to change history. You asked if Stephen and Matilda were married to each other. No they weren't, but Stephen was married to another woman called Matilda. And then there are stories floating around about what King Henry actually made the barons promise. Some said he forced them to promise that Matilda would be queen, and so the promise was invalid. Others said that he changed his mind on his deathbed. Then, in the year that King Henry died, Stephen seized the treasury with the support of his brother, who was also called Henry, but later on this Henry changed sides and supported Matilda. That's something else you see when skifters meddle—people changing sides again and again for no especially good reason. Then there was another Henry, who became Earl of Northumberland. The story ends when Matilda—not the one married to Stephen—had a son also called Henry, who eventually got the support of the Barons to become king after Stephen, and Stephen even adopted him as his son."

"That's very confusing. Did all that really happen?"

"It all really happened in the world we're in now, but I don't think it happened in the world we were in twenty years ago.

"But what I think originally happened—before someone started to interfere—was that Stephen married Matilda, daughter of Henry, and they had a son, also called Henry, who became King Henry the second when they died. But I think Stephen and Matilda's marriage was a disaster, perhaps because Matilda was Queen by birth, Stephen only King by marriage. Then some meddlesome skifter read in the chronicles that this marriage brought England to its knees. This skifter knew that Stephen would marry Matilda, but he persuaded him to marry Matilda of Boulogne, not Matilda of England."

"I suppose this skifter thought that if they didn't marry, there would never be any problem," said Scott.

"Exactly. But what this skifter didn't know was that Stephen was going to be king of England no matter who he married, and Matilda was going to be queen, and that Henry the second was going to be the son of Matilda and the legal son of Stephen. It took ten years before the skifter found out that he had made things worse not better. So then they tried to persuade Henry on his deathbed to change his mind and support Stephen, so that Matilda would never be queen at all. But this didn't work either. By this time the damage was done, but the skifter carried on meddling away, persuading the barons who crowned Stephen to change their minds and support Matilda."

"Do you know who this person was?"

"I don't. But I guess they are still there, vainly trying to repair the damage they caused. You may meet them, if you really are determined to go back to that time. Is that what you really want?"

"Yes," said Scott. "Yes it is. Do you know how I can get there."

"There is one way I know, if you are courageous."

"What is it?"

"Ten miles from here there is a deserted village. Or, rather, there is a village church which must once have had a village around it, but there are no houses and no sign of them. There is just one priest at the church, and he is so old that nobody can remember a time when he was not there. But they say that every Sunday, when the sun goes down, that church is full."

"Do people come from a distance, then?"

"The church is full with the spirits of the dead. They come shrieking out of the ground for miles around, and stream as one huge, grey crowd in through the doors and windows."

"It sounds horrid. How does it help me reach Stephen and Matilda's time?"

"A skift-door marks a very temporary opening. A haunting marks something more permanent, where catastrophe fractures time, and the spirits of the departed flit from one century to another. And you can follow them back, if you have courage.

"But won't I land in whatever trouble killed them?"

"The village was destroyed, but the church remained standing. It means that the church must have stayed safe. Perhaps the spirits go there because they remember it as a refuge, or perhaps they are angry with it for surviving when their lives and homes and families were lost. But if you stay inside the four walls of the church, I believe you will be safe."

"And how do you know it will take me to Stephen's time?"

"I have been looking at the records. There is a village in that place in the Doomsday Book. But by Henry the Second's time, all trace of it had vanished. The hauntings are week by week, which makes me think that the village was not destroyed in one go, but that people were murdered or tortured over many years. Between Doomsday and Henry the Second, there is only one time when such things were so common that they could have gone on unmentioned, unrecorded. That time is Stephen's time, where you must go."

"What will the ghosts do to me, if I wait there?"

"I never heard of a ghost harming anybody, except through fear. Are you afraid of ghosts?"

"I don't believe in ghosts—at least, I didn't until today. But, then, I never believed in skifting, and I suppose I didn't really believe in King Arthur and his knights. Now I don't know what I believe."

"That is perhaps a good place to start. There are many things in this wide world that you do not need to believe in until you meet them. The question is, are you willing to face ghosts to continue your quest?"

"Well, if it's the only way."

"Scott, I can't promise you that it is the only way. But it is the only way that I can promise you."

"Well, alright, I suppose. When should I go?"

"Tonight. Today is Sunday, if you had not forgotten. In a few minutes we must make ready to go to church, like all good Christian folk."

"And then?"

"We shall have luncheon, and some time for play. But the shadows draw in early these winter nights, and you will need to be on your way by mid-afternoon. And, Scott—you must slip away without being seen."

The castle did not have its own chapel. Sir Guy's library was in what had once been a chapel, but many years before it had been closed down by the bishop. Sir Guy did not know the reason. So, instead, the whole castle retinue assembled on Sundays and on holy days to process to the Collegiate Church in the town.

Scott had not done a great deal of processing in his life up to that point. It is not the sort of thing that you are called on to do in Stechford. In fact, aside from school occasions, he had seldom set foot inside a church. His mother always told callers who came to the door that they were 'religion: heathen'. After a while even the Jehovah's Witnesses had learned to avoid them.

If he had done much processing, he would have noticed that this was a rather unsolemn sort of procession. Everybody had put on bright clothes. The men at arms wore red tunics over their mail, emblazoned with Sir Guy's Bear and Ragged Staff. The younger ladies wore long, flowing dresses with numerous pleats. Sir Guy wore a dark cloak, but underneath Scott could see the rich embroidery of cloth-of-gold.

They set off at something between a march and an amble. It was a bright morning. Long winter shadows marked the cracks in the flag-stones. There was no trace of snow, but, for all that, there was a chill in the gusting wind. Scott drew his cloak around him.

Somewhere ahead, a bell began to toll, ring-ding, ring-ding, calling the faithful to worship.

Everybody laughed and talked as they went. Everybody except Scott. Partly it was that he did not know the languages they spoke. But mostly it was that he was beginning to think ahead to the night's ordeal.

So far in his strange journey through time, he had not once known what was going to happen next. It had unfolded for him as a series of marvels, guided here and there by Gawain, or by Sir Richard, or Sir Guy, or Marie or the roundhead soldiers, but always with no inkling of what was to come.

Now he had—if not a clear picture—a clear apprehension of what was coming. A deserted chapel at night. That was bad enough. He had once had to walk through a graveyard when it was quite dark. Every sound had set him flashing the torch here and there, his heart racing.

But ghosts! What would they be like? Would they seem like people? Or just lights and shadows? Would he see their faces—and would they be the faces of skeletons? Or, worse, would he see nothing, but feel them close by—an invisible hand brushing against his own, a whisper from nowhere, a pricking of the hairs on the back of his neck.

He shuddered.

"I missed you this morning, my friend," said a voice from behind him. It was Marie-France. She had come up through the procession. "I waited for you a long time at breakfast. Either you were very early or very late in rising."

When Scott did not answer, she went on: "I see you are caught up in your thoughts. Or are you preparing your soul for mass?"

"For mass?" said Scott.

"Ah, but of course, so much is still strange to you. We call the church service 'mass'. I think some still do in your time."

"I don't really go to church," said Scott.

"So modern. You will find this strange, then. Everything will be in Latin. As you will be in a stall with the nobles, you must respond as if you know what the priest is saying. You don't need to join in with the chants—only the clergy and the friars will do that."

They were now at the bottom of the hill on which the castle was built, and just beginning to climb up the cobbled street that led through the town.

"Ugh!" said Scott. As if they had crossed an invisible barrier, the stench of the town hit him again.

"It is a strong smell," said Marie-France. "I think we have just walked over a ditch they use as a sewer. At least you will not smell it in the church."

"Why is that?" said Scott.

"All you will smell is incense. They will swing it this way and that all the time we are there. The priests would tell you that it is for the glory of God, but really it is to keep out the smell of the town. It is also shows that the church is powerful and wealthy."

"How?" said Scott.

"The incense is brought by merchants from the Holy Land. It is very expensive, but the church here in Warwick owns almost as much land as Sir Guy does, and they get a tenth of everything he has as well.

"But see, we are now at the gate. Look how fine this building is."

It was a very fine building—delicately carved in many places with the figures of saints, and of angels, and of devils. Scott had been surprised at how haphazard Sir Guy's castle had seemed, but there was nothing haphazard about this building. Every line was perfect, every stone set true, and the saints were painted and gilded with their proper colours. It glistened like a great jewel in the low sunlight, and cast its shadow far across the town.

"Is this an old building?" asked Scott.

"Older even than me," said Marie-France. "They were building this while I was not yet born, before Steven's time."

"In Steven's time?" said Scott. His heart had suddenly caught in his mouth. "The one who fought with Matilda and married someone else called Matilda?"

"I did not know you knew our history so well," she replied. "Has this been a subject of special study for you?"

"It's just something we did in school," said Scott.

"Your school must be a good one. You are quite right. They were dark times, or I should say that they are dark times, since when I am not here and there they are my own times. And such things are hard to amend. But hush, for we must enter in silence."

Scott saw that the horses were already being led away.

Sir Guy knocked ceremoniously on the great wooden doors at the West end of the church. After a minute, they were drawn open by hands unseen. The bell, which had rung all the way from the castle, stopped tolling. Everybody became quiet.

There was a sound of singing from inside the church. Sweet singing, somewhere between chant and melody, accompanied by flutes and recorders. Something else was sweet—the rich, deep, almost sickly smell of incense. Light streamed through great windows on the south. And now they did become a procession—solemnly forming into two lines and making their way in slow steps to wooden stalls in the middle of the church. There they halted in front of a wooden screen, intricately carved with flowers and bears and the figures of bishops and saints. Through the carving Scott could see the high altar at the east end, where priests and monks moved back and forth.

Everybody kneeled, and Scott did the same.

It was not like any church service that Scott had been to. He had not been to very many, and only with the school, but he was used enough to hymn books and service sheets, standing when you had to stand and sitting when you had to sit.

This church had no hymn books, nor were there any boards with numbers on to tell you which hymns to sing. He wondered if printing had yet been invented, and decided that it probably had not been.

Everything was in Latin, and it was a Latin more intoned than spoken. In fact, there seemed to be little attempt to speak to the congregation at all. Through the wooden screen, priests continued to move back and forth, but it seemed to have little to do with the castle folk. Occasionally a bell would ring—not the great bell of the church, but a hand-bell, quite close.

Scott's mind began to wander. His eyes followed the curves of the carving on the screen ahead, while the half-sung Latin seeped sideways into his brain. The church was unheated, but he was dressed for outdoors, and between that and the thick, heavy scent of incense, he found it hard to stay wide awake.

At least, he was sure that he was not wide awake. The carvings in the screen had begun to move. First it was a surreptitious slide, which stopped as soon as he looked properly. But then the figures began to shift more confidently. Two of the carved saints turned their heads and began to talk to each other. Scott could not quite hear what they were saying—it was too soft under the Latin chanting—but he noticed their eyes glanced across to him every so often, so he guessed they were talking about him. A carved dragon which ran right the way round the screen was slithering into a position where it could get the drop on a disproportionately large rabbit. In the centre a man dressed only in a skin was juggling fruit while a woman with long hair clapped her hands in delight. Peering from the branches of a huge tree above, a snake kept time with the swishing of its tail.

Scott returned to the castle in something of a daze, once the service was finished. He had no real memory of leaving the church, or of the walk back. His companions at the high table were busy talking to each other, so he ate his luncheon in silence—a thick broth with some rather gritty bread to mop it up, and cold pheasant to follow.

Afterwards, Sir Guy called him into the courtyard for a fencing lesson. The practice swords were heavier than he was used to, shorter and less elegant, and there were no masks to protect the eyes. But Sir Guy was a good teacher. He had the trick—which all great teachers do—of noticing his student's mood and lifting him out of it. Within minutes he had Scott stepping up and down the courtyard, lunging, parrying, making hits to the side, to the chest, to the knees.

"Don't forget the knees, Scott. They are frowned upon in some circles, but if you are fighting a giant, the knees may be all you can reach."

"Are there really giants?" said Scott, breathing hard as he whipped Sir Guy's blade away from his chest in a last-moment parry and lashed out with the riposte.

"Bound to be," said Sir Guy, nudging Scott's blade away with rather greater ease. "I've heard stories that say I fought one myself. Now, as I move the blade, attack me in the openings."

"And did you?" said Scott, lunging in and out as Sir Guy opened up various lines to tempt him into.

"Never argue with the stories," said Sir Guy, half turning to give Scott an opening at the back. "Even if you don't remember it happening, it might still happen to you, and you'll look pretty silly if it then turns out to be true. Now, lunge to shoulder, circular parry and lunge to chest."

Scott had more difficulty with this move, and Sir Guy had to slow down the actions until he could do it. Finally, he added the balestra, which Scott had practised with Professor Sutton.

"Not that the stories aren't always—shall we say, 'improved' by the unscrupulous storytellers," Sir Guy added, as they took a moment's rest. "We had a lot of trouble with one of them—Thomas Mal Oreille, we called him, which is French for 'evil ears'. He took it as a compliment, and made it his family name."

"Was he a skifter, then?" said Scott.

"Of a sort," said Sir Guy. "He spent a week at Arthur's court, or so they say, and five years skifting here and there to avoid prison. They got him in the end, though, and that's where he wrote his book. Now, let's get back to that balestra—just the thing for fighting a giant."

By the time they had finished, a small crowd had gathered, and Scott was delighted that they clapped and cheered when he and Sir Guy made their final salute. He looked to see if Marie-France was watching, but could not see her.

"They don't see much fencing in these times," said Sir Guy. "Fighting, yes, but that's as often as not a big bloke walloping a smaller bloke with a very heavy, very blunt sword or axe. It's not pretty, but it wins battles."

"Will I fight in any battles on my way to save my mother?" said Scott.

"Do everything you can to avoid them," replied Sir Guy. "We talk about chivalry and honour and all those things, but when it comes to battle, it's about getting more of your men to attack less of them, or ambushing the enemy, or attacking when he is asleep or at a disadvantage. Men die in every battle: if you want to save your mother, stay out of the fighting."

"Then why are you and everyone else teaching me to fence?" said Scott.

"Sometimes you must fight. Skifting takes you to trouble, as you know. But other things than men find their way through the holes that skifting leaves."

"Monsters?"

"Dark things, strange things, things of legend, and things which are named in no story I have ever heard."

"And how do you fight them?"

"Ah, this brings us back to why you must practice your fencing. They are killed by a sharp blade, a bold hand, a pure spirit and a courageous heart. A pure knight, without fear, can kill a dragon with a single thrust of his blade. But any taint to that purity—be it fear, or dishonour, or worse—robs the steel of its potency."

"Can you shoot them?"

"No, you cannot. Neither arrow, nor javelin, nor bullet from a gun will do anything against them. It is you yourself that strike, and the weapon must be held in your own hand as you do it."

As they finished, a footman came to prepare Scott for his journey, taking him first to a wardrobe for thick clothes and sturdy boots, and then to a treasury, where an aged bursar wrote out a receipt in beautiful, elegant handwriting with a goose-feather pen, and gave to him a small bag that that was heavy for its size, filled with yellow coins, and finally to a stable, where a horse was ready saddled for him.

8 VILLAGE OF THE DEAD

It was late evening. Leafless trees reached into inky twilight. A harsh frost crept across the flinted road. Rooks shattered the evening calm, cawing and racketing in high branches.

Scott looked over his shoulder at his companion, charged with showing him the way. He was a young squire, talkative enough as they set off, though it was hard to pick up what he was saying among the strange words and stranger sounds. His name was Michael de Crowleigh, and Scott guessed that he must be eighteen. He had the manner of a school prefect, confident, showing off his knowledge and his skill—or, at least, that was how he was as they left Warwick. But now he lagged behind, cloak wrapped tightly about this chest, leaning hard over the horse's saddle as if he were riding into a high wind. But there was no wind, only the deepening, freezing dusk.

Scott understood. It was his adventure, not Michael's. He had chosen this path, and he would get the glory from it. Michael would ride back alone, reaching Warwick late into the night, contending with all the perils of the way, to receive muted thanks and no praise.

So Scott rode on, and Michael followed.

Presently they came to a fork in the road. To the right, the road entered thick forest, to the left, it picked its way through marshland. An evening mist was rising, its tendrils fingering their way across their path. Among the marsh-reeds, soft flashes of will-o-wisp.

Scott reined his horse in—despite the gloom of the journey and the grim destination, he was excited. He delighted in his new skill of riding, and his left hand kept straying to the sword by his side. Steel, a pure spirit, and a heart that knew no fear, and what might he not accomplish? But for now there was the question of the way. So he waited until Squire Michael caught up with him.

Michael was not long in coming.

"An mile, yon—" he said, throwing his arm out, uncertain that Scott would understand him. "Sinistra… gauche." Scott followed his arm along the leftwards path. His eyes now accustomed to the darkness, he made out the top of a church tower, silhouetted against the final gleam of the western horizon.

"I can find my own way from here," said Scott. "Je trouve mon chemin," he ventured, trying to make his accent sound like Marie-France. "Cognito viam," he guessed. Michael looked blank and shook his head.

So Scott took his hand and shook it—he was sure that this wasn't something that they did in these times, but he hoped Michael would understand.

"Goodbye, Michael," he said, and gestured back along the road towards Warwick.

Michael smiled. "God go with thee, Perceval," he said. Then, slowly wheeling his horse, perhaps fearful that he had misunderstood, he turned and set off back along the road. Scott felt that he was wanting to gallop off, but instead he rode with great dignity, until he reached a wooded copse, where, half twisting in the saddle, he waved. Scott waved in return, and Michael was gone.

Scott was alone. Biting his lip, reminding himself to show no fear, he spurred the horse along the leftward path, towards the dark church tower, over the marshes.

He, too, would have liked to have galloped, but the road was in no condition for it. A raised causeway in some disrepair, it was broad enough in the main, but here and there the sides had crumbled or been reclaimed by sucking, gurgling currents, leaving a narrow section with water on either side. Once Scott was forced to dismount and lead the horse by the bridle. He wondered if the horse could have jumped it, but, although he was now good at staying in the saddle, and could canter or gallop a little, he had yet to try any jumping. Night on a causeway across strange marshes was probably not the best place to start.

There were all kinds of noises in the marsh. Frogs croaking, crickets chirping, from time to time a splash, as though a fish had jumped. He could not see far to the left or to the right. The growing mist obscured everything that the starlight might have revealed, and now the last trace of light at the horizon was almost gone. He pressed on, eyes straining through the darkness, ears straining through the noises.

And then three things happened that set his pulse racing and his heart pounding and a cold sweat pouring down his back.

First, a light in the distance. Scott had once read that the human eye could see a candle flame at night a mile away. This light flickered like candle flame. He peered, and squinted, and tried to make out what it was. Not a flame, but a patch of light—light behind a window, or perhaps through an open door.

Second, while he considered the meaning of the light, he heard a new sound behind. A terrible sound. A great, ululating howl, splitting the night. He gripped the horse's reins. The howl was answered by a hissing all across the marsh. Scott could not imagine what the howl could it. It was surely deeper and more powerful than any wolf's.

And finally, but really almost no time after the first, a great bell began to toll ahead of him. And this was the worst, because Scott knew in his bones that the church bell was being rung to summon the worshippers. But what worshippers would come on such a night to such a church? Only the ghosts he had come to find.

He spurred the horse on—not a gallop, nor even a canter, but something between a determined walk and a trot. And he made sure that he looked neither to the left nor to the right.

The bell continued to toll, filling the night with its sound. But underneath it, all around him, Scott heard the hissing. It was almost a human sound, at times no more than a rush of steam, but sometimes finding its way to the brink of words.

Now the light was four patches of brightness: three windows, and a door, standing ajar, and letting out a long splinter of yellow-orange.

As he reached it he dismounted. The door ahead of him swung open. In it, framed in the warm glow of many candles, was a man in a monk's robe, hood thrown back, bearded, both grave and smiling.

"Welcome, my son," said the man. "Enter into this house of God."

Scott looked around for somewhere to tether his horse, but the man inclined his head and said:

"Do not worry about your animal. My acolyte will tend to him."

From somewhere—or perhaps nowhere—a slighter figure, also robed, the hood drawn across his face, came to take the horse's head.

Scott hesitated.

"Come my son, enter."

"How is it that you speak my language?" stuttered Scott. "And how do you know that that is what I speak?"

The man inclined his head again.

"That you may learn if you enter. Or, if you wish, you may remain outside. But I do not think that many would choose to remain outside on such a night as this."

Scott clenched his fist inside his glove, but he stepped forward, through the great door.

It swung shut behind him, as if propelled by unseen hands.

The church was tiny—scarcely bigger than a house, and it was filled with candles. Candles in candlesticks, candles hanging from the vaulted roof, candles placed on every pew, on the lecterns, on the window sills, in the aisles, and on the spiral staircase that led into the tower.

From somewhere, voices were chanting in Latin, but Scott could not see from where.

"Please sir," said Scott. "What is this place? Why is it full of candles?"

"The candles are for those who died."

"Do you mean the ghosts, sir?"

"They will not harm you, as long as you remain in these walls. They come here night by night to call before the throne of God for justice."

"Will they come inside?"

"They are already here. Can you not see them?"

Scott peered. It was hard to make things out among the flickering flames, but he thought he saw shadowy figures, or just the outlines of shadowy figures, filling the pews, and the choir stalls, and sitting in the windows, and standing in the aisles and on the staircase.

"You see well," said the man. "Everywhere there is a candle, for many died in these walls."

"What did they die of?"

"Of murder," said the man. "Some by the hands of Stephen's men. And some by the hands of Mathilda's. And some by the hands of men who served neither Mathilda nor Stephen, but only themselves."

"Are you a ghost, sir?"

"I? Do I seem a ghost to you? I am a poor hermit, living out my years tending to this place and contemplating the mysteries."

"And how do you speak my language?"

"Wisdom and insight into many things is given to those who meditate. Yours will be a long vigil tonight, as befits a knight on the brink of a great adventure."

"But I'm not a knight. I'm just a schoolboy," said Scott.

The man looked at him. It was the look you might call a 'hard' look, but there was nothing hard about the gentle face.

"Knighthood is not found in years, nor is it bestowed at the whim of kings. You came here, this night of all nights, of your own accord?"

Scott nodded.

"Then, Sir Knight, it is for you to maintain the vigil, unless others come to take this quest from you."

"What do I have to do, then, for the vigil?"

"Kneel at the altar, lay out your soul before God, confess your sins, for He is merciful."

At any other time Scott would have said that he did not believe in God, but it did not seem a particularly appropriate thing to say at that moment.

The hermit led him to a small chapel. It was strange that a church so tiny should have other chapels. This was little more than an alcove. A shield hung above the altar, and it was painted with a red cross on a white background.

Scott wondered how he was supposed to lay out his soul. All the sins he could think of at that moment to confess seemed rather trivial and insignificant. Was he supposed to pour out a catalogue of dog baiting, a collection of small lies told to teachers, a fight he had had with the boy who sat next to him in chemistry, and some sharp trading he had done over comic books? Chemistry and comic books seemed a very, very long way away from kneeling at an altar in a haunted church seven hundred years in the past.

The chanting grew louder, and he smelled the heady smell of incense.

He thought he might try his hand at confession. He had sat through some services at school, as well as the thrice weekly assembly, which as often as not finished with the singing of one of about five hymns from a small green hymn book, and the repeating of the Lord's prayer. He started on the Lord's prayer, which he did remember, and repeated several times the bit about trespassers. Trespassing was apparently a catch-all word for all kinds of sins, so it seemed a fair place to start.

Unfortunately, this took really no more than a minute. He wondered if repeating the prayer might be the thing to do, but then he hit upon the idea of going through the five favourite hymns, as much as he could remember. There was a rather odd one about fighting giants which had apparently come from a story, and another one about a fortress. Truth to tell he had not really been very taken with either of them, but both seemed strangely apt for the situation he was now in. As he was a little shaky on the words, and as the night ahead of him was set to be a long one, he decided to make do by manufacturing extra verses that might be appropriate as he went along.

So he launched first into "He who would valiant be..." which was the one that went on to talk about giants, hobgoblins and other heinous creatures. It was a good one for making up words to, because no matter how far you got from the tune, you could always finish each verse with a rallying 'to be a pilgrim!' Scott's version was really not very close to the original at all, but he had something of his mother's gift with words, and so he loped along something like this:

He who would valiant be

To rescue his mother ('to rescue' had to be sung rather quickly to get the words in)

Let him ride bravely (he lengthened 'bravely' so that it rhymed with 'dairy-lea')

Through all kinds of weather

He'll ride through ice and snow

Not knowing where he should go

In every kind of woe

To be a pilgrim!

Not particularly good, perhaps, but quite something for a beginner making up words on the spur of the moment in a church full of ghosts.

It was probably the longest version of the famous old hymn ever sung. Scott made it through at least a hundred and fifteen verses, which, if he had written them down, would have set out a fair account of all his doings since the snow began to fall in Birmingham and he met Gavin Knight on a train. Some of the later verses—once he had got into the swing of things—were not bad as poetry. He left 'to be a pilgrim' behind fairly early on, and sang instead 'a man of valour', as it seemed to fit his situation a little better.

One verse he was quite proud of (though he tried not to be, since he had heard somewhere that pride was a sin), went like this:

He shall skift to Stephen's time
To win his treasure
Hearing haunted church-bells chime
Will be his pleasure
He'll wield the sword of might
Though he is not yet a knight
He'll win in every fight
A man of valour!

Eventually he reached what seemed to be a natural place to stop, so he sang the first verse again, and drew out the final line as a kind of coda.

He had had his eyes tightly closed through all of this—partly because it seemed the sort of thing that you ought to do when vigilling in a church, and partly because it helped him to forget the hundreds of candles, each one the sitting place for a ghost.

When he opened his eyes, it was quite dark. The chanting of voices had ceased, and the candles were gone. There was a faint sheen of cold light around him, enough to still make out the little altar and the shield that hung above it. He might have got up to have a look around, but he heard the voice of the hermit quite close behind him.

"Keep to your vigil, if you would achieve this adventure."

There was a cold draft at his back, as though someone had left the door open, so he drew his cloak tight around him. Far away he could hear the moaning of awful voices on the wind.

He screwed his eyes tight again, and tried another hymn. This time he though he might try the one about a mighty fortress. He felt a little guilty about the previous hymn, as he somehow felt that hymns ought to be about God (not that Scott especially believed in God) and the Man of Valour hymn had really been all about himself. So he set off into the first verse, which, by the time he had reached the end of it, went something like this:

A mighty fortress is our God
A bulwark never failing
He'll help us overcome our foes,
Those wolves and witches wailing
Although it is midnight (this line didn't quite fit)
And we are weak with fright
Our arms he will strengthen (he put the emphasis on 'then')
To fight a thousand men,
He'll see that we don't weaken.

This seemed to be an altogether more satisfactory sort of hymn. Scott had a go at a good few more verses, though he did not equal the hundred-and-fifteen of Man of Valour.

By the time he had run out of words for this one, another hymn had popped into his mind. He had probably only sung it once in his life, but its strong tune and military theme brought it back to him as if had the book in front of him.

Stand up, stand up for Jesus
Ye soldiers of the cross
Lift high his royal banners
It must not suffer loss
From victory unto victory
His army shall he lead
Till every foe is vanquished
And Christ is Lord indeed.

This seemed too good to tamper with, but it was the only verse he could remember. Rather than abandon this promising vein, he sang it as a chorus between each of his own verses.

'Stand up with sword and armour' began his first additional verse –
'With weapons hard and strong
Stand up and face your future
And fight to right the wrong
To overcome the evil
That finds its way to Earth
To stand against the nightmare
And show them what you're worth!'

The rollicking tune was good for at least fifty verses, and he finished up singing the chorus five or six times, the last time very slowly and grandly.

His voice faded away.

Now that he was no longer singing, he noticed a couple of things. First, there was a difference in the quality of the air. The stone walls of the church had given an encouraging, resonant echo to his voice, but now it seemed to empty out into the wind. Also, it was getting lighter again, but not with the strangely eerie-cheery glow of ghostly candles, but with something much further away, and much more outdoors.

He decided to finish up with another Lord's Prayer, which he extended with a few extra lines about some things that had come to mind that he thought might well qualify as sins, and one final verse of 'Man of Valour'. When he had done this, he got up off his knees, and looked around.

The church was gone.

Or rather, most of the church was gone. Here and there were blackened ruins—a twisted pillar, an arch standing alone ready to topple in on itself, the remains of a spiral staircase. Only one part seemed to be intact—the tiny altar, surrounded by enough stones to make a kind of man-made grotto or cave, and the shield hanging above it. But even the altar and the stone-work around were blackened with soot, as if they had been covered with thick smoke. The shield, alone among all the wreckage, was clean, new, as if it had just been painted.

Over the altar, the sun was rising.

Scott heard a whinny and a neigh, and saw his horse grazing, tethered to an old stone, a few yards away.

He was glad to see the horse. There was some food in the saddle bags, which was enough to make a nourishing breakfast with something left for lunch. He gave the horse a rub down, which sent the warmth running back into his fingers. There was no sign of the hermit, nor of the candles, nor of anything much except blackened stone. There were ashes on the ground, which would have been enough to tell Scott—if he had known—that the fire which burned the stones was days or weeks gone, not months or years. He poked around for a few minutes, long enough to find the thick timbers of the great door, which the fire had charred but not burnt through, and long enough to find something else:

Two blackened skulls, smashed one above the eye, the other at the ear. The fire had picked them clean, but Scott could not help feeling that these were not old skulls, such as you might see in a museum. For one moment he saw vividly the kindly hermit and his young acolyte. Were these they? Had he then moved forward in time, to some terrible disaster after Sir Guy's day? Or was the church itself, with candles and all, no more than an illusion, an apparition, a haunting on a massive scale?

He shivered. He would have given a lot at that moment to know for certain. In a peculiar sense—which may not make sense to anyone who has not spent the night in a haunted church—it was more uncanny if the church itself were a ghost than if it had been a real building which just happened to contain ghosts.

But he would have given more to know when he now was.

There was really only one way to find out. So, mounting his horse, he rode once right around the church, and set off back the way he had come.

But before he did this, he took down the shield from above the altar, and fitted it over his shoulder. It fit well and snugly, as if it had been made for him.

Perhaps it was.

9 WHEN CRIST SLEPT, AND HIS ANGELS

Scott set off down the little knoll on which the church had once stood, looking for the causeway back over the marshes. But the marshes were gone. Instead, there were the scattered remains of huts, burned or smashed, with thatched roofs either gone or so caved in that they could keep out no water. There were ditches alongside some of the houses, perhaps irrigating crops or draining the land. But these too were in disrepair. The skeleton of some animal—bull, or cow, or horse—lay in one, picked clean by birds and insects. In another a cart had been overturned, while a third had turned into a stagnant, green pool, evil smelling.

Scott rode on. It was not a pleasant place to linger. He wondered what he would find if he went searching through the ruins. Best not to think about it.

The sun was rising in a clear sky, playing some warmth across his back, since he was heading for a while westwards, away from the dawn. There were thick woods ahead of him, where the night before it had been clear land. At the edge of the trees, there was something—or somethings—swinging in the wind. At first it was too far in the bad light to see what they were, but as Scott approached it became all too clear.

There was a gallows, roughly built onto one of the outlying trees. From it hung three cages, the size and shape of a man. A raven sat on one of them, idly pecking at something it had found.

Scott winced. It was the remains of three men, hanged and left to rot in the open, a terrible sign and portent for all who dared to disobey—but disobey whom?

He rode slowly past. The forest closed over him. The light under the trees was dim and green. Although most were shorn of leaves, the twining ivy was enough to block much of the early light. The trunks were close about the road, and after a few turns he lost all sight of the sun.

The memory of the village, and the gallows, coming after the ruins of the church, had settled on him like a thick cloud.

Since entering the past, he had seen two men shot, and one man executed—one in war, one in self-defence, and one through the action of law. These had shocked him, but for each there was a reason, a purpose, a form of justice or cause. But what crime could a whole village have committed?

In some ways he felt he ought to be glad, because this seemed to be Stephen and Mathilda's time, as Sir Guy had described it. It meant he was reaching his goal. But he had not reckoned with the brutality, the casual slaughter, the mindless, thoughtless evil which infected it. In his mind's eye he felt he saw a mist, like the mist that had flowed out of the marshes the night before, flowing up out of some dark subterranean water, poisoning all England. He wondered now if his mother were alive at all, and if alive, in what condition.

He was so wrapped up in his thoughts that he almost rode straight into a man gathering wood along the road side.

Scott reined the horse up sharply, and looked at him. He was small, dark haired, in a green tunic with a cloth hat that folded over. The man was as startled as he was. He dropped his wood, and stood stock still, glancing this way and that, not daring to move.

"Good morning," said Scott, too surprised to remember that the man would not understand him.

At least, "Good morning," is what he thought he said, and what he intended to say, and, part of him heard "Good morning". But another part of him distinctly heard himself say:

"West u hal."

And another part of him knew exactly what he meant by that, which was to say 'Good morning' and to put the man at his ease, and to bid him health.

"West u hal, thegn," said the man. And Scott knew exactly what he meant by it, which was 'good health, lord'.

"Hwilc is thissum gaer?" said Scott, by which he meant to ask what year it was. And a part of him knew exactly what the words meant, and how they should be said.

"Kenst thu nat, hlaford?" said the man, which Scott understood meant that he was surprised that Scott did not know what year it was, and that he thought Scott was an important person.

The rest of the conversation continued in much the same way, but I will set it out in the English that part of Scott thought he was hearing and speaking.

So the wood-man had just said:

"Know you not, lord?"

"I am a little lost, and out of my way," said Scott.

"The year is Anno eleven-hundred-and-thirty-seven."

"And who is King in England?" said Scott.

The woodman's face fell.

"Seek you to trap me, lord? I took you for one of our English thanes."

"I am a little out of my reckoning. I have come on a journey."

"The Crusade, my lord? And you are but lately come back. But you are so young, my lord. Know then that England has not king nor queen neither, but betimes one and betimes the other. First the usurper's son Henry fought with the church and levied cruel taxes upon the common folk, although he swore freedom for all when he looked for support against his brother Robert. Thus were many of our English thanes beguiled. But Henry's son drowned in the ice-cold waters of the North Sea, and he handed the kingdom over to civil war, giving it at the same time to Maud the Empress and Stephen of Blois to lay waste between them. And so it is that every kind of evil is now visited upon our land. All this was as the holy Wulfstan said would be.

"But if a Saxon lord were to rise in war, he could take England once more from the cruel Normans. Or if not a Saxon, some speak still of Arthur's return—"

"Arthur?" said Scott, interrupting what might otherwise have been a long speech. "What know you of Arthur?"

"I meant no harm, lord. I know only what every man knows, that Arthur sleeps and his knights, somewhere hidden, under a hill, awaiting the day of England's need. But no man knows the place, else had we waked him long ago."

Scott thought about this for a moment.

"Who rules these lands where we now stand?" he said.

"This we know not well, lord. Since Henry's death one comes and then another. We pay taxes to Maud, and taxes to Stephen, and taxes to any man who rides through the forest with four men at arms and calls himself our liege."

"Who was it who laid waste the village beyond the forest?"

"Thieves and murderers leave no names, lord. We live deep in the forest, as did our forefathers. When soldiers come, we keep far from the road. There was a terrible burning some months back, and again later. Some took refuge in the forest, and of them there is no trace. Some stayed to defend their homes. There are none there now."

Scott looked at the man, his pile of sticks scattered on the forest floor. He noticed that even as he spoke, his eyes were flickering backwards and forwards, darting this way and that, like a frightened animal.

"I thank you for your help," he said. "God go with you. This is for happier times." And—not knowing quite why he was doing it, except that it seemed to go with the words he had found himself saying, he pulled out the bag of coins and handed the man a single gold piece.

The man stared at it, and then doffed his cap. He called down many blessings on Scott's head while he carefully gathered up his sticks, still clutching the coin, and made his way backwards into the forest shadows.

Scott spurred his horse on.

In all of his strange and remarkable adventures, this was definitely the strangest and most remarkable thing. He had managed fairly easily to get his mind around skifting. He wasn't necessarily sure he understood how time was like a roll of silk, or like a chess-board, but the idea of finding a doorway and going through it and arriving not some-where else but some-when did not really bother him too much. He had not much liked the idea of ghosts, or of other things slipping into our world from other places. But it was not such a strange idea.

But this was very strange. Other words were going through his head than the ones he spoke. Stranger yet, as the conversation had gone on, he had found the part of him that was saying the strange words begin to take charge, and continue the conversation of its own accord, with the English speaking part of him listening in like an interested by-stander. But, at the same time, he did not in the least feel that someone else was talking through his mouth.

The sun reached its highest point in the winter sky, sending dappled light through bare twigs. Scott would have stopped to eat lunch, but something impelled him on. For the first time he felt that what happened next really was up to him. Until now he had been ward and pupil to anyone and everyone he met. First Gawain, and then Sir Richard, then Marie-France, Sir Guy, even Squire Michael, and finally the hermit. Each had explained the journey and pointed the way.

Now they were gone. He was alone in Stephen's time with little chance of meeting anyone able and willing to help. But neither was he quite the same person he had been the day before. The strange thing about language aside—and he was aching for another chance to try it out—he had done something brave all by himself, not because he had to, but because he intended to.

He rode on, eating from his saddlebag as he went.

Eventually he came to a fork in the road. Someone had planted an oak tree there, perhaps fifty years before. There was no signpost of any kind telling him which way he should go.

"I wish this tree could talk," he said out loud, half hoping that this would in fact be the case. The tree, however, remained stubbornly silent.

He set about considering the points of the compass. He had ridden north, and then east, and then finally towards the west, as the road snaked across the marshes, on his way to the haunted chapel. He assumed that he had taken the same road back, but he was now no longer sure. Certainly Warwick must be to the south, but Gawain had said that Kenilworth was where his mother was kept. He tried to think of his earlier journey. Had he gone south from Kenilworth to Warwick? He thought he had. But was he now between the two, or to the north of both?

By the time he had worked this out he was no longer sure of it, so he got off his horse and allowed it to graze for a while. Taking a stick he started to work out the points of the compass in a patch of dirt. Warwick to the south, Kenilworth to the north or to the south, the unnamed church and burnt village to the north-west.

Which meant that he should take the left hand road, because it was going south and a little east. Unless, of course, he was nowhere near

Warwick and Kenilworth, and the left hand road would take him past Kenilworth without ever seeing it. In which case it would be safer to continue on until Warwick, and then double back almost due north. But this did not satisfy him either. To begin with, he was not sure that there even was a Warwick in this time. And then there was the question—was the left fork a south-east fork and the right fork a due-south fork, or was the left fork the due-south and the right fork a south-west road which would take him away from Warwick, Kenilworth, and any other places he might once (in the future) have known.

He was still scratching in the ground when a figure came into view from the right-hand road. It was a monk, dressed in a white habit—or as white as the dust of the road had allowed it to stay.

"Benedicite," said the monk.

"Benedicite, frater," replied Scott. "Oro beneficium. Ignoro viam ad Kenilward et Warwici…" And then he stopped, because he realised he was speaking Latin.

"My son," said the monk, also in Latin: "Warwick is a simple matter, since I have this very morning come from there myself. But of Kenilworth I have no knowledge, not having heard such a name in this or any part of the world. Unless you should mean the new castle, which has risen up in just one year, and holds this little land in its own grip, while the king and the empress are busy about their own affairs."

The monk had a sing-song quality to his voice, as though he were as much used to chanting as to speaking. But he stumbled over his words in the final sentence, as if he had just said rather more than he had intended to, and wanted to draw it back.

"Forgive a humble brother of Bernard's order the impertinence, but are you of the faction that is at the new castle?"

Scott shook his head.

"Tell me about this new castle, brother monk," he said, hearing again what he meant to say echoing around Latin words. Scott had once watched a film on the ferry back from France, where his mother had taken him on holiday. The film had been made in English, and then loosely dubbed into French, and then subtitles had been added in English. This was something like the same kind of experience.

"It is truly a magnificent castle. Of finely carved stone the like of which is seen in Rome but rarely in England. It stretches in every direction as far as the eye can see, and is surrounded by a lake of great magnitude. I am but a humble brother of my lord of Clairvaux, and am unused to such works of man. But if I were knowledgeable about such things, I would dare to say that no fortress of such magnificence exists in England in our time."

"In our time?" said Scott, sharply. "What do you mean by that?"

"But my lord is surely not unlearned, since he knows the Latin tongue. This island was once wholly in the domain temporal of Rome, just as she remains to this day in her domain spiritual. And at such times the fortresses and cities at Viroconium, at Deva, at Verulamium, and indeed at Londinium were surely of great size.

"As one of the English poets has written, unlearned as he was in the histories, that their walls were carved by giants' hands, so great did they seem to the Saxons who came to these shores after, all as the noble Bede has written. The castles and strong places of our own day are but toys compared with those, excepting the White Tower of London. But this new fortress of which we speak is greater still than London's. Less high, perhaps, but with thick curtain walls surrounding baileys, around a strong keep. And all in red stone, so that it shines like blood in the evening light."

"And how did such a great fortress come to be raised in so short a time, brother?"

"My lord should know better than I, for surely my lord is a soldier of martial stock. But it is a mystery to myself, since no great army of workmen has been encamped in these parts, and even if it were, a castle is a thing of many years labour. There are some, my lord—" and he took a step closer to Scott, as if he was afraid of being overhead, "—there are some who speak of magic, witchcraft, and the foul dealings of sorcery."

"And what is your opinion, brother monk?"

"These are dark times, my lord knight. Every kind of pestilence walks this land. Neither the king nor the empress finds power of arms sufficient to impose their will on the other. How then can a fortress of great splendour be raised, except by the operation of the powers of darkness."

"And have you seen this fortress with your own eyes, brother monk?" Scott would not normally have been this direct—or this rude even to one of his school mates, let alone to a grown-up. But the Latin words seemed to be getting the better of him, pushing him on to say things that he might at other times only have thought.

"My lord, sir knight, I have seen it at a distance. But members of my order are not welcomed there, nor any order, nor priests, abbots, bishops nor any of the church. And this leads me most of all to suspect it of being a work of darkness."

Scott chewed his tongue, considering.

"My thanks to you, brother. Here is for your trouble." And he fetched out a gold piece from his money bag.

A look of bewilderment, and then something like cunning, and finally satisfaction passed across the monk's face.

"Brothers of my order may not accumulate wealth, my lord. We are sworn to a life of poverty. But if I may take this as a gift for the poor, I will see to it that the first penniless individual that I find has the benefit of it."

He bowed low, and Scott bowed too. It was a good five minutes before he worked out what the monk had actually promised to do with the coin.

Scott stood at the fork a while longer, wondering. He could set off towards Kenilworth, and ride straight into whatever trap or adventure was waiting for him there, or he could ride to Warwick. But there was nothing particularly in Warwick that would help him.

He felt he ought to at least try to have some plan. People in books always had a plan. But no plan seemed to spring to mind. It was at that point that Scott realised that, all along, he had had no clear picture at all about what he would do if he ever found his mother. Once he had lost Gawain, all that he had thought about was getting to the right time and the right place. But what then? What then?

There is only a certain length of time that you can debate something with yourself. Eventually you run out of arguments, for and against, and are left with the decision you first started with. What had Sir Guy said? Skill with a sword, a pure spirit, a courageous heart. This was not a question of skill, or of purity, but—and Scott could see this now—one of simple courage. The Warwick road would do no more than keep him from danger a little longer. So he should take the Kenilworth road, and face whatever he had to face.

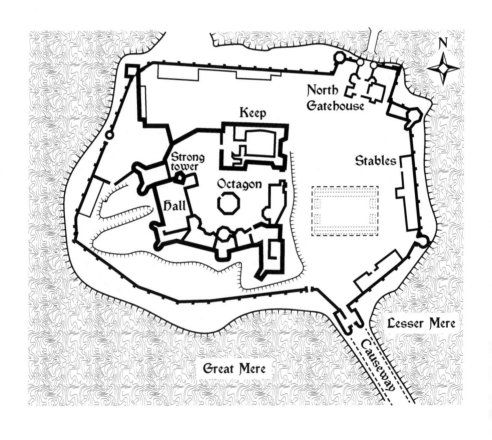

Fitt 2

The Red Castle

10 THE VISITOR

cott set off along the left-hand, eastern path. It was not in any sense a road, only a well-trodden way through the forest. It must have been used a great deal at one time, because it was broad enough—he guessed—for four horsemen. But it was now thoroughly covered in grass, making a green-way among the trees.

His horse made hardly any sound, and there was a delicious smell of winter forest air. He could almost feel the world tingling around him—the scent of leaf mould, the sounds of small animals, somewhere the bark of a fox, perhaps deep down the snuffling of badgers. There were squirrels in the trees—not the grey squirrels that he had seen in parks in Birmingham, but the golden-russet red squirrels which are now almost extinct.

It was because he made hardly any sound that he heard the jingling ahead of him long before he saw what caused it.

In the winter quiet it was a sound both enticing and frightening. It was alien to the forest, just as he was. He halted, and listened, moving his head this way and that to catch it.

It was not the clanking of machines, nor was it the clicking of chains, nor the metallic rustle of armour. It was the tinkling—surely—of tiny bells. Not the dull clang of a cow bell, nor the sweet chime of a hand bell, but the merry, jostling sound of tiny bells no bigger than your thumb.

The bells grew fainter—so whoever it was, was moving away from him, and he had been catching them up. What to do? Whoever it was, if they were going that way, must be going to the castle. So he would meet them sooner, if he caught them now, or later, if he waited. His first thought was to let them get well out of the way.

Mmm.

"Courage," he muttered to himself, and spurred his horse to a canter.

It was not long before he came upon a lady, dressed entirely in green, riding a milk-white mare. There were bells stitched onto her tasselled bridle, and she rode side-saddle, with a slow, measured elegant walk and a high step. All of Scott's riding had been of the practical kind, and the slow, courtly elegance of the milk-white mare entranced him.

"Good morrow, sir knight," called the lady. Strange as it may sound, Scott could not just make out what language she was speaking when she said this. Almost it entered his mind without going through his ears.

"Good morrow, fair lady," he replied. It felt as though he was speaking his own, native English. But perhaps not quite. 'Fair lady' was, of course, what you were supposed to say, but now that he looked, she was indeed a very fair lady. Her golden hair fell in tresses down to her waist, her face was a gently shaping triangle, and her eyes were lucid blue.

She looked away, as if shy, when she saw him staring.

"Good sir knight," she said. "It seems to me that I know you, and yet I cannot say where we have met. Are you of Arthur's court?"

Scott's heart leapt. But he shook his head.

"No, my lady. I am but a wanderer." It struck him as he said this that it was just the right sort of thing to say, but, at the same time, not the sort of thing he had ever found himself saying before.

"That is a pity, good sir knight, for Arthur's court is passing fair. But you are surely of the company of his company? Your face reveals you—your face is so like..." she paused, taking a moment to look at him carefully, but then she shook her head, glistening tresses following her motion in the dappled light, and said "— but no matter. You are a traveller, surely, yes, a skifter, as am I, seeking your quest in many turning times, as the years fold this way and that. Surely it is so?"

Scott stiffened. "How do you know me, madam?"

"How should I not know you? First, by your words—you speak, as I speak, words that drop into the mind without language, the language we call Cortayse. And the words you use are courteous and knightly, such as none in this miserable time when fools reign has learned. And second, by your attire. I see cloth of gold in your cloak, and the blazon of the earl of Warwick, Guy de Beauchamp on its clasp. Such things would not trouble a man of this time, but to another traveller they are as clear as day. And third—" She stopped.

"Third, my lady?"

"I should not say it. You ride well, and with great pace and vigour, and I doubt not that in battle you are storm and whirlwind and lightning and thunder to your enemies. But—" Again she paused. And almost smirked, although 'to smirk' would not be a word Scott would have put with that perfect, elfin face. "But, you see, you sit forward in the saddle, as if you were at a race, or about to give battle. Forgive me, for it is a fine way of riding, but if a riding-master of this age were to see you, he would disdain you for a barbarian or a fool."

Scott blushed.

"See, now I have offended you," she said, quickly, "and my words are clumsy beside your courtesy. But, if it please you, ride with me to the castle where this path leads, showing that you forgive me for my foolish talk, and I will assure you of the welcome and protection of the folk there, who are my kin and my friends."

"Gladly, my lady," said Scott, and then added "If I may but gaze on your loveliness as we ride."

The lady made as if to look bashfully away—but Scott caught a gleam, just a gleam in her eye that said that this was what she wanted him to say, and was expecting.

"My lord must do as he sees fit," she said. "While I am under my lord's protection I am in his hands."

Scott did not understand what she meant by this, but he was happy enough to ride beside her and look at her face. She was neither old nor young. Her skin glowed with soft light, and her voice rose and fell like the gentle ripples of a lake.

"Sir knight, you must tell me your name," she said, after a while.

Scott had no intention of telling her his real name, but, before he had quite decided what to say, he realised that he was already answering:

"My name, my lady, is the Chevalier Desconnu, but where I have needed to give a name, the name I have given is Perceval."

A pang of fear gripped him. He had been happy enough when his mouth seemed to be in charge of the Latin conversation with the monk, or the Saxon conversation with the woodsman. And he had been especially happy with the flow of courtly, chivalrous words which had seemed to charm the lady. But it had not occurred to him that he might give out valuable information before his conscious mind—the part that was listening to both sides of the conversation—had a say in the matter.

'But, Chevalier Desconnu, I have heard of you. Are you not Sir Gawain's companion? Word of your exploits has already reached us— how you broke the curse of the haunted chapel, and rescued a maiden from a mob, and how you found a skift-door into the past that none other could see."

And now Scott really was alarmed.

"But, my lady, how can this be, since I only come this day from the haunted chapel?"

"Because, my Chevalier Desconnu, although your exploits are your own, their stories are part of legend and history. No skifter can keep a secret from another."

"My lady, I do not understand."

"Yesterday, you set off from the castle of Guy de Beauchamp to spend the night at a haunted church. The story of that church has been known for a long time—that a knight would break the curse by holding vigil there alone. But nobody knew who that knight would be, because in skift-time it had not yet happened, even though in world-time, it happened long before." She smiled bashfully, as if she felt she was teaching him something he already knew.

"But does that not mean that men can know the future?" said Scott.

"The knowing of the future by this means is called prophecy, and the skift-days of Arthur's folk and Morgaine's folk are full of them," she replied, "yet prophecy is seldom clear, and thus our future always surprises, and prophecies conflict, and not all come to pass."

"My lady, I think I begin to see. But tell me, what is your name, since I have given you mine?"

"That you may not yet know, but I will tell you this—I was known to Sir Gawain, and dear to him too, if the tales tell truly. But that time is now no longer, and I search for a new paramour, if one be found worthy."

Scott did not know what a paramour was: It seemed that word was familiar to him, but he did not know of a meaning that went with it.

They rode on for a while in silence, Scott now all too aware that he sat forwards, almost on the horse's neck, while the lady sat exactly upright, her horse carefully pacing to smooth her ride.

At length they caught a glimpse of a banner, fluttering over a hillside. Soon the top of a tower, and then many towers came into view.

Now, seeing this gave Scott the strangest sensation. Because here was the same Kenilworth castle where he had stayed just a few nights before. But it was not the broken down ruin of his own day. Nor was it a tiny fortress like Sir Guy's castle in Warwick. This was Kenilworth at the peak of its grandeur—tower upon tower of red sandstone reaching into the winter sky. Bright banners flew from every turret, and men at arms in shining mail stood on the battlements. And white swans—brighter than the eye could look on—swam serenely in a huge lake.

He rubbed his eyes. Was this illusion?

The drawbridge was down and the portcullis open.

"A penny for your thoughts, my Chevalier," said the lady, seeing the confusion on Scott's face.

"I marvel that you need to ask" said Scott—once again with the feeling not that he had found the words, but that the words had found him.

"And why is that, fair sir?"

"Because in all my travels in this hinterland that we in my time so simply call the past, I have seen only that life is more brutal, more abrupt, smaller and less noble than the reputation which history has given to it. But this, your castle, is none of that."

She clapped her hands in delight.

"My good Chevalier, how truly you speak. For this castle is of all times and no times, being raised by the holy arts out of the pure picture in our mind's eye, and not the meagre work of hands toiling on the hard earth."

"You mean magic," said Scott—for once getting in his own thoughts before the fine words could get there before him.

"Good knight, do not start so. Our world of skifting and traffic between times and places is made by just such arts. But this little, little house is as nothing compared to the castle of Camelot that Merlin raised for Arthur. Do you not know it? This lodge is but a toy compared with the keeps, parapets, machicolations, the earthworks and barricades, the look-out posts and great engines of destruction which guard Arthur's throne. And all made by Merlin's art."

They were almost on the drawbridge and Scott hesitated.

She was ahead of him now, turning back in her saddle, beckoning him with her eyes.

"My Perceval, my knight protector," she said. "Surely you do not believe this to be an illusion? See, it is daylight. This is no chapel of ghosts, but a house of the living."

She flicked her hair as she said this, almost as if she were challenging him. And then she rode sedately across the drawbridge, looking neither to the right nor the left.

Reluctantly, Scott set off after her. His horse's hooves clattered solidly enough on the timbers. He could not help looking up as he rode through the gatehouse. The sharpened stakes of the portcullis hung evilly above.

Frowning, he set himself to ride onwards—not too quickly, but not too slowly either.

The scene that greeted him, though, when he left it, was enough to make him forget his terror, at least for a while.

To the right was a high keep, set in its own inner bailey with walls and turrets. Flags and banners hung from the windows, as if it were a cruise ship decked out to welcome passengers. Ahead were low buildings—stables and kitchens and kennels and barracks and armouries and more. There was a delicious smell of roasting meat, and hunger welled up inside him.

Between the keep and the outbuildings, the castle grounds were laid out as if they were a huge park. There were marquees and pavilions to the right and to the left, with musicians and conjurors and jugglers and jesters and every other kind of entertainment. A stretch of grass was set out with pennants and ropes, and rows of racked seats. Scott guessed that these were the preparations for a tournament.

A servant ran up to take the reins of Scott's horse while he dismounted. The lady's horse had already been led away, and she herself was standing in a small knot of ladies dressed like herself, in long flowing robes like the paintings of King Arthur's court in the Birmingham Museum done by a man called Jones.

All of a sudden they turned towards him—giggling—and waved. And then they picked up their skirts and ran, so that Scott was quickly caught in the middle.

"Are you the Sir Perceval of the Conte du Graal?" said one, "or should we expect someone else?"

"They say that you no know fear," said another.

"They say you ride at all times as if ready for battle," said a third.

All the bright faces bobbing up and down were too much for Scott to take in at once, but he did notice that these women seemed to be of very different ages, although they all shared the same stateliness and girlishness at one and the same time. But surely that girl giggling and batting her eyelids was older than his mother, while the lady who stayed aloof was barely in her teens.

"My ladies," he said, raising his voice, and noticing that it was agreeably deep. He had been developing a low alto voice, but he had had a tendency to squeak when he tried to talk loudly.

"My ladies," he said again. "I cannot answer even one of your questions, let alone all. And if I could, I would be caught by your flatteries in the grip of the grievous sin of pride. So let there be no more questions until such a time as there is peace to answer them."

This seemed to rather satisfy them—although Scott was left wondering what exactly he had actually meant by it.

"Ladies," said his hostess. "Our lord Perceval is doubtless fatigued from his journey. He will certes be wanting a little peace before the evening draws on. But have no fear, Chevalier—" she said, turning to him, "our damsels will find a way to steal your heart, even if they cannot yet have your conversation."

The lady clapped her hands, and a servant, splendidly dressed, ran up.

"My Lord, the Chevalier Desconnu, has need of rest," she said. "Bring him to a guest chamber, and attend to his needs."

The servant led Scott past a high keep to a round tower built onto the inner bailey. There was great arched doorway with wide steps running up to it, and carvings on either side and in the arch. Scott did not know much about castles, but it seemed to him that this castle was not wholly built as a fortress. He could not imagine men standing anxiously on guard from these towers, the way they must stand night by night on the walls of Sir Guy's castle. He followed the servant inside, up a gently stepped spiral staircase.

The guest room was comfortably furnished, and marvellously warm— warmer than any place he had been since he set out on his travels. It was as large as Scott's whole house, hung with tapestries, and set about with sofas and magnificent chairs. Behind the tapestries was oak panelling, and the ceiling, too, was oak, carved in great detail with the leaves and branches of an enormous tree. The carpet was a rich forest green.

Here there was writing carved into panels, and there words embroidered onto tapestries. Scott looked closely, but he found he could not read them. One was surely in Latin, because he could make out the words 'sed' and 'etiam', which he knew meant 'but' and 'because'. But he was disappointed that his new gift of language only went as far as talking. He felt that there was probably a lot he could have learned in this place if only he could read.

The servant stood deferentially at the door. A few days earlier this would have bothered Scott, but now he barely noticed.

At one end of the room steps led down into a sunken bath. At the other there was a great bed. It was carved in one piece into the panelling of the wall with curtains that hung from the ceiling. These were thickly embroidered as with leaves, and the bed was carved like a tree trunk.

Scott was still looking around when there was a heavy rap-rap at the door. The servant opened it, and spoke for a moment in a hushed voice with someone else. Then he turned to Scott.

"My Lord, you have a visitor. The Lady Ragnall. Will you speak with her?"

The 'Lady Ragnall' was a name he had heard before. Surely this was the lady from Marie de France's story at Sir Guy's banquet? He thought for a moment. The lady he had met on the way to the castle had said that she had been close to Sir Gawain. Was she now going to reveal herself with her true name?

It was then that Scott realised that he had not really believed the story that Marie de France had told. It was somehow hard to imagine someone as solid and real as Gavin Knight actually mixed up with women who changed from horrific hags to heavenly beauties in a moment. But he had come to understand who Gawain was only gradually. Now he would meet a figure of legend, knowing who she was.

It sent the slightest shiver up his spine.

"My Lord," said the servant again, "will you speak with her?"

Scott was on the point of blurting out a boyish 'Yes', but his mouth said:

"By all means I will speak with her, for fain would I discourse on many diverse matters."

There was a rustle of dresses. A woman's voice spoke to the servant from the stairs, telling him to leave them while they spoke.

And then the Lady Ragnall entered.

Scott gaped. It was a most unknightly thing to do. But, all the same, he gaped.

She was indeed a vision of loveliness which the eye seldom sees. Her golden hair fell in tresses over her shoulders, and she was dressed in a flowing green silk gown which perfectly set off her figure. She was more lovely than Marie de France, more lovely than the unknown lady on the road, more lovely than any of the ladies who had greeted him inside the castle.

But this is not why he gaped.

He gaped, because she was his mother.

She raised an eyebrow. Clearly she had not expected to see him either. In fact, Scott was not entirely sure that she recognised him at all.

"My Lord Perceval," she said.

"My Lady Ragnall," he replied.

"Art thou Perceval?" she said. "We have heard many tales of your exploits. But perhaps there is another?"

"Art thou Ragnall?" he countered. "I have heard but one tale of the Lady Ragnall, but it was so passing strange that I can scarce countenance that this lady should now stand before me."

"My Lord must believe what he will," she said, looking round the room. "This Lady Ragnall cannot speak for a tale told to my lord Perceval where she was not present. But I know of only one Lady Ragnall, and only one tale of a Lady Ragnall, who was delivered from a strange enchantment. And this is the Lady Ragnall who now stands before you."

"Then you have the better of me. For I am merely a Sir Perceval, who has had but few adventures, and none glorious. Whether others will befall this Perceval in the days that are before him, and whether these will become tales worth telling, is a mystery to which he cannot answer."

"Come, sit with me in the window seat," she said, taking him by the hand. "Let us look out at this castle, which is passing fair."

And so they sat in the window seat, looking out across turrets and bastions and curtain walls, across a wide moat and to the hills beyond.

"I marvel at you," she said, raising an eyebrow again. "Because you are the very image of my son, whom I left in a far away place."

"And I marvel at you," he said. "Because you are the very image of my mother, whom I have come to seek, and to rescue, and to return to her own time."

"Then let me pretend for a moment that I am your mother and you are my son," she said.

"And what would you say to your son in such a game?" he said.

"First"—and her voice somehow changed.

"First," she said again, "I would tell my son that I never meant him to be caught up in any of this." He was about to reply, but she put her finger over his lips.

"And second," she raised her voice, just a little. "If I really were speaking to my son I would tell him—" and her voice slipped in a moment from the fair, courteous, medieval English which his mind understood even though he did not know the meaning of the words, into the sound of words he had grown up with "—I would stop his pocket money, and ground him for the rest of his life." But there was a glint in her eye, the faintest hint of a wink.

"And third, because in all tales there are always three, I should say that the father who dragged him through time is a good-for-nothing scoundrel, and I should ask where he is hiding, so that I could tell him exactly what I think of him."

Scott thought for a moment. He had never had a conversation like this with his mother. To be fair, he had never had a conversation quite like this with anyone—sitting fifteen miles and eight hundred years from the house they both lived in, in a castle room which should not have been built for another three hundred years, and both pretending to be (or perhaps being) people quite different from the people they thought they were.

"But already the game is broken," said Scott, carefully and slowly. "Because I know that I have never met my father, nor has my mother ever spoken of him."

She looked away. And Scott saw there were tears in her eyes.

Then she took his hands in hers and said, in quite a different voice:

"Scott, Scott my love. I'm so sorry. So sorry. How could I have told you? How could it have made any sense at all?"

"But mum—" he said. And suddenly all the game or pretence of a noble knight talking with a noble lady had fallen away.

"When Gawain turned up, why didn't you tell me then? And why did you disappear? What happened to you? And why did you leave him in the first place? Or did he leave you?"

She frowned.

"I suppose I ought to answer your questions," she said. "But it's a long story."

151

11 THE OTHER STORY OF SIR GAWAIN AND THE LADY RAGNALL

"It all began," said Scott's mother, or the Lady Ragnall, "when I was a student at Oxford. I was studying medieval English, and my tutor was a lady whose name was Morgana Laufey, and she had long red hair. She was a striking woman in many ways. What she taught was not strictly in line with the thinking of other scholars, but she had such a detailed knowledge of medieval languages and texts that it was very hard for anyone to argue with her.

"There was a little group that used to meet at her house. It wasn't the kind of group that you could just join, but by the little things that people said, it was clear that this was where all the interesting discussions took place, and where people made the kind of friends that would help them get on later in life.

"Once a term Morgana had an open-house, which meant that the people who weren't in her group could come to her house and drink tea and talk to each other. I guess that she was eyeing us up, checking us out for possible inclusion. But all we thought of at the time was that we were at her house, almost inside her inner circle, although not quite. And we desperately wanted to be inside.

"You're probably wondering what was so special about being inside. All I can say was, at that age, and in that time, we almost worshipped Morgana, and we wanted to be like her and we wanted to be with her.

"So I worked hard, and tried to get noticed. But as hard as I worked, I saw that other students, the ones who were in her circle—she was only interested in the girls, the boys quickly dropped out of her lectures and found other tutors—wrote better essays than I did and learned the old languages faster, even though they seemed to be doing less work. It made me feel very stupid, and sometimes I used to lie awake at night crying myself to sleep. It all seems silly to me now, but at the time it was the most important thing in the world.

"At the end of my second year, which was a year in which we didn't have exams, I found I was even further behind than I had been at the start of the year, try as I might.

"I trudged up to Winchester Road, where she lived, for the end of term open-house. But when I got there I discovered that the day had been changed without anyone telling me, and I'd missed it. I was really, really miserable, and I was sure that everyone else had been told and that they had deliberately left me out.

"It wasn't Morgana who answered the door, but one of her graduate students who was having a tutorial. I was trying to hide my misery—I don't think I was doing it very well. Then Morgana came to the door, and the other girl explained what had happened.

"'You must come inside,' she said. She wasn't the kind of person you argued with when her mind was made up. 'We will be finishing our tutorial in twenty minutes, and then we must have tea together, just the three of us, to make up for the open-house you missed yesterday.'

"So they led me into a sort of living room, as big as the room we are in now, and left me there while they finished their tutorial. The room was full of books, and after five minutes of sitting fidgeting in the arm chairs, I went over to the shelves to see what she had.

"There was row after row of priceless manuscripts. Not prints or editions or facsimiles, but actual manuscripts, straight out of the middle ages, in huge leather bindings, written in perfect tenth and twelfth and fourteenth century handwriting. Each one of those books must have taken a year to make, and I took one of them down very, very carefully.

"At first I thought it had been rebound recently, because the cover seemed quite new. But, the funny thing was, the pages seemed new as well. I wondered if they were some strange kind of modern copy, but the handwriting, the binding and everything was too perfect.

"Scott, you have to understand how valuable these manuscripts are. Only the most famous libraries in the world have more than three or four like that: fabulously illustrated, in gold, and azure-blue, and malachite-green. But here they were, dozens of them, together in someone's house.

"Then I heard rustling in the hall, and I hastily put the book back on the shelf and sat down.

"'I hope you've had a chance to look at some of my manuscripts,' said Morgana, while the other girl brought tea. It was fine Earl Gray tea, served in porcelain cups. 'There really isn't anything to rival them. I bring back what I can, you know, each time I travel. Very few would have otherwise survived.'

"I'm sure all this makes sense to you now, but I was completely mystified. I drank my tea and wondered what she was going to say next.

"I stayed exactly one hour. She seemed to have the time precisely marked out, almost as if she had been expecting me. Just before she sent me away, she said:

"'You've worked hard this year, but your languages are still not up to scratch. If you would like to join me and some of the others over the summer, we are starting out tomorrow. You had better warn your family that you won't be back for a few weeks. We will meet here at eight p.m. Bring a change of clothes and a toothbrush. You won't need anything else.'

"You can imagine that this was beyond anything I had hoped for. I hastily gabbled my thanks, and promised to be there without fail.

"I was there at eight prompt the next evening, with a change of clothes in a little rucksack. It took until midnight for everyone to gather, and I wondered when it was all going to begin.

"At midnight, Morgana led us into the cellars of her house. It was a very strange place. The cellars went on far beyond the walls or even the garden. They say half of Oxford is hollowed out with tunnels and underground rooms which house the stacks of books in the Bodleian library. I guess that Morgana's cellars eventually met up with those. But the rooms themselves were not library rooms. They were marked with strange symbols on the doors, and there were things in the rooms—animals, or maybe people. If I had had half a brain I would have known that I was walking into trouble, but I was so desperate to be part of it that I didn't think.

"Eventually we came to a room where we all had to change our clothes. They were Anglo-Norman, like the dress I'm wearing now, although at the time they just seemed to me to be 'medieval'. It was strange that, in those days, I knew a great deal about medieval literature, and almost nothing about medieval life. We left what we were wearing—and the change of clothes—in that room. Then, in a larger room, which was rough, like a cavern, Morgana made us do some things which I won't go into now, but which were fairly clearly some kind of magic ritual.

"I didn't believe in magic, and I thought that this must be some kind of feminist-deconstructionist-poststructuralist way of setting aside our preconceptions about the text. I was very naïve.

"Then she took us up a winding, spiral staircase. We must have gone miles underground, because we found ourselves coming up inside Oxford Castle. Oxford Castle has been—or had been then, which is to say, will be, from the present—a ruin for many years. I'd never been inside it. But we came up among guards and attendants and orderlies, and everyone was bowing to us. I thought it was some kind of medieval pageant. But, of course, it wasn't. It was Oxford Castle in the time we are in now, but twenty years before.

"I expect you would have worked out what was going on straight away. But I spent weeks at Oxford Castle improving my early medieval English, and learning to be an Anglo-Norman lady, without ever realising who Morgana was or what her intentions were.

"We were there the entire summer, and we only went back to our own time ready for the start of the next term. Your grandparents thought—and I guess they still think—that I'd been on an intensive language course. Which was true enough, I suppose.

"When term started again I was one of Morgana's group, no mistaking it. I'd never been in the 'in' crowd before. All through school I'd been the clever girl who worked hard and didn't have many friends. The friends I did have were girls like me who studied a lot and never got invited to parties. So it was something new to me to be inside looking out, not outside looking in. There were other students who I always thought were Morgana's favourites who I suddenly saw as outsiders.

"I'm sorry to say I rather made the most of it. I enjoyed saying the things that made it absolutely clear that I was in and they weren't. I must have made them as miserable as I'd been before.

"I couldn't wait for term to finish, because it was pretty clear that we would be setting off again. There was a big dinner in hall, and we were all to meet again at midnight. This time it wasn't at Morgana's house, but at New College, which is one of the oldest. I still didn't understand how it was done, so I followed the others through vaults into a wine cellar the size of a five-a-side football pitch. Once again we changed our clothes, and when we went out the other side, we were in the fourteenth century.

"This time we were allowed to move about freely. Not that we could move very far or very fast. London was three days journey for us. But we got to mix with more people, and I saw some things that should have woken me up to what we were really doing.

"But they didn't. I missed Christmas at home, which your grandparents didn't like. Once again we got back for the start of term. This time I began to imagine that I was rather a favourite even among Morgana's select group. Of course, reading, and speaking, Middle English was now second nature to me. The spring term—we called it 'Trinity'—raced past, apart from one thing which rather brought me up sharp.

"I was taking a course in archaeology. It was my one act of rebellion, because Morgana had made it clear that she didn't hold with archaeology and she especially didn't hold with the Institute of Archaeology, where we had our lectures. I was having tutorials with a famous archaeologist, and we were studying the times of Arthur and of the Anglo-Saxons.

"The way we did things at Oxford was that we had to read out our essays each week. I had got into the habit of reading them out—for anyone except Morgana, that is—with a rather disdainful, arrogant air. I thought I knew better than my tutors. After all, I had actually been to the middle ages. But there was something about my archaeology tutor that made me just a little bit careful with her. She knew things which I didn't.

"I was reading out my essay, and she began to tell me about some excavations she had done into the very earliest Saxon settlements. She had spent ten years there, digging through each of the summer holidays.

I thought this was rather a long time to spend on one site, but I didn't say so. Anyway, she was talking away, looking out of the window as much as at me, and then suddenly she turned to face me straight on.

"'You're very taken with Morgana,' she said. It was completely unlike anything she had ever said to me before. Normally if someone had said something like that I would have instantly jumped in to tell them how much I thought of her. But she surprised me, so all I said was, 'I suppose I rather like her. Don't you?'

"Then she looked me straight in the eye. 'It's all very well to go digging around the past,' she said. 'After all, that's all that most of us do here at Oxford. But it's quite another thing to go and live there. Few do, and survive. And it's yet a third thing to start taking sides and meddling. If you must take sides, my girl'—she used to say 'my girl', which was a rather old fashioned thing to say even then—'then you owe it to yourself at least to listen to what the other side has to say, and see what they have to offer.'

"'I don't know what you mean,' I said, which was partly true. 'Well, I'm sure you know your own business,' she said, in the voice that says exactly the opposite.

"I didn't say any more about it, and neither did she—ever. She died just a few months later. But it gave me an uneasy feeling. If nothing else, it told me that more people knew about Morgana and skifting than I had believed.

"Skifting was a word I only learned during the Christmas holidays, and I still didn't really know what it meant, beyond that it was about travelling through time.

"After that, I began to do my own research, alongside the things that Morgana and her group were teaching me. Students didn't have computers then, and there was no internet. So I spent many days locked in odd corners of college libraries, poring over old manuscripts until the librarians came to chuck me out.

"Don't think that I was beginning to doubt Morgana. If anything, I was doing my own research as a way of worming myself even deeper into her favour. The Easter holidays were the last before my final exams. There was just one paper I wasn't doing well in, and that was Anglo-Saxon. I begged Morgana to take us to see the Anglo-Saxons, but she made no promises.

"When the day came though, we set off on horses out across the Port Meadow. I think she had the horses from a riding school. She told us that where we were going we wouldn't find much that we didn't take with us, and so we made sure our saddlebags were filled with food and warm clothes.

"One of the girls had brought a gun—a revolver that she had somehow got from her brother who was in the army. She showed it to Morgana, who pulled it out of its holster, and hurled it into the river. 'You must not take machines back with you in time,' she said. 'Do not try to do so again, at your peril.' The girl was crestfallen.

"This was the first time I'd been skifting outdoors and in daylight. So it was the first time I saw the air shimmer as we passed through the skift-door. And it was the first time I saw what was happening on the other side. We arrived at the scene of a battle. Not a pitched battle between two armies. It was a battle between a family of British tribesmen and an Anglian war-party. We rode straight past them, looking neither to the right nor to the left. There were children dying, and we rode on.

"Anglo-Saxon is a much harder language to learn than medieval English, and there were far fewer people around to teach it to us. The truth is that we were less than a century after the first Saxon invasions of Britain. There were no Saxon towns, only scattered villages, with dwindling Romano-British cities between them.

"We rode across downs and through forest until we found a road running north and south. It was hard going—I'd barely been on a horse before, although at least they didn't make me ride side-saddle. The road was easier, and we came to a tiny settlement which I think is now Alchester. We spent the night there, half-sleeping, half-waking, uneasy for fear of attacks.

"From there we rode at a good speed to the town of Verulamium. It was a walled settlement, and Saxons, Romans and British all seemed to meet there without fear or anger. Verulamium is what we would call St Albans. It's one of a very few places that have continued right the way from Roman times to our day.

"We were three weeks in Verulamium, and that is where, for the first time, we met Arthur's people. We did not know who they were. To us they were just Romano-British, speaking something like Welsh half the time, and bad Latin the rest. Few of them spoke Saxon. But we noticed something strange about their clothes, and we saw that people hushed and drew back as they passed—in much the same way that they hushed and drew back when we passed, except that we had been too full of ourselves to notice it.

"We had hardly met them before it was time to be moving on. Morgana took us back through Alfred's time and Canute's time and right up to the eve of the Norman conquest, to give us a taste for the different dialects. Or so she said. But it was immediately after Arthur's folk started to appear that she took us away.

"What this did do, though, was show me much more about skifting than she intended. I began to learn how to see a skift door forming, and it didn't take me long to work out that we always arrived in the middle of trouble—a fight, a murder, an execution, a house burning down. Skifting is not what you would call a lucky art.

"Term began again, and I knuckled down to work for my exams. I needn't have worried. We all sailed through Anglo-Saxon and early and late Middle-English. I also did well in archaeology, which I can't imagine pleased Morgana.

"All this was important, because I was hoping to stay on to begin work on my doctorate. That would mean I could stay at least another three years at Oxford, which meant I could keep inside Morgana's group and go skifting in the vacations. But to do that, I had to get top marks on all my papers.

"And now this is where the story begins to turn.

"Do you believe in magic, Scott?"

Scott didn't at first answer the question—he had been so wrapped up in his mother's story, although there were names and places and ideas that he did not know or understand.

"Well, I suppose so," he said. "Isn't skifting a kind of magic? And aren't ghosts and monsters magical?"

"None of these are magical, Scott. At least, the people who know most about these things don't talk about them as if they were. Skifting and monsters belong to the world of knights. And ghosts belong to the world of priests. Both of those are strange worlds. But the world of magic belongs to wizards and to witches. And neither witches nor wizards are welcome folk in most of the parts of history that you can visit.

"I did not believe in magic. I imagined somehow that skifting was something with a sound, scientific explanation, perhaps cooked up in the university nuclear physics department.

"But when I started work on my doctorate—of course Morgana was my supervisor—I also began to learn about magic. At first she called what we had to do 'experiments', and called the results 'effects'. But then we began to study in old Latin books—books which had been banned and ordered destroyed long before the age of printing. She taught us strange words that are not found in any dictionary. Dead words, relics of dead tongues. Things better left forgotten.

"We also began to make weekend visits. To attend a battle here, an execution there, to visit a pagan shrine, or see an old ritual performed at dead of night by people in masks.

"Part of me hated every minute of this. But part of me wanted it. I was thirsty for knowledge.

"The first 'experiments' we did were very simple, and the effects were hardly worth the effort of gathering the ingredients. But as things went on, our hands touched more power.

"As we became more adept, Morgana opened more of her mind to us. All along I had imagined that she was travelling back with us in time, showing us paths that she had discovered. But now she revealed that our time was for her the far future. She was in truth Morgaine— Morgan Le Fay—half sister of Arthur, terrible and splendid.

"She told us many things. She explained how confused the world of Arthur was, with people skifting this way and that, trying to discover the past so that they could change it, and making everything more confused, pulling in disaster over their heads. For this she blamed Merlin. Merlin, she said, was a proud enchanter who intended to rewrite history, and leave Arthur on the throne for ever, holding back the future of Britain.

"It was from that time that she began to send us out, one by one, as spies or secret agents in her work. Our job was to lure knights onto her side who might otherwise join Arthur's. Arthur, she said, was not choosey about where he got his knights from, but would happily pluck them from any time and any place if only they extended the glory of his kingdom. Many, she told us, were little better than criminals. Arthur did a little to civilise them, with his long talks on chivalry, and the round table, and elaborate courtesies. But what—she said—he was really looking for was results. That's why he kept Kay, and Lancelot, and many others who were fighting amongst themselves and, likely as not, fooling him.

"One knight who would probably have fallen into Arthur's hands eventually was a man of the fourteenth century whose name was Sir Gromer. He was a gruff man with a bleak outlook, so we called him 'Sir Gromer Somer Jour', which is a mixed up way of saying 'Sir Gromer Summer's Day'. Gromer had a long-standing grievance against Arthur, to do with land rights in a piece of trackless forest that nobody every visited. But those were the things that concerned people like Sir Gromer. It was not hard to persuade him to fall in with our plans. We lured Arthur and Gawain into the fourteenth century to the exact spot where Sir Gromer had his fortress. Some people said that Arthur behaved like a coward on that day, but, in truth, he was unarmed, facing a man in full armour. He knew his job was to keep Britain safe, at least for a while, and he could not afford to throw his life away as a gesture. So he agreed to bring back the answer to the question 'what do women want above all things'.

"Morgaine told us that no harm would come to Arthur—a year would elapse, and he would be unable find the answer, and so he would not keep his appointment, and would be shamed, and his hold over men would be broken, and Britain could return to its right course of history.

"But the day I saw Arthur make the promise to return, I knew that he would not break it. And by keeping his promise, I knew he would lose his life.

"And, suddenly, for the first time, I found myself choosing a side. Up till then, I had been happy to go along with things. I didn't particularly believe in Morgaine's plans, but I didn't not believe either. It was part of a university game. Except, from the moment I saw Arthur, it was no longer a game.

"And, perhaps, not just Arthur. That was the day I first saw Gawain.

"My year passed slowly enough. I was wrestling with some difficult Latin texts. I don't know if you have realised, but Cortayse—the trick of language which you seem to have picked up—only works when the other person is actually present. It will not teach you to read books. This is why Morgaine had been so keen to have us learn the languages properly, though she shared the gift with us when she sent us out as spies. Reading and writing was the advantage she would give herself over Arthur's side.

"Then, one day, I woke up and I knew what I wanted more than anything else in the world. I wanted to save Arthur's life. And maybe there was Gawain in my mind as well, though I didn't let myself think about that. But a year had almost passed, and, if I didn't do something soon, it would all be too late.

"It was an eight hour train journey to Carlisle from Oxford. I ran to the station. Somebody must have seen me leave college in a hurry. It was then that I discovered for the first time how dangerous and ruthless Morgaine was. All kinds of things happened as I ran. Three cars on three separate roads almost hit me. A load of bricks fell from a workman's hod three storeys up. They missed me by inches. There was a sudden, unexpected flood, which sent water bubbling up out of the drains in Hythe Bridge Street. And, as I finally reached the station, magpies came hurtling down, biting at me with sharp beaks, pecking at my eyes.

"Somehow I fought them off and got to the ticket office. The ticket clerk's machine first wouldn't work, and then it wouldn't accept my credit card. Eventually the ticket clerk gave up. He smiled, and pushed the ticket into my hands without payment. Somebody bundled me onto the train, moments before it pulled out.

"I caught a glimpse of two tall men rushing towards the train, but they were too late. We were gone.

"I kept on looking out of the window at every station, wondering if they were on my trail. But there was nothing, and I decided that I was safe. How wrong I was.

"I'd worked out exactly what I needed to do. I only needed to be at the side of the road as Arthur rode by—six hundred years earlier. The trouble he was in, and my connection to that trouble, would be easily enough to open up a door. All I needed was to skift through, and give him the answer, and skift back before the door closed. I would have to keep out of Morgaine's way for a while, but I thought that we would patch things up eventually.

"I was full of confidence as we pulled into Carlisle. I'd eluded all of Morgaine's traps, I'd kept ahead of her mob, and I was about to single handedly foil her greatest plan. I wasn't thinking about the fact that I had been on Morgaine's side, hatching plots and practising black magic, right up to that very morning.

"Carlisle station is beautiful—it's like something out of one of Arthur's adventures. This is something that often happens in places where a lot of skifting goes on. Time gets mixed up, and people start building buildings that belong to another age.

"I hired a bicycle, and set off pedalling towards a village called Cald-beck, which would put me on the road where I had to be. It was more than twenty miles, and hilly as well, but I was so close to my goal now that some hard cycling wasn't going to hold me back.

"I stopped just once, and the memory of it still makes me shudder.

"It was in a tiny place called Welton. I knew there was a funny kind of double back in the road ahead of me, and I stopped at the well house, which is what Welton is famous for, to ask the way. There was a woman standing there, almost as if she was waiting for me. I noticed she had deep red hair.

"The moment I looked into her eyes I knew that something was terribly wrong.

"'You should not have come, Anne Raynall,' she said. It was Morgaine's voice, dripping with disdain. 'I will not detain you,' she went on. 'But if you skift, you will feel my anger. And see if your love will have you then. And he will not, and woe betide you when he does not, because my anger will rest on you all the days of your life.'

"And then the woman turned away, as if she had just been passing the time of day, and started telling an old man about her cabbages.

"I had no idea what she meant, but just the fact that Morgaine was able to take over someone else's speech, and know where I was, and what I was doing, and even why I was doing it (which I had not admitted to myself)—all that shook me. I got back on the bicycle and pedalled off unsteadily.

"The rest of the story I think you know.

"I skifted as I intended, but as I stepped through the door I felt a terrible weight fall onto my shoulders. My back ached so much that it bent me double, my heart was racing with the effort of walking, and there was a terrible smell all around me—the stench of flesh rotting in open wounds. This is what I had become. I was twenty-three years old, but my body had become a hundred. There was a pool by the roadside, and, horrified by what I knew I would see, but unable to hold back, I peered into it to see my reflection.

"It was unspeakable. I wanted to hide, but at that moment I heard the jingling of riders, and the golden voice of Arthur, filled with sadness, but great nobility. He knew that he was riding to his death, but he rode anyway, preferring death to dishonour. And with him rode Gawain.

"Gawain! To see him was to love him! Even today it is hard not to fall under his spell. The kind, gentle features, and behind them a man who had fought countless foes, who put dragons to flight and struck down were-wolves and woses and ettins and worse. His eyes were like the sea, but his sword was like lightning, and his strength grew with the sun until at midday no weapon could bite him nor foe prevail. At least, such was his reputation.

"I stepped out in front of them. I meant to greet them courteously, after the fashion of noble ladies. But my mouth let out a loud cackle, and my voice was harsher than a raven.

"Morgaine's words echoed in my mind. I was in some way aware of part of the story, and what I had to do, although I did not know what the result would be. But there was simply no way that Gawain would have taken me willingly.

"So I bargained. I promised Arthur his life if Gawain would make me his wife. It was a horrible thing. I saw the look of dread on Gawain's face, and the look of pain on Arthur's, but both knew they had no other choice.

"I told them the secret of what women desire above all things—or, at least, I told them Morgaine's version of the secret, because it had to be her exact words to save Arthur's life. And they rode on. Gawain even thanked me, although he knew that if Arthur's life was saved, his own was as good as ended.

"I sat down by the road to wait for their return. A few woodsmen passed me on their way somewhere. One made the sign of the cross to ward me off. A dog came sniffing, and ran away with its tail between its legs.

"It was an hour later that they came riding back. I wouldn't have blamed them if they had taken another road. But Gawain was as good as his word, just as his uncle had been. Seeing I had no horse—I left the bicycle back in our time—he swept me off my feet and onto his horse behind him. The horse broke into a brisk trot, trying to escape. We rode to Carlisle. Mercifully they found me a room where I could be on my own.

"They let me eat in my room—I slobbered over half a pig. And I ate the lot. There was such a hunger eating at me that I had finished it before I realised what I was doing.

"The next day they arranged a carriage to take me south. A cart would have done just as well.

"And so we rode down, by easy stages, to Camelot, or to the Camelot of that particular time, because it did tend to move around a bit. We skifted here and there to get to where we had to go, and each time Arthur and Gawain fought an enemy or rescued a traveller, they would bring me a glove, or a scarf, or some other token of their victory, as if I were some great and noble lady, and not a reeking half-carcass of foul meat.

"Gawain insisted on the fullest preparations for a wedding. He had had ladies before, but none became his wife. I kept myself in strict seclusion until the day came. I didn't want people talking about me and gloating over me, and, if the truth be told, I wanted to keep the shame of such a creature away from Gawain as long as I could.

"And so the day came. I was dressed up in the purest white samite, which is a material that they were fond of. But no sooner did I put it on, than my sores and wounds started to pump out pus, and huge sweat weals began to form around every joint.

"A huge gasp went up from the crowd when they saw me. They were expecting to gasp, since it's only polite to pretend that the person who is getting married is the most beautiful, the most ravishing creature in the world. But they didn't gasp for that reason. I heard afterwards that some of them were physically sick, while others laughed out loud, believing that I was the comic relief, sent ahead to offset the beauty of Gawain's true queen.

"I hated everything about that day. I hated the procession, I hated the ceremony, I hated the guests who watched me gulp down wine and throw food over myself as if I'd never eaten before. Most of all I hated myself for forcing it on another human being."

"Then why didn't you stop?" said Scott.

"Stop? Scott, haven't you realised what things are like here, in skift-time? Once you have started something you cannot simply stop. Once a promise is made, it cannot be easily broken. If I had tried, Gawain would have been shamed for life. A knight who breaks his word is worth nothing. Do not forget that.

"The dreary day dragged on to its conclusion. But most of all I dreaded the night—"

"But didn't you know what would happen, once the marriage had taken place?"

"Know? How should I know? All I had was the curse of Morgaine. The curse of Morgaine, and a half-remembered story which might have been my tale or might have been someone else's, or might have been a fabrication to conceal a wretched truth.

"It was not until we were alone, in the wedding chamber, and he planted a kiss on my foul forehead, and turned away because even he could no longer bear to look—it was not until then that the truth began to dawn.

"As he turned away, I felt the weariness fall from by arms and my legs. My back began to straighten. My skin tingled. My lips became soft. My throat, which was raw with croaking, was soothed. Then I knew in my bones that that story had become my story. But there was one de-tail left incomplete.

"Gawain turned back to me. He summoned up the courage from some deep place to try once more to show love to this filthy thing he had married. When he saw me, I could see many thoughts cross his mind. I could see that he longed to have what he saw, not what he had married. But his honour held him even then, and he told me to leave and let him have his wife.

"And so I gave him the final choice—the choice on which the story turns. Would he have me fair by day but foul by night, or fair by night and foul by day.

"And he, for his part, gave the choice back to me, and so the curse was broken."

She stopped, and looked out of the window. The sun was beginning to fall, reflected in the moat, enriching the red stone of the castle with a glow like fire.

"Is that what women really want?" said Scott. "The choice?"

"How should I know?" she replied. "It was what this woman wanted at that particular moment. But do all women want that above all things? Who can say?"

"And did you live with Gawain, as his wife?"

"I did."

"And was he everything that you dreamed of?"

"My son, no man is that—nor no woman neither. Do not forget that, if you should one day marry. No woman stays fooled for very long once they are married, though some men do. Marriage cuts heroes down to size."

"And what happened then? Why didn't you stay together?"

"Scott, Scott," she said, and sighed. "I left him because of you. When I knew that you were going to be born, I sat at my window in my tower for many days, considering. Your father was away on a ridiculous quest, from which there was little chance that he would return. And then word came back to me, through one of Morgaine's people who I still saw from time to time, that he had denied me and fallen into the arms of another woman.

"It was like waking up from a long dream. I knew then that I was not part of this world, and never had been. And I did not want my child— son or daughter—to be part of it. So I set off at dead of night, following a skift trail through the snow, and many bitter winter days, through Alfred's time, and Harald's time, the days of King John, and the Black Death. I twice escaped being burned as a witch, and once as a heretic, and as a Catholic, and as a Protestant. I was robbed in Queen Ann's time, and jailed as a thief in Victoria's. They tried to intern me as a German in the Great War, and to recruit me as a spy in the Second.

"But eventually I found my way back to our time. I had been away for five years, and neither the police nor social services ever believed any of the stories I told them."

"What did you tell them?"

"I said I'd been backpacking in Australia. If I'd told them the truth they would have had me permanently locked up."

"And did you tell Gawain that you were leaving?"

"I left him a letter. Explaining everything, and leaving the strictest instructions that he was never to come looking for me. But I didn't really believe that he would anyway."

"But he did come."

"Yes, he did. Twelve years later. And he brought a heap of trouble with him, as errant husbands do, when they return."

"But you were the one who left him."

"I did. But I stayed faithful to him even when I left him, and never went looking for another. You can ask him the same question, if you like."

"And what kind of trouble did he bring?"

"What kind? The day after he arrived, Morgaine's people came to me at the University. They told me that they had left me alone because I had relinquished all contact with skifters and skifting. But now—they said—I was using the University computers to research skifting. This was completely untrue—"

Scott gulped inwardly. He remembered vividly logging in as his mother to search for 'skifting'. Was all this, then, his fault?

"—but they said I needed to relearn where my true loyalties lie. So they brought me here to this castle. I don't know what year we are in, but by the look of it, we must be late, perhaps the fifteen-hundreds—"

"It is Stephen and Mathilda's time," said Scott.

His mother looked at him, and frowned.

"Not to mention the disastrous trouble he has brought on my son by taking him skifting and then abandoning him in some god-forsaken century. But you are quite wrong, Scott. The castles in Stephen and Mathilda's time were primitive things. Little more than mounds with a single tower, or perhaps a keep and curtain wall. This castle has a moat, and a portcullis, and a drawbridge, and many towers and bastions."

"But it is Stephen and Mathilda's time," said Scott.

She looked at him again.

"You've grown up five years in as many days, Scott. I've heard that skifting can do that. Have it your own way, then. But either you are not in the time you think you are, or this castle is hundreds of years early."

"Couldn't Morgaine have brought it here?"

"A million tonnes of dressed stone? I think not. But, Scott, tell me about your adventures. I will try to listen like the admiring lady I was sent here to be, and not like the mother who is furious at her ex-husband's foolishness, and her son's."

Scott told her, in fewer, but more rambling words, about his adventures since setting off from Stechford eight hundred years in the future.

She occasionally interrupted him, and filled in parts of the story that he did not himself understand.

"Ah, Sir Richard Lovelace. He was a famous poet—perhaps more famous for what he might have written. He fought for King Charles, you know," she said. And later: "Marie de France? Yes, I knew her. And she guessed that you were my son. So you did not recognise your own mother when she told my story? Guy of Warwick, though, teaching mathematics at your school? I would never have let you go there if I'd known it." And later still: "A night in a haunted church? It seems strange that Sir Guy would send you there. And they gave you Cortayse? It was cheap at the price."

She was especially interested in all the things that Gawain had done and said, but she looked out of the window whenever she asked about him, so Scott could not see her face.

By the time they were finished, the sun was sinking across the low hills. The sky had emptied of clouds, and the stars were coming out.

Then, swiftly, and in as few words as possible, they discussed escape. And this really was the weak point in Scott's plan. He had set off confident that Gawain would be able to arrange a rescue. But, having lost Gawain, there did not seem to be a lot he could actually do.

This slowly dawned on him as they talked, and he began to expect that at any moment his mother would become exasperated with his stupidity—because all he had really done was put himself in the same danger that she was in, whatever that danger was.

For some reason she did not say anything of the kind, only concluding:

"Escape must be something for tomorrow. Tonight there is a great banquet, and the castle will be a blaze of lights. There is no hope of a way out tonight. But tomorrow we may outfox them."

Then she sat up straight, and became business-like.

"Now, Scott, we must quickly concoct some story to explain what we have been doing here the last hours," she said.

"But why?"

"Because Morgaine's deputy, who sent me to you, is expecting to grill both of us about what we spoke of. She will let your tongue run away with you, and she will question me quite carefully. In this way she will hope to discover if I can now be trusted, and if you are a person of significance."

"What do you mean by significance?"

"There is a Perceval in the Arthur stories. Your middle name is from his name. But nobody in our skift-time has yet met this Perceval. Some stories make him the greatest of all Arthur's knights, although others make him no more than a bystander. She will want to know if you are this Perceval, and if you are, what kind of Perceval you will be."

"And am I?"

"Not if I have anything to do with it."

"What's our story, then?" said Scott.

"Let us say that you have told me your story, just as you told it now. And I have teased you, and tested you, to see if you are the Perceval of the stories. But you have refused to give any such answer, and have instead tried to turn the conversation to compliments about my hair, and my eyes."

"What kind of compliments?" said Scott.

His mother shook her head in disbelief.

"Scott, I may no longer be quite the woman I was seventeen years ago. But you have sat for three hours with a woman who was once called the most beautiful in the world. Surely even you can think of something?"

12 Mortain

They stood at the bottom of the steps into the great hall. The sun had sunk beyond the horizon, leaving the sky glowing with its last light. The courtyard was lit with many torches, dancing in the eyes and faces of fair folk who thronged up to the feast.

Scott saw many ladies, and also knights and squires, old lords and young princes. One in particular he noticed: black-haired, hawk-nosed, thin of face but with powerful, piercing eyes.

His mother squeezed his hand.

"Medraut," she said. And he took it as a warning.

The guests were led one by one to heavy oak tables, set with a dazzling array of gold and silver, candlesticks, chalices, salvers, and many other items for which Scott—bizarrely—knew the names, but could not guess the purpose. There were torches in sconces and fires in braziers, and a great fire as large as a bonfire, sending sparks upwards, dying as they flew. Musicians played from a gallery, and jesters and tumblers and conjurors conjured and tumbled and jested in the aisles.

The hall was immense, reaching further upwards than the light could reveal. Scott did not count, but he thought there must be at least a thousand at the feast. It was in every way far grander, more sumptuous, more thrilling and more perfect than the banquet at Warwick.

This time he was not led to the high table. There were other guests present more important than he. But neither was he allowed to sit with his mother. Instead he was given a place at a table near the front. Two ladies sat beside him on either side, and one opposite. Diagonally on the left was a perfectly preened young man, perhaps twenty years old. Diagonally on the right was an older man in a black gown. He had a stern, sour face, and Scott did not much want to talk to him. The ladies around him were a few years older than he was, he thought.

A hush fell over the assembly. The musicians quieted, the tumblers fell silently to their feet. A tall man stood up at the high table, and pronounced a blessing in Latin. Scott gathered only the vaguest impression of what the words meant, and he took this to mean that the man pronouncing them was only marginally interested in what he said.

Gongs sounded, and with a crackle of trumpets and the booming of kettle drums, the first course was brought in.

It was soup, and it took a long time to serve.

"Are you the knight errant we have heard so much about?" said the lady opposite him. She leaned forwards, and her long golden hair seemed to float in the torch-light.

"Yes, are you the Chevalier-Desconnu, of whom we have heard?" said the lady to his right. She had jet black hair, which swept down to her waist, and seemed to flow like dark water. No light escaped it.

"Is it true you overcame ghosts?" said the lady to his left. She had hair which was neither dark nor light, but shone like copper, reflecting the firelight. She seemed the youngest of the three, but she had very deep eyes, deep green-brown, and he felt them boring into him.

"My ladies," he said, "I know nothing of such jests. I am but a poor traveller who has come seeking solace in your home. And if any such things became me, then I remember them as little more than a dream. Perhaps it was my dream of which you heard?"

Neither the young man opposite on the left nor the older man seemed particularly pleased with the attention Scott was getting.

"What need have we to fight with ghosts in these times?" said the older man. "It's the living we should fear. This very day I fought off four who came plundering as I rode along the way."

"You fought four men?" said the lady beside him. Her eyes seemed to open wide in wonder and adoration. But Scott saw, or thought he saw, a smile flit across her lips before she said it, and her eyebrows flickered upwards. Out of the corner of his eye he saw the ladies to his left and right return the smile.

"Four men?" joined in the lady to Scott's right. "Surely you are a master of the blade? Tell us by what means you dealt with four? Did you strike one first, and with the backstroke take the head of the second, throwing up your shield to take the blows of the third and fourth, and hurling them backwards to take their heads at your leisure as they lay prone?"

"They lived, yet, when I left them," said the man, shortly.

"I fought five, this very week," said the perfectly preened young man. He had a high voice, which squeaked a little, and whenever he squeaked, his fingers pointed involuntarily upwards. Scott bit his lip and tried not to laugh.

"Five?" said the first lady, turning to him from the older man.

"You are a greater master of the blade than our friend here. But, say, friends, what are your names? For surely we have heard of you?"

"Sir Jean Mortain," said the younger man. "Sir Mortimer fitz Mortimer," said the older man.

"And we are Blaise, Blanche and Benia," said the lady, pointing to herself, and the lady with the dark hair, and the lady with the chestnut hair each in turn.

"And your name, our young chevalier?" said Benia. "Or do you rest with the name of Chevalier Desconnu?"

Scott smiled, and shook his head.

"But it is said to me that you are the truest master of blade," said Blanche. "I have it from Marie of France that you move like the wind and your sword is a sliver of lightning. Is it not so, for she has seen you practising?"

Scott shook his head again.

"Every swordsmen is a master in practice," said Mortimer. "But when a man faces death, his true worth can be better accounted."

"It is even so," said Jean Mortain. "No man who has not risked his life should dare to measure himself with one who has."

"A wise thought," said Blaise. "And we who are but weak women can know little of the ways of warriors. So tell us, Jean Mortain, tell us of your battles, of your skirmishes and fights."

Mortain seemed to be a little taken aback by this. He pursed his lips and pushed his fingers together.

"Ask him not for tales of battles," said Mortimer, leaning across the table and scowling. "But you young fellow," he said to Scott, not unkindly. "You say little, which befits your age. Where have you come from and where are you going, and whose son are you?"

"The Chevalier has made a vow to be a warrior unknown," said Benia, before Scott had a chance to speak. She laid her hand on his, and a little thrill, like electricity, seemed to pass between them. "He is surely son of a mighty and most noble warrior. A prince, or perhaps a king. See you not how he gently parries each of our questions, yet in full courtesy?"

"Well I think a man should say who he is," said Mortain, his voice rising even higher than before.

"Humph," grunted Mortimer. "Sometimes a man does better to say nothing at all."

Scott thought Mortimer might have more to say, but at that moment the soup arrived. It was followed by strong wine, which Scott did not touch. Nonetheless, the wine clearly had its effect on Mortimer and Mortain. Mortimer's mood mellowed, and more wine eventually sent him into a kind of doze. But it had the opposite effect on Mortain.

At first it made him garrulous. He began to tell funny stories. Scott noticed that Blaise, Blanche and Benia each pretended at first to laugh, but as the stories went on, cut the laughter short, so that it was clear that they were mocking. Mortain did not notice at once, and when he did, he did not seem to know what to do. He spoke more quickly, rushing from one story to the next, and his voice became louder.

His final story met with nothing but blank silence. Not only from his three tormentors, but from the entire table, and the tables round about.

The silence lasted perhaps for just a few seconds. But it was a most unwelcome silence in a hall suddenly emptied of talk and laughter.

Then, slowly, like a puppet being pulled up by strings, Mortain rose to his feet. He lifted his cup to his lips, and drained it in one go. Then he turned it upside down and banged it onto the table.

"My ladies, lords, gentlemen of renown," he began, as if he was making a speech. Now every eye was fixed on him, not just from the tables round about, but from the entire hall.

"Renowned gentlemen of renown," he said. "I thank you for your hospitality. I thank you for my supper. I thank you for this castle. I thank you for this wide land of England. We are all here friends. All except one. One except for all here as friends. One mocks. My friends, for your honour, and for my own, and for the honour of these three gallant ladies. And for the honour of this castle. And for the honour of England. And for the King. And for the Empress. And for their uncles and aunts and cousins and relations. For all this, I now challenge, and provoke, and defy, and call a coward, and a knave, and a rascal, and every other kind of thing, the one who sits here mocking us all."

He drew a glove from his belt.

"You, Sir Knight, who will not tell your name. You I challenge."

And he hurled the glove at Scott's face. Scott was so stupefied with the speech that he did not immediately react. But he reacted a moment later when Mortain followed up the glove with the remains of a flagon of wine from the table.

Scott sprang to his feet.

His hair was wringing wet, and the wine stung his eyes.

He saw in an instant the red, furious face of Mortain, and the blank, shocked faces of the people at the tables all around. But he also saw the faces of Blanche, Blaise and Benia. And these faces showed neither shock nor surprise.

It was then that Scott understood that this was exactly the turn of events which they had planned and expected from the very moment that they sat down.

Mortimer stirred himself from his doze.

"Gentlemen," he said, rising slowly to his feet. "We are all shamed by this disturbance at our table. Such shame can only be removed by the trial of combat, I shall stand second for this unknown knight: he seems to me a worthy fellow who keeps his mouth shut when he has nothing to say. Who will stand second for this drunkard?"

Somebody called from one of the other tables that he would, and stepped up to lead Mortain away.

Mortimer went round the table to stand beside Scott.

"Come away, lad," he said. "You cannot remain at the feast now. We will have food sent to your room. I take it you know how to fight? Now is not such a good time to be learning."

He led Scott out of the hall, and down the steps, where they were joined by the servant who had first shown Scott to his tower.

The air was frigid, and the castle reached like a dark hand up into the night. The stars shone very brightly—brighter than Scott had ever seen them. He brushed the hilt of his sword, and wondered how good Mortain was. And he wondered how good he was. He had been playing at sword fights for as long as he could remember. He had worked hard at his fencing. But even in the last few days, he had never really believed that he would be fighting another human being. Sir Guy's words came unbidden into his mind.

At the foot of the tower, Mortimer promised to make the arrangements in the morning, and to rouse him in good time. The servant, torch in hand, led him back up the staircase, and stirred up the fire in the grate. A little later other servants arrived with a huge tray from the feast. Scott was no longer really hungry. He pecked at some goose, which he thought was very fatty, and gave up. Suddenly he felt tired. Without pausing to get undressed, he lay down on the bed and pulled the blankets over him.

Moments later he passed into a deep sleep.

13 BY THE SWORD

Anne Raynall slept little that night. From the day that she had first known that Scott was to be born, this was the day that she had dreaded. A part of her had always known that it was coming.

She had seen Gawain fight a thousand times. With swords long and short, heavy and light, in armour, and without. And she had seen him ride out to battle on a morning, and return, late in the evening, bruised, battered, and dark with blood. Those had been terrible days. But Gawain was already a knight when she first met him, already a skilled warrior, without equal in his day. So she always reminded herself that of all people, he was the most likely to live.

But this was her son. A child. Untrained, except for a few fencing lessons which she had not wanted him to have. She had never seen him fence, but in a single term, what could he have learned?

She paced backwards and forwards. Her first thought was to somehow smuggle Scott out of the castle. In truth she could not have smuggled herself out of the castle, let alone Scott. But, deep down, she knew that they didn't care about Scott either way. They were using him to flush her out—they knew, or guessed a connection between them. If she did something to save Scott, then the connection was proved. And then they would use him to break her, and through her Gawain.

So the only thing to do was to do nothing.

But nothing is often the hardest thing to do, and it is the hardest of all things to do well.

She did not dare keep a candle burning in her room—Anne Raynall knew that there would be many watchful eyes trained on her window. She could not even listen for the slow ticking of the clock, because there were no clocks. All she could do was watch the slow turning of the stars, until the cold light of morning crept like a sliver of silver from across the village, over the castle walls.

The sun rose in gold, and was answered instantly by a thousand reflections from the many facets of the castle windows. And it was the answering reflections that planted in Anne Raynall the seeds of an idea.

Scott's breakfast was waiting for him when he woke. He would have given a lot for a cup of tea and cereal. But there was a bowl of milk, broiled ham, a stewed apple broth, and thick crusty bread. A fire burned brightly in the hearth, and a large copper pot of hot water stood ready for a bath.

He felt wonderfully rested, and enjoyed his breakfast, and his bath, before dressing in fresh, crisp clothes that had been laid out for him.

Last of all, he strapped his sword and scabbard onto his belt. Then he drew it, and felt its weight. It balanced beautifully. Double-edged, razor sharp down both sides, it was thin and finely crafted.

He tried a couple of steps across the room. They had given him high boots, of the kind you can roll up for wading through water, or roll down at other times. The soles were soft, which he thought might give him a better grip if the fight was on stone, but they had no particular tread, which would make things hard if he had to fight on grass. Then he lifted his shield from where the servant had hung it on the wall. It fit snugly, but when he tried to lunge it overbalanced him. Regretfully, he put it back in its place.

It was then that it occurred to him that they were surely expecting him to fight in armour.

He had never worn armour, though he had lifted some up in a museum once. He once heard that in the Crusades, the Saracens defeated the Crusaders by fighting unarmoured with fast, light swords. But he did not much like the idea of fighting in his shirt against a man dressed in steel.

He clenched his teeth, and thought of Sir Guy of Warwick. Purity of heart and a courageous spirit.

He pushed the blade back into the scabbard.

There was a knock at the door.

"Mortimer fitz Mortimer at your service, young sir knight," shouted a voice, and the tall, grim figure of Sir Mortimer pushed its way into the room.

"You've slept well I see," said Mortimer. "That speaks for courage."

Scott nodded.

"I have made the arrangements for the combat. We have marked out a space on the flagstones. There will be weapons set out to choose from, or you may use your own if you wish. I see that you have not come here in harness, nor is there time to find any that would fit you. A shield we can find. For the rest, you must look to your luck."

Scott said nothing.

"I would not want to impugn your honour by offering advice. But you should know that Mortain is no fighter. He was drunk last night, and they taunted him until he broke. Even now his fear works on him. He will seek any advantage, by means fair or foul, and that can be your advantage, if you seize it."

It would have been ten minutes to ten—if Scott had known the time—when Mortimer came to call him to the 'lists', which was the area marked out in the courtyard. This was not the long causeway along which mounted knights would joust with each other, which you can still see if you go to Kenilworth today, but a paved space inside the inner bailey, in front of what—if it had been in its proper time—would have been called the 'Whitehall'.

Somebody had been busy. Raked seating which had stood ready for a spectacle had been turned or moved so that it now stood on all four sides. On one it was set against the wall of an outbuilding, and on the other a high stage or dais had been set up. Banners, flags and pennants hung, flew, or fluttered, as the fitful breeze gusted, guttered, and fell still. A crowd filled the stands, and Scott saw many of the guests from the previous night.

Mortain was waiting at one end. He was dressed from head to toe in mail, and it glinted in the low sunlight.

A hush fell as Scott strode in.

179

"Hear ye, hear ye, hear ye," called a herald. "In the matter of Mortain against the Chevalier Desconnu, let us be of one mind and one accord. The combat shall begin at the third bell. The combatants shall fight until the combat is finished, or else the sun shall set. The combatants shall now choose their weapons, and swear to fight chivalrously, and to the honour of all."

There was a row of weapons laid out on a trestle table in front of the high dais. Scott looked briefly at them, and felt their weight. There was a short pole with a heavy, spiked ball on a chain. He had seen something like it in a book, and guessed it was a 'morning star', which in the right hands could disarm a man and kill him in two blows. There were heavy swords, and long swords, and great two handed swords with hilts a foot long. But all—even the light swords—were too heavy for Scott. He drew his own sword, and showed it to the herald.

"The Chevalier Desconnu will fight with his own weapon," cried the herald.

Scott looked round to see what Mortain was doing.

He had promised himself that nothing that Mortain said or did would bother him or upset him. But something did bother him, very much. Mortain was standing talking to a woman, who seemed to be whispering in his ear, and the woman was Anne Raynall, the Lady Ragnall, his mother.

Then Mortain began to pull off his armour, piece by piece.

The crowd did not exactly laugh, but a whisper of amusement seemed to float around the stands.

Mortain was fully ten minutes taking his armour off. When he was ready, he walked quickly up to the table of weapons. He looked carefully at each one, also testing its weight, and in the end he chose the lightest—a sword scarcely heavier than Scott's own.

"The combatants will fight without armour and with the light swords," called the herald.

As he spoke, Mortain was busy fitting a shield to his arm, but when he saw that the Scott was not doing the same, he hastily put it down.

A bell rang once.

Twice.

Thrice.

Scott raised his blade to his nose, and swept it down past his toes, in the formal salute that was the first thing he had learned in fencing lessons.

Mortain made the same movement—but slowly, clumsily, as if he were not used to it.

There were ten paces between them. Mortain stepped forward. Scott noticed that he was leading with the wrong foot. This of course—although Scott did not know it—is how you move when you are fighting with sword and shield, so that you keep your shield forward. When you fight with just a sword and no shield, you keep the right foot forwards and the left foot back, so that the sword is always between you and your opponent. (All this is the other way round if you are left-handed).

Scott came on guard in the way he had been taught. Left foot at the back, at right angles. Right foot pointing forward. Knees bent. Sword in the position which is called 'sixte', guarding the right side of the body. Other arm held behind to balance.

And then a remarkable thing happened. Mortain stopped, stared at Scott, and then switched his stance, putting the right foot forward, and the left behind. But he did it poorly, leaning forward heavily, so that he was almost hopping on his front foot.

Scott advanced. So did Mortain.

If it had been a fencing match, with masks and protective jackets and blunt weapons, Scott would have immediately stepped, lunged, and—hopefully—hit. But advancing on an enemy who can kill you is a very different game. So Scott took a slow step forward, and stuck his arm out.

Mortain did exactly the same thing.

They were now only the distance of the blades apart.

Scott took a half step nearer. So did Mortain. This brought them into lunging distance, which is the most dangerous distance, because your opponent can hit you in a single motion.

Scott took a half step away. And so did Mortain.

This was now beginning to be a little ridiculous.

Perhaps less than thirty seconds had passed, but it already felt as though they had been messing around all morning.

So Scott stepped in again, and banged his blade against Mortain's. This is called a 'beat', and it should be done as much with the fingers as the wrist, sharply knocking the other blade out of the way. But because Scott's weapon was much heavier than he was used to, he had to make the beat with his whole forearm.

He didn't move Mortain's blade very far, and almost instantly Mortain banged back. It was no more a correct 'beat' than Scott's, but it was the first clash of blades, and the spectators leapt to their feet.

Scott beat again, this time with more control and more confidence. Mortain beat back.

Now a 'beat' is what is called a preparation. That is to say, it is not an attack in itself. Fencers may use a beat to find out what the other person will do, but most often they use it to clear the way for an attack. Scott was perhaps being over cautious with his beat, but he couldn't understand why Mortain did not himself attack.

He stepped back, to get out of harm's way. It was no surprise when Mortain also stepped back.

Something which had been at the back of Scott's mind since they began was his grip on the flag stones. They were quite smooth, with no great gaps between them. They had obviously been swept that morning, and fresh sand scattered. He pushed his feet a little. The grip was nowhere near as good as in the school sports hall, which had a rubberised floor, but it was better than it might have been.

It was time to try something a little more adventurous.

So he stepped in, stuck his arm out, and lunged. It was only a short lunge, not enough to reach, but it was a rapid one for all that.

What Mortain should have done—if he'd had the same lessons that Scott had—was to either step backwards to get out of the way, or to parry the blade, and return the attack, which is called a riposte.

What he actually did was to flail out his own sword, and make a half step, half jump forwards.

The blades passed each other, and Scott's point hovered for a moment an inch from Mortain's chest. Scott was just about to push himself a little further, completing the action and finishing his opponent, when he glanced down, and saw Mortain's own point resting on the cloth of his tunic. If he had moved any further forwards, he would have been dead. Panicking, he pulled himself out of the lunge and sprang backwards. Mortain did the same thing.

Now a plan began to form in Scott's head. It was already completely clear that Mortain was doing only exactly what he was doing himself. More slowly, and more clumsily, but Mortain had more strength and a longer reach. Scott's arm was already beginning to ache with the weight of the weapon. If he did a fast step-lunge, he could be on Mortain and run him through before the other could escape. But if Mortain imitated the move, however slowly, Scott, in killing his enemy, would be killed himself.

He thought quickly.

Then he stepped in, quite slowly. He waited until Mortain had finished his own step, and then he gave his blade a huge beat. It wasn't anything like the kind of beat that a fencing-master would have approved of. He began with an out-swing, which you should never do, before walloping his blade onto Mortain's with all his might.

Mortain did well to hold on to his weapon. Half turning, he grabbed hold of the hilt with his left hand, and with both hands he swung back for an even huger beat-back, easily enough to knock the blade flying out of Scott's hands.

He never made contact.

As Mortain swung, Scott lowered the point so that the other's blow passed entirely above it. Then he brought it back up in a circle, and lunged.

There was no time for Mortain to even try to do the same thing. He saw the point rushing towards him. He flailed helplessly with his own blade, and felt Scott's point pushing onto his jerkin. It was too late to think about parrying, and he did the only thing he could have done—step backwards to get out of the way. But he was already overbalancing from his uncontrolled swing. The step—coupled with the force of Scott's blow, although it had not pierced the leather—was more of a panicked stagger, and, as beautifully as you could wish it, Mortain's body went backwards at twice the speed of his legs, and he toppled over, as neatly as if he had been pole-axed.

And there he lay. He had let go of his sword as he fell, else even sprawling he might have been a dangerous man.

As it was, he was helpless.

Scott pulled himself to his feet. He had over-lunged, and if Mortain had kept his own feet and his weapon, Scott would have been hard-pressed to avoid the riposte. He stood, looking at Mortain, breathing hard.

Mortain did not move.

Very slowly, but quite deliberately, Scott walked up to him, and put his foot on his chest. He was wary of Mortain grabbing hold of his legs, which he had seen in films, but Mortain's hands were wide of his body and they did not move.

He was not quite sure what he should do now. In films, Roman gladiators killed their defeated enemies if the emperor put his thumb up (or in some, if the emperor put his thumb down). He had no intention of killing Mortain, but he did need to find some way of bringing things to a halt.

He need not have worried. The crowd were on their feet again, cheering and stamping. The roar was deafening. He had won.

He stood for a long moment bewildered, and then, slowly, he stepped back, raised his sword to salute his opponent, and lifted his left hand to acknowledge the crowd.

They were still cheering as the herald came to lead him onto the dais. He stood there, facing the multitude, while the chief herald read out a list of his accomplishments. It had been hastily cobbled together from various accounts of his brief adventures, and Scott scarcely recognised himself.

Looking at the crowd gave him an opportunity to see something that he had missed. The outbuilding at the back of the stalls opposite had the tops of arches at its base. And these arches were barred, like a prison. If fact, they clearly were a prison, because at least one prisoner had his head stuck between the bars and was clapping and cheering with the best of them.

But it was a face he knew. Black haired, showing the effects of two days' beard: Gawain.

14 The Enchantresses

And now we must return to Anne Raynall. When she first arrived, she had been bustled through time firmly but not roughly and brought to the castle under cover of darkness. From her arrival they had treated her with deference, and given her the freedom to move around inside the walls, but not outside. She had seen Morgaine only once.

"I am glad to see you again, Anne," Morgaine said.

"Doctor Laufey," she replied.

"Come, Anne," Morgaine went on. "We know each other better than that. I always knew that we would be friends again, one day."

"Are we friends, then?" she said.

"Anne, Anne, that is for you to decide."

"We were not friends last time we met."

Morgaine drew closer, and took her hand.

"Anne, you have grown up while we have been apart. But you have grown colder, too. Do you not remember the first thrill of skifting? Do you not remember the wind on your face when we first rode into Camelot? Can you have forgotten how you jested and—shall we say?—flirted with Arthur's knights, each one a legend, each one a model of perfection for the centuries to come?"

"I remember your curse."

"And by that curse you became part of the legend. Sometimes to go forwards we must first go back. Would Gawain have looked at you, among so many other beautiful faces? Would his heart have stayed true to you even for a day without it? And remember that you betrayed me, which is how you came by that curse."

"And do you not hold that as a grudge against me?" countered Anne.

"A grudge? My dear girl, how cold you are in your new century. The pieces move around the chess board. You were in my way, or I was in yours, and so we fought. But did I move against you in all the years you were with your knight? And was it not you yourself who left him? Did I have a hand in that?"

"Tales say that you did."

"Tales, Anne. How seldom they are true. But you must understand one thing: I am your one true friend in this place, in this time. Everything else you may mistrust. But I, have I ever lied to you?"

"I do not know, Morgaine."

"Then know it now. Or not, as you wish. But, Anne, stay here with us a little while, and be my friend again. For, see, you are quite grown up, and I still have many students. Stay, and teach them, as I taught you. For skift time is moving on, and, young as I seem, I grow old."

They had parted with a show of affection on Morgaine's part, and doubt and questions on Anne's. The doubts and questions became fears when she found her son, unexpectedly, in the tower, and anger when she saw how they had conspired to bring him—as she believed—to his death.

But she still had hope, and, as we earlier heard, in the small hours of the morning, a plan formed in her mind.

Prisoner of a powerful enchantress in a terrible fortress though she was, she was by no means as weak as she perhaps seemed. She was intelligent and resourceful, and her beauty was a thing of legend, even among those who lived daily among legends.

So it was perhaps no surprise that when she chose to sit with Jean Mortain at breakfast that morning, his mind was temporarily distracted from the combat he was about to face.

"You are Jean Mortain," she said. She did not do anything as obvious as flutter her eyelids or twist some strands of hair. But Morgaine's school, in which she had been an apt pupil, had prepared her well for capturing a man's attention. Jean Mortain was not a difficult subject.

186

Before long he was pouring out to her his hopes and fears. He had no idea, of course, that she was the Lady Ragnall of the famous ballad, and he would probably not have believed it if someone had told him. Jean Mortain did not know anything about skifting, and did not believe in King Arthur or any of the others. But he was a young man, and she was a beautiful woman.

"You are very brave, Jean Mortain," she said.

"Brave, my lady?" he said. "My lady is too kind."

"But, no, Jean Mortain," she went on, repeating his name as if she were stroking it. "Last night you challenged a man to combat, knowing him to be a famous warrior, a lightning blade, a man who, they say, has fought with ghosts and driven away wild men. No other dared challenge him, except you alone." She let that sink in, and then went on.

Mortain flushed. He had one of those faces which goes red too easily.

"So, Jean Mortain, I see that you yourself must be a master of the sword, veteran of ten, nay twenty, nay, surely a hundred combats, to dare to match yourself against him."

Mortain blanched—the colour drained from his face as quickly as it had come.

"I am but a humble knight, my lady. I know nothing of ghosts, and wild men, and have fought seldom."

"Then, Jean Mortain, you are all the more courageous for it."

"But—my lady—" and he looked at her with appealing eyes. "He seemed so young, how can one so young be all these things you say?"

"Do not let looks deceive you, Jean Mortain. A lad he may seem to you, but he is one schooled in every art of the sword. His waking moments are dedicated to its practice and perfection. At night he dreams only of the scream of blades. And he knows no fear."

"You know this, my lady?"

"Yesterday afternoon I spent two full hours in his company, and questioned him most closely. He disguised nothing, having no care for his own safety. He is one who longs for battle, and honour, and the praise of men, and fallen foes."

"Then how must I fight such a one, my lady?"

"What had you thought to do, Jean Mortain?"

"He is slight, though tall. I would come at him with a mighty sword, in full armour. I will swing this way and that. If he chooses a heavy sword and heavy armour, he will not be able to lift them. And if he chooses the light sword, I shall knock it from his hands."

"Mmm," said Anne Raynall, pressing her hands together and pursing her lips.

"What does my lady mean?"

"I have heard that, in the Holy Land, our Knights go in full armour and with swords that can break through stones or bend iron. But they are defeated by the Seljut Turks, who ride swift ponies, wear no armour, and carry the lightest, sharpest of blades."

"And the young man knows this, my lady?"

"I know not, Jean Mortain. But he spoke highly of the Seljut Turks, and expressed the longing to fight against them hand to hand. And I have seen—have you not?—that he carries a sword so light that he can lift it with his fingers. And who has seen him in armour? I have not. It is my belief that you will face him, clumsy in iron, swinging the great weight of a battle-sword until your hand can barely lift it. What will become of you then, I do not know, but I am certain that you will not engage him until he wishes to be engaged, and then on his terms."

"But, my lady, what must I do?"

"As to that, I cannot help you. If I advise you to go in light armour, or in full armour, or in no armour, and with the mace, or the morning-star or the three-chained flail, or the great sword, or the lesser sword, or the small sword—which ever way I advise you, he may choose that which I do not expect. And then your death will be on my head."

"My—my death, my lady?"

"Assuredly, for if you draw blood from him, he will most certainly kill you. No knight has ever drawn his blood and lived, that much is known."

"But, my lady, if you will not advise me, and that lack of advice leads to my... my death, is my—death not then as much on your head as if you had advised me and been wrong?"

"I see your logic, Jean Mortain. But I am but a weak woman, so how should I advise a warrior?"

"My lady!"

"Very well, I will say what I can, though I condemn my own soul. If you wear armour, and he none, then be certain that he has prepared for this, and is ready to show the world how easily a man may be disarmed. But if you wear none, and he wears armour, he will doubtless be showing to the world how, even weighed down with iron, he can outfight you. So, my advice must be this: whatever you see him wear, wear only that. Whatever weapon he takes, take a weapon which is like it. In battle, if he moves forward, do you move forward. If backward, backward. If he attacks, attack in return. That way he cannot gain an advantage."

"But I cannot gain an advantage either, my lady..."

"Jean Mortain, you have pressed me for my unwilling advice. Will you now reject it? But it is all one to me—" she stood up, as if to go. "If you wish to follow your own counsel, it is nothing to me. How foolish I was to even—"

"My lady, no. I have offended you. Forgive me. Forgive me."

"We shall see," she said, and walked slowly, measuredly out of the hall.

Anne had done her work well. Mortain took the trouble to apologise to her several times before the combat began. She watched with wry satisfaction as he went through the ritual of putting his armour on, and then taking it off, in order to obey the letter of her instruction.

She sat to watch at the lower end of the raked seating, but after a few minutes there was a tug at her elbow, and an elaborately dressed messenger requested that she join the ladies at the high seat. So, a few moments later, she found herself beside Morgaine. This she did not like.

Morgaine was nothing if not subtle.

"I hear that you favour the older, Mortain, Anne?"

"I have spoken at length with both, my lady," she replied. "Mortain asked for my advice, and I gave it."

"Ah yes, your advice. You have never been able to hold back from giving advice, Anne. What would you say if I asked for your advice now?"

"On which topic?"

Scott and Mortain were circling each other. Morgaine paused for a moment to watch the first clash.

"I have a man in prison here," she went on. "A knight. One known well to you. What should I do with him?"

"Who is this knight?"

"It is my nephew, your former husband, Gawain."

"Gawain?" said Anne, and made a show of pursing her lips. She wondered if Morgaine knew that he had come to see her in Stechford.

"Yes. It is quite a surprise that, after seventeen years, I should be entertaining you both in my castle. I think for some reason you failed to invite me to your wedding. A small oversight, though I came anyway. But you never visited me, though I saw Gawain, I think, round about the time you left him. I do not believe that I have seen either of you since then. So how would you advise me, now that you have both appeared, quite separately, together?"

It was then that Scott lunged at Mortain, and almost impaled himself on his opponent's weapon. Anne gripped the arms of her chair, then forced herself to relax.

"I should begin by asking why you imprisoned him," she said, forcing her voice to stay calm, "and what you were hoping to gain from it?"

"My dear child, I imprisoned him because I was able to. What more justification would be needed? And what I intend to gain from him is information about my half-brother Arthur."

"And what information is this that you wish to gain?"

"Why, child, his location, his whereabouts, whether he lives or is dead."

Just at that moment Scott made his final move, which sent Mortain sprawling. From Scott's point of view it was clumsy and badly executed. But to the spectators it seemed both fluid and (as it indeed was) successful. Suddenly everyone was on their feet. Partly they were cheering the side that won, and partly because they wanted to see whether the stranger knight was going to chop off Mortain's head, or let him live.

The clapping and cheering went on for a long time, and it gave Anne a space to organise her thoughts.

"Is Arthur then missing?" she said, once the din had subsided.

"Ah, how foolish of me, Anne," said Morgaine. "How could you have known? I wondered perhaps if you had been in contact with people from our side, or from his—but, no… well, listen then. You know that for years I pressed my half-brother to be more fierce in the defence of this realm against the Saxons. If I had had my way there would have been fortresses on every headland, and garrisons on every road, as there were in the days of Rome. But Arthur preferred to constantly send his knights out to seek adventure, and, once Merlin opened the matter of skifting to him, to send them across the centuries, rather than guard our own Britain in our own day. Then, as you know, in the five hundredth year Anno Domini, which was 1253 in the Roman calendar, Arthur fought the first of what were to be twelve battles against the Saxons."

"I remember some of them, but not that there were twelve."

"You left us when they had fought but six. But six more there were, and at the twelfth the Saxon army assembled and marched on Aquae Sulis. We joined full battle on Badon hill. The Saxons were scattered, and the British rode home rejoicing—Arthur's men, and my men, fighting shoulder to shoulder. But Arthur was lost to us."

"Lost to us, Morgaine? Now I know that you play with me. Do you not have him? Did you not take him with you to Avalon, to heal his wounds, and to remain in enchanted sleep until Britain's hour of need? This much is known. Or was that account in error?"

"Clearly, my dear child, it was in error, else I would not be asking the question. But other accounts say that Arthur's reign ended a generation later at Camlann. And then there is the matter of the Grail. All the stories tell us of the Grail quest, yet we who are the central actors have never seen it. Indeed, the young man who just defeated Mortain may well be—though he does not himself yet know it—Perceval of the Grail."

She raised an eyebrow as she said this, and Anne had to concentrate very hard not to react.

"He fights well, don't you think, Anne?"

"His opponent was a fool, Morgaine."

"We shall see. But you have not told me what you think I should do with Gawain. How shall we discover what he knows?"

"We could ask him."

"We could. I will see to it that he dines with you tonight, in your chamber. You may question him there. See to it that you do not fail me."

"And what will you do with the young knight?"

"He too can serve our purpose," said Morgaine. "How do you like my ring?"

She showed Anne a gold finger ring, set with a single opal, which seemed to glow in the sun. The gold was very red, and, for a moment, it put her in mind of another ring of which she had heard but could not quite remember.

"It is very fine," said Anne.

"I shall give it to our young Chevalier. We will see where it leads him."

"A magic ring, Morgaine?"

"A trifle, Anne."

And then she clapped her hands, and said:

"I'm so glad that you have decided to join us again. You will let me know swiftly what Gawain tells you."

That was the sign for Anne to leave. But, as she left, Morgaine called her back for one final word:

"Anne, if you have ever doubted me, then test your Gawain with the tale of how he betrayed you. See if it is I or he you should mistrust."

After luncheon, snow began to fall again. Anne Raynall stood at her window. It was glass—an extraordinary expense and luxury. Through the window she looked out on the mere—a vast expanse of water, a hundred times the size of the castle, grey under the low clouds. In the deepest winter it might perhaps freeze, but for now, the gentle waves silently accepted the gift of snow.

Anne's state of mind was far worse than it had been the previous night. She did not at all like Morgaine's hints. But she had not dared to ask more. She had first planned to spend the afternoon in her room, waiting to see Gawain in the evening. But she quickly realised that her mind was too full of conflicting thoughts and feelings. So, wrapping a thick cloak around her, she set off across the bailey.

She had known Kenilworth castle well in her own century. Even so, it was not necessarily easy to put the ruined buildings of her memory together with the castle of the present, and she felt that this castle was grander, fuller than the 'real' castle of history. Most particularly, she was almost certain that the short, octagonal tower directly ahead of her was not one of the later buildings. There was what is known as a scriptorium at the lowest level, which was a place to write, and to copy manuscripts. The copying of manuscripts meant that there had to be manuscripts, which in turn meant that the upper floors must contain a library of some kind.

She did not at first have any particular purpose in exploring the octagon, but as she approached it, she thought of one book which might interest her very much.

The Scriptorium was largely empty. A fire burned in the grate, and a few candles guttered as she opened the door. Anne looked around casually, and saw that there were just two ladies working nearest the Southern window, where the light was best. She guessed that both were of the age to be doctoral students, and were probably in just the same frame of mind that she had been in all those years ago. The stairs were in the very centre of the room. Rather than walk directly to them, Anne nonchalantly looked around the unfinished manuscripts lying on the desks. But she kept to the north side, so that the staircase was between her and them.

When she was quite sure that they were not looking, she trod softly up the stairs, taking care to make no sound.

The first floor was better lit. Anne was disappointed to see that there were no shelves of books. She was about to continue, when she saw what looked like a chess set on a solitary table, about half-way towards the north wall. It interested her a little, so she stole quietly across the sandstone floor to look at it.

It was the strangest thing.

A normal chess set has sixty four squares, eight rows of eight columns, thirty-two black, and thirty-two white. This set was eight sided, with little trapezoids instead of squares, eight along each side. The number reduced towards the middle, and they were smaller, so that from eight, the board went to seven, to six, to five, and so on, down to one for each side, and a single, octagonal space right in the centre. The colours were white, and black, and green, and red, and the single octagon was blue.

Perhaps you have sometimes seen the curiously ornate chess sets which have models of kings, queens, knights, castles, bishops, and tiny soldiers for pawns. This set was of that kind, except that there were many more pieces, and, when Anne looked closely, the faces were incredibly detailed, and there were names on the bases of the figures.

The pieces were in four colours like the board. The red queen was labelled 'Le Fay', while the white queen was labelled 'Mathilda', and the black king 'Steven'. The game seemed to be a very unbalanced one. The white and black pieces seemed to have a full complement of pawns, bishops, rooks, and so on, but green and red were arranged on different lines. Red had just one castle, a few pawns and one knight. But it had a large number of pieces alongside the queen which seemed to be between the size of a queen and a pawn, although they wore crowns or coronets, and were all of different sizes. The green king was missing from the set, but there were a large number of knights, and the queen was carved with her hands up covering a sorrowful face. One of the green knights was labelled 'Gawain', and this knight was threatened by the red queen and castle.

Anne had a terrible desire to move the green knight out of danger, so much so that she clasped her hands to stop herself reaching over the board.

Looking at the knights, she saw other names that she knew: Kay, Bors, Lancelot, Gareth, Yvain, and many more. But most were near the sides of the board, and seemed to be taking no part in the action.

An hour-glass stood at one side of the board. It was a foot high, and let through one grain of fine sand at a time.

"It might take days for the sand to trickle all the way," she said to herself. Be that as it may, the sand was already half through. She wondered what would happen if she rearranged the pieces, or upset the board, or turned over the hour-glass. Again she clasped her hands to hold herself back.

For the rest, the room, which occupied the entire floor, was empty.

Reluctantly, she returned to the stairway. It was not until she was half way up to the third storey that she saw something else. The floor was marked out in a tight spiral, with other grooves radiating from the centre, all marked in green on the red sandstone. The chess table stood exactly on the spiral. Anne took all this in without understanding it, and without expecting to. But she fixed in her mind for a moment the exact position of the table.

The third floor was the library that she had been looking for.

It was simply furnished—unusually simply for a medieval library. The bookcases, which lined the outer walls, broken only by windows, and made an inner octagon around the staircase, were plain oak. Candles burned in holders at intervals along the shelves. These shelves were lined with books: great, heavy books, a foot high and six inches wide, bound in leather and with pages which, Anne knew, would be made of the thinnest, whitest leather which is called vellum or parchment. Few people have ever handled such books—libraries which own them are careful not to let the public touch them, and the people who are allowed only see them after hundreds of years of heat and cold, and damp, and dry, and book-worms and insects and thousands of hands, themselves long since turned to dust, all dulling the ink, softening the lines, greying the vellum. Anne was one of the fewest, fewest people who had seen, touched and read such manuscripts when they were new. Each one would be a work of art, each one would have cost a year of the life of the man who had copied it. She would have loved to have spent hours taking down these volumes one by one.

She read along the titles as fast as she could. Some of them were well known to her, and were the medieval equivalent of 'best-sellers'—De Civitate Dei, Confessiones, Historia Ecclesiastica. Some were a little more esoteric: De Excidio Brittaniae, and one of her favourites, Sermo Lupi Ad Anglos, next to De Amore—on Love, by one Andreas Capellanus, whose real name was Andrew Chapel. There were other books: De Consolatione Philosophiae, De Administratione, and Historica Calamitatum, the touching story of a diastrous love between a scholar and his pupil. She hesitated for a moment beside the Historica Calamitatum. Surely, if this was Stephen and Mathilda's time, the book could be no more than a few years old, its author either still living or not long in his grave.

Her hands strayed, and a moment later she found herself holding the book, which was tiny compared with the others, and reading, as if for the first time: "Saepe humanos affectus aut provocant aut mittigant amplius exempla quam verba."—"Often a person is stirred—or soothed —more by actual examples than by words."

"It was one of the greatest romances of its age—of any age," she said aloud. And without meaning to, or wishing to, the story of another romance came into her mind, a poem she had read when she was a student, a story that had become her story.

She was sure that that particular book had not been on the shelf, but when she pushed Historica Calamitatum back, there, nestling beside it, was a thin volume, with a simple title: Ragnell.

Her hands trembling, she took it down, and let her eyes glide over the fateful verses.

"Lythe and listenythe the lif of a lord riche"—it began—"wake and listen to the life of a noble lord."

As poetry it was nothing special, but it seemed, at least in parts, to be written down by someone who had seen it first-hand. She had not intended to spend time on it—after all, who knew the story better than she?—but within a few stanzas her eye was caught, and she found herself living again those terrible days. The poet seemed to take particular delight in describing in the smallest detail her eyes, her teeth, her hair, her smell, her terrible manners and hideous voice.

By the middle of the poem she felt sick, but—perhaps because of the power of memory, or perhaps because of the magic of that library —she was unable to stop reading. She reached the wedding, and saw in her mind's eye the choking faces of the courtiers. Her face reddened as the wedding reached its conclusion, and a sort of mist came over her eyes.

Suddenly she found herself committing the ultimate act of sacrilege for a scholar: she was tearing a page out of that priceless manuscript, trying to tear it apart in her hands, but, being leather, it was too supple. She pushed the offending page into the pocket of her dress, and began reading again. Now they were in the bed-chamber, and suddenly, it was the moment when she felt all the age, and the filth, and the hideousness falling from her, and she was beautiful again, more beautiful than she had ever been. A wave of relief, and delight, and triumph rolled over her.

She read to the end, or almost the end. Three lines caught her eye, and held it there, while a single, hot tear welled up, and spilled onto the page below:

"She lyvyd with Sir Gawen butt yerys five
That grevid Gawen alle his lyfe."

From there she followed the poem more swiftly to its finish. The poet was in prison, and asked for God's mercy. She thought of Gawain. Was he, imprisoned, also asking for God's mercy?

She looked up. The sun had set, and there was only the flickering candlelight to see by. How long had she been here?

Too long. Swiftly, she searched now as much with her fingers as with her eyes for one book, which she knew must be there. It was almost the last on the shelf, also very new, a book of home medicines for the wealthy, black-bound, untitled, small enough to be hidden in rafters, because such books could prompt uncomfortable questions about witchcraft.

Fumbling fingers worked to separate the pages, eyes straining in the candlelight, until she found what she needed, on the ninety-first page.

"How to make a drynke that men callen dwale to make a man to slepe while men kerven hem. Take thre sponful of the galle of barrow swine…"

It was an old, old recipe for a draft by which a surgeon could put a man into the deepest of deep sleep.

She tried to fix the ingredients in her mind. Gall…hemlock… neep… lettuce, pape, henbane, and something called eysyl, which was a word she did not know. Neep was bryony, and pape was poppy. Was 'eysyl' perhaps vinegar? She seemed to remember that there was vinegar in dwale…

"Will you be leaving now, my lady?" said a voice from the other end of the aisle. It was a man's voice, a country voice, a workman's or a farmer's.

"Who are you?" she said, snapping the book shut and pushing it back onto the shelf.

"I mean no harm, my lady," said the man. He came a little into the light, and she saw that he was short, and old, with a bushy beard. He had a hammer in one hand, and a fine wood-chisel in the other.

"What is your business here?" she said, imperiously.

"I's Tom, the carver," he said. "I goes wherever there's trade, carving my faces wherever there's wood."

"Faces, what faces?" she said. "Show me!"

"I means no harm, my lady, They call it a 'green man'."

197

He showed her a bushy bearded face, rather like his own, which he had just finished carving at the end of a row of shelves. The carving went more than an inch into the wood, a face surrounded by wooden leaves, twining through its hair, around its ears, under its chin.

"I have seen these before," said Anne, slowly. And then, more sharply: "What do you mean by carving these in this place?"

"I means no harm," he said once again. "Her ladyship lets me come and carve for a while, and then she sends me away. I goes wandering across time and place, and sometimes I comes back and carves more. It's what old Tom does: is carve, and what Tom carves is the green man. That's all there is."

She looked at the carving for a while, reminded of something else.

"Will you be leaving now, my lady?" began Tom again. "It's just I mun blow the candles out."

She nodded and set off down the stairs.

She intended to hurry on down to the Scriptorium, when something on the middle floor caught her eye.

The chess table had moved.

It had not moved far—just one ray further along the spiral. But it had moved.

"Who's there?" she said. "Is there anyone there?"

There was no reply.

She wanted to hurry on out, back to her room, where perhaps Gawain already awaited her. But, once again, she felt compelled to look. Her footsteps were like hammers on stone, and her heart was hammering too. She took in the position almost immediately. The green knight marked 'Gawain', had jumped over another piece to put itself out of the threat of the red queen. And the hourglass had been turned over— it was now almost full at the top, with only the slightest trickle of sand beginning to pile up at the bottom.

Could somebody have come up without her noticing?

She had had enough. Picking up her skirts, she ran back and clattered down the stairway. The Scriptorium was empty. Wrapping her cloak tightly around her, she stepped again into the thickening snow.

15 MORGAINE THE GODDES

Luncheon for Scott was not in the Great Hall, but in the Keep. He had evidently risen in rank as result of the morning's adventure. A trumpet sounded as he entered the hall, and he was led straight to the high table. To his left an imposing knight of enormous size brooded over a flagon of ale. To his right was an empty chair—larger than the others, its heavy wooden arms intricately carved. The midday meal was cold meat, bread, ale, and a kind of pie with a rich crust on the outside, but which seemed to be stew inside.

Light streamed through the southern windows, making the dusty air sparkle in endless swirls. The Keep was a more imposing place than the Great Hall. Fully four storeys high it was, with galleries set at each level. Around the walls a staircase ran, unrailed, a narrow three feet of perilous stone, from one floor to the next. But even in the daylight the highest point of the hall was hidden, shrouded in shadow.

For all the improvement in his status, Scott felt strangely alone. The man on his left hardly said two words, and the chair on his right remained determinedly empty. He was glad enough to eat his fill of pie, though he left the ale and drank only water, but he was more pleased when the trumpet sounded for the finish.

It seemed that he was expected to process out, but only as far as the great door. There, a servant tugged at his arm.

"If my lord pleases, the lady of the castle will see him at this time." There was no menace or threat in the man's voice—but Scott felt, somehow, that this was not an invitation, but a command.

He allowed the servant to lead the way.

They wound their way through many passages, until they came out on one of the galleries which he had seen earlier looking over the hall. The balustrade was richly carved and limned in green and gold, but it was to the flight of steps at the end that Scott's eye was drawn. This was the same narrow stone stairway that he had marvelled at earlier. It was barely wide enough to plant both feet, unrailed, with a fifty foot drop to the floor below, sheer wall on the other, without so much as a hand hold to steady yourself.

He followed the servant along the gallery, and waited for him to lead up the steps. The servant had other ideas.

"My lord will continue alone," he said. "Only the queen's guests may ascend here. I bid you farewell."

Scott eyed the steps. They were smooth, but crisply cut, and with little trace of wear. Clearly this was a path seldom taken.

"Courage," he muttered, and started, as steadily as he could, on the first step.

He knew that he should not look down, but looking up, to the top of the stairs, was almost as bad. In fact, apart from down and up, there was really nowhere to look. The dimly lit stone to the left seemed to push his eyes away, and to look right was to look across the enormous expanse of empty space, dragging his eyes downwads.

He looked at the step five steps ahead, and resolutely set one foot after another.

They were steep steps. He felt he must be half way up when he decided to risk another look at the top. But the top seemed barely nearer. He had an almost uncontrollable urge to turn and look at how many steps he had ascended, but there was no room to turn at all.

The steps were steep. It seemed almost that they were becoming steeper with every one he climbed. Surely they were becoming steeper. He pressed on. Although there was no reason for speed, he felt he wanted to go faster. He had to hold himself back from scrambling from one to the next. And now it was no longer your eye on the step five steps ahead, but four steps, and then three steps.

He climbed into a patch of shadows. Even when his eyes grew accustomed to the light there was little enough to see. Grey stone in grey shadow beside grey wall.

He pressed on. Now he was climbing almost in darkness, each step a huge lifting of the leg and planting of the foot—steadying himself for the pull upwards, not daring to touch the wall in case the impetus pushed him off the stairway altogether.

Bang!

His forehead struck something solid. For a long second he swayed. He started to stagger, he felt the world twisting, he was falling, falling…

He had fallen onto more steps, upwards to his right. For a moment, bewildered, he did not understand. Then it dawned on him that he had reached the next wall, and the staircase had turned right to follow it. Peering around he saw the outlines of a small landing—little more than the size of a sofa, but immense and comforting after the narrowness of the steps.

He steadied himself for a moment, and then turned to face the new flight of steps. He wanted to stay longer on that landing, but he knew that the longer he stayed, the harder it would be to begin again, and begin he must, either onwards or back the way he came, unless he wanted to sit and starve on that ledge.

There was light at the top. This was comforting in many ways. He could make out a doorway, and a second landing.

The climb was easier—perhaps the steps were gentler, or perhaps the light gave him something to aim for.

One step at a time. One step at a time.

The landing was railed on two sides, and the light that spilled from the doorway showed it to be new cut stone. The rails were exquisitely turned metal, glistening with chrysoprase and garnet and malachite. A woman stood in the doorway, the light behind her, so that the silhouette revealed her form but little more.

"Welcome, my young champion," she said. Her voice was soft, with the same strange mixture of Irish, and Welsh, and Scottish that he had noticed in Gawain's.

"Please," she went on, "there are no servants here. You must follow me to my parlour."

She turned. Scott felt the faintest tingling as he crossed the threshold of the doorway—at least, now that he was there he saw that there was no door, only a simple archway into a corridor set with lanterns.

There were doors to the right and to the left, but it was a door straight ahead that the lady opened. Instantly, Scott knew that something very, very wrong was happening. He knew it with the certainty that you sometimes have when you don't know the reason for it, and not knowing the reason makes you all the more sure.

Perhaps it was the quality of the light. It was not daylight, nor was it candlelight, nor was it moonlight, or the light of any of these reflected on snow, nor yet marsh light. All these lights had been around him for days now. This was a harsh light, too white, and yet a thin, greyish white for all that.

Scott felt a tingling again as he crossed that threshold. He blinked for a moment in the brightness, because for all its harsh greyness, this room was lit more brightly than anything he had seen for—well—hundreds of years.

There was an overstuffed leather sofa in one corner of the room, and the walls were covered in grey-green paper. The floor was carpeted with a pile that glistened slightly with the glisten of ... something that seemed terribly familiar.

In the other corner was a desk, and on the desk was an angle-poise lamp, which is a lamp that can be moved into any position with springs, and a small portable typewriter, such as he had seen in a museum. Underneath, in the light of the lamp, was a book, about the size of a school notebook, except it was much thicker. Scott noticed that the open page was a very clear blue, but it was too far to see what it was. Another book, which looked like it might once have belonged on a coffee table, lay next to it.

The woman turned to face him. She had long, copper-coloured hair. Her features were finely made and in their way beautiful, and her eyes were fiery green. But her clothes were grey, plain, austere: tailored jacket and pencil skirt. And, although she was far older, he knew her for the young woman at the feast the night before, who, with her disdainful praise, had taunted Jean Mortain into a fury. Something, though, told him that she did not expect to be recognised.

"You seem surprised, my young knight," she said, and Scott heard her words directly, in what he would almost have called ordinary English. "But surely," she went on, "you have skifted this way and that. Have you not visited this time? It's the time they call 'after the war'. Is it so unfamiliar to you?"

Scott stood silent for a moment. What would happen if he spoke? Would she hear instantly that he was speaking his native language, and know the century he came from? Was there a way to trigger the thought-language, disguising his origins.

"You stand as one dumbfounded," she went on. "Yet, my ladies tell me that you are as gallant a knight as any in the world. But come, sit with me."

Scott thought furiously. When he spoke with his mother, he had slipped naturally into plain English. But when she had begun again in the old tongue, he had followed her as easily. What was the trick...?

"Je suis très content de vous rencontre, madame," he began, stutteringly. He did not know much French, and perhaps this is what saved him. Like a cog clicking into its wheel, he felt something shift in his mind, and the odd echoes of talking while he was talking began again.

"Your ladyship must forgive me," he found himself saying, "but I have not learned your name."

She studied his face for a moment before answering, and then looked away.

"Young chevalier—" she said, and she was back to Middle English. "I am the lady of this house, queen of the twilight world, goddess of battle and love. And I believe you have heard my name: Morgaine La Faye, sister to Arthur who is lost, now protector of Logres and the realm of Britain."

"My lady," said Scott, "your ways are very strange. What is it that you desire of me?"

"Oh, to pass a dull and dreary hour in the pleasant company of my newest champion. To divert myself with the tales of your adventures. Is that not a worthy purpose for one burdened with the weight of state-craft?"

"And this room, my lady, which is from another time, why do you bring me here, and how is it that we have travelled so far and so fast, for I think that this time is far from the time of the castle without?"

"My chevalier, I am Morgaine, and all times are alike to me. The greyness of this place offends you? I have other rooms that lead to other times. And not only other times, but other worlds."

"Is your highness thus so powerful that she keeps worlds locked in rooms?"

Morgaine laughed.

"Perhaps. But I have given my name, would it not be courtesy to give your own?"

"My lady, I am on a quest, and cannot reveal my name."

"Just so. But the tales give your name as Sir Perceval."

"Perceval, my lady, is but a travelling name."

"Perhaps. And perhaps not. Perceval the Grail Knight, Perceval the brave, the perfect knight of Logres. Are you that Perceval, or another?"

"My lady, such I cannot say."

"But tales already follow you. You rode with Gawain, you fought with ghosts, you defeated Mortain with a single blow."

"My lady, tales multiply when truth is scarce."

"A response of great courtesy and modesty. And yet what I have seen with my eyes I cannot forget. Almost you recall Arthur to me, when he was young."

Once again, she looked at Scott very carefully. Scott could not work quite see what she was looking for.

Then she turned away, and was silent for a moment.

"My Chevalier," she said. "I see that I weary you. You have fought for your life this day, while I and my ladies have but idled and marvelled. Shortly we will return to the castle. But first, you must crave a gift."

"A gift, my lady?"

"How could you complete your quest and return to your own time, whenever that may be, and know that you met Morgaine, of whom the centuries whisper, and yet took with you no memento? Come, what is it to be? I have at my command all the worlds of knowledge, and of weapons, of victory in battle, of monumental feats, of exploration, of rulership over mind, and over matter. And of love, my chevalier. Speak only what your heart desires, and it shall be yours."

Scott stood quite still, like a chess player whose hand hovers over a piece, ready to make a move, suddenly seeing the trap he is to fall into.

"Choose, my Chevalier," she said, moving towards him. Her voice was soft and smooth as fine silk, and as she drew closer a smell like cinnamon and the freshness of a mountain wafted over him.

"My young knight—" she was saying, and she was now very close, and he felt the warmth of her breath, and the age faded from her skin, so that she was young, and beautiful.

For a moment—just one moment—he looked into her eyes. In an instant he was almost caught: the desires of men rolled over him. He felt himself drowning in a sea of ambition: power in war, greed for gold, the patient search for hidden knowledge, the dark writing on blank pages of the magician, conquest and domination, the power of love. Each one presented itself in his mind as something bright, and good, and infinitely to be desired. And all the while—all that instant that seemed to last for ever—she was drawing closer to him, so that her body pressed against his.

And then he saw something, deeper, once more something that she had not intended him to see—beneath all the desires that she paraded before him. It was something writhing, twisting and turning, like a flame, like a serpent, like a column of thick smoke. Without knowing what it was, the words of Marie de France about Morgaine came back to him: For to her, in all the world, this was what she most sought—to have mastery over Arthur, her brother, and to rule Logres through him.

He stepped abruptly away.

"My lady," he said. "How can I, who am unworthy, dare to select a gift from all these things? I will ask for one thing only: that you yourself choose with which gift I should leave. That will be enough."

"My Chevalier," she said. Her voice was golden, and she put her arm onto his shoulder. "My young knight, you are yet new in this world of ours, and do not know which way you should choose. I will perhaps one day offer again what I offered to you today. But, for now, I will give you some little thing that will please us both. Give me your sword."

Scott hesitated—then, not knowing how to blankly refuse her, un-buckled the scabbard and gave it to her.

She drew it out, half-way, and ran her finger along its edge.

"You are indeed courageous to have fought Mortain with such a blade. Let me give you another—one that will serve you against man, and against monster."

She pushed the weapon back into its sheath, dangled it, and then let it fall to the floor.

He stooped to pick it up, but she took his hands in hers.

"Let it lie. It is no more than a toy. Come."

Without waiting for yes or no, she led him back into the corridor, and stopped in front of a heavy door. He felt his skin tingling, and it tingled all the more when she put his hand onto the great iron ring that opened it.

"Have no fear, my Chevalier," she said. "Through this door you will find another, and then a third. And beyond the third is a sword, such as few have ever touched. Take it, it is yours. When you have received the sword, you will see another door. Go through it, and take whatever adventure befalls you. Goodbye my Chevalier."

"Will you wait for me at this door, my lady?"

"My Chevalier, there is no way back for you through this door. When you pass through this door, you leave the castle, and this time, and even this world. But you are of great courage, and I know by my arts that we will meet again. Now I bid you farewell."

With those words she kissed his forehead, and turned the iron ring, so that the great catch on the door lifted. But before she let him go through, she did one last thing:

"Stay a moment, friend," she said, "and take this from me." She pushed onto his finger her ring. The band was very slim, and the opal was tiny, and Scott forgot about it almost immediately. If he had known the trouble that it was going to cause, he would have looked for some excuse not to take it. For now, it was the door, and what was beyond, it that troubled him.

With great misgivings, he pushed it open.

16 DWALE

The fire in Anne Raynall's room was a welcome sight after the bitter black and white of night snow. A servant stood ready, and a tray of steaming vegetables and sputtering meat was laid out on the table.

The fire was the only light, so it took her a moment before she made out the form of Gawain, sitting bolt upright in a wooden chair a few feet away. The servant did not ask her where she had been—it was not his place to, and Anne offered him no explanation.

"You may leave us now," she said. The servant bowed his head, and went and stood beside the door. But he did not leave the room, and Anne guessed that he had orders from Morgaine to overhear their conversation.

She looked at Gawain. They had chained his wrists and his ankles to the chair, which made him sit bolt upright.

"Have you no keys for this?" said Anne to the servant, but the servant made no reply.

"Go, quickly," she said, "And call someone who can free this man." Once again, the servant made no reply.

She pursed her lips. Then, heaving, she dragged the heavy wooden table where the food was laid, creaking and scraping across the flag-stones, and pulled a chair beside it, until she could sit with the food to her left and Gawain to her right.

"My lord Gawain," she said, bending her head to his, as if to whisper. Instead she touched his chin, and, feeling something she had not felt for many years, she bent further and planted a long, slow kiss on his lips.

"My lady," he said.

Then, without saying another word, she fed him, morsel by morsel, from the food on the table beside her.

But as she fed him, she mixed in words, and as he ate, smacking his lips and chewing loudly as no knight should, he mixed in replies. And this went quite undetected by the servant, who had been told to listen, but not why.

It would be too tedious to recount that entire conversation, so I will only give you the gist of it. And it was this:

"Gwalchmai," Anne Raynall began. "Morgaine has sent you to me so that I can learn your secrets."

"And will she learn my secrets, if I tell them to you?" said Gawain.

"My love, my lord," she said. "We must trust each other. I am perplexed."

"What troubles you, Anne?" he asked, using her first name, which he seldom did.

Then she told him all about the castle of Kenilworth with its myriad of glazed windows, which should not have been anything more than a wooden fort on an earthen mound. She told him about Scott's adventure with the ghosts, and how he had learned Cortayse, to speak and understand many languages, but could not hold his tongue in any of them. She told him about the duel with Mortain, and how she had tricked Mortain into only doing what Scott did. Then she told him about the chess set in the tower, and how it had moved when she was sure that nobody had moved it. And finally she told him about Morgaine's ring, that we was giving to Scott as she sent him into some dark quest.

Gawain asked many questions, especially about the chapel of ghosts. He had known all along that Scott was his own son. His reaction to Scott's adventures was very different from the reaction of a normal father in our time. He was proud of Scott for having gone so far on his own, and especially proud of the adventure of the haunted chapel. The single-combat did not interest him so much—he felt that she spoilt it by interfering. This might well have caused an argument, but it seemed that Anne Raynall was, at least for the time being, willing to make some allowances.

"Were all of Arthur's knights on the chess-board?" he said.

Anne thought for a moment.

"Most of the usual ones. Some of the later knights were missing."

"Was Perceval on the board?"

"Perceval? No. But Gawain, understand this: our son is not Perceval. As soon as this is over he is going back to the twenty-first century, and he is going to grow up like a normal boy, and he is not coming back to this time or any other time. Ever."

"But Perceval was not on the board."

"No."

"And was the name Scott on the board, or the Chevalier Desconnu, or Desconus, or Hibernius?"

"He seems to have picked up a lot of names. But none of those were on the board."

"And was your name on one of the pieces?"

"I don't know—I only really looked at the knights."

"But you are sure that the green king was not on the board."

"Absolutely sure."

"Then I think I know at least something of what Morgaine is about. I cannot believe that Morgaine's chess set controls our actions. But, I think, by some means, she has managed to mirror or match them. She also follows the movements of Stephen's people and of Mathilda's. But there is one person that she had no knowledge of."

"Scott?"

"Who could have imagined that Scott would come travelling through time, daring strange adventures, and would pitch up at this castle at just this moment? Nobody knows who he is. Is he Perceval? No one can tell her. So the first she does is send you to find out. Does she know that he is your son? Perhaps. Marie de France was with us at the beginning of the journey—I do not know how closely she is in Morgaine's wiles. Has Morgaine received a message from her? She may know, or she may suspect, but that is not what troubles her. What concerns her is not who he was, but who he will become. First she tries to have him killed. Now she sends him away, and she sends you to me to find out what I know of Arthur."

"But why does she need to know about Arthur?"

"Because Scott cannot become Sir Perceval of Logres except by the hand of Arthur."

"But nobody knows where Arthur is, or if he is alive."

"True. And it may be that Scott is not and never will be Sir Perceval. But while he is here among us, he is still the one thing that Morgaine could not reckon on. And of that she must be afraid."

"Then, my lord Gawain, it is time for you and I to leave this place, if we can. We sit here like caged birds, while our son risks his life."

Gawain was bone-tired, but not sleepy, when they led him back to his dungeon. Despite the discomfort of being chained to a chair, and his powerlessness as a prisoner in Morgaine's castle, and the danger to his new-found son, he had enjoyed the evening more than he had enjoyed anything for a very long time.

He knew that his best chance of escape was on the way to somewhere, or on the way back. Chained to the chair in Anne Raynall's room, or in his cell with the door locked and bolted, there was little that could be done. But the castle courtyard was not quite the place for it. In the snow, which made the world as bright as daylight—there was too much chance of being seen. And, just as importantly, his sword, cloak, and various other items that he valued were locked up in the guard room near the dungeon, while his horse was somewhere in the stables. Getting out of the castle at night with a horse would be difficult, but he knew all too well that, once outside, their chances of escaping on foot in the snow and ice were next to none.

Neither the two guards nor the servant who led them had much of a notion of military discipline. The servant wrapped his cloak tightly around him and trudged ahead as fast as he could. The guards lagged a little, prodding Gawain with the butts of their spears.

"Where d'you think they got this one from?" said one, and gave Gawain another prod, making him stumble all the more.

"Beats me," said the other. "Found him in the woods, they said."

"Put up much of a fight, did he?"

"Broke five heads is what I heard, and then he put down his sword and surrendered as quiet as a rabbit."

"Rich, then? They say it's the rich ones who put up a fight then surrender. Afterwards money changes hands, and they're out again. It's your poor merchant or traveller who fights tooth and nail."

"I suppose so. Not much fight left in him now, either way."

"You're right there."

But they weren't.

The guardroom was on a lower level, with a narrow door at the top and stone steps leading down. The door was wide enough only for one person, so the servant waited outside for the guards to lead in the prisoner.

At the top of the steps, Gawain hesitated, and lurched as if he was going to be sick. The guard behind him did not want to stay in the cold longer than he had to, so he gave him a shove that would probably have sent him hurtling down if he had not been ready.

But he was ready.

Grabbing hold of the man's belt as if to steady himself, he pulled him off balance, twisted out of the way, and sent him flying down the stairs to land in a moaning, injured heap at the bottom.

The other guard rushed to help, making a really vicious elbow jab at Gawain's face as he went. This was a mistake. Gawain grabbed the elbow, turned the man against the wall, and then, with a long, slow kick to the stomach, sent him tumbling down the stairs to land on his fellow at the bottom.

The servant had not yet realised what was happening.

"What are you—ow—no—stop it—that's not funny—" he said as Gawain pulled him through the doorway and rolled him over the wrought iron banister, leaving him hanging on for dear life.

He was still squealing and squawking as Gawain closed the door behind them and turned the key. He did not want to be disturbed until he was quite ready.

There should have been other guards on duty to come and help the two at the bottom. But, as is the way of these things, they had got into a game which involved beer, dice, and copper coins, and they had no intention of leaving it no matter what noise their comrades were making on the stairs.

They did not pay much more attention when someone in a long cloak wearing a guard's helmet slipped into the room where they were playing, picked up a few things, took them outside, and came back for

211

the massive bunch of keys that were lying on the table. The slamming of the door was enough to give one of them a start. But he looked up only in time to hear the sound of the key turning. It was too late.

As for their friends, Gawain dragged them into his own cell, while the servant hung desperately to the bannister. In truth the drop was not a huge one, and he could have quite safely let himself down and raised the alarm. But he was not the sort of person that naturally takes risks. By the time Gawain pulled him back onto the stairs, he was willing to do whatever he was told.

"Where are the horses?" demanded Gawain.

"In the stables, my lord," said the servant desperately. "My lord's horse is in the stables nearest the gatehouse," he gabbled. "They are not locked, but a stable hand keeps watch."

"But my lord is not thinking of escaping through the gatehouse?" he said in horror. "The gates are locked and guarded, and none may enter or leave during the hours of darkness by my lady Morgaine's sternest decree. And there is a portcullis, which can be dropped at a moment's notice, severing a man's limbs or crushing his steed…"

He carried on talking, very rapidly, in much the same way, while Gawain locked him in with the two guards. But he left them a flagon of ale and a loaf of bread, and so they probably passed the night as comfortably as they would have done anywhere else. But they would face the wrath of Morgaine in the morning, and the fear of it was enough to keep the servant, if no one else, awake until the first cold fingers of dawn came sliding through the iron grill that served as a window.

Gawain was a good twenty minutes saddling his horse and another, a snow-white mare. The stable-hand was nowhere to be seen. He was curled up high in the hayloft, drowsing in the warm air and the smell of horses, nestling against the world's bitter cold.

Anne Raynall, too, had been busy. She had chosen warm winter boots, and a thick dress, and sturdy riding gloves, and a deep red cloak with a white fur lining, which she put on inside out. As soon as Gawain's guards were out of sight, she set off across the courtyard to the gatehouse. It would have been a very attentive watcher who saw that figure cloaked in white against the snow.

Underneath the gatehouse was a cellar. Anne had already spent a little time looking around it, and there were two things that she particularly wanted. One of these, tucked in a far corner, was a cask of mead, which is a strong drink made from honey and water. Somebody had broken open the cask, and there was a copper flagon standing beside it. Anne looked inside the cask. It seemed that a mouse had climbed in and drowned. It was floating upside down, paws splayed. The mead was probably strong enough to sterilise the mouse, but it was not the sort of thing you would have wanted to drink. Anne had no intention of drinking it herself.

She quietly filled the flagon, and then pulled down a small casket which was gathering dust on a shelf high above it. She opened it, and instantly her eyes began to water. In tiny compartments, here were herbs and spices worth their weight in gold in the winter of Stephen's England. The casket contained two trays. The first was ginger and caraway and cardamom and cloves and cumin and juniper and saffron and anise and cinnamon and galangal and myrtle and fenugreek. Long miles they had come, from India, through Byzantium, over the Alpine passes and up the winding roads of France. Nothing for her there. Underneath, the second tray was what she sought: hemlock, white bryony, mandrake, henbane, laurel, toadstool, valerian, foxglove, aconite, yew, holly berries, and in the last compartment, the precious seeds of the opium poppy.

There was a tiny measuring spoon clipped inside the lid. With it, she measured out hemlock, henbane and poppy seeds into a pestle which stood on a lower shelf, and ground them up with a mortar. She looked carefully around the shelves, but could see no sign of gall. The other ingredients from the book, she was fairly sure, were harmless and ineffectual.

She tipped the contents of the pestle into the flagon of mead, and, wrapping a rag around her hand, she held it into the flame of a torch which gave the cellar its light. There was a swift, choking smell as whatever was on the bottom of the flagon burned off, and then, for a while, nothing, except the rag around her hand becoming hot. As it became almost too hot to hold, she heard the crackling, popping sound as the mixture began to boil. When it was ready, she took it out into the snow, cooling it swiftly.

Then she made her way up the staircase to the first floor, towards the voices and laughter of the gate guards. These guards took their job more seriously than those of the dungeon. They stood to attention when Anne entered, although they relaxed when they saw the flagon of mead.

"Captain, my lady Morgaine bids you good cheer on this grim night," she said, placing the flagon on the table near the man who seemed to be in charge.

"My lady," said the captain, "your lady is most generous. I drink her health—" and he took a tankard from the table, poured himself a good measure, and then held out the flagon for the sea of hands that were suddenly thrusting their cups at him "—as do my men."

They did not fall asleep straight away. She stood, smiling gently. First their conversation became lively, and then extremely odd, and finally their voices slowed, while one by one, their heads drooped to the table.

It took her a long time to slowly winch up the portcullis. It was held by two great chains, drawn through pulleys to a huge wheel, with spokes for handles, like the wheel of a sailing ship. She had first to draw one up a few inches before changing to the other, and then returning to the first. The drawbridge was an easier matter. It was balanced on counter weights, and lowered to the softest touch.

Ten minutes later, Gawain and Anne Raynall rode out of the gates together, into the snowy night under a clear, inky black sky. The stars and moon shone down brightly on them.

They rode very quietly until they were among the trees, out of sight of the castle. Then they spurred their horses on to a canter, going south and east, following much the same path that Gawain had followed with Scott just five days before. They hurried on for four miles, before slackening, first to a trot, and finally to a halt at the edge of thick woods.

"What do we do now?" said Anne.

"We are near a place called Guy's Cliff," said Gawain. "There is, or will be, a hermitage there. There may be a hermit, or it may be deserted. But there was also a mill, which was here in Saxon times, and was certainly here a few hundred years later. The miller may give us a place to stay for the night, for gold, if not for love."

He dismounted and led the horses through the trees. After a while he stopped to look up. The field of stars was no longer to be seen. Instead, clouds scudded across the sky, covering the moon. Snow was falling again.

After a while they reached a tiny hump-backed bridge over a river. The air was filled with the sound of water, which went rushing under the bridge, churned brown and swollen with flooding. It was built at the river's narrowest point, before it spread into a wide pool. Across the water was a long, low building with a shallow sloping roof. It was a water mill, the huge wheel heavy with snow. But there were no lights, and no smoke from the low chimney. The door hung half on its hinges, and snow had blown inside. It was an abandoned and desolate place.

"This doesn't seem much," said Anne.

"It is shelter, and it will keep us safe from prying eyes, at least for a while," said Gawain, but his voice was uneasy.

17 THE GOLDEN HILT

Scott found himself in total darkness. The air was cold, and damp.
The door boomed shut behind him, sending echoes rattling and
scurrying through the blackness.

He reached forward. On the left he felt nothing, but on the right he
brushed against a wall of some kind. He turned to face it, running fin-
ger-tips across the surface. Not quite a wall—something smoother, but
less even. A cave, perhaps? He had once been in a cave with the school.
They had had to put on hard hats, which he thought was silly until he
banged his head against low rocks more than a dozen times. If this was
something like that, the floor might drop away suddenly, or the roof
might become a wall. Neither were chances he much wanted to take.

Very slowly, he turned round. With his back to the wall, he felt ahead
with his right foot for the ground underneath, and with his fingers for
the roof above. The floor was solid enough, but his groping hand did
not find a ceiling.

He edged slowly along, until, after what might have been an hour, or
might have been ten minutes, a wall crossed his path. He felt around
it, and guessed that it made a right-angle. Right-angles were encouraging, because they suggested construction. So he turned and felt his
way along until he came to a lintel, and beyond that the wooden frame
of a door.

His senses were sharpened by the darkness. The door within the
frame was rough wood, but smoothed as if with much use. There was a
faint smell—no, it was gone. After a moment he found an iron ring,

gnarled, rough, he imagined it being black, wrought iron. Should he open the door, or continue to explore?

A sudden gust of air. Something very large, bellowing and snuffling, rushed past him on hoofed feet. His hand froze on the ring. He wanted very, very much to tell himself that it was a bull, or a cow. But his mind went back to the bull-headed figure in Oliver's time. There was a heavy smell of fat, and incense, and something he could not quite place. He did not like it at all.

He did not have long to think about it: the sound of hoofed feet was returning, sending echoes along the tunnel.

Biting his lip, he turned the ring and pushed the door open.

The new room was less dark than the cave. It was grey and dirty, and light streamed dimly from a high place, cutting a shaft through spiralling dust.

He stepped quickly through.

Crack!

His right boot went straight through a rotten plank and he overbal-anced, which sent him sprawling into a wooden rail that gave way under his weight, sending him in turn tumbling onto hard flag-stones.

His first thought was to somehow get back to the door and close it before whatever was in the cave followed him. He tried to stand, but pain shot through his left ankle.

He let out a groan, and looked desperately back.

The door had closed of its own accord. In fact, looking more care-fully—and it was very poor light—the door seemed to have closed right into the wall, leaving no sign of frame, lintel, or threshold.

The plank he had fallen through was part of a low platform, two steps above the stone floor. He saw that he had completely broken the rail, which was splintered in two pieces. He wondered if the longer piece might make a rudimentary crutch, but, when he managed to drag himself back to it, not trusting his weight on his left foot, it was soft and rotten. The wooden planks were in the same condition, though, strangely, they showed no other signs of age: the edges were good and square, as if they had been fitted recently by a carpenter.

His eyes travelled across the room. The source of light was an opening high in the wall, and although the room was dim, the light was too bright to look at. There were no furnishings, but there was another door exactly opposite where he had entered.

He pulled off his boot and rubbed his foot. Wiggling his toes he was able to find the exact spot where it most hurt. His ankle was swollen, and the flesh was soft and puffy. He pulled the boot off and stuffed it into his belt, and tried to stand again. This time it was a little better, and he managed to limp across to the third door.

It too was fitted with an iron ring, and reinforced with heavy iron plates. For the third time, he put his hand to the ring, and turned it.

This time, he waited a moment before going through, which is why he saw something which he would otherwise have missed: the wall had no thickness. On the one side, the door was set into a heavy wooden doorway, made from massive black oak. But from the side, it was thinner than cardboard.

Through the door was a chapel. A heady smell of incense filled the air—though quite different from the smell in the cave—and stone knights lay at rest on old tombs. A knight in partial armour knelt at the rail near the altar, and he was so still that he might have been stone as well. It was lit by the flickering glow of candles, but there was also a dim light, perhaps from a window behind the altar, that gave Scott the impression it was late evening.

Gingerly this time, feeling with his left foot while keeping his weight on the right, Scott slipped through the door and into the chapel. It did not really surprise him when he put his hand out to close it that there was no longer a door to close.

The instant he was inside, Scott knew that this was a place like nowhere else he had ever been. Something pulsed through the air, like an impossibly deep note on a cathedral organ, shaking the floor but barely heard.

"How is your foot?" said a voice. It was a rich, warm voice, neither young nor old. Scott looked around him. The knight at the altar had not moved, but there was no one else.

"My foot?" he said. His voice was trembling.

"When you came in, you limped on one foot. Now, how is your foot?"

Scott tried his weight—the pain was gone. Not gone, leaving a soreness, or a memory of pain, but gone completely, as if there had been no pain. He knelt and put his boot back on.

"Good. I think," said Scott. "Who are you?"

At this the knight turned, but only a little, and Scott saw that he indeed must be the speaker.

"There are no names in this place," said the Knight. "And no pain, no death, no decay. But no life either. Come and kneel with me at this altar."

Softly, because the place he was in was surely sacred, though he did not know quite what 'sacred' was, Scott made his way to the altar rail. He noticed that a shield lay at some distance, and, a little further, a helmet. Both were dented, and glinted in places, as though they had recently been scratched. The knight had a chain-mail hauberk, and Scott saw—with horror—that it was torn in one place, and wet blood glistened from a deep gash.

"You're hurt," he said, as he knelt.

"A deadly wound," said the knight, not as though he were pleading, or afraid, or wanted to impress him, but as if it were a dry fact.

"I must get help," said Scott. "Where can I go?"

"There is no need," said the knight. "Here we are outside time. I feel no pain, and I can last here until the end of the world."

"Oh," said Scott. He did not really know what else to say.

"If I were to leave these walls," said the knight. "I should die swiftly. And when you leave, some of the pain in your foot will return. But, until then, you, and I, may have peace."

"What is this place?" said Scott.

"I do not know its name, if it has one," said the Knight. "But how came you here? Were you seeking me?"

"No, Sir," said Scott. "I was looking for my mother, and I found her in the castle of Morgaine, and Morgaine said that I must go this way."

The knight looked at him strangely for a moment. And then:

"It is well," he said. "It is not yet the time that one should come seeking me. But, this Morgaine, who is she, and is she a friend to you and yours?"

"Morgaine is an enchantress who kidnapped my mother." And then something cleared in Scott's mind, and he said: "But she tricked me into coming into this place, and I am sure she meant my death."

"It is well," said the knight again. "But perhaps Morgaine did not wish your death by sending you here. She had other plans, maybe."

"Please, sir," said Scott. "Will you tell me who you are?"

"I cannot give you my name, nor should you give me yours," said the Knight. "But I will give you something else, if you will give me something."

"I haven't got anything," said Scott. "Morgaine took my sword and said I would find a better one here. And all I have beyond that is the clothes I'm standing in, and they wouldn't fit you."

"Then I must give you two things," said the knight. "But you do have something which I very much want."

"What is that, sir?"

"Your word, as a knight."

"But sir, I'm not a knight."

"We shall see. Reach before you, to what is lying underneath the altar rail. What do you find?"

Scott peered over the rail, and saw the hilt of a sword. A golden hilt, on a long, keen blade, which reflected back the flickering candlelight.

"A sword, sir."

"Give it to me."

Scott lifted it gently, and placed it into the hands of the knight.

Very slowly, the knight rose to his feet. He did it not as if he were stiff, or old, or hurt, but as if he had not practised the movement for a long time.

Taking the blade in his right hand, he touched Scott's left shoulder, then his right, and then the top of his head.

"Arise, Sir Knight," he said. "I dub thee the Unknown Knight, until thou shouldst find thyself in a place where names are used." He smiled, and his tone changed. "And now, since I have given you a gift, I call upon you to swear me an oath, and I require that you swear it on your sword."

"But, Sir, I don't have a sword."

"Let this then be your sword, until such a time as you are able to return it. And may you bear it valourously, and to good fortune. Do you swear?"

"What should I swear, sir?"

"That you will say nothing of this place to anyone, living or dead."

"Yes, sir. I promise. I mean, I swear, by my sword."

"It is well," said the knight, and he remained standing for a long while, as if the experience were a new one, and he wanted to savour it. But, eventually, he knelt again beside Scott, leaving the sword between them, propped up against the altar-rail.

"In a little while you must leave me, my knight," he said. "But first, since it is so long since I have spoken with anyone, tell me of your wanderings, and how in turned times many you have come to this place."

Scott was uncertain about how to begin, but the knight listened patiently, and eventually Scott told his story, much as you have read it here.

The knight was an attentive—and, it seemed, well informed listener— he nodded at the names of Richard Lovelace, and Guy de Beauchamps, and Marie de France, and occasionally made comments such as "He is a good man" or "she has not changed". But Scott did not include his mother's story, nor did he say that Gawain was his father.

The knight stayed silent for a long time after Scott had finished. Normally this would have been strange and embarrassing. But in this place it seemed quite right. He said later that the chapel was a place with all the haste taken out of life.

"You have travelled far and fast for one so young," he said at length. "And there is perhaps more to the story than you have told me, and more than you yet know."

"Can you advise me, sir?" said Scott.

"Advise? I have been away from the shifting world for too long to give advice. Nor was I ever such a one to give it, but rather to receive it. So what can I say? Fear nothing, be always generous, be chivalrous to damsels, treat everyone with courtesy and respect, offer your trust freely, even when you know that it will be abused. Do not keep a count of wrongs done to you, but work always to set right such wrongs as you commit. And remember that it is better to die honourably than to live shamefully, but better than both is to live with honour and in grace. There. I have told you as much as any man should, and perhaps more than I ought. But when we meet again, I shall want to hear the rest of your story."

"When we meet again, sir?"

"Do not doubt it, my Unknown Knight. In this place, or beyond the end of the world, or somewhere in between, as fate and fortune would have it. But, for now, good bye. Goodbye."

His voice faded, and he closed his eyes, bowing his head to continue whatever meditation it was that Scott had first interrupted.

Scott picked up the sword. It was heavy in his hand, but not as heavy as he had imagined, and it balanced beautifully, so that he could make the tiniest circles with only the strength of his fingers. The hilt was wrapped in soft, red leather for a better grip, but the inside of the guard, and the pommel, were golden. He wondered if they were real gold, or gold plated, or simply some metal that looked like gold. There was writing on the blade, but it was in a script that he found hard to make out, and the words appeared to be Latin words which he did not know. He put his finger to the edge, and drew it back almost immediately. A single drop of red blood welled up, and stopped, as if it refused to bleed any further in that holy place.

Scott looked up at the altar. There was a single cross, with the dim evening light behind and above it—light that had not changed all the time they had talked—and a painting in three parts. In the left part people in different kinds of clothes—some Roman, some medieval, some it seemed from Scott's own time—kneeling. In the right part people were standing and cheering, some were knights, and some were ladies, and one appeared to be a modern general, and at least one seemed to be a tramp. But in the centre a lamb stood, glowing with rays of light pouring out of it.

"You should salute before you leave, Scott," said one of the knights from the right of the picture. Scott raised the sword and saluted first the people to the left, and then those at the right, and finally both the lamb and the cross.

"And now you should be on your way," said the tramp. "Time was when I tramped across all of England. And all you need to do to do that is to put one foot in front of the other and keep walking."

"Right," said Scott, a little bewildered by the talking pictures. "Do you know where the scabbard for this sword is?"

"You'll not be finding the scabbard," said one of the ladies. "That much is known."

"Hurry along there, my man," said the General. "No call to be dawdling, what?"

Scott nodded. "Goodbye people in the painting," he said. "And good bye Lamb. And good bye Sir Knight. Goodbye."

Neither the knight, nor the lamb, nor the people replied.

So, balancing the sword over his shoulder as if it were a length of wood, he turned his back to the altar and cast about for a way out.

The chapel—as chapels so often are—was in the shape of a cross. Scott had entered first along the long section, which is called the nave, and he now looked from side to side at the shorter sections, which are called transepts. To the right there was a door, and to the left another. He felt he ought to take the right-hand door.

"But is that right looking towards the altar, or right looking away from it?" he said out loud.

"Take me!" said a voice from the door to his left. "No, take me!" said a voice from the door to his right.

"I am the door that you must take," said the left door. "The other door leads to ruin."

"No, I am the door that you must take," said the right door. "His door leads to ruin."

"You cannot believe him, he always lies," said the left door. "Whereas I always tell the truth."

"He lies," said the right door. "I am the door that tells the truth, he is the liar."

Scott thought for a moment. He had heard of something like this before.

"You must let me ask one question," he said.

"Yes. One question. But only one, and only of one of us," said both doors in unison.

"But there's no point asking him, because he will definitely lie," said the right hand door.

"In saying that he lies," said the left hand door. "That is the only thing you can count on with him—he always lies."

"Quiet," said Scott. He knew more or less what the answer to the riddle was, but he wanted to be absolutely certain. The doors, however, were getting impatient.

"Ask us, ask us, ask us," they chanted in unison.

"I will ask my question of this door," said Scott, pointing to his left.

"You fool!" said the right-hand door.

"Quite right," said the left-hand door.

"My question is this. If I were to ask your brother door which door I should take, what would he say?"

"He would tell you to go through his door, as you already know he would," said the left-hand door, testily. "And he would say it because he is a liar."

"No, no," said the right-hand door. "He is the liar not I."

Scott thought hard for a moment. Sitting safely at home, or wherever you are reading this book, you have probably already worked out what Scott should do. Scott knew too, but it is very different to solve a puzzle in the comfort of your home, or to do it in a strange, sacred, magical and perhaps dangerous chapel.

"If you are the truth-telling door, as you say," said Scott, "then you will have truthfully told me the lie the other door would have told me."

"No, no, he is the liar!" butted in the right-hand door.

"But if you are the lying door, as your brother door insists," he went on, "then you will have lied about the true answer that the other door would have given me. So, therefore, if you are the truthful door, then the answer you have given me is the wrong door, because you have truthfully told me the lie, but if you are the lying door, then the answer you have given me is also the wrong door, because you will have lied to me about the truth. And therefore I must take your door, and not the other door."

"You'll regret it for ever," called out the right-hand door, but Scott was already lifting the latch on the left-hand door.

18 THE TALE IN THE MILL

Snow had drifted into the mill, and there was more snow falling from a hole in the roof. Gawain drew his sword, but the dank smell of ash had already told him what he needed to know.

"What's there?" said Anne.

"Cold smoke," said Gawain. "Weeks old. Nobody here. Not for a long time."

There was a sound of a match striking. The flame guttered up for a moment in Gawain's hand. Anne watched the light moving across the empty darkness until it hovered around an old oil lamp. The wick burned black for a moment, but by some miracle of chance there was enough oil for the flame to catch. It was a very lonely flame.

In its dim light, she saw tables, a cot, a loom, a chair and two stools on the floor, overturned as if a fight had broken them.

"Hello," she called softly. "Is there anyone here?"

"There's no one," said Gawain.

Presently, he found another lamp, and the darkness receded a little.

The horses were champing at the bit and stamping in the snow. Anne led them inside.

Gawain went from window to window—they were empty spaces, not glass—pulling the wooden shutters closed.

"Dare we light a fire?" said Anne.

"It will be a cold night without it," said Gawain. "There is nothing more bitter than winter to the traveller."

"For werre wrathed hym not so much þat wynter nas wors," said Anne—"for war tested him not so much that winter was not worse".

"What's that?" said Gawain.

"It's from a poem. Don't you know it? It's about you. The adventure of Gawain, and of the Green Knight."

"The adventure I remember well," he said. "But not the poem. Who wrote it and when?"

"Nobody knows. Perhaps you will write it, or perhaps I. I often wondered how much of it was true."

"Perhaps you can tell it to me, and I will tell you how much is true," he said.

"But if I tell the tale true, will you truly tell me the truth of it?" she said, playfully. "But, first fire, and then my tale."

I would like to write that within a few moments Gawain had a merry fire burning in the hearth. But anyone who has ever tried to light a fire in an abandoned building in the dead of winter will know that this could not be the case. It was almost an hour—and endless amounts of not quite dry kindling, and endless re-lighting, before Gawain, covered in soot, eyes blinking with smoke, had coaxed enough flame to set a log burning. By this time Anne had reset the tables and the chairs, and brought food out from their saddle-bags, and a pitcher of wine.

"Come, my lord Gawain," she said, looking him up and down. "You are quite the picture of chivalry. I bid you, eat, and I will tell you a tale, after the manner of the ladies of Avalon." And she sat him down on a rough wooden chair, in front of a half-plank table, such as you might find in a garden, rough and covered in dust. But, for all that, she sat him down as if at Arthur's court.

And so the tale began.

I will not give you all of it. It would make this book far, far longer. And you can go to the public library and find a copy for yourself. But I will give you a glimpse of it, because it is important, as you will see.

Gawain did not see and hear the story in quite the way that Scott had seen and heard Marie-France's tale of the Lady Ragnall. Much—if not all—of the tale were things that were in his own memory, some buried very deep. So he experienced it as something like a waking dream.

"The King was at Camelot at Christmas," she began, and instantly Gawain was taken back to that Christmas, his last with Anne before he set off into the wilderness, and before she left him, returning to her own time.

He was in the great hall at Camelot. There were jugglers and musicians and knights and courtiers and ladies fair (one fairer than Guinevere, Arthur's queen), and young lads running errands who hoped to be made squires, and squires standing to attention who hoped to be made knights, and knights from other parts of the country who hoped to be made knights of Logres. And in the centre of the hall, surrounded on all sides by trestle tables, because the place was filled to bursting, was the most famous table of them all, the Round Table of King Arthur. It has been said of this table that no matter how many knights were appointed to it, it would always be big enough. Round it was, so that no knight might have precedence over another, and the names of each knight were written in silver by magic. In this way, news always returned to Camelot the swiftest if a knight should die, because his name would fade from the table as if it had never been.

In those days there were a hundred or so knights, and Arthur sat with Gawain on his right and Kay on his left. The joy of those days came flooding back to Gawain like a sharp agony of pain, because he knew that, without Arthur, they could not return, and he was doomed to be a traveller all the days of his life, searching for a king that all others had forgotten. "For all was this fair folk in her first age, with joy," Anne was saying. But then he lost the words again, and fell back into the dream-story.

Dinner was served—such a dinner as would surpass any dinner of Morgaine's castle, just as hers surpassed Sir Guy's. Those forgotten smells were in his nostrils again. But Arthur would not eat nor his knights, because he had vowed never to begin until some marvel presented itself.

And so it was that, while they were discussing amongst themselves what might occur, a mighty stranger rode into the hall. He was half a giant, if ever there was one, and his horse was a half-giant horse. But it was not his size—nor even the huge axe, razor sharp, that he carried in his right hand—which made them gape. From head to toe, the stranger knight was green. His clothing, his weapons, his hair, his eyes, his skin. He was somewhat like the green men carved in the bookcases of Morgaine's library, and in other places across our tiny world, because ivy and mistletoe seemed to curve around him, and he carried in his left hand a holly stick with red berries.

"Where is the governor of this gang?" he said. He did not shout, or bellow, or raise his voice, but his words were so deep that they shook the ground on which he stood. Everyone was terrified. Everyone except Arthur. He rose to his feet and offered the man food, or fight if he preferred. But the green man laughed.

"Fight? With you, little man? I come but with a Christmas game. There must be a man who will take my game—a simple game, a child's game of tit for tat. Your man shall strike a blow at me, and, later, I shall strike one in return. Come, who will take my game?"

Gawain saw again the shrinking looks of fear and dismay around the hall. He tasted his own fear. He wondered what blow a man could possibly strike that would do this fellow any harm. But something larger than fear took hold of him, because he saw Arthur rising to his feet to accept the challenge.

Arthur! All who knew him loved him. His beard was golden, his eyes tawny, his hair chestnut. With Excalibur, that fabulous sword which he received from the Lady of the Lake, he was invincible to all enemies. Wise in judgement, skilled in strategy, patient in adversity, merciful to his enemies, bountiful to his friends.

And suddenly Gawain found himself standing.

"Give me this quest, my lord Arthur," he said. He remembered saying the words long ago, but in this dream-story he found himself saying them again, just as Scott had found himself speaking first and catching his own meaning afterwards.

So he stood with the giant's axe in his hand. Arthur was urging him to strike true, so that there would be no return blow. He raised the axe above his head, mindful of what it would mean if he were to receive a blow back with that same axe. There was a terrible moment when it shook in his hands over his head, then he brought it down on the giant's neck.

He struck true.

The head went bouncing off the block, rolling around the floor among the legs of the nearest diners. Everyone was too shocked to cheer.

Axe in hand, Gawain stared at the bleeding, headless body.

It twitched. It twitched again. Then it drew itself together, standing up on stiff legs. It strode to the front trestles and picked up its head.

"You have struck well, Sir Gawain," said the head. There was a shriek from somewhere, and someone fainted. "Come to my Green Chapel at New Year, a year from now, and I will give you my return blow. Fail not herein, at your peril."

And, leaping onto the back of his horse, he rode out through the great gates.

There was consternation in the court. Everyone talked at once. Some said one thing, others another. All agreed that Gawain had been cruelly tricked, and was destined to die at the hands of that enchanted knight.

The voice of Anne Raynall paused for a moment. Gawain stared at the flames of the fire. He was like a man caught in a nightmare from which he could not wake, no longer remembering the rest of the story, but doomed to relive it.

When she began to speak again, she was no longer telling the story, but reciting the words of the great poem, line by line.

"Though the end be heavy, have no wonder… a year turns eagerly, and yields never the same, and from its begin to its finish it twists full often… After Christmas comes austere Lent, which tests the flesh with fish and food more simple, but then the weather of the world contends with winter…"

Gawain saw the bustling spring world awaken, clouds rising in the sky, cold dispersing, sheer sheets of rain falling in warm showers on the dark earth. Flowers opened, and the trees put on leaves and buds. Birds hurried to build nests, singing brightly as the soft summer came rushing in with blossoms and blooms on every hedgerow and across wide hills and meadows. Cows lowed in the fields, and the wind blew gently across the land, filling the air with freshness. He smelled new mown grass, and the heavy perfume of lilies. The bright sun burned, drying crops for harvest, hardening the seed. Labourers toiled, working late into the long evenings to bring the harvest home, while the great harvest moon hung low over the dry earth to light the way. The winds blew again, bringing a first rumour of cold. Green leaves turned to brown and fell from the trees. The forest floors became a rich carpet of yellow and ochre and russet and fawn, crackling under a pony's feet.

The last fruit ripened, and fell to earth. Leaves, apples, twigs returned to the soil from which they were born.

"And thus turns the year in yesterday's many, and winter wails again, as the world wants… so Michaelmas morning came with winter's wages, then thinks Gawain full soon of his wearisome voyage…"

It was feast again around the Round Table, and Gawain sat beside Arthur, laughing and joking for the sake of the guests, but even in the laughter his heart ached. The smiles around him, too, were hollow and forced. So he took his leave of his friends, Yvain, and Eric, and Lancelot, and Lionel, and many others. He wandered listlessly around the castle, and went to bed early, and slept fitfully, and rose before dawn and called for his armour.

It was brightly polished, and he put each piece on with great care. When he was ready, he went to bid the king and the court a final farewell. The lords and ladies laughed and cheered, and some clasped and kissed him. And so he mounted Gringolet, and they handed him his shield, which had a five pointed star painted on it, whose points were to remind him of honesty, and fellowship, and purity, and courtesy, and compassion. And, thus arrayed, he spurred his steed and sprang onto the road. He was eager to be gone, but he was not gone so fast that he did not hear sad voices behind him: "He is certain to lose his life," said one, "It would be better if he had gone out to fight a battle, not to lose his life in this Christmas wager," said another.

Gawain rode through the realm of Logres, searching for the Green Chapel. Everywhere he went he questioned the people, but no one could say that they had ever seen such a Green Man, or such a Green Chapel. He took many strange paths, and visited many a dark dell, his heart sinking lower with each new disappointment. He climbed many hills. At every river crossing an enemy stood ready to oppose him, armed with cunning and with magic. He fought serpents, and wolves, and wild men that live in the cliffs, and bulls, and bears, and wild boar, and giants that came stalking him as he rode as a stranger through their lands.

"…for werre wrathed him not so much that wynter nas wors…"—
"…for war tested him not so much that winter was not worse…" and for a moment the words took him back to the firelight, and the mill,

and two horses stamping and snuffling. Faithful Gringolet, old friend of many quests, was flecked with foam as if from a gallop. Did Gringolet, too, relive their darkest adventure? Then he melted back into the wild winter's tale.

Rain fell, and snow, shuddering down from the clouds onto the fallow earth. Sleet froze him, and many nights he slept in his armour, finding a little shelter among the naked rocks, often waking as a new stream found its way from the hills to drench him in icy water. More than once he woke with hard icicles hanging over his head, and so in peril and pain he came to Christmas Eve. Somehow that cheered him, and he rode all morning through a deep forest, with hills on either side and ancient oaks standing together, with hazel and hawthorn and rough, ragged moss. Birds sang pitifully on bare twigs, and trembled in the cold.

But Gawain rode on, thinking of a child born, so many Christmases before, son of a virgin. He reminded himself that he rode to serve that Lord, and he prayed for some shelter, where he could attend the midnight service, and the matins of Christmas morning. And so he prayed as he went, and was reminded of many misdeeds.

And suddenly, where he was sure that there had been none before, a castle rose up before him out of the forest. It was the most beautiful that he had ever seen, set in a spacious park. It shimmered and shone through the oak woods, scarcely two miles away. He spurred Gringolet on, anxious to reach the castle before the vision faded.

Thus he came riding in haste to the moat. But the drawbridge was up, the gates were locked, and men stood at arms on the walls. It was a fortress of sheer stone, fortified in every way, ready to resist an army.

Gawain called to the men on the walls, and a few moments later a porter came to the battlements and asked what he wanted.

"Shelter" said Gawain. Without argument the porter welcomed him, and within moments they were ringing down the drawbridge, and a crowd of squires and knights and ladies opened the gates and welcomed him in. They helped him from his armour, and brought him into a bright hall. They already knew his name, by the devices on his shield and armour. They took care of Gringolet, and treated Gawain like a prince, taking him to their lord.

Clean clothes were brought for him, richly made in silk and cloth of gold. Swiftly they led him to the feast, and gave him a chair nearest the fire. Gawain marvelled at his host, more kingly than Arthur, and his host's lady, more beautiful than Guinevere. There was another lady, too—as old and rough as the other was beautiful and young. They treated her with even greater honour, though Gawain could not see why.

The younger lady smiled, flickering her eyes, touching her lips with the tip of her tongue. Behind him, someone said "This is surely Gawain, the most chivalric, and the most romantic of all knights. What will he show us of love-talking tonight?" The lady's lord inclined his head. Taking it as leave, Gawain went up to the lady and kissed her on the cheek, and took her arm, and said "My lady, let me be your servant, while I can."

Time moved on in an evening full of mirth. Gawain went to bed that night with a glad heart, and slept until the morning. He woke from a long dream, and opened his eyes thinking of Christmas, and all it meant. He went to the service in the chapel, and found himself beside the lovely lady. At luncheon, also, the lord of the castle sat him beside her, while he himself ate with the old woman.

They passed the day, and the next, in innocent delight. Indeed, Gawain stayed with other guests until there were only three days left before the new year.

"This is the greatest honour of my life," said the lord of the castle, "that I have had Gawain at my Christmas feast."

"It is I who am honoured," said Gawain, "but now I must be leaving." With great courtesy the lord tried to persuade him to stay, and in the end, because he pressed him, Gawain told him the story of his quest, and that he must set off once again into the winter to find the Green Chapel.

"But my good fellow," said the lord, "nothing could be simpler. I know this Green Chapel—none better. It is half a morning's ride from here. You must do this: stay here at your ease, forgetting the hardship of winter, laughing and dancing and feasting, until New Year dawns, and then my man shall show you the way—it is not two miles from here."

Then Gawain was glad, and thanked him heartily.

"But there is more," said the lord of the castle. "While you stay, lying at ease, and talking with my wife who will welcome the comfort of your company, I must be about early hunting. So let me make a bargain with you, an exchange of winnings, if you like: whatever you win in the castle during the day, you must give to me in the evening. And whatever I win at hunting, I will give to you as my honoured guest. A sweet swap, to liven up our Christmas days."

And Gawain agreed.

So they ate, and drank, and dallied, and made merry long into the night, and Gawain went to bed with a glad heart, and slept softly through the long hours until dawn and after.

The people of the castle rose early. The lord of that land was about before first light, eating a hasty breakfast, preparing his horses and his many men, opening kennels, blowing bugles. And so they set off, a hundred hunters.

At the first rumour of that quest, the wilderness quaked! They rode like the wild hunt, through hill and dale, taking stags and deer, and filling the forest with the sound of trumpets until the cliffs resounded. And so, with great greyhounds and tireless horses, they drove through the woodland until night began to fall.

Gawain, though, lingered in bed, staring peacefully at the curtains and the rafters, while daylight gently played on the walls.

There was a sound at the door. A small sound, as of someone who tries to enter a room making no noise. Very cautiously, Gawain lifted up the curtain, and saw that it was the lady. She closed the door with silence and secrecy. Gawain was ashamed that he had stayed in bed so long, but he did not know what to do, so he lay down again under the blankets and pretended to sleep, hoping that she would go away.

She did not go away. Instead she walked softly to the bed, pulled up the curtain and crept inside, and stayed there watching to see when he would wake. Gawain did not know what to think, much less to do. She showed no sign of leaving.

He made a show of waking up, and being surprised. But he saw in her face that she was not taken in.

"Good morning, Sir Gawain," she said. "You are a very trusting sleeper, if anyone may slide onto your bed. And now I will stop you getting up, as a punishment."

"Good morning, beautiful one," said Gawain.

And then she began to tease him, and to taunt him, and to tempt him, and she made him offers which were quite inappropriate for a wife to make to her lord's guest, but all the time in such a teasing way that Gawain could not tell if she were serious or not.

Now Gawain was renowned for his courtesy but he could not find a way to rebuff the lovely lady, and send her away. So they fenced and played with words until mid-morning was past. And then she got up to go. But, just as she went, she turned back to him with a twinkle in her eye.

"If I did not know for certain," she said, "I would be certain that you were certainly not Gawain."

"Why?" said Gawain, quite forgetting his courtesy, afraid in case he had in some way failed his reputation.

"The real Gawain could surely not have gone all morning with such a one as me and yet not crave a kiss, as a mark of courtesy."

Gawain had no answer to this, so he took her in his arms and kissed her. And then she took her leave.

Once she was gone, Gawain quickly called the chamberlain and chose his clothes. From there he went at once to the chapel, and knelt before God, and tried to forget the sweet taste of that kiss. But afterwards he went to luncheon, and watched the lovely lady and the old, ugly lady making merry, as if they were sisters.

In the evening the lord of the land rode through the castle gates. He was bloody with the blood from the hunt, and he had already cut up much of the meat. But he called Gawain to him, and solemnly showed him the fresh venison, which is the meat of the deer when caught wild.

"Now, tell me, have I won the game?" he said. "Of a certainty, this is the finest day's hunting I have had at Christmas in seven years. Come. Tell me, what have you won?"

So, unsure of what to do, but seldom at a loss, Gawain stood on tiptoes (the lord of the land was a tall man) and kissed him on the lips.

"This is all I have to give you," he said, "because this is all I gained— a kiss which I now present to you."

The lord of the land laughed loud and long, and so, in friendship, they went at length to supper, and thence each to his own bed.

By the time the cock crowed, the lord of the land had already leaped from his bed, and his men from theirs. With hunt and horns he descended once again on the woodland, this time armed with boar spears, hunting the wildest and most dangerous of woodland game: the wild boar. The boar himself is no hunter, but he is armoured with a thick hide, and has stern tusks, and his way of escape is to charge down the hunter, and woe betide the man who stands in his way, because a boar's tusk will pierce chain armour and gore a man to death.

Thus the hunters were well matched with the hunted. Again and again they brought the boar to bay, and again and again the boar broke out, wounding the hounds, shaking off arrows which bounced harmlessly from his thick hide. Then, at last, when both men and hounds were tired and wounded and longing for home, the lord of the land on a light horse himself chased the boar, and took him on the end of his lance, and himself blew the bugle that signalled the end of the day. And the end of the day it was, for the shadows were lengthening fast, and the sun was dipping behind the hills. Thus, grim, but triumphant, the hunters returned to the castle in the twilight.

Gawain, though, lay long past first light in bed. And the lady came to him again, and teased him, and tested him, and tempted him. But this time he was a little prepared, and so, when she came to leave, he gave her two kisses, but no more. Afterwards Gawain went again to the chapel.

In the evening, when the lord of the land returned, Gawain gave him two kisses, straight on the lips, and the lord gave him the wild boar, which had cost them so much pain. And the lord laughed again, and said:

"By saint Giles, you are the best I know! You will be rich soon, if you carry on with such bargains."

At length, they all went to eat, and to drink, and to make merry through the long winter's evening. But before they went to bed, the lord of the land took Gawain on one side, and said:

"The day after tomorrow is New Year's day, when you must be at the Green Chapel. So tomorrow is the last day of our game. I will once more to hunt, while you must gather your strength. So far I have tested you twice in our game, and I have found you faithful. But 'third time throws best', I think. So, tomorrow we shall see who has won the most."

Once again Gawain slept long and soundly, but the lord of the land was up before first light, taking a morsel after early prayers with his men, and setting out once more into the wild wood to find what there was to find, and to bring it back for Gawain. At length the hounds picked up the scent of a fox, and the huntsmen set off with a will, for though the fox has little to make him worth catching, the skill to take him is greater than for any other animal. And so they followed him through forest and field, over hill and dale. Many times the wily fox doubled back, sending the hounds off on a false scent, and many times the lord of the land winded his horn to bring the wayward hunters back.

Meanwhile, Gawain lay sleeping, or not quite sleeping, because he knew that the lady would return to test him. He was confident now, having resisted her on two occasions. But he had not reckoned with all her charms.

When she entered the room she was dressed in a rich gown, open at the back and cut low at the front. There were jewels in her hair and at her throat. She came softly into the room and opened a window.

"O, man, how can you sleep on such a perfect morning?"

Now Gawain was not quite asleep, but not quite awake either, and his wits were not quite ready. His thoughts were on the adventure ahead of him, and what was going to happen at the Green Chapel. And so he misread the lady's strategy.

This time she attacked him full on. She offered him her love, called him a coward if he would not take it, kissed him all over his face and his neck. Laughed at him, and cried for him, and pretended to be angry, and yet all the while with the slightest trace of merriment at the corner of her mouth, and the hint of cunning in her eye.

Gawain was on the point of giving in, but something held him back. He reminded himself of courtesy, and chivalry, and his duty to his host, and to his promise.

Then she changed tack.

"Is it that you have a mistress, a lover, someone who is dearer to you than me?"

"In faith," said Gawain, "nothing like that. That is not it at all."

"Then that makes me even more miserable. But kiss me now, and we will call this game at an end."

So Gawain kissed her, three times. But the third time she turned away sadly.

"Why are you sad, my lady?" said Gawain.

"Because I would give you a gift, but not one to return to my husband." And she handed him a rich ring of red gold, with a single stone, set like a star, that sparkled and shone in the bright daylight.

"Lady, give me nothing, because I have nothing to give you in return." And he handed the ring back to her.

"I don't want anything back," she said. "But let me at least give you this." And she took off her belt, which was a thing of green silk and lace under her gown, finished with the finest, reddest gold.

"Not even that, my lady," he said.

"You would not say 'no' if you knew what it was," she chided. "For whoever wears this belt cannot be killed, no matter what another does to him."

For a moment Gawain was caught. She had had already put the belt on his waist, and tucked it under his shirt so that it could not be seen. His mind was racing to the Green Chapel. Was this a way to escape death at the hands of the Green Knight?

She begged him not to reveal the belt to anyone, least of all to her husband, so that no one except they two would ever know.

Then she took her leave.

Gawain got up as before, and dressed. But this time he took care to hide the green belt. And then he went off to the chapel. He stayed there long, confessing his sins, and calling on God's help. But he perhaps neglected to mention the belt.

That evening the lord of the land returned, and this time Gawain gave him three kisses, but no more.

"Now this time I have the best of the bargain," said the lord, "for all I have is this fox-skin." And he gave Gawain the skin of the fox which, at long last, they had run to ground. That night they feasted, and blessed each other, and made ready to part as friends.

Gawain—the Gawain listening to the tale—woke from his reverie with a start. The voice of Anne Raynall had fallen strangely silent. The fire had burned down to little more than a glow. The horses moved nervously. Outside the wind had got up, and roared above than the rush of the mill-water. It was very cold.

He stood up and put more logs on the fire, and stirred it up until there was a crackling of spark and flame.

Anne Raynall began again.

"Now the New Year nears, and the night passes
The day drives back the dark, as God commands it,
But the wild weather of the world wakened outside
Clouds pushed the cold keenly onto the earth…"

The pictures began to form once more in Gawain's mind. Spiteful snatches of snow, the wind whipping about, blowing more snow from the deep drifts.

He was springing out of bed, afraid that he had slept too long. He called for his chamberlain, and dressed swiftly, taking care to wrap the green belt out of sight under his tunic. They helped him quickly into his armour, and he was glad to see that they had cleaned it and polished it as if it were new.

Thus he was ready to ride, and they brought Gringolet to him, and he called down blessings on all the folk of the castle. They let the drawbridge down, and unbarred the broad gates, and Gawain set off, with one man to guide him.

It was a hard road after the ease of the castle. They climbed alongside cliffs, and rode through misty moorland. Every hilltop was shrouded in clouds. At length they came through a wood, and onto a snowy hill, and the guide asked him to stop.

"I've brought you this far," he said. "Now, if you take my advice, you'll be off back to Arthur's court. I'll tell no tale, I swear. But if you go down to that place below us, the Green Chapel, and meet with the one who lives there, then neither magic nor any other thing will save you, even if you had twenty lives. Give up the game, Gawain, and go home!"

"You're a kind man," said Gawain. "And you wish me only good. But I could not return to Camelot—I could not live with myself, and I could not serve God, if I turned coward now."

They spoke a good many other words, but in the end the guide set off to return to the castle, and Gawain took the difficult path down the hillside into the valley of the Green Chapel.

It was not much like a chapel. Rather, beside the bubbling of a brook, so fierce that it seemed to boil, there was a green mound, with a hole at either side and at one end, all hollowed out inside. Gawain walked around, wondering what it might be. It seemed to be nothing but an old cave, overgrown with grass. But there was no doubting the unnatural chill.

"Is this really the green chapel?" he said out loud. "More likely a place the devil would come to say his prayers at midnight. But this is just the sort of place where the green man would come. A chapel of mischance, the most accursed church I have ever been inside."

Then a noise chilled his blood. "Quat!" it went. It was the noise of a great blade being sharpened on some enormous grindstone. "Quat!" it went again, echoing around the cliffs like water in a mill race. "Quat!" it rushed and rang.

There was no doubt: it was the sound of a mighty axe being sharpened. The lady's belt no longer seemed much protection. So he called out, to challenge whoever was there. "Gawain is here!" he shouted. "I have kept my promise."

"Wait!" boomed a voice from the hillside. Into sight came the Green Knight, taller than Gawain remembered him, and carrying an axe even huger than the one he had left at Arthur's court.

"You have done well, Gawain, to keep your end of the bargain. Now, make you ready for my return blow."

And now there was no time left, nothing for it. All excuses were in the past, all hopes and fears were gone. So Gawain laid his head on the wooden block, and drew back his collar, revealing the bare flesh of his neck to the cold winter air.

He closed his eyes.

With a soft whoosh, he heard the axe begin to fall. He shrank a little from the blow.

Then—nothing. The axe had made no contact.

"What!" roared the knight. "Are you really Gawain? You flinched when I brought my axe down. I did not flinch when you struck me. By that token, I am the better knight."

"I flinched once," said Gawain, "I won't flinch again. But remember that when my head falls on the stones, I cannot put it back on."

He bared his neck again, and closed his eyes.

Whoosh! He heard the soft parting of air as the axe began to fall. This time he did not flinch, but he felt no bite of the axe. The Green Knight had let the blow go to one side.

"Good," said the Green Knight. "Now I know that you will not flinch. Prepare for the true blow."

This time Gawain knew that he really meant to take his head. He closed his eyes tightly, and tried not to listen for that first soft sigh air.

Whoosh! He felt the cold steel of the axe break his skin, cutting into his flesh, sending blood pouring away from him…

But…

He was not dead. He was cut, but his head was still on his shoulders. He leapt up, grabbing his sword, ready to do battle, giant or no giant.

"You have had your return blow," he said, breathing hard. "Now prepare to fight, if you are not a coward."

The Green Man leaned on his axe and laughed, long and hard. The hillside shook with it.

"Fight you, little man? Why would I want to fight you. We were having a Christmas game, and you have proved yourself the most noble knight in the world.

"Know then, that I am Sir Bercilak of Hautdessart, and I am the lord of the land who has entertained you these last days. All this was planned by Arthur's half-sister Morgaine, to test the prowess of the knights of Camelot, and to frighten Guinevere, whom she hates. Three times at my castle we made a bargain, to exchange our winnings, and three times I took my axe to you on this very ground. On the first day, I gave you the venison which I had hunted, and you faithfully gave me the kiss which my wife had given to you. And so, when I struck first, I did not harm you. On the second day, I gave you the boar, and you faithfully gave me two kisses, which you had had from my wife. And so, on the second blow, I did not harm you. On the third day, I gave you the fox-skin, and you faithfully gave me three kisses. But —" at this the colour drained from Gawain's cheeks, "— but, you neglected to give me the belt, which she wove at my command for this very purpose. You see that it bears my own colours, green and red, which are the colours of myself, and the holly bobbin I carried to Camelot. And so on the third blow, I nicked your neck, because you were almost faithful to your promise."

Gawain felt hot shame burning inside him, to have been thus tricked, and exposed as a coward and a liar.

"But I forgive you that—it is no great sin to love your life, and you did nothing shameful, nor did you try to take my wife away from me. Now, please, do me the courtesy to return to my castle, and we will feast merrily and praise your honour. For no other knight in all the world could have succeeded in this quest as you have done."

"I cannot return with you," Gawain replied. "I am shamed for ever, as no knight should be."

"Fie," said the Green Knight. "It was a little, little thing. The old lady that you saw—that is Morgaine. Few can escape her traps, and she has taken a special interest in entrapping you. But you are so almost perfect that to be any more so would mean you would have had to leave the world altogether."

Silence.

Not only the voice of the Green Knight, but also the voice of Anne Raynall had ceased. But the story was incomplete.

"And so Gawain rode sadly back to Camelot," said Gawain, looking around him. "He carried with him the mark of his shame, the green belt, which he has worn to this day to remind him of his weakness..."

He was going to carry on, when something small but moving very fast flitted by the corner of his eye. Quick as a flash he turned and leapt to his feet, to be rewarded by a sharp slap across his face.

Then another.

Then another.

It was Anne Raynall.

"Ow! What! Stop!"

He saw that there were tears in her eyes, and her face was red. And now she was hammering with both fists on his chest.

"Anne. My lady. My love. Stop. Stop. What is the matter?"

She stood back from him, eyes wide, staring, furious.

"You don't know, do you?" she said.

"My lady, what don't I know?"

"You don't know what you really did?"

"My lady, what? I admit that I failed. I told all the knights of Camelot about my shame—"

"You did not! Even now, you have no idea!"

"What then? What have I done?"

"Because all the time you were dallying with that woman, you were married to me!"

"But, my lady, I was faithful to you!"

"You were not!"

"My lady!"

"You really don't understand, do you?" Her anger was beginning to subside, but, somewhere, Gawain saw the signs of deeper hurt. "When you married me, you promised to be true to me and no other. What were you then doing, dallying and flirting with that woman? What were you doing kissing her? When she asked you if there was another, you said there was not. You betrayed me—"

"But Anne, what I meant was that that was not the reason—"

"Well it should have been the reason. What?" Now it was Anne's turn to see a change in Gawain. "What?" she said again.

Gawain shrugged and sat down. The life seemed to have gone out of him.

Very gently—she was still angry, but she had the not uncommon capacity to be angry with someone, and yet care about them deeply, and be sorry for them, all at the same time—she knelt in front of him.

"Gawain. Gwalchmai—what is it?"

"It's you."

"Me?"

"You. All of you. Women. How is it any surprise that I was fooled and made a fool of by a woman? What do you do all day long except beguile and entrap us? What have I had but sorrow at the hands of women? Like Adam, who was betrayed by Eve, like Samson, who was betrayed by Delilah, like David, who was betrayed by Bathsheba, like Solomon, who—"

She put her fingers on his lips.

"Like Gawain, who would prefer that it simply was not his fault.

"Listen, Gawain, my love. There were two reasons why I left you— you remember that you returned from this adventure to find an empty home. Perhaps you told yourself that I was already gone when this happened. But I was not. I got word—from Morgaine's people, but you have confirmed today that it was true, all the same—of what had happened at the Castle of Hautdessart. I might have stayed for you—I might. But the second was that I knew by then that I was expecting our child. I did not want my child to grow up in the world in which you live. I wanted my child to go to school, and have a career, and perhaps be an artist, or a musician, or a writer, and not end his life spitted on a lance at some foolish tournament, or bleeding to death in a lonely forest. Perhaps I would have stayed to explain this to you, perhaps even to take you to my time. But, the two together—that is why I left. For my part, and with so many years between, I forgive you. But—" She paused.

"My lady, I still love you," he protested.

"Gwalchmai, do you even know what love is?"

"My lady!"

"Yes, yes, I know your reputation. Gawain, the knight of courtly love, the most chivalrous, the one that all women desire. But that is not evidence that you know how to love, only that you excite love in others. Tell me, if you can, how you are more than Andrew Chappell, who knows all there is to know about love except what it is like?"

Gawain breathed deeply.

"My lady, just five minutes ago, you told me that I had betrayed you in loving another. How can you now say that I do not love at all?"

"Because you did not love her. You found it entertaining to dally with her, to see how far you could take yourself and yet remain a perfect knight. In doing so you showed that love is to you just a game. You are charming, you are respectful, you are courteous, you are past-master at all the things which make women believe that you love them, and for this reason it is hard now for me to believe you. You say that you love me, but you are so advanced in the arts of pretending to love that neither I nor anyone else can tell if you really love. Perhaps you are so far advanced that you yourself cannot tell."

"Would you prefer a more simple man? A peasant or a farmer who speaks gruffly?"

"Do not look down on the simple peasant, Gwalchmai. If you were a simple man, I would know if you loved me."

"But would you love me?"

"Would you have loved me if I were not—how does the poem put it, 'more beautiful than Guinevere'? Judging by these two tales, you love anyone, as long as she is 'more beautiful than Guinevere'. Is that love, to possess the most beautiful thing in the world? Or is it merely greed?"

Gawain spread his hands, in a gesture of loss.

"My lady. I can say no more. If I speak for myself, then I am using my skills of courtly love-talking, and so my words have no value. But if I say nothing, how can I persuade you?"

She shook her head, and stood up, wrapping her arms around his head and pressing it against her body.

"You poor fool," she said. "Tonight there is no answer for you. Perhaps one day there will be."

Fitt 3

Time Out of Joint

19 THE BOOK OF HOURS

ain like a knife drove through Scott's ankle as he stepped across the threshold. He did his best to avoid falling, and he did not at first take in his surroundings.

When he did look, the first thing he saw was men and women dressed in beautiful, brightly coloured clothes. They all had a 'medieval' look about them, although Scott would have been hard put to pick a century. There was a monk in white robes and a red surplice, and a young man in an impossibly blue garment that looked rather like a shapeless dress. He wore odd socks, one green and one white. There was a whole crowd of such people, standing in the chilly air around trestle tables covered in white cloths and laid with foods of many kinds. One man in brown and red was feeding a white dog.

There was a sort of pavilion with an open front set up on the other side of the trestles, with a brazier lending some kind of warmth. Everybody was talking, and eating, and many were giving or receiving gifts.

Scott leant on his sword to take the weight off his foot, and wondered if anyone would notice if he helped himself to the food. It seemed a long time since lunch.

Before he could do this, he felt someone tugging at his shoulder.

"Once again, I am pleased to see you," said a voice in his ear—a voice with a soft French accent.

It was Marie de France.

"My lady de France..." began Scott, eagerly gushing out words in Cortayse.

She waved her hand in a circle, closing it when she reached the centre, and said:

"It's ok. I'm ok with your English. Do you know where we are?"

"I know not..." began Scott, and then lapsed into modern English. "I don't," he said. "I just got here. Do you know where we are?"

"I think..." she said, overemphasising the 'th' sound, "that we are not anywhere, at least, not in a real place. I think we are trapped inside the pages of a book."

"Why do you think that, Marie-France?"

"Look in the distance. What do you see?" She gestured beyond the pavilion.

"Knights jousting on horse back," said Scott, peering, "and hills. And in the distance a castle."

"And beyond that?"

"The sky?"

"Yes, exactly. The sky. It is very blue, don't you think? And here it is bright as day, but where is the sun? There are no clouds, we are all lit up, and yet no sun. And look, again—do you see the blue of that man's robe, and that other man's head-dress, and that other man's cloak? They are exactly the same blue as the blueest part of the sky. Have you ever seen that in real life?"

Scott thought about this for a moment.

"Also," she went on, "I think I know the book. I think this is the page for Janvier—that is, January—of the Très Riche Heures du duc de Berry. It is a famous book."

Scott thought a little longer.

"Does this happen a lot?"

"What do you mean?"

"Well, I only learned about skifting a few days ago. It was surprising, but it seemed to make sense. We move from layer to layer of time when trouble opens up holes and we fall through. But this—do people often fall out of time and into books?"

"I have never heard of it happening."

Scott chewed his tongue. He did not really want to believe that he had somehow fallen out of the world altogether, but the more he looked, the more he had to agree that their surroundings had a certain air of unreality. The colours were too bright, the shadows wrong, and the perspective was all mixed up.

"What shall we do?" he said.

"You are the knight," she said. "Are you not a knight? Something has changed in you since we last met. Yes, surely you are now a knight. I am but a woman. It is for you to decide what to do. You have surely come to rescue me."

"What would happen if we walked out of the picture?" he said.

"We can try," she replied. "Do you have a horse, or do you really mean walk? I think in the next picture—if it is possible to walk there—it is snowing."

Scott did not really know what to say to this. He remembered leading his horse while Marie-France rode, and he did not much fancy the idea of doing it again with his foot as it was.

But, even as he thought about it, he heard a soft whinny behind him, and turned to find two horses—a white mare, already set side-saddle for a lady, and a grey charger. The charger was trimmed with blue and gold, and the mare with gold and green. He helped Marie-France onto the mare, and pulled himself onto the charger. The stirrups were already the right length, as if they had been made for him.

He turned the horse's head to ride to the right, and Marie-France followed.

Then something very strange happened.

Have you ever sat on a train, and watched the train next to you set off, and, for a while you think you are moving until it is gone? Rather the opposite of this was happening to Scott. The horses trod as they should, but he had the distinct impression it was the ground that was moving, not the horses.

For a little less than an hour, they remained under that impossibly blue sky, with the castle in the distance on green hills, and then, very suddenly, they crossed what was evidently a border of some kind. There was not a sharp dividing line, but the blue sky became grey cloud, and the green grass turned to thick, powdery snow. At first that was all there was: grey sky, snow on the ground, snow on the hills. But after ten minutes they saw a thicket of leafless, spiky trees, and, in the distance, a village with a church spire.

By and by they came to a farm. Sheep were bleating in a covered pen, jackdaws pecked at something in the farmyard. Beehives stood, like soldiers at attention, in front of a short tower. A peasant was making his way up the hill, beating a donkey which carried a load of sticks towards a village. Through the window of the farmhouse he saw people warming themselves on a fire. There was a harshness to the landscape, and a cruel wind blew, freezing Scott's ears and nose.

Marie-France had drawn her cloak tightly about her, and the hood over her face. For a while they had ridden side by side, but she dropped behind when the chill set in. Scott wanted to hurry up, and he spurred the charger on. But, although the horse doubled his efforts, they seemed to move no more swiftly than before.

It was perhaps an hour later that they came to another division of the land. The snow thinned, giving way to patches of down-trodden grass and muddy, brown earth. The sky was at first grey and cloudy, but, quickly, the clouds floated upwards, giving way to clear blue.

"This is March," said Marie-France, catching up with Scott. "We are riding through the months of the year. Each month, I think, is taking an hour."

"So it will take us twelve hours to ride out of the book?"

"We may hope so. But this book has more than two-hundred pages, and in the final pages they are martyring the early Christians. Let us hope that we do not have to ride through those."

Presently they came to a farmer, ploughing with a rudimentary plough and two oxen. His back was bowed, and his surcote was patched in several places, protecting a blue tunic underneath. Elsewhere labourers were trimming vines, and in the distance, two shepherds played with a dog in a field of sheep.

"Look," said Marie-France, "that monument at the cross-roads is a Mountjoie, and behind is the castle, called the Château de Lusignan."

Scott looked. There was something flying about one of the towers. Something golden, with great wings, surely—it was—it was a dragon.

"What is that?" said Scott, "flying above the castle?"

"That is the fairy Melusine. Melusine promised to make Raimondin, son of the king of the Bretons, the first nobleman of the realm if she married her, provided that he never saw her on Saturday. Raimondin could not suppress his curiosity, so one day he watched her. But Melusine saw him, and flew away in the shape of a golden dragon.

"But, Scott—"

He started, hearing her use his own name

"—I think you know all about magical ladies who change their shape, do you not? Anyway, Melusine will hover around the castle to protect it—Except..."

Just at that moment, flame came pouring out of the dragon's mouth, blackening the red tiled roof of the tower.

"That is not right—" said Marie-France.

The dragon's tail swept across that same roof, sending tiles and bricks flying. It breathed again, and flames sprang up from the lower castle roofs. It raked them with its claws, and turned to deal with a taller, strong tower. It was answered by dozens of tiny flashes of light, as if people were firing arrows or throwing spears. Then something seemed to catch the dragon's eye. Dragons have great, beady eyes, which are sharper than hawks' eyes, and can spot an enemy at a great distance.

Turning head on, it began to fly, on huge, barred, golden wings, straight towards them.

"Quick, ride, Scott, it has seen us."

She spurred on the mare, but, just as before, the ground seemed to move no more quickly. Scott rode after her, though he turned in the saddle to watch those golden wings. The dragon must be further away than he thought, or else was having the same difficulties increasing its speed. He looked again, and saw the next month, only a few hundred yards ahead of them.

The dragon put on a burst of speed. It had been as big as five-pence, and now was as big as ten pence, and was fast becoming the size of a fifty-pence piece. They were five minutes from the border, and the dragon was already veering to head them off before they reached it.

"Come on, Scott. Come on," shouted Marie-France, seemingly unaware that she was going no faster.

Now Scott could begin to make out the dragon's features—the terrifying teeth, hundred-fold, dripping with venom. He saw that the dragon was not entirely golden, but greenish gold above, and whitish gold beneath. Its claws were the size of scythes, and sharper than razors.

There was no mistaking its speed now. It would catch them perhaps fifty, a hundred yards before they reached the break in the green grass which would be the month of April.

Now Scott could hear the rush of the heavy downbeats. Soon he would smell the fiery breath—

Suddenly, without knowing why he did it, he stood up in his stirrups and raised his sword, as if issuing a challenge. The charger reared as he did so, almost sending Scott tumbling, but he kept somehow upright and stood, like a softball player waiting to receive the ball.

The sword glinted in the sunlight.

The dragon stopped in mid-air, pushing its legs towards him, flapping its immense wings to halt itself. And then, ponderously, as if infinitely weary, it turned on its tail and flew back again.

Scott rubbed his eyes.

"Is that what usually happens?" he said, a minute or so later, when he had caught up with Marie-France. She made no reply. Perhaps she had not heard.

They crossed into April. There was no mistaking the richer green of the new grass. Leaves thrust themselves out of winter twigs, and the warm sun looked down kindly on the land.

Presently, they came upon a charming group of courtiers, exchanging rings, and gifts, and playing in the grass. One of them had a face a bit like a skull, thought Scott. Two, at least, looked scarcely older than himself. They were babbling away merrily in French, but, to his dismay, he could not understand them.

Marie de France must have guessed at his difficulty.

"You cannot understand them, because they are not real," she said. "They are only pictures in a book."

They rode on. It was pleasant just to ride in the balmy spring air.

"Something is wrong," she said, abruptly. Just at that moment, there was a gasp from the group, which was now behind them. Scott turned to see that the woman with a face like a skull had fallen to the ground. Others were helping her, but their faces showed shock and panic.

"Ride on, ride on," she hissed. Scott was for turning back, but Marie-France came alongside and took his horse's reins.

"You can do nothing, here," she said. "It is the Black Death. Ride on, or we are lost too."

They saw no other people in that April land. The green-way through the woods was strangely silent.

There was only the slightest line when they crossed into May. Here the forest was thicker, the air warmer, the grass greener, the wind fresher. Through the trees, to the left, were roofs, towers, and the tops of tall buildings. Marie de France stopped once and leaned longingly on her saddle, looking.

"It is Paris—" she said, and then sighed. "But it is not real." And then: "Hurry, Scott. We must hurry. By now we should have met people—merry courtiers with trumpets and horns, and knights and ladies Maying. This whole woodland should be filled with their sound. Something is terribly wrong."

So they rode on in silence. Indeed, the silence of May was even deeper than April. Scott looked around as they went, but he saw no sign of man, or beast, or bird, or any animal of any kind.

The full warmth of the sun hit them as they rode into June. It was the middle of the day, the middle of the year. They were in a wide, fertile land. But as they went on, blackened stumps began to appear. There were whole fields which had been burned. Scott at first thought this was straw burning—his mother had once explained to him, on a visit to the country, how farmers sometimes burn off fields of straw after the corn has been harvested. But as they went, he saw cracked, burned seed still on stalks that had escaped the flames. Here and there were the remains of scythes and sickles, burned or bent and useless.

"War has passed over this land," said Marie-France. Indeed, as they came up on a walled town, they saw the streaks of smoke on the stones. No flags flew from the towers, and there were no banners on the battlements, and, though they came closer than they had come to any town, there was no sign of life.

20 The Valley of Death

July was desolate. A heavy scent of burning hung in the air. The remains of sheep lay by the wayside, as if their coming had disturbed whatever feasted on them. By and by they came to the ruins of what must have been a beautiful castle, constructed as a triangle in a lake, with white walls and graceful white towers at each corner. But the walls were broken down in many places. Nothing more than stakes remained of a wooden bridge.

"What did this?" said Scott. "Is this part of the book?"

"This is the work of cannon," said Marie-France. "See, the walls are first broken in rough circles, and then the stones above them have collapsed. But this is no part of the book, no more than the burnt fields and the black death. I fear what we shall find in August."

Her fears proved well founded. Plumes of smoke rose from a wrecked castle on the August hillside. But the worst was far worse. Their path followed a long, gentle and shallow river. It would have been a nice place to bathe, and Scott was wondering if it might not be a good place to stop in the heat of the day, to rest the horses. Then he saw something white, floating. He reined the charger in and looked.

It was a body. A young man, naked, floating on his back. There was a trickle of blood from a gash at his neck. A little further along the river there was a bend, and a number of things seemed to have been caught in an overhanging root. Now that he had seen the body close up, there was no mistaking what the things were: corpses, piled up like dead fish. As he watched, he saw a vee of ripples headed towards them. Something thrashed for a moment in the water, and then a huge pair of jaws appeared, and in one bite severed one of those bodies, and vanished under the surface.

Scott blinked. Marie-France had come up behind him, and her face was white.

There was nothing to do but to ride on. Eventually the road left the ghastly river behind it. Marie-France now rode close beside him.

There was a guardian at the crossroads into September. In the distance it seemed to be a spindly man, wrapped in a white linen or cotton shawl, or perhaps a cloak.

As they drew closer it seemed to be a very thin man. He had no hair at all on his head, and his face was drawn and blotchy. He made no sign that he had seen them, though he seemed to face in their direction. If he had held a scythe, Scott would probably have guessed straight away. But he—if 'he' is the right word—did not hold a scythe, but a sword. Five feet long it was, yet the figure seemed to hold it effortlessly in one hand.

"Hoi!" called Scott, as they approached, in what he hoped would be a jovial, but at the same time martial, voice. The figure made no reply.

Now it was much easier to see what kind of person it was. It was skinless, red flesh, barely covering the skeleton, but with sinews clear and active. The white clothing was a shroud, or winding sheet, which is used to wrap a body when it is placed in a coffin.

Marie-France clutched Scott's arm.

"Mon ami," she said forgetting her English, "c'est la Mort!," which (as Scott understood it) means, 'my friend, it is Death!'

"Will you let us pass, or must we fight you?" said Scott, as they rode up. The figure said nothing, but bowed, mockingly, and gestured as if to welcome them in. And it pointed to a sign, written in huge, ugly red letters, which said: "Allen zijn welkom!" Scott looked at Marie-France, but she shook her head.

"I think it is Dutch, or maybe Flemish. I do not speak these languages. But it puts me in mind of a Flemish painting, and it is not a place we will be wanting to be."

"What other path do we have?" said Scott. And then, to the guardian: "Will you swear to let us pass unharmed, if we enter your country?"

Once again, the figure said nothing, but it chattered its teeth as if laughing, and stood back, beckoning them on.

"Wait on this side," said Scott. He felt very knightly, and proud (but in a humble way), and both brave and frightened at the same time, as he set his horse to cross the barely visible line into the land of September.

He watched the guardian out of the corner of his eye as he crossed. And it was a good thing too.

No sooner was the horse completely over the line, than the figure of death sprang at him. It was lithe and powerful, and jumped six feet across the ground and five in the air, bony fingers reaching out with the left hand to throttle, sword raised in the right hand to bring across his throat like a garrotte.

Scott turned in the saddle, and the horse, who understood mounted warfare perhaps better than he did, wheeled with him. He brought his own blade up to meet the other, catching it in a wide sweeping parry.

There was a flash of light, as metal hit metal, and a splintering shriek. Scott's blade cut straight through, sending shards in all directions, and buried itself for a fraction of a second in the dead flesh of his enemy.

Against a man this would surely have been enough, but the dead thing hacked at him with the remains of its sword, clutching with its left hand for Scott's throat. A stench of decay and rotting flesh filled his nostrils, and it made him want to retch. The skinless head was now very close, and he looked into the red, staring eyes, and the loose, rotten teeth in fleshless gums.

He wanted to scream, but instead he snatched his sword back, and swung once more, catching sword hand, neck, and left shoulder in the same sweep. That was an amazing sword! It cut clean through the un-flesh and un-bone as if they were barely there. The grotesque head went bouncing off among the stones, while the sword hand fell heavily to earth. The other arm fell at his horse's feet, and was pinned down by heavy hooves.

Even this was not enough. The headless body was now astride the back of the horse, trying to wrap its handless right arm about Scott's throat, and its legs about his chest. The feel of that clammy flesh on his skin seemed to draw strength from him. There was not much space to use his sword, but savage desperation welled up in answer to that touch, and he somehow twisted it back, through the headless torso, to rip upwards, cutting the thing in two. Then, with a last gasp of strength, he swung his left leg up and kicked the remains backwards over the horse's tail. A stab of pain went through his foot, which went instantly numb, and he slumped over the horse's mane.

The dismembered corpse lay twitching on the ground.

Marie de France rode over the line. She was careful to go nowhere near the juddering remains. Scott's skin still crawled with the horror of that touch, but a delicious warm feeling came over him when she laid her hand on his.

"Now you are truly a knight in my eyes," she said. "But tell me, where did you get that sword? I have never seen one like it."

If Scott had been speaking Cortayse he would have probably blurted out the whole story. But he was mindful of his promise to the un-named knight, and, in his own English, knew how to hold his tongue.

"Oh, somebody lent it to me. But I promised not to say who, or how, or where, or even why."

"That then leaves only the question of 'what?'. May I see it?"

Without waiting for his reply, she peeled open his fingers, which were weak and soft after the fight, and took the weight of it in her hands.

"Scott," she said very quietly, "do you not know what this is?"

"What do you mean?" he replied.

"You have not looked carefully at this blade since you had it?"

"No."

"And—let me ask, did you also receive a scabbard, to go with this sword?"

"No."

"Look then, here—" and she held the weapon up, so that the light glanced along a fine inscription at the base of the blade. Scott's eyes went wide when he saw what it said. There, as clear as day, was a single word: 'EXCALIBUR'.

"Scott, this is the sword that cuts through steel, that splits a hair on water and draws blood from the wind. The Lady of the Lake gave it to Arthur, at Merlin's command. There is no scabbard because the scabbard, which could prevent a man from losing blood, was stolen and cast away. This weapon of all things Morgaine desires to have—to destroy it if she can, or to keep it from her enemies if she cannot."

She balanced it in her hand for a moment, chewing her tongue and sucking in her cheeks.

"Here," she said. "You must have it back. If you will not tell me where you got it, nor how you came by that knightly look, then I cannot force you to, nor will I trick you. But I am a storyteller, first and last, and above all other things, and if I ever come to tell this story, I will say that, in some strange time or place, you met with Arthur, and he made you a knight of the round table, and lent you his sword, that else only he and Gawain had ever used."

She pushed the sword back into his hand, and he felt a lump rising in his throat.

"Listen; to me you will always be Scott, the young boy that I met on the road to Kenilworth. But to others you are now Sir Perceval, knight of the Round Table, and of Logres."

"And will you be my lady, Marie de France?" said Scott. The words sounded like the courtly words he had spoken without learning and often without intending, but this time they were his words, and spoken from the heart.

"You are so quick to choose! And maybe, when you see other ladies, you will wish to choose differently. But, for my part, yes I will be your lady, if you will be my knight. Come, we must exchange rings."

Scott was about to protest that he did not wear a ring, when he looked down and saw Morgaine's ring, still on his finger. He had quite forgotten it. It did not seem entirely right to give something away which he had only so lately received, but Marie de France was already pulling the ring from his finger and placing it on her own, and taking her own ring and placing it on his. Scott was tall for his age, but thin with it, otherwise this would not have worked. As it was, the rings fitted like a charm.

"And now, Sir Knight, lead on," she said. "I am quite emboldened in my spirit, to know that I have such a protector and lord."

They rode on through an eery quiet. At length they passed a ruined castle, set among desolate fields. From time to time they saw gaunt sentries at distant crossroads, and once they came across a high gallows, on which hung nine bodies. Marie-France counted them carefully, but Scott did not ask why.

In time they saw an enormous darkness across the landscape ahead. It was thick cloud, and smoke, and soot, and all manner of black mist and fog.

As they crossed the line, they found a world lit by uncontrolled fires. After a few hundred yards, they reached the top of a ridge. Below was a valley the like of which they had never seen: to the left, to the right, and straight ahead—everywhere—figures fought. Many lay already dead. In the smoke and fume it took a moment to see, but Scott soon made out the familiar half-alive, half-deadness of the corpse-men. There were thousands of them. Some were pouring out of the ground, others arrived by boat, and yet others were arrayed as armies, carrying huge coffin lids for shields. There was no end to their numbers. But the others—the others seemed to be ordinary men and women, rich, poor, old, young. The corpse men were busy slitting their throats, or hurling them into pits of fire, or drowning them in water, or hanging them on gallows, or hewing at them with swords. Here and there a gallant few resisted, but the killed were more numerous than the living, and the corpse-men more numerous still.

Marie-France touched Scott's elbow.

"Scott, I know this picture. This is not part of the Book of Hours. This is the painting called 'The Triumph of Death'."

"We must ride down and rescue them," said Scott.

"Rescue them? Scott, these are not real people. This is a painting. How we come to be here I do not know, but somehow this painting has overflowed into the pages we already travelled. The most we can hope for is to pass through unharmed."

"Is there nothing we can do?"

"Against these legions of death? What could we do? But let us ride— do you hold Excalibur ahead of you, and I will ride behind. Look neither to the left nor to the right, and speak to no one, not even if they call you by name."

Scott looked down the hillside. He spied a pocket of resistance: one man with a long sword was standing, ready to fight, another dealt a blow to a shrouded corpse man, while his friend, who had fallen to the ground, prepared to parry a blow from a great scythe. Yet as he looked, he saw that the numbers of dead were not increasing. All was activity, everywhere was wild movement, but the corpse with the scythe never seemed quite ready to strike the man on the ground, and the man with the long sword never quite fully drew it from the scabbard, and the man preparing to slash never quite moved his blade. There was the completest sense of hurry, but nothing quite happened.

He bit his tongue. The new Knight in him wanted to ride down and take Excalibur to those undead things. The schoolboy in him wanted to skirt right round the edge, perhaps find a way beyond the valley, where none of this was happening. But another part of him saw the wisdom of Marie-France's words.

His chest tightened, and his mouth was dry. But, letting his horse find the best path down the hillside, he set off, holding Excalibur aloft.

The press of knives, scythes, swords and bodies did not open to allow them through, but somehow, there was a path for them to find between it all. Once a skeleton came running at them, but it veered away at the last moment. A man caught in a trap called out to them pitifully. Fires sputtered, but did not burn. In one place a great, nameless beast lay across their path. Yet as they reached it, it rolled over and moved sluggishly away.

Scott's arms were tired long before they were even half way across that valley. But the further they went, the more he was sure that Marie-France was right: as long as they took no part, turning neither right nor left, they were safe.

They climbed the steepening slope on the other side, towards a hill of gallows. The sound of slow, sombre drum beats echoed from a cave in the rocks, and out of it streamed untold more skeletons and corpse men. They shook their spears and chattered their teeth, but did not follow.

As they reached the edge of that valley, a single figure barred their way. It was cloaked in black, with a black hood hanging low over its face—if there was a face under that hood.

Scott rode directly on, but the figure did not move. At the last moment the charger shied, and turned to one side. The hooded figure neither spoke nor attacked, but, as Scott and Marie de France passed, it turned, and watched them leave that land. As they topped the ridge, Scott looked back. The hooded figure raised its hand.

"Fare ye well, Scott Perceval Raynall," said a dry voice, soft but not gentle. They were a hundred yards away, and the voice was barely more than a murmur, but Scott had the strongest sense that it was the figure that spoke: "Fare ye well," it said, "we shall meet again. Goodbye."

It was twilight in the month of November, and they were in thick forest. Owls hooted from the trees and evening insects whirred comfortingly around them. There was no sign of Death nor his legions.

Marie-France rode alongside Scott and was inclined to talk. She explained much that had been mysterious: tales of Arthur, and the way in which Logres and Avalon were intermingled, sometimes by alliance, sometimes by marriage, and often by intrigue. Scott's family tree was more complicated than he had imagined, because Arthur was Gawain's uncle, and Morgaine was his aunt. Morgaine's sister Morgause was Scott's grandmother, and his grandfather was Lot, King of Orkney, who fought against Arthur and died in the battle. She spoke of Merlin, the great enchanter at the back of so many of the stories. She spoke of Guinevere—Arthur's Queen—who these five years stood night by night on her tower at Camelot, looking out across the dark landscape, with its dwindling Roman towns, and petty chieftains one by one raising again their own standards, as the word went out: 'Arthur is lost'.

And so at last she came to Arthur.

"History is full of his legends," she said, "yet most were never fulfilled. Some say that somewhere his tomb lies with the words 'hic iacet Arthurus rex quondam rexque futurus'—'here lies Arthur, king once and king future', but no one can say where that grave is, or when he will come again.'" Scott begged her to describe him, and she did her best, though she had been no more than a child when she was at his court. As she spoke, the picture of the wounded knight in the chapel formed vividly in Scott's mind. He bit his lip and said nothing.

In time they came upon a turreted house in the forest, and swineherds feeding bristle backed hogs with pellets under the trees. There was a lake through the trees, and Marie-France said that they were now back on the right track.

Finally, they came to their own proper month of December. It was no longer twilight, but true night, and the trees crowded closely around them. A vague anxiety settled over Scott: what would they find after December—would it lead the way back into the real world, or would they find themselves in more pages?

They came upon a boar hunt in the forest. It was very like the boar hunt that Anne Raynall had described to Gawain, if only Scott had known. But they had come at the end of it, and a pack of hounds were tearing at the Boar. The hunters stood by, ready to pull the hounds off when the boar was quite dead. Scott—who had never seen a hunt before, and (although now it seemed a different world and a different lifetime) would have complained if his mother had served up food with the slightest red in it—thought it a very ugly spectacle, but Marie-France rode on unconcerned.

At the end of December, the forest thinned, and became a wide plain, and the plain, which was flat, with bright, short grass and black earth, met the edges of an expanse of water. There was scarcely any difference between the level of the grass and the level of the water, and Scott, who was by now very sleepy, rode onto it without noticing. The horses hooves splashed softly. The bottom shelved off so gently that it was ten minutes before the water was knee high, and another ten before it was haunch high.

"What shall we do?" said Scott. "We can't go on for ever."

"Look!" said Marie de France, and she pointed ahead. In the near distance, a huge cliff rose up, and dead ahead was a waterfall, spilling spray and foam in a gushing torrent onto the lake below.

By the time they were twenty yards from the waterfall, the horses were almost swimming.

"I think we go through," said Marie-France. "There is space behind the waterfall." Scott looked and saw that there was at least a small patch of sand, big enough for a horse to stand on.

"Here goes, then," he muttered to himself. It would have been more comforting to gallop through the sheer wall of foam ahead, but the water was too deep to get up any speed.

Going first, he found himself (as did the horse) drenched by a vast pounding rush, like rain heavier than hailstones. He was pressed down in the saddle, and thought he would fall. Then he was through. The horse stood on white sand, and ahead lay the blackness of a cave. Or the blackness of something. As his eyes adjusted he realised that it was not white sand, but white snow, and the blackness was not the unlight of a cave, but the inky-blue blackness of a starlit night.

Marie-France came up behind. She was drenched and shivering with cold. Not knowing quite what to do, he clambered off his horse and climbed up onto the neck of the milk-white mare. She clung to him for warmth, and, rather clumsily holding the charger's reins, they set off into the night.

Within moments they were out of earshot of the waterfall. Looking back, the waterfall had become no more than a spring, tumbling down from the face of a cliff. Ahead was another sound: the low rushing of a mill race. The mare trod softly across the snow, and found her way over a little bridge. And so at length they came to a mill house, with a pleasant smell of wood-smoke. The snow had drifted deep around the walls, but somebody had stamped the doorway clear.

Not knowing if they were in a dream, or another picture, or in real life, Scott slid to the ground and pushed open the door. It moved only a little, and grated, as if it were off its hinges—and then it sprang suddenly backwards. Behind it stood a man with a drawn sword, ready to strike.

It was Gawain.

21 THE BESTIARY

Scott led Marie-France and both horses into the long, low mill-room. Without speaking, Gawain led both of them straight to the fire. Scott was barely conscious of a familiar figure wrapping blankets around him. In the warm, safe heat, he began to drowse, and in moments he was asleep.

They woke him just once, to feed him hot honey-water and warm, flat bread. For the rest, he slept throughout the rest of the day, and all that night, and did not wake until late the next morning.

A ray of sunlight woke him, a thin sliver escaping through the trees, through the shutters, to gently stir him from slumber. His eyes focussed gradually, and what he saw first was a soft halo of gold around a dim face.

"Good morning, sleepy-head." It was his mother. She rolled him over and pulled him out of bed. They had somehow managed to move him from in front of the fire to a tiny bed in a tiny bedroom. The boards of the bed were padded with straw and heather, and the only covering was a thick cloak, lined with white fur. The original owners of the mill had left their bedding behind, but Anne had put it all on the fire: it was thick with fleas, lice, and other vermin. She had also washed and dried (though, of course, not ironed) Scott's clothes, and they sat ready for him beside the bed. It was so strangely like just being at home that for a moment Scott wondered if he had dreamed the last few days.

One look around the mill room, with horses at one end, and a very smoky fire at the other, told him that it was no dream.

Gawain sat at the table. He had already had one breakfast, but was hoping for a second, and counted on Scott to be the excuse for it.

He got his wish, and soon he, and Anne, and Marie de France, were gathered round the table going over their adventures. Scott's tale—or, a version of it—they had already got from Marie de France. But Scott was more interested to find out what they had been up to.

"This is now the third day that we are in this place," said Gawain. "The mill is set between the river and a cliff, which is called Guy's Cliff, after Guy of Warwick, whom you met. There used to be a hermitage here somewhere, although we have seen no sign of a hermit. But it is naturally defensible, and the cliff is a good vantage point to see comings and goings in the lands nearby. I also climbed Blacklowe and saw what there was to be seen.

"Strange things are happening in this land. I saw a conturbernium of Roman legionaries marching northwards, and a Viking raiding party scouring eastwards. I heard—but did not see—the sound of muskets and small bore cannon. I also found a gang of men carrying bronze swords and spears, speaking a language I had not heard before. I saw darker things moving in the snow: hill-giants, a were-wolf howling at the moon, and once, a great loose-limbed creature prowling the marsh-land beyond the forest, which reminded me of the monster of the fens. And I saw traces in the snow which reminded me of something else I had forgotten—the Wild Hunt."

Anne Raynall took up the story.

"Something strange is going on. The walls between different worlds and different times seem to be breaking down.

"Guy of Warwick believed that someone had meddled during the years of Stephen and Mathilda. But I wonder now if the anarchy which England finds itself in is just a symptom of a deeper trouble. Two strands of history are interwoven, or more than two. But the question is: will all this just peter out, or is time itself unravelling?"

"Is all this Morgaine's doing?" said Scott.

"Perhaps, and perhaps not," said Gawain. "It would be hard to believe that she intended to bring worlds and time crashing down about our ears. But she may be attempting some enormous work of magic which has somehow gone wrong. Or she may yet have chosen a time in which it was already beginning to go wrong in order to harness it."

"Or, she may indeed be working with all her powers to prevent it, and to save the day," said Marie de France. "She has done us no wrong, that we should thus accuse her."

"She imprisoned me," said Gawain.

"Yes, yes, and the stories say that you once threatened her with the sword, is that not so?" countered Marie de France. "But she did no harm to you in prison."

"She sent Scott into danger," said Anne Raynall.

"Or, she sent Scott to where he could meet Arthur and receive the sword Excalibur, at least for a while, and be made a knight," said Marie de France.

"What?" said Gawain. "Is this true, Scott?"

"My lord Scott has sworn not to speak of it. But look at the sword and see for yourself."

She carefully lifted it from one of the long trestle tables, and held it up in the firelight. Gawain let out a low sigh.

"Caliburn!" he said. "Does Morgaine then have Arthur imprisoned in the castle?"

"There you are again, jumping to conclusions," she replied. "Scott was no longer in the castle when I met him, and I do not believe that he was in the castle when he found Arthur. In any case, if Morgaine had imprisoned him, she would have taken away Excalibur long ago."

"So you think we should just trust Morgaine?" said Scott.

"Perhaps, and perhaps not. But two of us at least are still welcome at her castle. Why should not you and I ride into the red castle and find out?"

There was a silence.

"You're still very taken with Morgaine, aren't you, Marie-France," said Anne.

"My lady Ragnell must forgive me," said Marie de France, meekly. "I have never been transformed into a hag, but neither am I nor will ever be the most beautiful woman in the land. I am plain of face and my hair is dull. In your future time, nothing about me will be remembered, not even when I lived and how I die. So how can I argue with you? Morgaine has been kind to me. More I cannot say. But if you will allow me to be part of your adventure, I would risk my life to ride to the castle and see what is to be seen."

Gawain smiled.

"We have been ungracious, Marie-France. Yours is a generous and noble offer, and we may sit here a long time and find no better plan. You shame us with your courage—and your loyalty. The Lady Ragnell and I will wait here while you two reconnoitre."

Anne gave him a sharp look, and was about to interrupt. Scott guessed (though probably not exactly right) what she was thinking, and jumped in:

"By all means will I ride with you, Marie de France. We have ridden so far together, and have I not made you my lady?"

Scott was for riding out straight away. But by this time the wind had whipped the snow into a fierce blizzard, and it was impossible to see even a few yards ahead. "You would quickly lose yourselves," warned Gawain, "and only the wolves would find you." But he spent the rest of the afternoon instructing Scott in many finer points of knighthood. He showed him how to grease the horse's hooves to help them in the snow, and he also showed him how he should stand if he fought with sword and shield, which is something that Scott had never learned.

Marie de France sat gazing through the place where the shutters did not quite reach the window sill at the swirling world outside. Anne Raynall came to sit next to her, and for a while she said nothing.

"Marie-France," she began eventually, "I was wrong to chide you."

"You are not pleased that your son has chosen me," Marie de France replied.

"I did not want my son to be part of this world. He was safe in his own time."

"That must be very fine, to be safe in your own time."

"Why do you say that, Marie?"

Marie-France shrugged.

"The year we are in is 1137. I was born in Paris in 1120, the year the White Ship sank off Normandy. I skifted since I was ten. The knights of Arthur skift to seek danger and glory, but I have skifted hither and thither to escape it. I lost everything when Stephen and Mathilda's war began. When Gawain and Scott first found me, a mob wanted to burn me for a witch. You are from a happy time, and happiness follows you. I am from this wretched anarchy, and trouble follows me. They say we will endure it for another seventeen years—until I am twice the age that I am now, if I should live so long."

"But your poetry and stories will be read for centuries, Marie-France. Is that not something?"

"It is a little. But now I have found of all things in the world that which I most desire, and you begrudge it to me."

"My son is so very young. He may change a great deal before he is old enough to love you in return."

"But he loves me now."

"Marie-France, he loves you as a child loves—for friendship, and companionship. No more than that."

"But are not friendship and companionship the basis of love? Or am I as foolish as Andrew Chapell, and do not understand true love?"

"Marie, Marie," said Anne. "Which of us truly understands true love? Listen, I will make a bargain with you: ride with my son for now, and be his lady. If—let me see—when he is as old as you are now, and you still love him, and he you, then I will not stand in your way."

She would have said more, but at that moment there was an enormous cracking sound, as if a bolt of lightning had struck the mill. Scott and Gawain came running to the window, and Gawain pulled back the shutter to see what had happened

Instantly, a rush of snow came pouring through, covering the floor five feet around.

Scott, Marie-France and Anne spluttered (more than one of them had snow in their faces).

"Hush," said Gawain. "Listen!"

They listened. There was no sound.

"What?" whispered Scott. And then it struck him. There was no sound—no sound of the fire gently crackling away, and no sound of the roar of the mill-race. It was very, very cold—far colder than it should be, even with the draught from the window. He looked around, and saw that the door—which was already broken—had been somehow pushed open, and a large drift of snow had collected inside. And he saw that the fire had gone out, and there was snow in the fireplace.

Very carefully, Gawain climbed onto the window sill, and lifted himself out into the world. A minute later he lowered himself, and did his best to push the shutters closed. Then he went over to the fireplace, cleared away the snow, and set about lighting the fire again.

The others gathered round.

"Something strange has happened," he said. "Outside, the mill-pool has frozen over, which is why we do not hear the mill-race. And snow has fallen, deeply. It seems that in a moment of time, two, three, maybe four days of snow fell. And then there is the fire. Five minutes ago it was burning merrily, and the smoke was blowing around the room. But now the smell of smoke is gone, this wood is stone cold, and wet, and this place is as chill as when we first found it."

"It is as if the world has moved on without us," said Marie de France.

"Time is unravelling," said Anne.

There was silence.

"That settles it," said Gawain. "We have been too timid in our dealings with Morgaine. We will all ride to the red castle, and see what can be done there."

"Will she not imprison you again?" said Marie de France.

"We must risk it," he said. "But I do not think she will breach the laws of chivalry so directly. It is one thing to capture a man in the forest, and another to mistreat a guest."

"The laws of chivalry are very strange," said Scott.

"So it may seem," said Gawain.

They saddled the horses, and by dint of lifting the door off its remaining hinge and using it as a sort of snow plough, Gawain forced a passage outwards.

The snow had drifted steeply around the mill, but beyond the bridge it thinned into little more than a dusting. The road sparkled and shone, and the horses' hooves crunched on frosty stones. Scott and Marie de France rode ahead, but Gawain and Anne Raynall lagged behind.

"Tell me, Scott-Perceval," said Marie de France as they rode. "What is life like in your time?"

Scott screwed his face up. 'His time' seemed a very long time ago.

"It's... nothing much goes on."

"Do you live in a palace?"

"No, not really. We live in a little council house in Stechford. My mum—the lady Ragnell—has a part time job teaching English."

"The people do not speak English?"

"It's at the university. I think it's mainly medieval English."

"I see. Your mother does not like me, I think."

"She's just like that sometimes. She pretends not to like Gawain."

"Ah, but she is so in love with him. That is easy to see."

They were deep among the trees.

"This forest is called the forest of Arden," said Marie de France. "They say that druids used to worship the oak trees in hidden clearings. Mister Shakespeare wrote a play about the forest, but not about the druids—mon Dieu, what is that?"

'That' was something very familiar to Scott, but not at all to Marie-France.

"It's a police car," he said. More exactly, it was two police cars, one much larger than the other, which looked strangely old-fashioned. The larger, newer one, was halfway off the path, and seemed to be tangled up in the undergrowth. The smaller, older one had its lights flashing.

There was nobody about.

"Something from my time," said Scott. "And something from a little before. They must have skifted through. Or slipped through, perhaps."

"That's a 1970's police car," said Anne, coming up beside them, "but the crashed one is much newer."

"It is a sort of carriage without horses, no? Does it also go without a driver?" said Marie de France.

"Perhaps the cars came through but not the drivers," ventured Scott. By now, they had come up to the cars. There were footprints all around.

"No, I think the drivers arrived as well, but they have gone," said Gawain. "But how is it that two cars from different times are at this same place?"

"Radios. The police have radios," said Scott. "They can call each other for help."

"Across time, do you think?" said Marie de France.

"Not usually," said Scott.

"Let us hope, then, that they came to no harm," said Anne.

They rode on.

It was not the only wreckage on the way. War had passed through the forest. Here and there were broken weapons, shields of different types and designs, and, once, a richly carved helm. Gawain got off his horse to look it at. For a moment neither he nor Anne noticed that Scott and Marie-France had continued on without them.

"Saxon work," said Gawain. "The signs of bloodshed are everywhere, but no trace of the wounded."

"This battle is days old," said Anne. "And they are not all Saxon. Look." And she pointed to a scar of splintered wood on one of the trees.

"That is the trace of a bullet," she said—"or, perhaps," and she too dismounted to look more closely, "a shotgun."

"This I do not like," said Gawain. "Morgaine has found a way to bring the weapons of later time to destroy the people of this present."

"Perhaps," said Anne. "But if she is so powerful, why would she need such weapons?"

The conversation would have continued, but at that moment there was the sound of a scream from further along the path.

Instantly Gawain sprang into the saddle and galloped off towards it. Anne was a whisker behind him. They were too late.

This is what had happened:

A few yards further on Scott and Marie-France heard the sound of metal on metal. It was a sound they both knew: fighting. Scott gripped Excalibur and spurred the charger on. He felt its sides throb: the horse knew the sound too.

He came quickly on a clearing in the trees. Two men were fighting, one with a short axe and the other with a long knife. A cart was over-turned. Small, heavy chests lay tumbled across the frozen grass. One part of the grass was stained red, though neither man was bleeding.

They seemed to be having a rather abrupt conversation between blows:

"You are the most stupidest man alive," grunted the axe-man.

"That's rich, coming from the stupidest man who'll soon be dead," shouted the knife man, jabbing.

"You said they was money."

"And I said slit his throat. He'll 've had the money in his purse."

"'Ere, who's this?" shouted the axe-man. Both men turned to face Scott. The horse reared, and the men stood a moment looking at the the steel-shod hooves. That was enough for them. The knife-man did a backwards somersault and set off among the trees. He seemed to be spectacularly agile. The axe-man tried to run but slipped and went crashing into one of the cart-shafts. It broke under his weight and he lay quivering for a moment. If Scott had known what to do, he could have pinned the man to the forest floor. But he was too slow, and the man pulled himself up and went slithering off after his brother, or friend, or enemy, or whatever he was to him.

Marie de France came up behind.

"Pah. Bandits," she said.

"I don't think they got what they wanted," said Scott. The action had given him a warm, pleasurable feeling, but he was disappointed not to have got more out of it.

"No, indeed," said Marie de France, dismounting. "But what they could have had was precious indeed." She lifted the lid on one of the chests and pulled out a thick, leather bound volume. "These were for our lady Morgaine, I think. She is a great collector of books. Scott also dismounted, and eased open another chest.

"Books it is," he said.

"But there is something very strange about this one," she replied. She opened, and Scott saw that the pages were blank. At least, the first pages were blank, but after that there were pages with faded writing, and, towards the back of the book, beautifully written pages with rich illustrations. The pictures were strange animals—the Sea Pig, the Siren, the Torpedo, the Two-headed serpent, and the Unicorn.

"It is a Bestiary," said Marie de France. "And a good one. But what is happening to the pages?"

As they looked, the writing seemed to shimmer, and lift from the parchment, and slide softly into the pictures. The pictures themselves grew more distinct, more colourful, then they in turn slid, wafting off the page into the air. For a moment the faded writing remained, like a shadow, until, after a minute, that too was gone.

"That explains why the other pages were blank," said Scott. "What is a Bestiary, anyway?"

"It's a book of strange and mythical beasts. Very many of them have been written, of which the most famous is the Natural History of Pliny the Elder…"

"Does one of them have a head like a badger, a body like a lion, and a mouth that opens from ear to ear?"

"That would be the Leucrota, it is the swiftest of all animals and can… why do you ask?"

"Because there's something very like that on the other side of the clearing—look, there, in the shadows."

Under the trees, something the size of a donkey, with a golden body, mane and tail, and a black white striped head, sat grinning at them. At least, it seemed to grin, but instead of teeth a single bone white bone flashed softly at them.

"Coo. Talk to you. Who knew?" it said.

"What's it saying?" said Scott.

"Nothing. Everything. Just words. The leucrota makes the sounds of human speech, but it does not speak."

There was a sudden flurry, and the creature was gone.

"That is so strange," said Marie de France. "I have never seen a leucrota. I thought they were imaginary."

"What—what other beasts were in the book?"

"The books vary—the alerion, the barghest, the bishop-fish, the caladrius…why?"

"We found our way into a book. What if the leucrota found its way out?"

"That is not a very pleasant thought."

"Come on then, let's get to the castle while we still can," said Scott, and he spurred his horse back along the path.

Marie de France made to follow him, but she seemed to be having trouble with the reins. Scott turned impatiently to urge her on, which is when he saw something that he did not quickly forget:

The whole of the clearing was glowing. At first the tips of leaves, and the white mare's hooves, then the wreckage of the cart, and the scattered chests, then the trunks of trees, and the earth itself. The air sparkled as if it were filled with fire-flies. Marie de France glowed more than any of them, a fierce white-gold radiance that seemed to flow from her finger. In moments it was too bright to look at.

That was when she screamed.

Scott stared in horror. He tried to raise his voice to warn her, and spur his horse to save her, but neither his voice nor his muscles obeyed him. The light pulsed through his flesh, and the intolerable brightness filled his world until he could think of nothing else.

The brightness began to fade. The air thinned, the earth dulled, the leaves and the trees and the grass returned to their natural colour. Everything became as it had been, except for one thing: the saddle of the white mare was empty. Marie de France was gone.

"Scott, what is it?" shouted Gawain, galloping into sight. "Where is Marie-France?"

Scott gestured.

"Gone," he said.

They searched the clearing for ten minutes, and then made Scott tell the whole story of the books and the leucrota again.

"Perhaps she skifted," said Scott, mournfully.

"That does not sound like skifting," said Anne. "I have heard of something like this once before. But..." she took his hand. "What is this on your finger?"

"Marie-France's ring. We exchanged rings when —"

"But Scott, you don't own a ring."

"It was—oh." Scott's mind went back to the part of the story he had forgotten to tell. "Morgaine gave me a ring before I set off through the three doors."

"She gave you a ring? Did you give her nothing in return?"

"I left my old sword behind. She said I would find a better one."

"Cunning," said Anne.

"Cunning?" said Scott. "Why do you say 'cunning'? What do you mean?"

"Magical gifts of this nature cannot simply be given," said Anne. "They must be exchanged for their power to be effective. She tricked you into leaving a thing, so that you could receive a thing."

"This ring, what was it like?" said Gawain.

"It was gold—I think—with a single stone, very bright, like the sun."

"'That bore blushing beams, as the bright sun'?" said Anne. "I know this ring. Morgaine showed it to me, but I forgot about it. Gawain knows it too, I think."

"I do, if it is the same one. A lady tried to give it to me once. But I had nothing to give to her in exchange."

"What does the ring do?" said Scott.

"It draws the wearer back to the person who enchanted it, no matter where in time or space they are," said Anne. "Morgaine, I think, sent you through the door to find Excalibur. And now she thinks you have it, and she has reeled you in. Count on it, we will find Marie de France at the castle."

"Well, what are we waiting for?" said Scott. Without stopping for an answer he set off at a gallop along the forest way.

22 THE SHIELD AND THE STAIRCASE

Leading the milk-white mare, Gawain and his mother caught up with Scott a bow-shot from the castle walls. The forest road had brought them to the south gate, which was separated from the outer bailey by a long, walled causeway across the mere. The drawbridge was up, the portcullis closed, and the last of the light had caught the gatehouse, so that it seemed to glow in the twilight. In the distance they could see the towers of the inner bailey, still sunlit in the growing gloom, windows twinkling.

Scott was in the middle of a conversation with a man on the battlements.

"Chi est là?" called a man's voice in broad Anglo-Norman—'Who is there?'

"Sui li chevalier Perceval. Pais soit à chescun de vus. Jo ristourne de chivauchier, et jame parlez avec la seignouresse de ceo chastel," replied Scott,—"I am the knight Perceval. Peace to you. I have returned from errantry, and desire to speak with the mistress of the castle."

His voice echoed off the walls, but there was no other answer.

Then, after a long time, there was a rumble, and the drawbridge at last came crashing down.

The portcullis rose to reveal the figure of a lady in a white dress and a thick fur cloak. Scott spurred his horse across the drawbridge. Gawain and Anne followed. As they dismounted, the lady was already greeting him.

"My lord Perceval," she said, taking his hand. It was the lady who had ridden into the castle with Scott just a few days before. He was struck in the evening light by how much she looked like his mother, though younger—long tresses of curling golden hair, and a delicately triangular face. "You left us in such haste, without a good bye. Now you return on this shortest day of the year. I hope you will stay with us longer. But who are your friends?"

She turned to greet Gawain and Anne, and for a moment her face fell.

"My lady Ragnell," she said, "and my lord Gawain."

"Blanchefleure," said Anne. "So lovely to see you."

Gawain took her hand and kissed it. "My lady. I never learned your name, but you I have not forgotten."

Anne looked sharply at him.

"Do you know this lady, Gawain?"

Gawain blushed. "This is the lady of the castle Hautdessart—" he began, and stopped. He stopped because Anne had stamped down hard on his foot.

"Blanchefleure," she said. "My oldest friend. We have pressing business with the lady Morgaine. Can you take us thither."

"Assuredly," she said, and smiled. "I see you have a spare horse. It is some distance across the causeway, and cold in this winter air. May I ride with you, to show the way?"

"Assuredly," replied Anne.

Scott wanted to ride beside Blanchefleure, but his mother held him back. Blanchefleure, it seemed, preferred in any case to ride with Gawain.

"Do you know who that woman is?" said Anne.

"I met her on the way to castle when I came here first," said Scott. "I didn't know her name, but she said she knew Gawain and was dear to him."

"More than dear," said Anne. "Blanchefleure was my oldest friend. It was she who wrote to me from Morgaine's party to advise me that Gawain was betraying me."

"Oh," said Scott.

"More than 'oh'," said his mother. "It seems she knows Gawain too. While she was writing to tell me that Gawain was dallying with another woman, she was the woman who was trying to seduce him!"

"What shall we do?" said Scott.

"We shall retain our composure at all times," she said, and she spurred her horse on to catch the other two.

There was a second gate at the end of the causeway. It was made up of two short towers at either side of a tunnel. The gates stood open, but something on the other side sent Scott's heart beating. Nine feet high it was, with a heavy, thick bladed sword, six feet long, stuffed carelessly into its belt, and cast iron plates stitched to a leather jerkin to make crude armour.

"A giant," said Scott. You would have thought that someone who has ridden through the valley of death would have not been bothered by a giant, but there was something deeply unnerving about its sheer size. The huge sword was more than Scott could have lifted with both hands, but beside its owner, it was little more than a long dagger.

"An ettin," said Gawain. "True giants are taller. Ettins are hill-giants. Do nothing to annoy it. Ride by looking neither to the right nor the left."

Scott rode nervously past. He thought for a moment that he saw Blanchefleure smirking at his discomfiture, but when he looked again she fluttered her eyelids and smiled.

"My lady Morgaine is in the Strong Tower," she said. "Go you three ahead, for I think that she too is anxious to see you. I will see to these horses." And she clapped her hands, which brought two stable lads running.

Scott, Gawain and Anne dismounted, and Blanchefleure went off to the stables. The final gate, into the inner bailey, stood open, flanked by men at arms. They made no sign as the three entered.

The Inner Bailey was not so much a wall with towers, as a large number of towers with interconnecting wall. The Strong Tower was opposite the gates, but immediately to the left was a tower which Scott recognised.

"Wait a moment," he said, pushing Excalibur into Gawain's hands, and dashed off up the tower staircase.

"Scott—no—what are you doing?" shouted Anne, but Gawain put his hand on her shoulder.

Scott pelted up the staircase to the room which had been his. There was something which he hoped would be there which he very much wanted: the shield from the haunted chapel.

The room had been tidied and cleaned since the morning he fought Mortain, but it was otherwise untouched. The shield was where he had left it, hanging beside the fire place, just as it had hung over the altar when he found it. He took it and fitted it snugly over his shoulder.

Then he ran back down the stairs.

Running down the stairs did not go quite as he had wished. Spiral staircases are not made for running, and Scott slipped, staggered, and tumbled head over heels.

It was the shield which broke his fall, lodging itself in the masonry, and bringing him to a booming, thudding halt, though it pulled his shoulder horribly. Bruised, Scott pulled himself to his feet, furious and afraid that he had somehow damaged the shield. He looked carefully along the rim and across the face, but saw no mark.

But there was a mark on the stone-work. A deep, fresh groove, long and smooth. Scott rubbed his fingers along it. On the surface was the rough, crumbly texture of sandstone. But underneath it was smooth. His mind went instantly back to the sound he made as he fell. He had once before fallen on a stone staircase, running up the steps at the university as a small child. Back then he had come away with a nasty bruise which lasted for days. But the sound had been quite different.

He felt the back of his head. It had caught the edge of one of the steps, which by all rights should have cut it right open, and possibly fractured it. There was some blood, and a small bump, but no more than he would have got for banging his head on the fridge door at home.

He pushed against the wall again. Surely stone should be stone cold? There was the slightest give where he pushed.

It was a puzzle, but there was no time for it now. Going more carefully, he made his way down to join the others. Gawain handed him back Excalibur.

"I had to get my shield," he said. His mother raised one eyebrow, reprovingly, but she said nothing. Gawain smiled.

A man-at-arms stood at the foot of the staircase into Strong Tower. He had evidently received no instructions about their visit.

"You may not enter," he said. "My lady Morgaine is within, and she will see no one."

"She will see us," said Gawain.

"She will see no one," said the man.

Just at that moment there was a sound, like a soft shriek or a cry, from two floors up.

"Marie-France!" yelled Scott. Without waiting he pushed past the soldier and up the staircase.

"Oy!" said the man, and grabbed at Scott. But his flailing hands snatched at air, and Gawain walloped him in the chest with the pommel of his sword. He fell backwards down other steps that ran to the basement. He had just time to shout before he hit the bottom.

Gawain leapt after Scott, who was already at the landing of the next floor. A man-at-arms blocked his way, raining blows on Scott's shield from above. The blows bounced off harmlessly enough, but Scott was struggling to get his sword anywhere near the other man, with the pillar of the staircase between them.

"That's not how you fight on a staircase!" bellowed Gawain, pushing past Scott.

"How then?"

"Like this!" Quick as a flash Gawain switched his sword to his left hand and jabbed the man in the arm. There was a cry, and he dropped his weapon. Instantly Gawain changed hands again, grabbing hold of the man's now weapon-less arm, pulling him forwards, so that he fell sprawling onto the landing, straight into the arms of other guards who came running out of their guard room to help him.

Gawain turned to face them, bristling and breathing hard.

"Do you wish to fight?" he roared. "Know that I am Gawain, the Hawk of May, the King of Gododdin, the lightning blade."

For a moment, not one of them moved. But then, at the back, there was a crackling, ratchetting sound.

"Part lads, and we'll show this wild man what we do with intruders," said a voice. They broke to reveal a black haired man fitting a bolt to a cross-bow.

"Lightning blade you may be," he said. "But I do not think you will defend yourself against this."

He levelled the weapon.

23 TO UNFREEZE TIME

"**E**nough," boomed a voice from far above. It was Morgaine. "Let these guests ascend."

The man lowered the crossbow.

"As you wish, my lady," he muttered. For a moment his eyes met Gawain's, and then he looked away.

One by one, Scott, Gawain and Anne climbed the stair.

Morgaine stood aside from the doorway to let them enter.

The chamber ran the entire length and breadth of the tower. Deeply set windows stared blankly into the darkness. The walls were covered with thick tapestries, except where sconces held great torches that gave a heavy, flickering light. There were many shadows, but little furniture: no more than a single table, shaped as a crescent moon. The table was bare, except for a small book and a golden cup. A five-pointed star was painted on the floor in blue, at the very centre of the room.

In the middle of the star, stood Marie de France, absolutely still. A faint glow clung to her, like the glow in the clearing.

"What have you done to her?" demanded Scott.

"I?" said Morgaine. "Nothing whatsoever. But she is not quite here, not yet. Perhaps it has not occurred to you that you cannot get something for nothing. It takes time to travel by magic. You have galloped, and ridden, and fought, and so you have overtaken the one who, coming directly but slowly, you meant to find. In a moment or so, she will arrive. Watch."

As she spoke, the last golden glow faded. Then, with a lurch, Marie de France staggered, as if she had missed her step. She looked around, startled, and then ran to Scott, burying her head in his arm.

"As I say, quite unharmed," said Morgaine. Marie de France began softly to sob.

"But now," Morgaine continued. "Come into the light, so that I can look at you all. What a delightful family group—you thought I did not know, Anne? A washed up, discarded husband, a girl who has yet to learn our first mysteries, and goes scuttling around time because she cannot bear the home she left behind, and a boy who thinks he is a knight. But you, Anne, I had thought better of. Have you no care for your son that you let him wander through the centuries unsupervised? And you left me in such haste. I would gladly have given you a horse, if you wished to leave. Yes, and given you this man, if that was what you desired. But perhaps you were ashamed to ask?"

"Not ashamed, Morgaine," said Anne. "Else, why would I choose to ride with him back to your castle. And, see, I have returned your horse. She is even now in your stable."

"Then, Anne, we are all friends again. Shall I call for wine, that we might pledge one another?"

"Perhaps," said Anne. "But first, I would rather do what you always urged me."

"And what is that, sweet Anne?"

"To seek for knowledge, Morgaine. There are answers to questions that only you can give."

"My good Anne, when have I ever denied you the answers to your questions?"

"I do not know, Morgaine. Perhaps never. But at times, I feel you may have diverted me from the best questions."

"Ask, then."

"Tell us what you are about. What you are doing, how is it that this castle stands here centuries before it should, why time is unravelling, and, most of all, what your intention is with all of this."

"Oh my, oh my," said Morgaine, pressing her hands together and making a steeple with her fingers. "If I told you that, I would tell you everything. But how can I resist, having said that I will answer your questions? But it is a long tale, and I have no chairs. Are these questions yours alone, Anne? Your—shall we say—associates, may wait below in comfort if they wish."

"We want to know too," said Scott. He was suddenly conscious that the whole conversation had been going on in ordinary English.

"Ah!" said Morgaine. "He speaks! And in his native voice. You did well when you tried to disguise yourself before, Scott Perceval Raynall, except that I already knew. And you were cunning to give away my ring so that I could not find you, but it is no matter, since you have brought me what I wanted anyway. How well you have grown up, and in Stechford! If your mother had not so stubbornly refused my help we could have done better for you. No matter. So you too wish to hear the answers. Very good. And does that go for the French girl and for my nephew? You are losing your touch, nephew Gawain: I lost many ladies to your gentle manner and dark good looks, but during your last stay at my castle, you scarcely turned a head. No wonder you must trail around this one who has discarded you."

"I thank you for your interest in my welfare, aunt," said Gawain. "But I too would like to hear your answers."

"Very well, then. Know that this very spot on which we stand is the exact centre of England."

"I thought that was Meriden," said Scott.

"There is an oak near Lillington which also claims that honour," said Gawain.

She sighed. "Seas change, and so do lands.

"But know further, that, by my arts, I have discovered that this very year is the mid-point of skift time, which stretches for forty years before us and for forty years behind us. And, know that this century is the mid-point of all centuries in which we may skift. And this very night, which after midnight will be the fifteenth of December, is the winter solstice, the shortest day, and is therefore the very centre of the skift-year—"

"The fifteenth isn't the winter solstice," said Scott. "It's the twenty-second of December."

Morgaine raised her eyes heavenwards, with a look of great patience.

"My dear Anne, did you not teach your son anything?"

"Hush, Scott," said Anne. "I'll explain later."

"Thank you, my dear. So, you see, we stand at the centre of things. Of all times and places, this is the most satisfactory for my—shall we say?—my experiment."

"And what experiment is that, Morgaine?"

"A sensible question at last. You saw, I think, my chess set? A fine piece of work. It follows the pieces across both time and space. I was many years perfecting it. But the chess set is good only to follow the action, and it is hard to interpret. Many days I have pondered it.

"So I set myself to make a better instrument, an instrument capable of showing not only this moment in skift-time, but all moments, and, more than that, an instrument capable of bringing about the most subtle changes in time itself."

"You want to interfere with time?" said Anne.

"But, my dear girl, why ever not? You of all people must see the benefits. Consider this time, this anarchy, which is destined to last through seventeen more winters of misery, suffering and torture. Would it not be the greatest humanity to subtly rearrange it? Could we not go back to the wreck of the White Ship, and keep the king's son from going aboard? Would not that most subtle change have the greatest benefit to all?"

"But what other changes might occur if you meddle in this way?"

Morgaine clapped her hands together.

"Anne, Anne, how I have missed you. You reason with me, as few others dare. But, consider: could not the same argument be made to doctors, to scientists, to explorers? It is in our human nature to change the universe. We can, therefore we must."

"I see. And how would such an instrument to rearrange time be constructed?"

"This castle is like—is like—Anne, you know as well as I do that it is impossible to describe the workings of magic simply. But imagine that the castle is like a great bell, that will resonate if struck in exactly the right way at exactly the right time."

"And that is the secret? Building a castle here at this point gives you control of time. It's surprising that not everyone is doing it."

"Anne, Anne. Have you any idea how hard it is to build a castle of this size, at such a time in history? But you are quite right. There is more to it. These walls are imbued with all the magic I can muster, and even then, one thing was still lacking. A bell must have a hammer. I needed such a trigger for the experiment—the most magical thing in Arthur's realm. Lacking, that is, until now."

"Excalibur."

"Exactly. It was fortuitous that your son arrived. I had expected Gawain, which is why I had my men waiting for him in the woods. It was a simple enough matter to pass word to him that you would be here. I knew where Excalibur was, but I needed someone to collect it. Gawain would have been acceptable, but your son was perfect: he knows little, understands less, and suspected nothing when I gave him my ring. After that, I no longer needed Gawain, and it was more convenient to let him go than to keep him."

"Why did you arrange for him to fight Mortain?"

"My dear girl, what gave him the confidence to attempt the adventure? In any case, a basic level of ability was necessary. I couldn't have a complete fool going after the sword. I admit I had a moment of doubt when I summoned the ring and the French girl appeared. But, by that time, you had conveniently arrived, bringing the sword to me."

"I'm not going to give it you," interrupted Scott.

"My dear young man, you don't need to give it to me. You are in the castle. I don't need to actually have the sword in my hand."

"Then we'll leave," said Scott.

"You would not escape from these walls. And, in any case, the magic began to work the moment the last rays of sunlight faded. By the time you escaped, even if you could, Excalibur would no longer be needed."

"Supposing we killed you?" said Gawain.

"Always the man of action," she replied. "Did you see the lake as you came in? It is completely frozen over. Fish swim under the ice, but it is of no use to man or beast. Time, too, is frozen. We move underneath its surface, but we cannot break through. With, or without me, this magical castle has begun to unfreeze time. Now that it has begun, only I can control it. If you killed me, it would unfreeze uncontrolled. First it would grow warm, and then it would begin to boil. Do you know what would happen if time boiled?"

"Then we will make you stop it," said Gawain. Grabbing Excalibur from Scott's hand he threw himself at her across the room.

He never reached her.

Morgaine made a peculiar motion with her hand. Gawain stopped, flailing in the air, as if he were still running, but unexpressably slowly, making no progress.

"Enough of this," said Morgaine. "There is nothing you can possibly do."

"Perhaps not," said Marie de France. "But perhaps." She opened the book which was on the crescent table.

"Put that book down, you silly girl," said Morgaine.

"Ah, you are perhaps afraid of the French girl after all?" said Marie de France. "Let me see—" and she began to read: "Sed etiam tempus..."

Morgaine flicked her wrist again and muttered something. Marie de France gasped: "Mon Dieu!" The words which had been so clearly written on the page slid and slithered around, and one by one glided into air. In just a few seconds the page was completely blank.

"Finally, enough," said Morgaine. "Do you imagine I would have told you all this if it were not too late? Anne, at least, you do the courtesy of reasoning. True to type, Gawain attempts violence. The French girl thinks to out-spell me. But neither reason, nor the sword, nor magic can stop this. It is begun. You are too late."

"You are determined to carry on with this?" said Anne. "Don't you realise that already time is unravelling in the woods around this castle?"

"Such things are inevitable. The ice begins to crack first around the flame. When the water is warmer, such effects will cease."

"You think they will cease," said Anne. "But you don't really know, do you?"

"On the contrary, my—what are you doing?" She whirled to confront Scott, who had lifted a torch from one of the sconces on the wall.

It was heavy in his hand, and the tarry smoke made his eyes water.

"The magic has begun," he said. "And you no longer need the sword. And you have begun it, so even you are no longer needed. But the castle—does it work without the castle?"

"What are you talking about, Scott?" said Anne.

"The castle is in the wrong time," said Scott. "But how do you build a castle quickly, so that no one notices? Isn't it easier to steal it?"

"I have no idea what you are talking about," said Morgaine. "Now give me that torch." She moved across to take it from him.

"Not so fast!" said Scott, and wafted it out of her reach, pushing the shield between them. "When I wasn't thinking about staying on my horse, or surviving in a duel, or escaping through a book, I was thinking about the castle, and how it got here. I thought about machines, but I've heard you allow no machines back into the past. I thought about giants, but now I've seen a giant I know that you would still need a lot of giants to build this castle. I wondered if the stones could have been quarried in the future, and then sent back. But, even then, you'd still need an army of men to put them together.

"But when we got here I dashed to my room to get my shield. Like an idiot I tripped on the way back down, and I went flying down the steps. I should have cracked my head, but all I got was a bump. And when I looked, the shield had carved a deep groove in the stone work.

"It's not much fun growing up in Stechford, you know," he said. "I remember the time my class at Junior School went to see Santa's Grotto in Birmingham. It looked like stone, but, in one place, somebody had run a trolley into it and made a groove just like the one my shield made. It wasn't much of a school trip, and it got worse when one of the boys set light to the grotto with a cigarette lighter and some cardboard boxes. You see, the grotto was made out of resin, which doesn't burn if you put a match to it, but if you get something else that burns really well—

"When I banged my head, I remembered something I read, I don't know where, about a whole film set, of a castle, being stolen. I think they make those sets out of the same kind of resin as the grotto..."

He began to waft the torch to and fro along one of the tapestries.

"NO!" screamed Morgaine, and twisted her arm over her head to cast a spell. Light leapt from her hand. Scott threw up his shield. The light crackled around it, like an electrical storm. But it went no further.

Snarling like a cat, Morgaine leapt at Scott. This must have broken her concentration, because, instantly Gawain, who was still held motionless in the air, went skidding into the table, knocking it over.

Flame sprang out of the tapestry. Marie-France, Anne and Gawain seized other torches and followed Scott's example.

"NO!" screamed Morgaine again. Now the flames were climbing up three more tapestries, and the first was well and truly ablaze. The air began to fill with a thick, choking smoke.

"Get downstairs," yelled Scott. "The walls are beginning to go."

They scrambled down. Guardsmen were waiting for them on the first floor.

"Run, you fools," screamed Anne. "The castle is on fire."

They might not have believed her, but black smoke was billowing down the stairs after them.

"What about Morgaine?" shouted Gawain as they clattered to the ground floor and spilled out into the courtyard.

"I think she is looking after herself," said Marie de France. "Look!" She flung her arm pointing to the pinnacle of the Strong Tower. A huge cloud had scudded down from the heavens, and sleet was pelting onto the roof.

"Will she put the flames out?" said Gawain.

"Not if we set light to the rest," said Scott.

"Each to a staircase, then," said Gawain.

24 THE UNLIKELY SWORDMISTRESS

Scott sprinted across the flagstones to the staircase his room was on. Grabbing a torch from the entrance, he hurried to the top.

"Everybody out—castle's on fire," he shouted as he went. People in various states of dress and undress came bustling onto the stairs. Before long there was a press of bodies struggling down. It gave Scott ample time to light the tapestries in each room on his way back down.

On the third floor an armed man barred his way to the tapestry—dressed in full armour, visor down, sword point on the ground. Gawain still had Excalibur: except for the shield, Scott was defenceless.

The armed man did not move.

"I'll have that," said Scott, grabbing at the sword while waving the torch in the man's face. The man made no sign, and the sword came away easily. It was not a man, but a suit of armour on a stand. Smoke rushed down the stair-well, so he threw the torch at the tapestry and ran back to the staircase.

At the bottom, for a moment, he was caught in the trampling, jabbing crowd. Smoke billowed, filling his lungs with acrid stench. He shut his mouth. Every instinct in him was to push his way through, but his heart told him to wait. The moment seemed to last for ever, until his lungs were bursting. A woman in front was on the point of fainting. Scott grabbed hold of her waist and dragged her through the archway into fresh air.

Flames sprang from the windows right around the bailey, and thick black smoke floated heavily in the air. The courtyard was full of people, but there seemed to be trouble at the gate. The gates were indeed open, but a monstrous figure, half again as high as a man, stood in it, swinging left and right with a huge sword. It was the ettin.

A circle had formed around it, just out of reach. Men-at-arms hurled spears. Some had long-bows, and the guard from the Strong Tower was taking careful aim with his cross-bow. But arrows, spears and bolts fell harmlessly from the ettin's hide. There was no sign of Gawain, but Marie de France and his mother were running towards the gate.

"Mum! No!" shouted Scott, but his voice was lost in the din. Sword still in hand, he sprinted after her.

"How do you kill a giant?" he said to himself. He watched the swinging of that huge sword. If he had Excalibur, he could surely cut through it, through it, and through armour and magical hide to the flesh and bone beneath. But he was too late.

His mother had come running up and was yelling at the guardsmen.

"Idiots! You must hold the weapon in your hand," she shouted. "Only your body's strength can harm it." The guards paid no attention. "Give me that," she yelled, and seized a sword. Just at that moment the ettin made a sally and plucked one of the men-at-arms up by the hauberk, swung him once around his head as if he were no bigger than a cat, and sent him flying into the crowd, scattering them like skittles.

"Enough!" roared Anne Raynall, in a voice which told Scott she was at her angriest. For a moment it caught even the ettin's attention. Then Scott watched in horror as she detached herself from the circle and ran straight towards it, sword out. Or she did not quite run.

Scott screamed, and burst through the outskirts of the crowd, desperate to somehow save her. The ettin paused to roar with laughter, and then brought his sword crashing down to cut in two the reckless woman that dared to come against him armed only with a sword no bigger than a knife.

There was a flash of light, and the blow struck stone, not flesh. As the sword came down, Anne Raynall was not there. Executing a superb double-balestra, she arrived in the spot where the giant's blade was, a moment after the monster expected it. Then, on the second step, she sprang forwards at twice the speed, finishing with a savage lunge. Her body stretched to its limit as she delivered the blow through the ettin's stomach, past its lungs and into its heart.

The monster fell. It crashed to the ground, like a factory chimney falling. Scott stood, mouth agape, while his mother pulled out the sword and wiped it on her enemy's greasy breeches.

"That's how you kill a giant," murmured Scott.

"Indeed it is," said Gawain, who had come up behind him. "She is good, isn't she?"

"But—she hates sword fighting. Where did she learn that?"

"No, Scott. She hates you sword fighting. Come on, there's no time to waste. These towers will be coming down any minute if we don't watch out."

Once again they were at the back of the crowd as it strained and struggled to get through the gate. It was too narrow for the fear and desperation of so many terrified people. Great gobbets of flame rained down, mixed in with the sleet which had spread from the strong tower and splashed down as rain, snow, and hail. It had little effect on the flames. Scott raised his shield to keep the molten chunks from reaching them. Others cowered beside them, until there was enough space in the gateway for them to shelter before they finally escaped into the outer bailey. The inner bailey was now well ablaze, all except the Keep, which was scorched, but did not burn.

"The Keep, I think, is part of the real castle, and will escape this," said Gawain, "but I do not doubt that Morgaine's plan is at an end. Well done, my son. Well done."

"What now?" said Scott.

"Our quest is accomplished. We must rescue our horses and be gone."

"What about all the people?"

"Some of them belong to this time, and they will scatter across the countryside. I don't doubt it will be hard for them, and they will make it hard for others, but we cannot stem this flood. Others came here skifting, and they will find their way back through the highways and by-ways to their own times, or whensoever the wish to go. We can be sure of one thing."

"What?"

"This great fire will open a skift door big enough for all to find a way through."

They were the last out of the gate. Scott turned back once to look at the raging blaze. Then he and Gawain ran down the slope towards the stables, skidding on the snowy grass.

At the stable gate another fight seemed on the point of bubbling over.

A golden-haired woman in a white dress—it was Blanchefleure—stood at bay in front of the stable door, holding off a woman—also golden-haired, who might have been her sister—in a red cloak. It was Scott's mother.

"Let me have those horses!" roared Anne Raynall.

"Not until you promise to take me with you," cried Blanchefleure. Her face was a mixture of anger, and fear, and self-pity. That is, until she saw Scott and Gawain, and her mood changed.

"My Lord Gawain," she called. "Help me! Have mercy on one who has loved you. Take me with you! This woman deserted you—but I offered you everything. See, my lord—" and she pointed to the green belt which Gawain still wore wrapped around his jerkin. "See, my lord, you still wear my girdle—for the love that you bear me, take me with you!"

This last plea seemed to enrage Anne Raynall even beyond her rage when she fought the giant. Seizing Gawain by the shoulder as if he were a child, she wrapped her fingers around the green belt, and in one movement pulled it free, snapping it as she did. Then, striding across to Blanchefleure, she grabbed her hand and rammed the girdle into it. Scott thought she was going to strike her.

"Enough! That is the last thing you will get from my husband, and that is the last you will get of mine and me. Now be gone, I care not by what route. But if you ever cross my path again, beware!"

Blanchefleure stood for a moment, then ran into the stable.

"I'll get the horses," said Gawain. But Anne Raynall thrust out her hand and grabbed hold of his collar.

"You'll get nothing. Stay out!" Her voice dropped. "Scott, Marie-France, perhaps you would be so good as to bring out four horses."

Scott looked at Marie de France, and Marie de France looked at Scott.

"What?" bellowed Anne Raynall.

"Madame, you called him your husband. I have not heard you use that word before."

"The horses!"

Marie de France looked at Scott, and Scott looked at Marie de France. But this time they said nothing, and slipped into the stable to do as they were told.

25 THE UNEXPECTED SUMMER

"**W**hich way shall we go?" said Gawain, looking at Anne. "Why are you asking me?" she said, still fuming.

"I had the impression that you were in charge," said Gawain. But he winked at Scott and Marie de France.

"Do we have a choice?" said Marie.

"Not usually," said Gawain. "But there will be hundreds of skift doors opening up here."

"I thought a knight was supposed to skift into trouble," said Scott.

"But Scott, we must think of the ladies." He winked again.

"Can we really choose?" said Marie de France. "Then I should like to go to the time of Queen Elizabeth. They tell me Kenilworth was beautiful in that time. I should like to see this place when it is made in stone—not in, what did you call it?—resin."

"And after that," said Anne Raynall steadily, "if we might, Scott and I will return to the time of Elizabeth the Second."

Gawain spent a few minutes casting around. The crowds were dispersing, some—as he predicted—vanishing into shimmering air, while others made for the gates. Almost the last to leave was a golden-haired woman on a chestnut-rowan horse, but she kept her face hidden.

"This way, I think," said Gawain, and led them into a broad archway of bright air.

They rode into the golden warmth of a late summer sunset. It was so rich that, for a moment, Scott thought that the towers were still on fire. To the east, the sky was a peerless azure, rivalling the sky of the Duc de Berry's book. All the space of the outer bailey was filled with bright tents, pavilions, gazebos and summer houses. Pennants hung from every wall, and flags flew from the towers. A vast crowd milled around, dressed in every kind of bright costume. Most had a vaguely medieval flavour to them, but Scott felt the details were not quite right.

They dismounted, so as not to attract attention.

"But, is this the right time?" said Marie de France, sounding suddenly very French. "Are we gone forwards, or did we slip back to the summer before?"

"Listen," said Anne, suddenly much more cheerful. "Hear the voices. That is no Middle-English. How we come to be in summer I do not know, but the words you hear are the language of Shakespeare, not Stephen."

"And you may see the young Shakespeare among the crowds, if you look carefully," said Gawain, "but he will be no more than eleven years old. For, if I am not much mistaken, these are the festivities that the Lord Leicester is organising for Queen Elisabeth."

"Then why is it summer?" said Scott. "Shouldn't we have arrived at the dead of winter?"

"As to that," said Gawain, "I cannot say. But many strange things were happening to time as we left. We should count ourselves lucky to have escaped so lightly."

Without warning, a huge cry went up behind them, and a voice shouted:

"Gawain, Sir Knight, prepare to guard thyself!"

Gawain spun round, drawing his sword (he had given Excalibur back to Scott). The crowd parted into a wide ring, and a huge knight in red armour was readying himself to strike on the other side of the circle.

Gawain was about to shout back a challenge when a man dressed entirely in green, with a green belt prominently tied around his waist, somersaulted into the arena. He sprang to his feet, drew his sword, and in the same movement, lifted his hat to all those around him.

"Fie thee, sir knight," he shouted back. "Wherefore challengest thou Gawain, most peerless knight of England?"

"I defy thee with all defiance," bellowed the red knight.

"Then have at thee!" shouted the man in green, and sprang forward to engage him.

Instantly, they were at it hammer and tongs, the red knight raining down so many blows on the unarmoured man in green that it was a wonder that he was not killed. The man in green, though, was not simply content to parry. He clattered his sword about the red knight's head, until eventually the helmet sprang off and went rolling among the feet of the bystanders. There was a sigh of amazement from the crowd. In the same moment, the man in green kicked the red knight in the stomach, sending him reeling backwards. Bystanders had to jump to get out of the way. The red knight staggered into an inconveniently placed log. He fell backwards, and landed perfectly spread-eagled on his back. The man in green leapt onto the log, and shouted

"Yieldst thou, knave?"

"Yield?" roared the knight. "Never!"

"Then I shall kill thee!" And he jumped lightly from the log onto the red knight's chest. He raised his sword to strike, and a gasp went up from the crowd. But he hesitated just too long, because the red knight wrapped his arms around the man's legs, dragging them forward, and toppling him backwards.

But the man in green did not fall. Instead, as lightly as a gymnast, he flipped over backwards, so that he stood upright at the red knight's feet. His sword went flying off and stuck quivering in the ground to the other's left. The red knight jumped up—a very sprightly jump for a man in full armour—and ran for his sword where he had dropped it on his right. The man in green sprang for his on the left, and, a moment later, they were at it hammer and tongs again.

This time the man in green ignored the head, and devoted his attention to the great breastplate. "He won't get through that," said Scott to himself, but, wonder of wonders, in seconds the man in green had snapped the strap at one shoulder, and then the strap below, until the breastplate swung loose.

The red knight roared, and raised his sword high above his head for one last great charge, hurling himself from one side of the ring to the other. The man in green stood to receive the charge, but, at the very last moment, stepped forwards and bent right over. As neatly as you could wish it, the red knight rolled over the top of him, burying his sword to the hilt in the turf, and landing flat on his back once again.

"Yieldst thou now, knave?" shouted the man in green.

"I yield to thee, Gawain," declaimed the red knight. "For thou art the truest knight in Christendom, as all well know."

Then the man in green gave the red knight his right arm to help him up, and both turned and bowed. There was wild applause.

"Thank you one, and thank you all," called the man in green. "We are Captain Cox and Master Williams, and we thank you once again for your patience. The sun shines in the sky, and we bid you a fine evening—but, soft, lo! What causes the sun to grow dim? A brighter light ascends in our heavens—"

The crowd broke to allow the entry of a group of ladies on foot, accompanied by a single gentleman in fine, brightly polished armour. They were so close that the armour brushed against Scott's hand. He felt it to be decorative rather than defensive, almost frivolous, but the gentleman had a stately bearing, perhaps even a swagger. He paid particular attention to one of the ladies, who had red hair.

"Sacrebleu!" whispered Marie de France in Scott's ear. "C'est la reine Elisabeth—it is the queen Elisabeth."

"Bien sûr, c'est la reine, ma petite française—of course it is the queen, my young French lady," said a voice. "Now turn this way and let me look at you."

It was the queen herself who spoke. She was perhaps the same age as Anne Raynall, thinner in the face, with a strong chin, and bright eyes.

"You, I do not know," she said. "But your friend—he, I know. Come. All of you. Walk with us. Somebody—" she snapped her fingers "—take care of their horses."

"You are his wife, my dear," she said to Anne as they walked. "That is plain to see. I knew him as a child. I thought, perhaps for a while, that he and I—but then I became Queen. A queen might marry a king, perhaps, or a courtier, in extremis, but not a legend. What is your name?"

"Anne, your majesty. Anne Raynall. The lady Ragnell."

"Yes, I thought you might be. Such beauty. You and I are almost of an age, you know. Do you know the phrase 'uneasy lies the head that wears the crown'?"

"That's not been written yet—" said Anne.

"You are a scholar, my dear. But I have spies, as a queen must. In other countries, in my own country, in the past, in the future. You know it, then?"

"Yes, I know it."

"It is false. At least, false for this head, and for this crown. But if the writer were to have written 'lonely lies the head that wears the crown', he would have been closer to the mark."

"It wouldn't scan," said Anne, forgetting herself for a moment. "It's a perfect iambic pentameter—"

"I know what an iambic pentameter is. I am asking your advice on a matter of state."

"A matter of state, your majesty? But you scarcely know me."

"All the more reason to trust you. You are not of this time—you gave yourself away when you knew my quotation. You have no reason to compete with me. I cannot match your looks, and you already have a husband. So I want your advice on a matter of the heart."

"A matter of the heart, your majesty?"

"My dear, you are far too clever to miss my meaning. This Robert Dudley, earl of Leicester, the owner of this fine house, who has bankrupted half his county to pay for these three weeks of festivities, all to woo me. Should I marry him?"

"What does your heart tell you, your majesty?"

"My heart tells me to trust no one."

"Yet you are trusting me?"

"You are my Lady Philosophy. In this age, you are no more than a character from a book. No more, and no less. So what must I do?"

"Your majesty, I cannot help you. I know too much. All I can say is, that you will make your decision, and it will turn out well."

"Then we are agreed."

They reached the end of their tour around the castle. Elizabeth stood on a flight of steps. Her ladies had gone ahead, and Dudley had remained with the festivities. So she addressed the four of them:

"My friends," she said. "I must bid you farewell. Your horses will be well stabled but first…"

Suddenly, she stumbled, and her face changed.

"Thus we meet again." The voice was the voice of Elizabeth, but the phrasing, the words, and diction were Morgaine's.

"It is fitting, perhaps, that I speak to you through the mouth of a queen. Her father killed her mother, you know. It could have been averted. England could have found its golden age, not once in ten generations, but endlessly, in every generation.

"Once more Gawain, my nephew, you have deprived me of my desire. And your son, also. On this occasion I cannot deprive you of yours, but I can deprive him of his.

"Fare you well, my friends. A little revenge, and we will consider our debt to one another cancelled. For the time being. And that is all the time there is. Goodbye."

The Queen fell to the ground.

Gawain knelt beside her.

"She has fainted. No more."

"What did she mean by that?" said Scott, who was less interested in Elizabeth and more in Morgaine."

"Something that—" began Gawain, but he stopped to point at Marie de France. "The ring."

The ring glowed.

Its stone sent out brilliant beams of light, filling the air with sparks like fire flies, until the ground, the air and the buildings also glowed. But Marie de France glowed the brightest. Scott ran to her, seizing the ring, but he could not pull it from her finger. He felt the pumping, pulsating light flowing through him, strengthening.

He leaned forwards to kiss Marie de France, and for a moment their lips met. And then he was clutching air.

She was gone.

26 Stechford

They skifted back in stages, finding their way through the Civil War, and the Black Death, and some rather unpleasant business around the time of Napoleon, and thence, eventually, back to Scott's Stechford. They left the horses at the very same inn where they had found Marie-France, though the innkeeper did not seem to recognise them. Gawain warned him strictly to take care of them. They took a lift in a carriage back to Blakesley Hall, and trudged along Stoney Lane until it became, in time and distance, Station Road. With each successive skift they moved closer to the proper season, and arrived on a snowy morning to find the streets deserted. Cars were parked haphazardly in strange places, and only Station Road was gritted.

"Has there been an invasion?" said Scott.

They found just one man to speak to as they climbed up the hill behind the swimming baths.

"Why are the streets so deserted?" Gawain asked him.

The man looked at him unsteadily for a minute, and they noticed that he had an empty bottle in his right hand.

"You're drunker than I am, mate," he said. "It's bleedin' CHRISTMAS DAY, that's what it is."

A few minutes later they sat round the dining table in number seventeen, Giles Close. Aside from the milk in the fridge, which had turned to yoghurt, the house did not seem to have noticed they were gone, although there was a large pile of letters waiting for them at the door.

Anne sat sifting through the post.

"There's still some things I don't understand," said Scott. "First, how was it that the winter solstice—the shortest day of the year—was on the fifteenth of December. It's always on the twenty-second, isn't it? And mum—" 'mum' seemed vastly more appropriate, now that they were home, "—how did you learn to fence? And finally, who was that lady Blanchefleure, and why were you so angry with her?"

"The Winter solstice is always at the same time of the year," said Anne, "but it's an unfortunate fact that the calendar which Julius Caesar established in 46 BC wasn't very good at keeping pace with it. By the time of the Anarchy, it had drifted a whole week, and eventually, in the 1590s, it was ten days adrift. That's when people began to use the new calendar, which we use today. Not everyone adopted the new calendar at the same time, but it's a safe bet that if you skift back before 1700, sooner or later you are going to have to subtract a week to make sense of where you are.

"The fencing is simple. You know that I stay late at the University every Monday, and most Thursdays. Those are fencing nights. That's how your father found me, though it wasn't me he was looking for. And that's why, when he turned up here he had his fencing kit with him."

"But mum, you hate fencing."

"I hate you fencing, Scott. Or, at least, I have no real objection to fencing, but I knew deep down that one day it would lead to real fighting, and I didn't want you ever involved in any of that."

"And do all of Arthur's ladies fence?"

"Scott, heaven forbid that you should meet any more of those ladies. That was what I hated most about Arthur's court: ladies chatting, ladies gossiping, ladies talking about clothes, and embroidery, and recounting to each other the sixth century equivalent of Mills and Boon romance. I was never going to be one of those ladies, and learning to fence was a way of getting out of their world and finding myself."

"And what about the lady Blanchefleure?"

"That, you can work out for yourself. Happy Christmas." And she handed him a small parcel, in green wrapping paper.

He tore it open. It was (as he expected, because it always was) a book. A green covered paperback: 'Sir Gawain and the Green Knight, Second Edition'. He opened it to somewhere near the middle. It seemed to be a poem, but the lines were in a language that he now recognised, but could not read.

"But mum," he said, "this is all in Middle English. How am I supposed to read it?"

"You should have picked up enough to be going along with," she said. "And it's time you learned some properly. Goodness knows, you won't struggle quite as much with French from now on. Anyway, every family has a heritage, and this is yours. When you've read it, you can decide for yourself how guilty your father is."

Gawain, who had been sitting looking at the titles of the books on the shelves, started at this.

"Not guilty," he said. "Tricked by one woman, discarded by another. But Scott, there's one question which I know is on your mind, and you haven't asked."

Scott bit his lip.

"Will I—we—ever see Marie-France again?"

His mother got up from the table, and pulled a book from the shelves that lined the walls. It was a thick, grey paperback, and it was in French. The title was: 'Les Laïes de Marie de France'.

"Marie de France did not write many of these down until years later," she said. "It's not always easy to find people in skift-time, and I don't want you to try. But you can know for certain, that somewhere, in time or space, and this world or another, Marie de France is alive."

That night Scott went to bed with two books, both written in languages he could not understand. The green book he put on his bedside table, but the grey book he wrapped his arms around, and thus went to sleep.

EPILOGUE

Scott Perceval Raynall returned to school at the beginning of the next term. He wondered if there would be a fuss about his unexplained absence, but it was all put down to a school skiing trip, which he and five other boys whom he did not know were said to have attended. As none of the others ever raised any doubts about it, he concluded that they, too, had been on some strange and mysterious adventures, and the school had a well-regulated and established way of dealing with such things.

That year he made surprising progress in spoken French, and to a lesser extent in written French and in Latin. His English teacher, though, suggested he should try for a more modern tone when writing dialogue, and confided to his mother at a parents' evening that he felt Scott was now a little old for stories about King Arthur. He got rather a sharp reply, and disappeared into the staff room for most of the rest of the evening.

For some reason Anne Raynall discovered that they were not as hard up as they had been before, and they moved out of the council-house in Stechford into an old farmhouse in Warwickshire. It made for a longer journey to school each morning, but there were other benefits.

There were stables with the farmhouse. They were in quite poor condition, and his mother insisted that they completely clean and repair them before they could even consider finding horses. In the event, they had half finished when one Saturday morning, Scott caught sight of a lone rider coming over the fields, leading a charger and a mare.

Gawain stayed with them more frequently from then on, and Scott noticed that his mother had begun to refer to him, at least on the telephone, as 'my husband'. Once or twice he attended a parents' evening, thereby dashing the hopes of many of Anne Raynall's admirers.

Anne Raynall remained fabulously (and, in academic circles, famously) beautiful, and time seemed to leave no mark on her. She relented on the fencing, and gave Scott lessons during the holidays when he could not fence at school. But she put an absolute bar on unaccompanied skifting, until the age of seventeen.

Everybody remarked how tall Scott had grown, and how confident, and people often mistook him for one of the sixth-form. He became the youngest person ever to win the school fencing championship. He was very popular with the girls from the Girls School next door, although he resisted all attempts to become anything to anyone which was more than friends.

The sword Excalibur hung from their mantelpiece. Whenever visitors asked about it, she told them that it was of 'archaeological' significance. Gawain continued to search for Arthur, though in time the searches became shorter, and the stays at Scott's house became longer.

Time passed, and things were set fair. Fair, that is, until one very hot summer.

But that is another story.

Made in the USA
Charleston, SC
13 September 2015